MAY 1 5 2014

THE HOLY MARK

THE HOLY MARK

The Tragedy of a Fallen Priest

GREGORY ALEXANDER

MILL CITY PRESS

Mill City Press, Inc.
322 First Avenue N, 5th floor
Minneapolis, MN 55401
612.455.2293
www.millcitypublishing.com

The Holy Mark originally appeared as a short story in Emory University's *Lullwater Review*, Vol. IX, No.1, 1998.

Cover image concept by Shear Grafix, LLC.

ISBN-13: 978-1-62652-499-6
LCCN: 2013919255

Cover Design by Mary Ross
Typeset by Kristeen Ott

Printed in the United States of America

For Wallace and Elaine Alexander—

for somehow managing to raise a son

who cared about words.

CHAPTER ONE

KATTANNACHEE

Clara let me sleep till nine today. She remembered what day it is—and not just that it's Wednesday and, praise God, not a Mass day for me. Every Monday, Wednesday, and Friday is like that, and I don't generally sleep past seven thirty. What Clara remembered is that this is a special day for me, or at least it should have been.

"Happy anniversary, Father," she greets me. Ordinarily Wednesdays and Saturdays are her days off, but she said she wanted to come in and fix me something special today. I suspect it will be her lasagna. Sweet woman, never stints on the cheeses either: a layer of provolone on the bottom, mozzarella on top, and, of course, the ricotta in the middle. I've always believed, like my dear grandmother, that lasagna without ricotta is simply not fit for a dog.

"Any messages on the machine?" I ask her. I hate to check that thing myself.

I'm forever pressing the wrong buttons. And the messages from these people are so absurd. One woman actually made her confession into that contraption. She said she was too sick to go out and didn't want to bother me to make a house call.

"Just Miss Gremillion," Clara says. "She wanted to know what time you'll be doing the rosary Friday."

"Does she have any reason to believe it won't be the same time it's been every Friday since I came here?" I ask without expecting a response.

Clara's good at letting me vent. I just roll my eyes and then turn my attention to the tray she's carrying with my coffee and some eggs and honeyed biscuits. Now don't get the idea I'm accustomed to breakfast in bed; even in New Orleans those little perks went out a long time ago—except perhaps for the archbishop. He may still command such privileges from that little nun/servant of his. This is just another of Clara's little touches to try to cheer me up. She knows how I feel about today. We've talked.

There are two slim newspapers on the tray, the *Clarion Herald*, the Catholic weekly from New Orleans, and the local paper, also a weekly, another pathetic reminder of where I am—a place so removed from the world that it can only manage to generate sixteen pages of newsprint every seven days.

"Father Gerald left you this," Clara says, placing an envelope next to the *Clarion*. I can tell it's a card. Gerald is a young priest who drives over from Monroe on Wednesdays to say Mass. My days are Tuesdays and Thursdays—and of course Sundays. The population isn't sufficient up here to offer a service every day.

I wait until Clara is gone before opening the card, not that there's any reason why I couldn't read it in front of her. But I wait anyway, fiddling with the coffee pot and shuffling the papers around until she's just out of the room but close enough to hear me slicing open the envelope. I know it's awful of me—making her think there might be something private about the card or that despite what's happened and how much they all know about me around here I might still have a secret or two. And there are so few like Gerald taking vows anymore—handsome and young with no obvious mental or physical debilities, not cross-eyed or stuttering.

Predictably all it says is "Congratulations." The event is left vague enough: "For Your Accomplishment." There are doves on the front. Is it my literary training that starts me wondering if they're a symbol of something? Does Gerald think I've lost my fervor, that I could use a fresh infusion of the Holy Spirit? Or is he wishing me peace—maybe to make peace with my past, with everyone in New Orleans?

Am I taking it all too far? How much does Gerald know about me? He's never asked about my past. Of course that could mean he already knows, maybe that he's gotten an earful from the bishop of Monroe, who probably knows everything. Gerald is from Texas. He's never been to New Orleans and doesn't seem to have much interest in the place. He probably just grabbed a card when he went to Walgreens for razor blades. He has one of those perennial five o'clock shadows. But it's becoming on him, no gray in it yet, dark and virile like a soap opera hunk.

I wonder how long Gerald will last—I'll give him five years tops. He'll meet a girl and want out. It happens all the time now. There was one in New Orleans they had just made assistant to a drunken old sot named Fendix, pastor of a small church with an elementary school. The girl was a pre-K teacher. I heard she told him how she felt in confession. Good thinking since he couldn't use it against her. Not that the thought ever crossed his mind, because they ran off without notice, leaving the archdiocese with a weekend to sober up Fendix and find a replacement to wipe the children's noses for sixteen thousand a year.

I can tell the type that isn't going to last; they get into it for all the right reasons: counseling, spiritual healing, the mystery of the Mass. Stars of their own Pat O'Brien movies, where expansive priests teach boys to box, they soon learn what it's really like and long for their days off like a store clerk.

Just look at me: Should I relish the thought of getting up at five thirty in the morning to say Mass in a trailer for five crones as old as Mother Seton and so deaf they don't know when to make the responses unless I hold up my hands like Arthur Fiedler? And do I get any help? Not even a nun to sweep that rusted-out eyesore they call a church. I once celebrated in Saint Louis Cathedral on television, for God's sake! I doubt there's a nun in this entire godforsaken Parish. (For clarity's sake, I'll use "Parish" to denote a geopolitical area—what the rest of the country calls counties; "parish" will mean a church parish.) And forget giving me an altar boy. Even if that weren't the last thing in the world they'd do if there were any around, I'm probably the youngest Catholic within twenty miles of here.

Northern Louisiana is absolutely nothing like New Orleans—a completely different culture. There's actually only one other church in the whole Parish. Its pastor, I heard, was sent there from Florida, for what atrocities I've not yet been able to ascertain. I did hear a rumor that it had something to do with rigging casino night at his church in Coral Gables.

We're both technically under the heels of both the bishops of Shreveport and Monroe, but I doubt that either of those eminences will stoop to come here if they can avoid it. They're probably keeping tabs on me in some way, though, no doubt apprised of my history by that malicious cabal in New Orleans.

No, this isn't how I expected to be marking the dawn of my second quarter century as an ordained disciple of Christ. Yes, as hard as it is to believe, today is September 27, 1995: twenty-five years to the day since I cast off the name Joe Broussard and became Father Anthony Miggliore (four syllables, please). It was my maternal grandmother's name, Mama Ellen Miggliore. The name "Anthony" was in honor of a beloved cousin who was taken long before his time. It's also the name of his father, my detestable uncle whose hateful actions I will get to shortly. Though bearing my uncle's name was on the one hand a constant reminder of his miserable existence, on the other it rather served him right—that for so many years his name was carried on not by his firstborn son, but by the most despised member of his extended family.

For religious, the Silver Jubilee should be a joyous occasion. If I were a Jesuit, I'd have my own page in their *Jubilarian*, but I'll probably spend the day reading Henry James. He's about the only passion in my life lately—he and Clara's cooking. Maybe I'll write something on him. We have much in common, James and I. He was always torn between two worlds. When he was in America, he said the only way to survive was to forget about Europe. I know I have to do the same thing—just put New Orleans out of my mind.

I did my masters thesis on James, you know: "Sexual Sublimation in *Roderick Hudson*." I'm surprised they didn't dig that up to use against me too. My argument—that the older Roland Mallet was everything the younger, romantic Roderick needed to avert his tragic fall had it not been for Roderick's stubborn denial fueled by hideous Victorian strictures—was, I'm not too modest to say, quite brilliant and original for its time and certainly would have supplied my nemeses with fodder aplenty for their cannon.

Those nemeses have seen to it that my little Jubilee go virtually unheralded: no gifts, no testimonials, no dinner with the community (indeed no community!), no Mass in my honor at the cathedral, no trip to Italy. Oh, how I would have loved that—the Spanish Steps, the Vatican frescoes, Michelangelo's *David*. James loved Italy too, you know. He spoke the language fluently, as do I. There's an extant letter he wrote upon first seeing Rome in 1869: "It makes London seem like a little city of pasteboard. . . . I've seen everything—the Forum, the Coliseum, Saint Peter's, all the piazzas and ruins and monuments (*stupendissimo!*). In fine, I've seen Rome, and I shall go to bed a wiser man than last I rose."

I, alas, will be no wiser tomorrow than I am today, nor am I likely to feel any more appreciated. That despicable archbishop in New Orleans did vouchsafe me a card—at least his office did anyway: "His Excellency regrets that service to the Holy Father will keep him away for the occasion, but he sends his best wishes and will keep the honoree [unnamed] in his prayers. Yours in the Brotherhood of Christ, Franklin Ratchett."

Service to the Holy Father indeed! He's probably toadying up to some wealthy parishioners whose church needs a new central air unit or cultivating ties with another influential family now that he's got the Miggliores in his back pocket. Or more likely, His Excellency is celebrating my humiliation with a certain uncle of mine. They must have had a good laugh over that card. The sanctimonious hypocrite Ratchett couldn't even be bothered to sign it. Somebody just stamped his name on the thing like it was a certificate from a weekend retreat.

On the other hand, I've got to hand it to them—when it comes to retribution, has anyone ever held a candle to the Church? Just look at this place. They couldn't have devised a more malign payback without strapping me into a time machine and whisking me back to the Inquisition.

Kattannachee Parish—that's what this place is called—is just below the Arkansas border. There's absolutely nothing here. Shreveport, the nearest metropolis that the rest of the civilized world might have heard of, lies nearly one hundred miles to the west. Even Monroe, where at least there are a few buildings taller than the pine trees, is nearly fifty miles to the east.

The Parish took its name, appropriately enough, from a tribe of backward Indians, the Kattannachee, who inhabited the region when the Spanish first explored it and, up until their merciful extinction shortly after the Louisiana Purchase, had still not emerged from the Stone Age. When I'm able to transcend the degradation, I can see the exquisite irony of it all: that someone who could have written a book on Henry James would find himself at this stage of his life in a place like this instead of doing the grand tour of Europe. I can only thank the mercy of God that my dear grandmother, whose name I meant to honor when I took it as my own upon my ordination twenty-five years ago today, didn't live to see the lot of her favorite grandchild.

CHAPTER TWO

THE MIGGLIORES

And I was her favorite, no mean distinction considering there were seventeen of us in my generation—my sixteen cousins and me. My parents might have added more to the mix if my father had managed to come back from the war. It was just the same to my mother's family, though, especially my godparents, who never approved of Josie's marrying a Cajun in the first place. Their only regret was that my father didn't ship off before siring me.

Paradoxically, Aunt Rose used to say that my not being a "purebred" was the reason Mama Miggliore favored me—that she really pitied me like one might a deformed puppy, not to mention my being fatherless and an only child. "She just feels sorry for him, not having any playmates at home," she used to say to my uncles, Paul and Anthony, her brothers, not caring whether I heard or not. She always seemed to be looking up from her compact mirror, one eye forever on her nose, which for decades was an expensive work in progress, until, as if revolting from the unnatural meddling of a parade of plastic surgeons, it finally rotted on her like a grounded fig. "And you know she's always had a soft spot for Josie, being widowed so young and all."

Josie, of course, is my mother. She and Anthony are the youngest of the Miggliore children and the only two still living.

Rose could be even less charitable when the mood struck her, as it often did at family gatherings. "He should get more exercise," she'd say, referring to my weight, a problem that has plagued me all my life. "Why doesn't he play more with his cousins instead of hanging around an old woman all the time? It's just not natural."

That was just a mother's defense mechanism. I'm convinced that my aunt's animus toward me was in great part a psychological reaction to the degeneracy of her own youngest son—my cousin Ronnie. What better way to draw attention away from one's own black sheep than by painting another's a darker shade?

They're both dead now, and I do pray for their souls: Ronnie the victim like so many of his kind in the eighties to his own tragic *joie de vivre*. We were the same age, so everyone expected us to be close. Besides, among the Miggliores, cousins were supposed to be as thick as siblings anyway. So I suppose comparisons were unavoidable.

My aunts and uncles could try to rationalize the family dynamics all they wanted; the reality was that Mama Miggliore considered me special from the moment of my birth, so it had nothing to do with my being fat or fatherless or an only child. The real reason I was destined for Mama Miggliore's favor was evident the moment my tiny head poked its way out of the sanctuary of Josie's womb that morning in May over fifty years ago. It was in my grandmother's house that I was born, in the great cherry wood bed where she had conceived and given birth to her own six children a generation and some years before me. The tradition of home birthing was waning in those war years, but Mama Miggliore badly wanted another child to be born in that bed. The last several family births—including Ronnie's just a few weeks before mine—had taken place in the antiseptic ambience of Touro Infirmary. My mother, without a husband around to consult, capitulated to her mother's wish. Uncle Anthony was there, standing in for my father, I imagine—and Rose too. They would be my *padrino* and *madrina*, my godparents. Rose, though, was useless as usual; she is said to have swooned at my dear mother's unanesthetized cries and had to be carried by Anthony to another bed where she lay until hours later when her scrubbed and tidied *figlioccio* (godson) could finally be presented to her.

So with Anthony tending to Rose in that other room, only Mama Miggliore and the midwife were on hand to witness my nativity. Anthony must have thought that a monster nothing shy of the Hydra itself was emerging when he heard my grandmother's cries echoing through the halls. "*Madre do Dio!*" she cried. And then, "*La testa! La testa!*" (The head!)

It wasn't that my head was abnormally large or small or misshapen in any way or that I had more than one of them that incited my grandmother's rapture. Rather it was what she saw on the top of my otherwise unremarkable noggin. I was born with very little hair, which trait served to elevate into prominence a peculiar birthmark at the crown of my head.

Actually birthmarks of this kind are not at all uncommon; it's simply a port-wine stain, the kind that Gorbachev would later make fashionable. *Nevus flammeus* is the precise medical term, and a malformation of blood vessels beneath the skin, the unromantic explanation. Its peculiarity lay neither in its type nor its size (it covered then, as it always has, about one quarter of my scalp), but in its shape.

It was a bit like having my own little purple Rorschach on top of my head: Everyone looked at the same thing and saw something different. Without digressing into subjective interpretations, I can tell you that the mark is of one continuous solid shape, wider at two opposite sides and tapering roughly symmetrically toward the center so that in the middle it is about one-half the length across as it is at its two opposite and widest extremes.

The bevy of descriptions I've heard over the years never ceases to amuse: It's an hourglass; a figure eight; no, a race track; no, the symbol for infinity. None other than Louis Prima himself, the famous jazz trumpeter, had an opinion. He knew the family through Uncle Paul, who was a musician, and paid a visit before I was old enough to remember. Prima said my birthmark looked like a trumpet poking out of the mouth of a megaphone.

Through my mother I learned the various family members' reactions. Uncle Paul took one look and saw the curves of Betty Grable. He was an insatiable lecher, dear old Paul, sire to four of my cousins and God only knows how many unacknowledged bastards. He was a clarinetist and played off and on with Prima. A couple of times he actually went on the road with Prima's band. My mother said he was always happier in a jazz club than home with his wife Nita—and she couldn't blame him because Nita was such a cold fish. Mama Miggliore said he had more mistresses than Mussolini. He died in bed with one of them when I was about nine. He wasn't even fifty years old.

Uncle Anthony was the one who saw the figure eight. He always thought about numbers; I'm only surprised he didn't see a dollar sign in front of it. Aunt Rose said it didn't look like anything. "It's just a birthmark," she said. "Why are you all trying to make it out to be something else?" But my mother said that everybody kept pressing Rose until she had to make up something. "All right," she finally screamed out (I can hear that shrill, hysterical voice of hers, though it's from my mother that I got the story). "It looks like a handbag!" Rose always loved to shop.

My mother herself told me when I was older that she thought it looked like two Hershey Kisses really kissing. "Two of the Christmas kind, so they'd be wrapped in red. And every time I looked at it, I wanted to kiss it."

Others have looked at the thing from a different angle, seeing the two wider parts as lateral sides rather than top and bottom. This perspective has yielded such responses as a bow tie and even a dog biscuit.

But none of those opinions are important to my story, for it was what Mama Miggliore saw when she first looked at my head that not only determined how all the others would view me, but in a way rendered my future as a priest a *fait accompli* from the beginning. Ironic, isn't it, that my fate would come to be shaped by a thing with no certain shape itself?

Born in southern Italy in the nineteenth century, it should be needless to say that my grandmother was a devoutly Catholic woman. She often lamented the absence of priests in the family. Her two sisters back in Sicily had produced three *pretes*. They would write her upon first receiving Communion from one of their boys or to boast about the number of marriages and baptisms their sons had presided over.

So forlorn did my poor grandmother feel and so badly did she want to compete with her sisters that she came to convince herself that her first male child, Little Joe, who died in infancy, must have been destined for the collar. He's already dead in the only photograph we have of him, fully dressed in what appears to be a new little suit not unlike what he might have worn had he lived to receive the Blessed Sacrament. He lies there on his mother's immaculate sheets, dwarfed by that great bed like a sleeping midget or ventriloquist's dummy. In that morbid nineteenth century tradition of posing the dead with props, he clutches the bronze crucifix his mother had brought with her from Sicily. She kept the framed image on a wall of her bedroom all her life. That crucifix still hung above her deathbed.

In her mind that child became, essentially, the one who got away. The question then was: Who would follow in Little Joe's aborted footsteps? Once her other sons, Paul and Anthony, had chosen business and music over the Church, that left the grandsons. One of them would surely not disappoint her. But which one? There would have to be a sign.

Enter me and my birthmark.

"*Il segno*," Mama Miggliore said of it that very first day. "*Il segno sacro!*"

The word *segno* can be translated as either a sign or a mark; thus my grandmother declared the nevus on my head to be no accident of genetics but a "holy mark." But what is so holy about a dog biscuit or a bow tie or even the figure of Betty Grable? Nothing, of course. Only to Mama Miggliore, the mark didn't look like any of those things. It was a chalice—a chalice full of wine, or better yet, the blood of Christ.

It was truly an ingenious interpretation. There's even a small "droplet" at what would be the base of the figure if one takes it to be a cup of some sort. The tiny excrescence is ignored by nearly everyone who looks at the thing, dismissed, as it were, like an insignificant bit of "noise." But not to my grandmother. To her it was confirmation that the thwarted destiny of her firstborn son would at last be fulfilled; therefore, this new child, she insisted, would be named Joe.

"Chalices don't look like that," my small-minded Aunt Rose said. "They're supposed to be wider at the top and fat at the base."

"No, no," said Mama Miggliore, pointing to my head. "*Chalice di Paradiso*." This is a heavenly chalice. "*Perfezione!*" She meant that it was not like the things of this world. Reading between the lines, I can see how she might have been subtly chastising her daughter, who was always a slave to fashion and the latest fads.

"She'd sell off anything Mama gave her if it didn't go with her house," my mother told me. "When Mama got wise and started passing things to me instead of her—like the silver set—Rose was furious. She thought she was entitled to everything since she was the oldest daughter. She could care less that it was her mother's or her grandmother's. She only wanted something if it was worth money, like all those yellow cars she bought every other year. Rose only liked new things."

My mother was right about all that. My aunt would live long enough for me to know her very well indeed. She even hated the nose her mother had passed on to her and spent years and a small fortune getting rid of it.

And as for the significance Mama Miggliore had ascribed to my birthmark, Rose would have none of it. "That color," she said, "it's all wrong. It's practically pink! No decent red wine is that light. Champagne maybe. But a chalice of champagne? It's ridiculous. And as for blood, well that's even stupider. Do you all know how dark blood is?"

Here Mama Miggliore stopped her again. "*Non importa!*" she cried with matriarchal finality. According to my mother, she caressed my head in the palms of her aged hands and said that the color didn't matter now; it would change to a deep crimson over time. "*Miracoloso!*" She was predicting a miracle, like the Consecration; the cheap wine would become blood.

Surely an uneducated woman from rural Sicily couldn't have known much about the behavior of port-wine birthmarks, but my grandmother's prediction was uncanny in light of the medical facts. The *nevus flammeus* is indeed known to change its color over time, something to do with the mutation of the broken vessels beneath the skin. In fact, they actually do become darker, more the color of blood. My mother tells me that I was in my second year when Mama Miggliore first noticed the color change.

"*Guardi,*" she said (Look here). She had me propped up in her lap, as was her way until I was too big for her—something she never did with Ronnie. "*Il color di vino. Guardi! Guardi!*" My mother says that everyone gathered around us except Rose and Ronnie; supposedly, Ronnie had wet himself.

The texture of the *nevus flammeus* is also susceptible to change. The nevus, which is simply a discoloration at birth, flat and undetect-

able to the touch like a shadow, will in some cases begin to acquire a
third dimension, growing thicker and standing out in relief above the
surrounding skin. Mama Miggliore had not predicted this phenomenon
as she had the darkening of the birthmark's hue, but she did not fail to
take notice of it or ascribe to it a miraculous explanation.

My mother kept my hair short all through my early childhood,
whether due to the style of the era or to Mama Miggliore's wish to see her
grandson's "holy mark" I still wonder. As my grandmother's eyes began to
fail her, though, she came to rely more on her sense of touch. When the
grandchildren were presented to her, she would put her hands on their
shoulders, rub her fingers over their faces, and say the Italian equivalent
of their names. In my case, though, the ritual was slightly different: After
touching my face, she always pulled me close to her body and cupped my
head in both her palms, like a priestess laying on the hands.

She had gotten immense in her last years. Her breasts were huge;
like her nose and ears, they seemed to have never stopped growing. She
wore the most cumbrous earrings—big, weighty loops and crosses like
Christmas ornaments that seemed to pull her fleshy lobes down to her
jaws. Bags collected in layers under her eyes, which drooped so that you
could see the bloody softness under her eyeballs. I thought it was the
weight of her ears and nose pulling down the flaccid skin of her face. She
always sat in the same great rosewood chair with its rococo designs and
delicate curving feet. It was upholstered in floral like the wallpaper of a
ballroom, similar to the huge, tent-like housedresses my grandmother
always wore so that as she got bigger, she and that chair came to be in my
mind one great sedentary idol.

I was seven when Mama Miggliore was first able to detect the
"holy mark" with her touch, so I can render that scene first-hand. It
was Thanksgiving and the family was gathered as usual at her house. In
addition to the major holidays, the Miggliores congregated one Sunday
a month to celebrate whichever grandchildren's birthdays had recently

passed. They were all there when Mama Miggliore went through the usual routine of grabbing me by the shoulders, smothering me in her breasts, and groping my head like a school nurse looking for lice. Only this time she detected something—not a louse, which I'm sure would have pleased Aunt Rose to no end, but a bump. "*Bernoccolo!*" she exclaimed.

At first no one knew what she meant. "What's wrong?" asked Uncle Paul. "Did he hit his head?" This is one of the few personal memories I have of Paul. He always seemed to be on the couch in the back room listening to jazz on the radio. Sometimes my mother would fix him a drink with three of those little white onions skewered on a tiny plastic fork and have me bring it to him. He always ate the onions right away, then thanked me and gave me the fork back. His wife, Aunt Nita, whom I can't remember ever speaking a word to, might be back there, but not on the couch with him; she would be standing, so I always had the feeling I was interrupting an argument, even back then before I knew about my uncle's running around. He would die his blissful death within a couple of years.

I suppose it's not really fair to judge people with so little evidence, but that's probably what I did with Uncle Paul, branding him a lecher based on family gossip. In truth, however, I've never held that against him. It's always been my opinion that the Lord smiles more benignantly on our transgressions when they're rooted in love and affection for others and not based on a grasping self-interest. It's probably not an inexplicable irony that the only one of my aunts and uncles that I have a jot of esteem for is the one I knew the least. I'll never know what role he would have played had he lived through the family machinations surrounding Mama Miggliore's death several years later, but I doubt he would have paid any of it much notice, as long as he had his clarinet and his women.

"No, I'm sure he didn't," my mother answered him. But Mama Miggliore kept rubbing my head and repeating her ejaculations. That's when Anthony stepped forward and put his rough and impatient fingers in my hair too. He didn't seem to know or care, as Mama Miggliore always had, how sensitive I was there.

"It's just that birthmark of his," he said, letting go of me again like I was a dumb beast he had just branded. "It's swelling up or something."

Mama Miggliore started prattling more Italian, much faster than I could follow at the time.

"What's she saying?" asked Aunt Rose.

Anthony was the only one of them who spoke enough Italian to answer her. "It's about the birthmark," he said. "She thinks it's changing, like it's turning into something." He stopped to listen some more. Everybody was silent, as if waiting for a message from Fatima. "She says it's like she predicted." He looked to Rose and my mother. "I don't remember her predicting that."

"I don't know," said Aunt Rose. "Who can remember everything she says about that thing. I asked Ronnie's pediatrician about those birthmarks. He said it's normal for them to change color like that."

"What about the way they feel?" asked Anthony. "Are they supposed to get bigger and thicker?"

"I didn't ask about that," said Rose.

Then Anthony turned to my mother. "You really should look into doing something before it gets worse and ends up covering his whole head. It could ruin his life. Maybe a plastic surgeon could burn it off or something."

Of course my mother wouldn't hear of putting her child through such a thing. "Oh stop it, Anthony, please," was all she said.

So how could I not have been my grandmother's favorite? After all, I was practically living proof of her powers of prophecy. Even though the seminary was still years away, my birthmark had already begun to set me apart at Miggliore gatherings. Once she realized that she could actually feel it, my grandmother was constantly tracing its outline with her fingers and muttering things in Italian, most of which I've forgotten, except for "*Segno sacro*," which I heard her repeat so many times that I believe they were the first words in her language that I learned.

Bacio became another, for not only did Mama Miggliore want to kiss my holy mark whenever she saw me, but she encouraged others in the family to do so as well, especially if they were ill or had some sort of special intention for which divine intercession might prove useful.

One of Uncle Paul's girls was an asthmatic child. She had an attack on the Fourth of July one year, and before Aunt Nita could fetch her inhaler, our grandmother grabbed the two of us and shoved the poor girl's wheezing mouth onto the top of my head. She wore braces and they scraped my skin, drawing blood, which Mama Miggliore believed to have flowed from the holy chalice. Her resulting ecstasies sent my cousin into a faint, which calmed her convulsions and convinced our grandmother of a miracle cure.

Unconvinced, however, remained Rose and Anthony. I often overheard my godparents huddling together after Mama Miggliore had made a fuss over me after another scene like the asthma incident. They were always smoking: Rose's long, skinny cigarettes she kept in a gold case with a rose emblazoned on its cover and Anthony's stubby cigars with their putrid licorice scent. It's a wonder my poor cousin didn't have an attack every time she was around those two.

"It isn't fair," Rose once said. "She treats him like some kind of saint just because of a scar that should have been removed years ago, if his mother had any sense."

"Josie's never had a mind of her own," said Anthony, typical in his disdain for my mother, who was probably in the kitchen helping Wanda, the colored sitter, clean up everybody's mess while they talked about her. "She's always done whatever Mama wants."

"All of our beautiful children," Rose went on, "and look what she latches onto—a fat little thing with a purple head!"

Whenever my aunt's mean streak started to show, Anthony would touch her on the shoulder or take his cigar out of his mouth just long enough to whisper something in her ear without setting her hair on fire. It usually didn't deter her.

"No, it's true," she'd say. "My Ronnie doesn't have a blemish on him, and Tony Junior is going to be as handsome as Tyrone Power. Doesn't that mean God favors them? Why can't she see that?"

"She believes what she wants to believe," said Anthony. "It's just the shape of that damned birthmark. If it had come out looking like a snowflake or a lampshade, we wouldn't have to go through all this."

"It should have covered his face," snapped Rose.

Even when she wasn't that vicious, my Aunt Rose managed to find little passive-aggressive ways to hurt me—like buying me hats practically every Christmas of my childhood. "I thought he'd need a new one," she'd say. "His head is getting so much bigger."

Mama Miggliore still loved me, of course. The time I spent with her through those early years may have inflamed my godparents against me, but it was incidentally how I came to speak Italian. That was the only way to communicate with Mama Miggliore, who, though she had left Sicily in 1895, could not, even at her death over sixty years later, speak a word of English. My mother used to say that that was my grandfather's, Papa Miggliore's, doing, his way of keeping his wife in tow despite all the freedoms and worldly temptations she might be exposed to once he had brought her over here.

"He wouldn't even let Mama listen to English radio stations," she once told me. "There was one station broadcasting in Italian in those days, and he glued the dial on her radio so it was stuck on that one. That was all the entertainment she had except for the Mario Lanza records Papa brought home for her when he was running the music store. And he didn't even let her keep them. He'd just let her listen to them for a few days and then bring them back to the store and pass them off as new."

My grandfather wouldn't let his children speak English to their mother. It was Italian or nothing, and none of them were close to fluent except the artful Anthony, who studied it at Tulane. Once Papa was gone, it was he who translated everything for her when the family was together—everything he wanted her to hear, that is.

"Rose and I weren't allowed to go to college," Josie said, "even though Papa could afford it. College was just for the sons in those days. Not that Rose would have gone anyway. She was too busy shopping and going out with boys. But I might have liked to study something, not to go to work or anything, but just to know more things. Paul went to Tulane, too, but he never studied Italian. He just took whatever courses he needed for his business degree. He was too busy playing his music and getting girls—like Rose with the boys, only worse."

My mother felt she never got to know her own mother, though she was past forty when the old woman died. How could she when they couldn't have a real conversation?

"I could speak a little Italian, but not much. Rose knew even less than me. She always carried around that dictionary so Mama would think she knew more than she did," she told me. "But that was the way Papa wanted it. Let Mama have the babies and take care of the house. If we wanted to talk about anything important, we should go to him. He never understood that there are some things a daughter needs to talk about with her mother."

Maybe Aunt Rose was right—that my affinity with Mama Miggliore was unnatural—but I was a fat little boy with no friends, so who could blame me? Besides, there was something else about the relationship that Rose, in all her self-centeredness, could never understand: In some way I was making my mother happy, filling a kind of emptiness, if you will, by getting close to her mother.

I took an early interest in Mama and Papa Miggliore's story. My mother told me that their families had been friends in Sicily, in the little village of San Guiseppe, some miles inland from Palermo. Once I was able to understand my grandmother's language, I could hear her own accounts of those early days.

"Everybody was poor there," she said. "Except the ones who were rich." As absurd as that sounds, she was making a keen point about southern Italy, the *Mezzogiorno*, as they called it then, in the late nineteenth century: You were either rich or poor, owned land or were virtually owned by those who did. There was nothing in between. "I picked olives and lemons from the time I was a girl."

She never gave me the impression that she was unhappy there, despite the privations that I know she had to live with—like no plumbing and working all day for the equivalent of about twenty-five cents. She never mentioned those things to me; I got them from my mother, who in turn had them from her father.

"He wanted to make sure we all knew what he had rescued her from," my mother said. "It was how he always shut us up when Paul or me said something to him about not letting her go anywhere. 'Don't you two brats start on me,' he'd say. 'She'd still be crapping in a hole by an olive tree if it wasn't for me.' And he was right, that's what they had to do over there. But you know, I don't think it mattered to her. In a way, she might have been better off. She just wanted to be with him, though."

That I knew. Of her devotion to my grandfather, there could be no doubt, even to someone who was just learning the language and could barely understand her. He was a great man, she insisted, so great that they even built a splendid "*monumento*" to him upon his death, or so she thought. As a child, I didn't doubt this; I even had a vague memory of seeing this monument myself, before I learned the real truth.

One thing was interesting to me about the way my grandmother spoke of her husband: She never used the word "love" to describe their relationship. Rather, she would say things like *protezione* or *appartenere*. It was as if, in her mind, he was more of a protector and she simply belonged with him, or perhaps even *to* him. I am not quite able after all these years to make that distinction, having been so young and naïve of the ways of the world at the time to have known what a critical distinction it was.

"*Acuto*" is what I always remember being her first reaction whenever someone mentioned my grandfather in her presence; how smart or sharp he was seemed to be foremost in her memory. "*A quello Angelo—acuto!*"

"She was right about that," my mother agreed. "Papa was one smart cookie, all right. And ambitious, too. He already started moving up in the world even before he left San Guiseppe." She would shake her head at this part of the story, where her father lifted himself above the ranks of the peasantry or "*contadini*." "It might sound like a good thing here, but over there it could only mean something bad."

She meant the *cosche*. Government in the Mezzogiorno had always been weak and haphazard at best, police protection a joke. Sicily itself was especially chaotic, practically the Wild West of Southern Europe. The few who had any property worth protecting were on their own. Hence the cosche, loose coalitions of wealthy families banded together to protect their own interests. They may have begun with the good intention of self-preservation, but in time their power became corrosive, and they began wielding it where it was not wanted, doing things like forcefully regulating prices and charging innocent people for their "protection."

"They were always looking for young men from the farms to join them," my mother said. "Young men who knew the poor farmers and could gain their trust. They would tempt them with money and things that they would never be able to have on their own. And Papa was just the type they could get to. There was no way he was going to spend his life with the *contadini*, picking somebody else's lemons."

Of course I never mentioned the cosche to Mama Miggliore, but I do know that her husband came to America two years before she did. That was rather common: the man making the journey first and returning for the woman or family later. My mother was convinced that the cosche paid her father's way, probably even arranging his eventual settlement in New Orleans.

It was 1895 when my grandfather returned to Italy for his young wife. She was only seventeen. "He had to marry her before he came over the first time," my mother said. "That was part of the control. Once they were married, she had to wait for him. There was no changing your mind in those days. She was just a girl."

He sent money ahead so she could meet him in Naples, the port from which most emigrants embarked for America at the time. My mother thought there was something a little funny about that. Why couldn't he have come to Sicily for her? He mustn't have wanted to have to explain to the families what he had been doing. "He knew Mama wouldn't ask too many questions. She wasn't the suspicious type. She just said how handsome he looked in his new suit."

As far as the actual voyage and arrival in America, I can relate the story as I heard it from my grandmother. "*Tre settimana*," she would say to me of the voyage, some six decades remote in her memory: three weeks. Sometimes she called them three lonely weeks: "They wouldn't let us together. Only during the day."

That was indeed true: The men and women were segregated by night and only allowed contact during the day; and even then it had to be out in the open on one of the decks they were restricted to. That rule, however, applied only to the masses crowded into steerage. In first class it was a different story, and on that my mother had her own opinion. "I would have never told Mama this," she said," but there was a picture of him on that boat, a photograph. It showed him with another woman. And believe me, they weren't in no steerage. They're sitting at a table in a dining room where everybody's dressed up like royalty. I know it's on the boat because its name is on the centerpiece of the table in plain letters—the *Reluctant Glory*. He's got his arm on her shoulder in a way that you can tell it means something."

She said she found the picture among some papers Papa Miggliore left, and she was convinced the woman was her father's mistress. "She was beautiful, too, with eyes like a young Gloria Swanson, only this was way before Gloria Swanson. She couldn't have been Italian. She looked more German or Russian or something like that. There was no way Papa could have married her, even if he wouldn't have already been married to Mama. If you wanted to get ahead in those circles, you better marry Italian. But it was okay to have a good-looking foreign woman on the side. God forgive me, but you know Mama was never nothing to look at."

My mother was certainly right about Mama Migglioire's looks. In the most flattering photographs I've seen, the best you could say is that she appears "handsome," like a younger Gertrude Stein before she turned into a man.

So it was my mother's belief that her father shared a first-class cabin with this woman while poor Mama Miggliore was herded away in twenty-dollar steerage like a cow. I have no idea if that could be true, having never seen the picture or spoken to anyone else on the subject. My grandmother, though, did survive whatever indignities came her way during those three weeks, including being checked for lice by the health officials in New York.

Her favorite tale of that first day in America is what the family has come to call the "Banana Story." I'm no authority on the flora of southern Italy in the nineteenth century or on the diet of its inhabitants, but apparently bananas were extremely rare if not nonexistent in Sicily. As incredible as it is to us in America today, where even in a backwoods dung heap like Kattannachee, Louisiana, Clara is able to get pineapple and kiwi fruit year-round, my grandmother at age seventeen had never seen a banana in her life.

"Bananas, bananas!" she'd scream whenever that first sighting came to her memory. The word is the same in English and Italian. They became a favorite food with her and a major contributor to her obesity in her old age when she couldn't chew anything. My mother and I would bring her a batch every time we visited. I'd watch her peel them and stuff them one after another nearly whole into her toothless mouth, smacking with her lips like a dog with a mouthful of peanut butter. It was quite charming, though disgusting. Once Rose tried to upstage us with a batch of her own, but Mama Miggliore put hers aside and would only eat ours.

"You see, I can't do anything right in her eyes," said Rose, the rejected Esau. "There's nothing wrong with these bananas." She held them up and shook them like something dead she had by the tail. "But she'd rather have those brown old rotten things just because they're from them. I got these from Langenstein's. Nothing cheap there—fifteen cents a pound."

And they were beautiful, as magnificently yellow as one of Rose's Cadillacs. The problem was that Mama Miggliore liked her bananas soft. My mother and I always made a point of going to the market exactly five days before a visit so they'd be just the way she liked them: half-brown on the outside and mushy on the inside. Rose didn't know that; she could never exchange more than a few shallow words with her mother even with that pathetic dictionary of hers.

My grandparents soon made their way down to New Orleans. Mama Miggliore told me it was because there were more *Cattolicos* down here. My mother said they had other motives.

"The Catholic thing was only part of it," she said. "The climate might have had something to do with it too. But he made up more excuses—like wanting to get her away from all the Jews up there, telling her they hated the Italians—just so she'd think he was trying to make her happy. The real reason was money and getting ahead. I told you he had connections that set him up over here?"

Again, she was referring to the cosche.

"I think they wanted to move into New Orleans, and they needed somebody they could trust down here. They probably told him either go to New Orleans or you're on your own. Papa said a Sicilian in New York could work like a dog all day and make less than a nigger."

My grandfather used his own initials to name the company he started in New Orleans. "If that doesn't tell you how full of himself he was, I don't know what would," my mother said. By 1910, A.M. Enterprises comprised several bars and liquor stores. With the advent of Prohibition, it branched out into a couple of movie theatres and a music store that sold phonograph records and sheet music as well as small instruments.

"You'd think he would have been hit hard when that Prohibition took over," my mother told me, "but we were better off than ever. He even renovated the house then. And I don't think for a minute it was because of the movie houses and the music store. He kept us all away from it while he was around, so we never knew what was really going on."

My grandmother bore him six children in all, the first two dying before my time. Little Joe, as the family would always call him, came first, in 1901. *Febbre di cervello* is what Mama Miggliore told me carried off her firstborn, the one that would have been a priest—a "brain fever." Grace came a year later, dying at age fourteen during the influenza outbreak a year after my mother was born. Uncle Paul came along in 1906, then Rose in 1911, Anthony in 1915, and finally Josephine two years later.

Incidentally, I'm the only one of my generation who would know these things. None of my frivolous cousins could care less about family history—or "trivia," as Ronnie used to call it. True, I haven't been in contact with any of them since Rose's funeral, but I don't have any reason to believe they've changed since we were children, when one of Paul's daughters—not the asthmatic, an older one, a vapid girl of thirteen at the time—told me that Mama Miggliore had been a slave in Sicily, which my cousin believed to be an island in the Caribbean, somewhere near Jamaica.

It must have been the girl's birthday, because I remember her being all excited about a gift she had received: some new Eddie Fisher record she was playing over and over on the Victrola. I had brought my own Johnnie Ray—"The Little White Cloud that Cried," I believe. I always liked Johnnie Ray. I remember a few years later when he came out with "Yes Tonight Josephine." I played that record over and over for my mother, and for weeks whenever she asked me to do something—dust my room, put out the garbage or milk bottles, or what have you—I'd say, "Yes, tonight, Josephine" and we'd laugh together.

"She wasn't a slave," I insisted, confident on the subject at age eight to challenge someone who to me was practically an adult. "Only coloreds are slaves. Wanda's grandmother was one."

"That's just here," my cousin said. "It was different in Sicily. Down there, anybody could be one. It went by money. They weren't prejudiced like us."

When I told her that Sicily wasn't "down there," but "over there" in Europe, she became angry and wouldn't let me play my record.

"Johnnie Ray's a sissy who wears makeup," she sneered.

No, my cousins could hardly be said to have developed much in the way of filial pride, but just ask them about the money and see how sharp they get.

And I don't just mean the five dollars our grandmother used to slip me at every visit while the others only got two. I actually felt guilty about getting more than the others because I could sense that it was exacerbating their jealousy of me. To make amends, I sometimes bought a little gift for Tony Junior, the only one who ever accepted me and didn't begrudge the special place I held in our grandmother's esteem. At first it was just a piece of fudge or licorice, but then Tony started smoking when we went behind the levee, and I started giving him some of my extra dollars to buy a pack or two.

The money I'm referring to—about which my cousins, I'm sure, are quite cognizant—is the *real* money, the sizable fortune Papa Miggliore amassed by way of his various business interests, investments, and four decades of schemes whose true and precise details perhaps the

Lord Himself only knows. My mother certainly didn't have a clue as she was growing up.

"Papa wasn't around very much except late at night and on Sundays," she said, "but that wasn't unusual. The men were like that in those days, working long hours and leaving the household things to the wives and daughters."

Many of these conversations with my mother took place in the weeks and months following Mama Miggliore's death in 1959, an event that precipitated the uncovering of a family secret that had remained hidden from me and the rest of my cousins all our lives.

"The only thing that was a little suspicious back in those days when Papa was around was that he gave Rose and me positions in the businesses, even though we never hardly did anything," said my mother. "Now Paul and Anthony—they really did work, everything from tending bar after the Prohibition was over to taking tickets at the movie houses. I think that's how Anthony started with those nasty cigars. They used to sell them at the bars. Nothing funny about that, though. Sons are supposed to learn the business like that. But why did Papa have to put me and Rose's name in the books? You know I was the manager of the music store when I was just eighteen! And I never even went in the place except on Saturdays to pick out a record or two. The boys took care of the music store just like everything else. That's how Paul met Louis Prima, you know."

The essence of my mother's point was that Papa Miggliore just wanted to have the children occupying important positions in the businesses so as to make the family's wealth appear less suspicious; he could pay them exorbitant salaries—at least on paper—and the Miggliore coffers would continually grow, apparently legitimately.

All that was expected of the two daughters was that they would marry boys from good families. "A good family meant two things to Papa," my mother said. "They had to be Italian and they had to have some money." Rose did fine on both counts, marrying one of the Cuchinotto boys, who ended up with a good share of the seafood business on Claiborne Avenue. She got a nickname from that: Uncle Paul started calling her the Fishwife after she got married. Anthony picked up on it too. I can remember him using it when she wasn't around. "When's the Fishwife getting here?" he'd say if she was late for something. "She's probably still putting on her scales." By that he meant her long orange fingernails.

"You know, the Cuchinottos were the first ones to ship fresh crayfish across the country," Josie told me. That's how my mother was—always willing to give credit to others, even to the family of a spiteful barracuda like Rose.

As far as marrying well herself, poor Josie had less to brag about. "It was bad enough your father was a Cajun from Lafayette," she told me, "but driving a bread truck for a living was more than they could put up with."

By "they," my mother meant Anthony and the Fishwife; Papa Miggliore was no longer around by the time my mother met Danny Broussard sometime around the beginning of the war. "They gave me a hard time about it, that's true," she said. "Especially Rose. She used to say things like 'I can't believe Josie's going with somebody named Broussard. Mama's going to be sick when she finds out. It's a good thing Papa isn't here to see this.' And things like that. Danny was a Catholic, thank God, so at least they came to the wedding."

Rose was wrong about her mother's reaction; Mama Miggliore was apparently quite fond of my father. "I remember when I was trying to explain to her what he did for a living," my mother told me. "'Ah, pane!' Mama said. That's bread in Italian, and Danny always brought her some whenever he saw her, before and after we were married. She might have thought he was a baker. I'm not sure."

I believe that Mama Miggliore must have realized by then that marrying Italian wasn't an infallible guarantor of happiness. Although everyone says she never complained about my grandfather, she must have been aware on some level of what her place was to him. Of course she knew about Uncle Paul's philandering and Anthony and the Fishwife's constant grasping for money despite "marrying well." There were good Italians and bad Italians, good Cajuns and bad Cajuns.

Having only one child didn't mitigate my mother's situation in the eyes of Rose and Anthony either. They were forever using their prodigious broods—in all twelve children between them—to ingratiate themselves to Mama Miggliore. Ronnie and one of Anthony's girls who was younger than I were the most shamelessly exploited, forced to put on pathetic little Christmas and Easter pageants for their grandmother's entertainment. They both took dance classes, so Anthony and Rose would have them dress up in whatever costumes they wore for their last revue. Never mind the absurdity of an Easter pageant featuring John Smith and Pocahontas.

It was all about the money, of course. And though we were all no doubt better off not knowing exactly how Papa Miggliore had amassed his fortune, it was quite a sizable one for its day. I'd rather not get into exact figures, even if I knew them, which I don't. Let it suffice to say that when my grandmother died, the amount to be distributed among her heirs was well into the seven figures, quite substantial in those Eisenhower days.

The manner in which the estate would be divided became a matter of great controversy even before Mama Miggliore's death, thanks mainly to Uncle Anthony. The facts seem uncomplicated enough: Four of my grandmother's children had survived childhood: Josie, Rose, Paul, and Anthony. Four children, four slices of the pie. A "no-brainer," as they say today.

But anyone who thinks the issue of succession in a large Italian family could ever be a no-brainer, especially when a great deal of money and a brace of greedy, backbiting dagos like my godparents are involved, should have his head examined. Anthony actually hatched his insidious scheme to grab the lion's share of the prize for himself years earlier.

My uncle's argument was that although four families indisput-
ably stood as heirs to the Miggliore estate, a strict mathematical split into
quarters would not really be fair because each of Mama Miggliore's children had not themselves produced an equal number of heirs. Anthony
had six children, as had the Fishwife; but Paul and Nita had only four;
and Josie, of course, might have been barren had it not been for me. A
truly equitable distribution of the family assets, my uncle maintained,
would take into consideration not just the number of children Mama
Miggliore had but the *size* of those children's families. The pie should
be divided not into four parts but seventeen, with Anthony, Rose, Paul's
widow, and Josie receiving one part per grandchild (or "blessing," as
Anthony put it) that they had added to the family.

It was obvious who the big loser would be in such a scheme.
With six children each, Anthony and the Fishwife would be looking forward to a windfall: not 25 percent of the family fortune as anyone can
see they were legally, as well as logically, entitled to, but over 35 percent.
Paul's widow would receive about 23 percent, and Josie would be left
with a preposterous 6 percent, the mere crumbs off her siblings' tables.

Obviously even the crookedest judge in New Orleans would have
laughed at such a proposal, not to mention whatever lawyer Anthony
could have found foolhardy enough to argue it. But my uncle never considered venturing near a courtroom with his scheme. He was far more
artful than that, as I discovered when my mother related the story to me
the day of Mama Miggliore's wake.

"Oh, no, he knew he wouldn't have a leg to stand on in court,"
she said. We were on our way to the funeral parlor in the old Plymouth,
one of those bloated old things from the early fifties. Josie kept it for
years. One reason it lasted so long is that we both loved to ride the streetcar so much. That was how we always went shopping or to the movies:
a little walk to Saint Charles and then the streetcar downtown. She still
had that thing after my ordination, but by the seventies, we had to get

her something new to drive to the malls after, as she put it, "The coloreds took over Canal Street."

"If Uncle Anthony knew it wouldn't work, why did he try to bring it up?" I asked.

"He was trying to get to Mama," Josie instructed me. "He thought if he could convince her that it was the right thing to do with the money and get her on his side, the rest of us would go along with it because it was what she wanted. But it never happened. They never got to her."

Not for want of trying. Throughout the last few years of my grandmother's life, I can remember the two of them managing to bring up the subject nearly every time the family was together. Rose, always the less discreet of the two, hardly bothered to conceal not only her delight at the prospect of the extra money but her outrage that I might ultimately be left far better off than her precious Ronnie.

"Ronnie deserves the best," she said. "His ballet instructor said he has real talent and it would be a sin to waste it. We could send him to New York to study with the best. It just isn't fair that Josie's boy gets all that. It would just encourage him to get lazier and fatter."

She even used her absurd choplogic to try to turn my mother's frugality and simple tastes against her. "What does Josie need with all that money anyway?" she said. "She never buys anything. How old is that car anyway?"

Anthony at least tried to assume the guise of objectivity, as if driven not by his own self-interests but by a laudable sense of democracy.

"I think we would all agree that this isn't about us," he said one day to his two sisters and Aunt Nita. Mama Miggliore was there, too, but by then she could do little more than sit in her great flowered chair and drift in and out of sleep. "None of us wants anything for ourselves. It's the kids we're looking out for." Here Mama Miggliore passed gas, a deep sonorous croaking like the angry voice of Mother Nature.

Anthony hardly paused. "The children are the real beneficiaries, not us, and I know we all want what's fair for them." He puffed on his stinking licorice stick and resumed his quasi-Jeffersonian dialectic. "Do we want this family to degenerate into groups of haves and have-nots? I don't think that's what Mama and Papa came to this country for."

Here we all looked instinctively to Mama Miggliore, her eyelids half-closed so we couldn't tell if she was aware of our stares or not. Naturally, we didn't think her capable of contributing to the conversation, so when a single word emanated from her ancient lips, we all took notice.

"What did she say?" asked Aunt Rose.

"She said *pudore*," said Anthony. "It means 'decency.' You see, sometimes she can understand us. She knows that what I'm saying is the decent thing to do." In his excitement, he bit down on his cigar so that it stuck out straight from his mouth.

"It didn't sound like that to me," said my mother. "It sounded more like a Z sound, something like 'puzarry.'"

The Fishwife started rooting through her handbag for the dictionary. "Is there such a word as that?" she asked.

"No," said Anthony.

"Maybe she meant '*puzzare*,'" I said, provoking my uncle to look my way.

"What does that mean?" asked Rose. Anthony continued to stare at me, the red-hot tip of his cigar leveled right between my eyes. He probably didn't know yet that I had become quite proficient in Italian, that the language was no longer their little secret.

"It means 'stink,'" I said.

"Stink!" screamed Aunt Rose. "Why would she say that? She can't think your idea stinks. It must be a mistake." She had the dictionary in her hands by then and was rifling through its pages, her orange fingernails like sparks shooting off the pages.

"She meant her fart," said Aunt Nita, who rose to leave the room laughing. "She doesn't know what we're talking about."

That humiliating setback most probably marked a turning point in my *padrino's* attitude toward his godson. Until then I was for the most part beneath his notice, except for an occasional comment muttered into his cigar about the preferential treatment I got from Mama Miggliore. After that day, however, I'm sure he began to see me as a threat. His contempt toward me culminated the day of the most memorable family event of them all: the death of Mama Miggliore.

There had been several trial runs in the four or five years prior to that day, each precipitated by some kind of medical "event" or other—a minor stroke or one of my grandmother's famous falls. There must have been a half dozen of these little stumbling episodes in the last eighteen months or so of her life, each blown absurdly out of proportion as if the Tower of Pisa itself had after nine hundred years finally come crashing to earth. It was the same thing when I worked at the retirement home for nuns, the last place the vengeful archbishop stuck me before my exile to Kattannachee. Why is it that these old women can't seem to walk from one place to another in broad daylight in a house they've lived in for years without falling flat on their faces?

"Ah! Mama fell again!" would come the shrill voice of Aunt Rose over the phone, and Josie and I would rush to the house in the Plymouth. During those last few years, we had a sitter staying with my grandmother, a huge black woman named Wanda whose husband had been a garbage collector until he slipped along his route in Carrollton one rainy morning and fell into the garbage hold of the truck. His colleagues managed to pull all of him out except for one arm, which was crushed by the mechanism. They retired him with a shamefully small settlement, only five thousand dollars, according to Anthony, who hired Wanda after one of her cousins, who did Anthony's yard work and some occasional odd jobs for Josie, told him of the family's misfortune. For years I assumed Wanda was a genuine healthcare professional: She was always wearing white, and we certainly could have afforded a nurse. Eventually I found out that

Anthony had bought the uniforms for her to make a good appearance before the neighbors.

Wanda always began the phone chain after every disaster involving my grandmother: She'd call Anthony, who'd call the Fishwife, who'd call my mother, who'd call Aunt Nita. By the time we'd all get there, the crisis had usually passed. Mama Miggliore would be snoring vigorously, the pieces of whatever she had broken during her fall neatly swept away by Wanda.

But on that last day of my grandmother's life, the phone chain was broken. Rose didn't call my mother. Instead it was Wanda who told us to get over to the house right away.

"Tell your mama to get over here as quick as y'all can," she said when I answered the phone.

"She's in the bathroom," I said. It was a Saturday morning and Josie was washing her hair. "Did Mama fall again?"

"No," Wanda said. "Tell your mama them two's already here and to hurry up. This could be it this time!"

It went without saying who "them two" were. Wanda wanted us there because she didn't trust my godparents, particularly Rose because of the plastic surgery. By 1959 the Fishwife was in her late forties. One facelift behind her, she had begun the work on her nose, which she would concentrate on through the next decade, once she had her share of her mother's money. She was forever dieting, too, further annoying the wide-hipped Wanda. "She just don't want to look like her mama," Wanda would mutter in the kitchen, where only Josie or I could hear her. "That all that's about."

When my mother and I arrived, there were two other notables in attendance in addition to Wanda and the family. One was a doctor, whose name I can't remember except that it started with a C and was very Italian, something like Aunt Rose's Cuchinotto, only with even more syllables—like Castigliano or Castrogiovanni but neither of those. I had never seen the man before and after that day would never again. The presence of the other watcher was alarming, though not unprecedented, as I had never seen him in the house except on Sundays or religious holidays. Unlike the anonymous doctor, however, I would never be able to forget the name of Franklin Ratchett, the future archbishop of New Orleans. Little did I know that this man, who was there ostensibly to comfort my dying grandmother, would eventually become one of the most redoubtable nemeses of my life.

He was just Father Frank to us then, a mere parish priest, albeit an ambitious and politically sensitive one. His first assignment was as assistant pastor at Mama Miggliore's neighborhood parish, Pope Pius. He was still a young man, perhaps in his late thirties if he can be believed, the day my grandmother died. A handsome man overall, he stood a good six feet tall and had more than his share of Nordic blond hair, most of which, incidentally, he still has today.

There's something wrong with his right hand, though. Excepting his thumb, the other four digits didn't completely develop, so that at a glance he always appears to be making a fist. It's the most odd deformity because each finger is only about a half an inch long yet has a fully formed nail, which if viewed from certain angles seems to be growing out of his hand. From the palm side of his hand, though, you can see the fingers, the tips so normal looking that it seems you could yank on one of them and it would pop out full length like the organ of an aroused tomcat.

Like all resolute opportunists, he managed to work his handicap to his advantage: It humanized him to the women of the parish, balancing his otherwise intimidating Nordic good looks. Tennessee Williams has a story about a boxer who turns to prostitution when he loses an arm. The men of the French Quarter find the beautiful Adonis all the more alluring for his imperfection, like Byron with his clubfoot or the damaged statue of a Greek god. Similarly smitten were the women of the predominately Italian parish that Father Frank first ministered to. He must have been the ideal foil to their fat, swarthy husbands. But it was just after the war when he came out of the seminary, not exactly the best time for a first-generation American with German roots to step into a position of trust. Which was precisely why the deformity came in, if you'll pardon the pun, "handy." It was exactly what the females of the flock needed in their shepherd: a reason to pity him.

The hand had always fascinated me as well, drawing my eye like an unexpected flutter of movement or flickering of light every time Ratchett was around. What would it feel like to the touch? I used to wonder if the little fingerlings ever moved. I imagined them wiggling futilely, like desperate, striving larvae.

I have had many reasons in the past handful of years to study the career of Father-cum-Archbishop Franklin W. Ratchett. (By the way, he'll say the W stands for William, but I learned he had it changed from Wilhelm while in the seminary sometime in the forties). His parents emigrated from Hamburg just after the First World War and made their way to northern Florida, where Ratchett claims to have been born. There have been some rumors, however, that he was actually born in Germany before the war's end. In all fairness, I have not been able to trace or substantiate that allegation, so I will assume a birth date circa 1920.

He chose a Louisiana seminary and, upon ordination in 1947, requested an assignment in New Orleans because he wanted to work in an urban area among a large immigrant population not a great distance from his family. The abundance of native Italians still around at mid-century made the city exceptionally appealing.

It didn't take long for his ambition and political perspicacity to reveal themselves. He used his good looks to his advantage with the women, but there was never the slightest hint of impropriety in his relations with any of them. This I find significant as it seems to be characteristic of the most ruthlessly career-driven: They are not about to let mere human frailties stand in their way. He learned some Italian to endear himself to the older generation. And most importantly, he quickly determined which parishioners to develop close ties with.

It may not be fair to maintain that Ratchett's rise was a *fait accompli* from the beginning. There certainly were parishes where he would have been more visible than at Pope Pius. Furthermore, it doesn't appear that he began to court the favor of my family until several years after his arrival there, and after more than ten years, he was still just an assistant pastor. On the other hand, there are a few noteworthy circumstances surrounding his story that give me pause for thought. By the time Father Frank started personally to look to the spiritual welfare of the Miggliores—namely by bringing my grandmother the Eucharist and hearing her confession once a week, as well as making hospital visits and baptizing Rose's and Anthony's youngest—he was by any account somewhere in his early thirties, that age when the romantic ideals of youth are just about to yield to the realities of middle age. But not quite. There exists a part of the man that still believes he's young enough, strong enough, attractive enough, innovative enough to try to make something of his life beyond the mundane. He takes a long, deep look at the two factors that most define his existence—his career and his marriage (or lack thereof)—and asks himself if he has made the right choices.

I was fortunate to be doing some of the most gratifying work of my life in my thirties—running a boarding house for homeless boys—so I never had to question the value of my own vocation; but I've seen priests at that stage of their lives go in every direction: Some come to feel guilty about the bourgeois comforts they fear they may be settling into and adopt a rigid asceticism, taking off to battle ringworm in some blighted Third World hole. Others who may have come to fraternize with wealthy and powerful members of their congregations may be pulled in the other direction—craving their own membership in the club.

I believe something like that drove Ratchett into the relationship he came to have with my family. At first we had to share his attentions with others in the parish. He'd often stop by only long enough to offer my grandmother Communion, apologizing that he had made dinner arrangements with some other family. As the years went by, though, that gradually changed until, by the end of the decade, Father Frank had practically become the Miggliores' private chaplain. He even kept a spare surplice in the hall closet nearest Mama Miggliore's room for convenience. We'd have it dry-cleaned for him periodically or whenever my grandmother drooled or spit up something on him when he leaned close to offer her the Eucharist or hear her confession.

Why we were singled out for such special attention is easy to understand considering the demographics of the parish: Pope Pius was never a wealthy population. Most of its parishioners were first- or second-generation blue-collar immigrants—truck drivers, butchers, roofers, and the like. Among these people, the Miggliores must have stuck out like silver thumbs, especially the ostentatious Rose and Anthony, with their expensive cars and wardrobes. Rose probably spent enough at her manicurist's every year to fund a Maryknoll mission for six months.

The house wouldn't have attracted a gold digger's attention itself. From the street it was just another wooden duplex on a one-way street off Magazine near the park. The only concession my grandfather made when he started making money was to tear down the dividing wall and merge the two kitchens in the rear of the house so that the family had the whole place. "He was too cheap to buy Mama a new house even though he could afford it," my mother said. "But what did he care? He was never there anyway."

I know Ratchett and Uncle Anthony were getting thick as thieves in the years prior to Mama Miggliore's death. Their conversations were always laced with allusions to parties and dinners at Anthony's uptown home or how much money they took in at the Saint Joseph's altar. What a scam that was. Every spring Anthony let Father Frank set up a tent by his pool. Ratchett would have a bunch of fat-ankled, goitered old women from Pope Pius bake Italian pastries—biscottis, cannolis, cucidatis (those fabulous fig cookies), ricotta pies—until the poor things nearly dropped from exhaustion, all to put together a sumptuous spread for Garden District socialites. The spectacle used to make the society page in the *Picayune*, with half of Saint Charles Avenue showing up—even the Jews. What became of the money is anyone's guess.

It certainly was ingenious of my uncle to have an ally like Father Frank on hand the day of my grandmother's death—a priest and therefore above disrepute, one who owed him more than a few favors and could conveniently understand some Italian. It wouldn't surprise me if my godfather had planned that day for years.

By 1959 my godparents' malignant resentment toward me seemed to be healing, but with Mama Miggliore's death, I realized it had just been in remission. Since my grandmother's health and state of mind had declined to the point where she was for the most part unresponsive, I was no longer treated as her pet grandchild. She hadn't mentioned my "holy mark" in ages and no longer insisted that Josie take me to the barber every two weeks to make sure my hair didn't grow out enough to obscure it.

For his part, Ratchett had never been impressed by the mark. Taking his cue from Rose, he called it my "birth defect," as if it were some kind of grotesque deformity like that stubby paw of his.

"Mama thinks it's a sign from God," the Fishwife said to him one day. It was the first Easter he spent with the family. Later that day she had the inspiration to try to use Father Frank to put an end to any credence that Mama Miggliore's belief might have had.

"Here, Father, take a look yourself and tell me what you think it is." She had led him by his good hand into the yard where the children were hunting plastic Easter eggs filled with candy and pennies. "Don't any of you say anything," she said to my cousins. "I don't want you to give anything away."

The priest looked at my head while my aunt held me fast by the shoulders. I was perhaps seven years old. "I don't know what you mean," he said. "The birthmark?"

"Yes," she said.

"I think the boy is very fortunate," Father Frank said. "I've seen them much worse, even covering half the face."

"That's not what I mean," Rose said. "Do you think it looks like anything?"

Ratchett had no idea what the silly woman was talking about.

"Eugene thinks it's a flounder with the tip of its head chopped off." Eugene was her husband, Uncle Eugenio Cuchinotto, the one with the seafood company. "Sometimes I think he dreams about fish."

When Ratchett still didn't respond, she went on. "All right, I'll tell you what Mama says. She says it's a chalice filled with blood. See, the fish tail is the base and the chopped head is the cup." I could feel her nails tracing around the top of my head. I probably had orange flakes in my hair. "She thinks it's a sign, like it's marking him as something special. I think she's just spoiling him, putting grand ideas like that in his head."

I got the idea then that she was attracted to him. He was in his shirtsleeves, and her hand—the one that wasn't scraping my head like a chisel—was resting delicately on the golden hairs of his forearm. What a contrast he must have been to Uncle Eugenio, who was maybe five foot four, hopelessly obese, and covered with fur like a Louisiana brown bear. "What do you think, Father?" she asked.

Ratchett had to be careful here. The wrong words one way or the other might have alienated him from one branch of the wealthiest family in his parish. "Well," he said, "if it *is* a sign, I guess we'll know soon enough."

CHAPTER THREE

THE DEATH OF MAMA MIGGLIORE

Father Frank's more or less benign attitude toward me, as well as the lapse in abuse from my godparents, would be over within hours of our arrival at Mama Miggliore's house the day she died. We raced over in the Plymouth as soon as I hung up with Wanda and relayed her news to my mother, who was still in the bathroom, setting her hair. So frantically did Josie turn into Mama Miggliore's driveway—a column of untidy grass betwixt two long rows of cracked concrete—that we nearly lost the Plymouth in the ditch that ran along the street in those days before the city hid it under a sidewalk.

The drive was already almost full. Rose's yellow Cadillac was in the rear with two black Mercedes ahead of it: The newer one belonged to Anthony; behind it was a nearly identical, but slightly older, model. It had once been my uncle's as well, but instead of trading it in, he had donated it to Pope Pius. Needless to say, Ratchett was driving it now.

There was another car in front of the ditch, presumably the doctor's.

Wanda greeted my mother and me at the door when we arrived. She hugged me and took both my mother's hands into hers and began crying.

"I'm so glad you's here, Miss Josie," Wanda said. "I don't like seeing her alone with them two. They been huddling together whispering and keeping me busy back in the kitchen so I couldn't hear nothing. Then they goes and calls that priest over here before they even calls you and Miss Nita."

"Do they know we're here?" asked my mother.

"No, Miss Josie," said Wanda. "I didn't want to give them no warning. I just knows they up to something. Best if you catch 'em off they guard."

Wanda was wise there. It was obvious to me what my godparents were up to. Anthony and the Fishwife wanted one last chance with Mama Miggliore to try to trick her into falling for their property division scheme without my mother or Aunt Nita around to argue against it. Anthony probably had some papers on him that he'd try to get his old mother to sign while she still could. Ratchett was on hand as an unimpeachable witness who conveniently spoke a smidgen of Italian so he could attest to whatever words Anthony wanted to place in the dying old woman's mouth. And without me around to contradict them, who could say it wasn't all true?

Anthony and Ratchett were the only ones with my grandmother when Wanda led us into her room. Everyone else must have been in the kitchen. My uncle didn't ask how we knew to be there, but one accusatory glance at Wanda told me he must have figured that out. With the most hateful look on his face, he appeared about to curse the three of us when Father Frank put his good hand on Anthony's shoulder.

"Perhaps we should let Josie and Joe be with her for a few minutes," he said.

The two of them probably joined Rose in the kitchen to plot strategy and try to salvage something of their foiled plan. A few moments with Mama Miggliore, though, and I knew what they must have known as well: The old woman was in no condition to make any kind of legal or financial decisions that would be binding in any court. From the moment we walked into the room, I heard her utter not one syllable to indicate that she was the slightest bit cognizant of what was going on. Her communication consisted mainly of moaning and groaning, with a few infantile nonsense syllables mixed in. Now and then an eerie type of humming passed her dry old lips—nothing recognizable to me; perhaps it was an old Sicilian lullaby or something.

In a few minutes we were joined by the rest of the attendants: Anthony and Rose, of course; Ratchett and that doctor; and some of my cousins, including Ronnie, who complained all day about missing his modern dance class.

Ratchett had donned his vestments but remained aloof from the family, taking a seat at the old rocker beside my grandmother's set of nesting tables in a back corner of the room, sipping a cup of Wanda's chicory coffee. He often said it was his only vice, that coffee of hers; and he could never seem to get it hot enough. A cup couldn't sit for five minutes before he'd ask her to put it back on the fire. She'd do so and bring it right back to him so that he could put it, almost boiling, to his lips. Their plot gone bad had cast a shadow over his demeanor. He was no longer his usual facile and collected self as he sat there staring into his steaming cup and drumming the top of the nesting tables with his deformed hand like a spiked mace.

The death scene was about to begin. Once everyone was gathered, my mother and aunt stepped forward and, as if taking a cue from an unseen director, assumed kneeling positions on either side of their mother's bed. Rosaries at the ready, they both took one of Mama Miggliore's hands and began to tell the beads through her apparently insensible fin-

gers, all the while sobbing pleas for forgiveness for a lifetime of unspeci-
fied transgressions.

Years later, as a priest myself, I realized that such scenes are more
or less stock at Italian deathwatches. Often they can be far more intense
than I witnessed at my grandmother's bedside. One particular incident
from the late seventies comes to mind. It was an otherwise happy time for
me, as my primary responsibility was overseeing a house for some wonderful homeless boys. I had been called upon to say the Mass before the
funeral of an elderly woman named Pizzo, from my grandmother's old
neighborhood. Her widowed daughter accompanied me in the limousine
from the funeral parlor to the mausoleum, along with her two grown
children, a black-eyed girl who was obviously destined to be the image
of her mother and grandmother—bloated ankles and all—and a younger
boy with the most splendid strawberry hair and bluest of eyes.

The casket was about to be slid into a vault, where it would take
its place among a marble wall of Pizzos past when the woman decided
the time was right to reveal her most private and agonizing secrets to her
mother and everyone else in the building. Namely, that she had aborted a
child in 1955 because she couldn't tolerate another seed of "that no-good
stinking bastard" (her late husband) growing in her womb and that she
had had a long-standing affair with her Swiss gynecologist, out of which
union had sprouted her beautiful son, he of the strawberry locks. I tried
to reason with her that perhaps the confessional, rather than her mother's
graveside, might be a more appropriate place for such revelations and
noted that a couple of nearby folding chairs flanking a potted hydrangea
would serve us well enough in that capacity in a pinch. But she would
have none of that (hence my liberty to relate the scene here) and proceeded to apostrophize her dead mother with the customary litany of
self-indictments; e.g., "I'm no better than the shit beneath your heel."
She then flung herself onto the coffin, beat her head against its lid while
synchronously striking one of the brass handles against its backplate to

heighten the effect, staggered a bit before falling senseless to the floor directly beneath the bronze epitaph of two baby Pizzos who had gone to God a half century before during the great pandemic of influenza, and, as if in keeping with the theme of dirt and filth, soiled herself.

Returning now to my grandmother's room . . . when it appeared that my mother and aunt might remain kneeling longer than their middle-aged knees could support them, two of my younger cousins came forward like ring bearers with cushions for the women's relief. These had no doubt been supplied by the ever-solicitous Wanda, who kept an eye on the goings-on in the death chamber via regular appearances to replenish Ratchett's cup with more scalding chicory.

There was a beautiful, almost regal symmetry to the scene at this point, with the two cushion-bearing children attending Josie and the Fishwife on either side of the bed and Mama Miggliore in the direct center, her great breasts made even more protuberant by her outstretched arms, each clutched by an opposing daughter. And looking down on it all from the space it had occupied above her head for nearly sixty years was the portrait of my infant Uncle Joe, the child who would have been a priest.

That theme of sorrow and disappointment occupied my grandmother's discourse when she did slip back into coherence:

"*Nessun prete*," she moaned at one point, bewailing that sad fact—disgraceful in her Old World eyes—that there were no priests in the family. "*Due filligi e nessun prete.*" (Two sons and no priests). And then "*Peccato*"—shame. When she said that word, she wrenched her right hand free, the one that Rose had been holding, and hid her face. My aunt seized the opportunity to grab the dictionary out of the handbag at her side and begin flipping through its pages to catch whatever bits of meaning she could.

When Mama Miggliore uncovered her face, it was to cry out the name Joe. At first everyone looked at me, but when she struggled to tilt her head back to focus her clouded eyes on the portrait of her firstborn son, everyone's eyes followed hers to the priest-child on the wall. "*I nipoti*," I heard her say quite clearly. She must have been praying through the intercession of her own departed child that one the grandchildren would take Holy Orders and make amends for the shame her grown sons had brought her.

Nearly in the same breath as her allusion to the grandchildren, my grandmother spoke two words that I hadn't heard from her lips in many months, perhaps years: segno sacro. Several in the room—Anthony, my mother, Ronnie—instantly looked my way. Even Rose didn't need her dictionary to discover that Mama Miggliore hadn't forgotten her favorite grandchild's "holy mark." I wondered what had brought it back to her mind now, at this critical time near the end. If the old woman's mind was lucid enough to form clear associations, then the cognitive path leading from the priest-child in the portrait to her disappointment with her sons to the grandchildren and an icon distinctive to me could only mean one thing: My grandmother was making a deathbed wish. I was to fulfill the thwarted destiny of her son whose name I bore.

The combination of my realizing that awful responsibility and all those eyes staring at me was nearly overwhelming. I started to get dizzy, blood rushing to my head. But just as I feared I might succumb to the vertigo, the room's attention was drawn away from me and back to Mama Miggliore, who was sitting up in the bed and reaching out with both arms to something invisible to the rest of us in the room. "*Mio marito*," she said softly. (My husband.)

We were about to witness a vision, or *visione*, as the old Italians called it, a phenomenon which, I would discover years later as a priest myself, is not at all uncommon at a Sicilian deathwatch. These visiones consisted of a supernatural appearance in the death chamber visible only to the one about to cross over. The appearance could be that of a deceased loved one or a noteworthy member of the Catholic pantheon—the Blessed Mother, Saint Joseph, or the like. They became as much part and parcel of an Italian death vigil as the self-flagellating daughters. People came to expect them. "Was there a *visione*?" they'd ask of the witnesses. Or "Did she see anyone?"

The specter that initially appeared before my grandmother's eyes, saving me from a fainting spell after the mention of my birthmark, was none other than my grandfather. "*Vengo, Angelo*," she called out to him. Her voice was clearer than I could remember it, even in my childhood. It must have sounded as it had to her husband's ears when last he heard it, some twenty-odd years before.

Her lucidity was even more astonishing when she continued: "*Vengo per essere con te dove appertengo*" (I'm coming to be with you where I belong). At those words my mother and godparents exchanged brief and furtive glances, which I believed at the time to reflect the same awesome fear of the unknown that was gripping me, but which I later discovered—after the whole story of my grandfather's fate came out—to be nothing more than the telltale signs of embarrassment and guilt. Anthony went so far as to turn his back on the scene and briefly leave the bedroom for a fresh cigar. Following him in and out of the room was the lackey priest. Was I the only one who found it odd that the feckless Father Frank would choose this spectacular moment to seek a change of air?

For the next several minutes, my grandmother seemed to be engaged in colloquy with her dear departed Angelo, who she seemed to think had come forward and was standing, or perhaps hovering in the air, at the bedside to her right. The subject of my grandparents' dialogue seemed to range among the various domestic issues of their many years together. "*Quaranta annos!*" she sighed at one point, although by my reckoning they had been married for at least forty-two years. It is the fact that my grandmother saw Papa Miggliore and not the particulars of what she had to say to him that is relevant to my story, so I will not recount those particulars in detail. She had quite the Sicilian memory, though, especially for slights. Let one example make the point: In between complaining about not getting an electric washer until 1935 and missing Caruso when he came to New Orleans in 1920, my grandmother mentioned a woman named Harriet. I looked to my mother and aunt, but neither seemed to recognize the name. This Harriet must have been known to my grandfather, though, for Mama Miggliore, by the casual yet presumptive manner in which she brought up the name, obviously took for granted his familiarity with the woman.

"*Perché, Angelo,*" she sobbed. (Why?) Then she threw in his face that he had spent his wife's thirtieth birthday with this Harriet, and if she saw the little *putana* in the next life, she'd spit in her face as she should have in 1908.

It is probably just as well that I will never know who Harriet was. For a man like my grandfather, who spent so little time at home and had the means to indulge in the many sensual pleasures that turn-of-the-century New Orleans had to offer, the possibilities are too many to count. Was she a family friend? The daughter or wife of an associate? A waitress in one of the many restaurants he never took his wife to? A Storyville prostitute? Or could she perhaps have been the unidentified woman from the *Reluctant Glory*? My mother said the face in the photograph didn't look Italian; perhaps she could have been a Harriet. If so, that meant that she and Papa Miggliore had carried on their dirty little affair right under my poor grandmother's Sicilian nose for at least a dozen years.

By the time my uncle and Ratchett re-entered the room, my grandmother had finished her harangue against her husband, forgiven the ill usage she had suffered at his hands, and was once again stretching out her arms in his direction and smiling beatifically. Her eyelids began to flicker, and we thought she might sleep awhile, but her *visione* was not yet complete.

Before her lids were completely shut, she seemed to hear something. "*Senta!*" she cried. (Listen.) Then "*Musica*" and "*Cora*" and finally "*Senta*" again.

"What is she saying?" asked the Fishwife, for the words were coming faster than she could rifle the pages of her dictionary without hazarding one of her precious orange nails.

"She wants us to be quiet," said Anthony, as if the words had an ironic relevance to his stupid sister. "She thinks she hears music, a choir of some sort."

"Oh God!" shrieked the Fishwife. "She thinks she's in Heaven!" Then she looked the word up. "*Cielo*, Mama, *cielo*! Yes, you'll be there soon!"

"Shut up!" ordered Anthony, and Mama Miggliore seemed to agree.

"*Senta!*" she cried once again. Her gaze went upward, toward the ceiling in the middle of the room. She crossed herself before stretching her arms out full toward whatever it was she saw.

"*La Famiglia Santa!*" she exclaimed. Enough of us understood the Italian for the Holy Family that a shudder was heard through the room. Even Ratchett seemed bedazzled, but only for a moment; from the corner of my eye I could see him shift in his chair, about to stand, but then checking himself as if the reaction had been inadvertent, like a reflex to a stimulus not quite extinguished.

Mama Miggliore's head suddenly lurched to the left so violently I thought her old neck might snap. Her eyes opened their widest and then teared. Could there be something before them more compelling than the Holy Family itself?

"Joe," she said, "*il mio bambino*." She was talking to the little priest-child, but not to the picture on the wall this time; it was clear that in her mind that uncle of mine, whom no one present (at least not the living ones) ever knew, was in the room. She reached out her left hand to him, her right to her husband. And then she fell quiet.

For a moment I thought she was dead. It seemed so irresistibly perfect: her husband and child coming for her; a choir of angels heralding the approach of Mary, Joseph, and the Baby Jesus to welcome her into Paradise. Again I was struck by the symmetry: the two compact little families floating away to a blissful Elysium, like a Raphaelite diptych.

The doctor snapped us all back to the reality of this vale of tears, rushing forward to apply his stethoscope to my grandmother's breast and assure us that for now she was only sleeping. He ordered everyone out of the room for the time being, except for Wanda, who had been standing in the doorway holding the coffee pot, wary of her place yet determined not to miss anything. The rest of us retreated to the big double kitchen in the back of the house and helped ourselves to the feast of cold cuts and vegetable trays she had prepared. For once I had no appetite, even for Wanda's cooking. I thought about that kitchen and of Mama Miggliore's chastisement of her husband as I stood there looking at the table, lit by the glow of a single bare light bulb hanging by its cord from the ceiling. That double kitchen that my mother said was his only gift to her when he got rich: What had it meant to her but double work?

I expected the conversation to center around my grandmother's visione, but surprisingly none of the adults mentioned it. Could not one of them have been affected by it? I shouldn't have been surprised at Rose and Anthony; nobody expected them to have anything on their minds except what they were in for after their mother's death. But how could my mother stand there chomping on a carrot stick after what had just happened? Was it some kind of egregious breach of the etiquette of the deathwatch to talk about a visione while the seer still lived? And why didn't my mother want me close to her after what we had just witnessed, as I wanted her near me, stroking my head and holding my hand even if no words were to be spoken. Surely she must have known how affected I would be by all this. Instead she seemed to be avoiding me and staying close to her perfidious brother and sister, who were talking about, of all things, Wanda.

"I don't like her being in there without us," said the Fishwife, spreading mayonnaise on a *pistolette* for Ronnie. She always prepared his plates for him as if he were a prince or an invalid.

"Would you rather stay in there yourself and change the dirty sheets?" said Anthony.

"No," said Rose, "but I think she knows something."

"Knows what?" asked Anthony. He was examining the broccoli on one of the trays, turning over one piece and then another with his stubby, tobacco-stained fingers.

"I don't know, but I think they talk to each other sometimes."

Rose was, of course, being irrational. Her newfound distrust of Wanda could only have been caused by the poor old domestic's getting my mother and me to the house and spoiling their plan to have Mama Miggliore to themselves before she died.

"Wanda and Mama?" said Anthony. "Don't be stupid."

"It's possible," said the Fishwife. "I know someone at the beauty parlor who has a colored maid who speaks Spanish."

"She's probably from Cuba," said Anthony. "Wanda can't speak Italian. She's practically illiterate in *English*." He seemed to have found a flower of broccoli to his liking and started rolling it like a candied apple in the cucumber dip. "Besides, what are you afraid they'd be talking about anyway?"

"You never know," said Rose. "She could be turning Mama against us. I don't think she likes me."

My uncle seemed to have something to say to that—he looked to my mother for a moment—but decided to let it pass.

"I heard on the radio," Rose went on, "where some wealthy woman turned against her family at the end and left everything—her house and all the money and valuables, jewelry and everything—to her maid." My aunt poured Ronnie a glass of iced tea. She always squeezed the lemon wedges over a strainer to make sure no seeds got into his glass.

"We don't have to worry about that," said Anthony. "Mama's got a sense of family, if nothing else."

"The woman's children didn't even get her clothes. She left them to the Salvation Army." Rose paused for a second, looking for a place to put the spent wedge. Finally she just left it on the table for Wanda to clean up. "They didn't say if the maid was colored, though."

"Where was that?" asked Anthony.

"Somewhere up north," said Rose. "New York or New Jersey maybe."

"See!" said Anthony. "That can't happen here. I checked with de Salvo." (Michael de Salvo had been the family attorney since Papa Miggliore's time.) "He says Louisiana has forced heirship. Mama couldn't cut us out if she wanted to." He licked his broccoli flower and took a bite. There was still so much dip on it, it looked like an ice cream cone. "It's the Napoleonic Code," he continued. "One of the advantages of living in a state that's a century and a half behind the times."

"Thank God," said Rose. "But I still don't think you should have hired a colored woman. They're always trying to worm their way into white families. And you should have gotten a nurse. Then people wouldn't feel so sorry for her."

"A nurse?" spat Anthony. "Do you have any idea how much a nurse would have cost?" he said, swallowing hard on his broccoli cone. "Especially a white one!"

After a few minutes, Doctor C. joined the family in the kitchen. He said a few words to Anthony and his sisters, fixed himself a plate, and entered into an extended conversation with Ratchett, who was also serving himself, piling meats and cookies onto a paper plate adroitly balanced on his stump of a hand. Once he had had enough of Rose, Uncle Anthony joined them.

There was a bottle of whiskey and a bucket of ice on the counter for their convenience. I assume Wanda had placed it there at Anthony's orders. Clearly iced tea or even her coffee wasn't potent enough to wash down whatever it was they were discussing. My mother was now alone with the Fishwife by the food table.

The doctor soon broke away from his little huddle with Ratchett and Anthony to re-enter my grandmother's room. A moment later he joined the family again and announced that Mama Miggliore had regained consciousness. We all put down our sandwiches and drinks in preparation for processing back into the death chamber. Even Ronnie, who was using the toaster as a mirror, stopped the little tap dance he was doing in front of it.

Anthony, however, wasn't about to let us all back into that room without a fight. I quickly learned what he and his two cohorts had been discussing.

"Everybody wait!" he shouted. "This might be the best time for Father Frank to have a private talk with Mama. She hasn't made her confession yet."

Of course their talk couldn't be exactly "private," as Ratchett's Italian was at that time by his own admission still rather rusty. Anthony would have to be present as well, offering his services as "interpreter."

I can see today what a transparent excuse that was. What sins could an old woman who can't talk to anyone and hasn't gone outside the house since her last trip to the emergency room possibly have to confess? My uncle's plan was obvious: He had had Ratchett in his pocket for years already, thanks to those lucrative Saint Joseph's altars and other favors like the car. The doctor, too, could obviously be counted on. His opinion was that it would be best for Mama if only Anthony and Father Frank went in this time. He wouldn't even go in himself, he said, but would wait outside the door in case he was needed (and no doubt to ensure the rest of us kept our distance). Rose incredibly didn't make a peep. That such a jealous, small-minded woman would suffer her younger brother to be with their mother while she remained in the kitchen was nearly unthinkable and could have only one explanation: Anthony had forbidden her to contradict any of his decisions that day.

It was an ingenious plan, especially impressive for being hatched at the last minute after Josie and I unexpectedly showed up. Anthony would now be able to say that Mama Miggliore, strengthened by the sacrament of Penance as death drew near, had had a change of heart regarding the distribution of the estate. Anthony's plan, she would finally admit, was the only true and just one for all of the children, and she embraced it with her last coherent breath. He and that priest would make it sound like the old woman had spoken with the infallibility of the Pope on a Vatican balcony.

I stood there aghast, hoping that someone would stop them, but lacking the courage to do anything myself. I looked to Wanda, who was standing by the sink, clutching a serrated knife like an outraged mammy, but she seemed as lost as I as to what to do. She and I, and I'm sure everyone else in the room, were shocked when my mother spoke out.

"Let Joe go in too," she said.

Anthony turned on his heels like a little Napoleon who had just been questioned by the lowliest gendarme. How dare his younger sister gainsay his decision! "Why him?" he said. "His Italian isn't as good as mine."

"It's good enough," she said. "And he's her favorite. Everybody knows that."

Out of the corner of my eye, I could see Ronnie standing by his mother. The Fishwife's head turned in my direction, but I didn't dare meet her hateful gaze. I'm sure her orange claws were fully extended, ready to poke out her fat little nephew's eyes, or at least scratch off that birthmark that was the cause of all this.

Anthony's allies rallied to his cause.

"We need to keep any unnecessary people out of the room for a while," said the doctor. "It could agitate your mother."

"Her confession should be heard in private," said Ratchett. "It would be inappropriate."

But Josie cut them off. "I want him in there," she insisted. "Either just him or all of us."

No one was more surprised than I at my mother's assertiveness in the face of this cabal of intimidating men. It was as if she had taken abuse from her brother for all those years, storing up her courage for the time when it would count the most. I was so moved by her strength that I actually lost my own fear. I followed my uncle and the two others into my grandmother's room, where of course nothing happened. Mama Miggliore just continued humming and babbling. Confession would have been obviously futile, so Ratchett merely anointed her. When the priest was done, my disgusted uncle called the rest of the family back in.

We've never explicitly discussed it, but I know he believes that Josie and I had it all planned: enlisting Wanda's aid to make sure that he and Rose never got to Mama so that we could selfishly keep the biggest piece of the Miggliore pie for ourselves. Never mind that we were legally entitled to it and there wasn't a state in the union—not even Louisiana with its corrupt judges and antiquated Old World statutes—in which he would have had a leg to stand on should he have tried to deprive us of it through the courts.

He didn't say a word to me that day, but I could read his thoughts in his malignant expression as he glared at me when the family re-entered the bedroom. I saw it in my dreams and in the dark for months—no, for years—afterward. Italians can be the most articulate of peoples with their curses, but sometimes even more so with their silence.

His unspoken thoughts wounded me more gravely than if he had cursed me and struck me across the face. "I'll get you for this, you fat little freak," they said. "You think you've won, but I'll make you pay in the end. If it takes the rest of my life, I'll make you pay. I'll outlive everyone in this family just to see you eat dirt."

My uncle did indeed wait me out, as a part of me knew, even back then, that he would. The actual passing of Mama Miggliore was, I am almost ashamed to say, practically an anticlimax considering the drama that preceded it. She died an hour or so after Ratchett anointed her.

I was outside on the porch with Ronnie when she passed. Not that I relished my cousin's company, especially after an incident that had happened behind the levee with Tony Junior a few weeks earlier. I just wanted to avoid my uncle, and I knew the last place Anthony would want to be was around this effeminate cousin of mine. Ronnie may have been Rose's pet, but Anthony had no more use for his dancing nephew than I did.

After Mama Miggliore had been pronounced dead, Josie and the Fishwife came outside to fetch Ronnie and me in to view the body. "Come look at Mama," they said, as if she were sitting up in the bed doing card tricks. We did as we were told. Following the adults' lead, I kissed my grandmother on the forehead. One of her eyes wasn't completely closed, and as I bent over her, she seemed to be peeking at me through it. It made me feel she would always have an eye on me, watching to see that I didn't disappoint her.

Everyone stayed until the people from the funeral home showed up to take the body. Josie asked them for a lock of her mother's hair. They told her she could take it herself, and she did. The doctor was the first to leave, then Ratchett, who stayed just long enough to accept an envelope from Uncle Anthony, no doubt filled with cash—the customary gift to a priest for a personal appearance, plus most probably a tidy bonus for his part in the aborted confession scheme. I would see him again at the funeral, but after that not again until I was several years into the seminary.

When it was time for us to leave, I went straight to the car. So anxious was I to get away from my uncle that I didn't even say goodbye to Wanda. It didn't even occur to me that without Mama Miggliore around, she would have no more business with the family and that I might never see her again. My mother managed to keep up with her through Wanda's cousin Wendell, who continued to be Josie's handyman through the seventies. Through him we learned that Wanda's husband, the one-armed garbage man, had died a couple of years after my grandmother and that Wanda had moved in with one of her children somewhere in "the country."

He always said he'd have to ask his wife, but he never got around to it, and Wanda lived out the rest of her life with no contact from us. I don't know what we would have written each other about anyway—short of what rats we both knew my godparents to be—or even if the poor woman could write at all. Wendell reported in 1969 that Wanda had died of what he called "female trouble." By then I was in the seminary, less than a year from ordination.

My mother knew how upset I was about everything that had happened—the visiones, Anthony's little power play, and finally my grandmother's death. We talked that night over leftover sandwiches Wanda had packed for us. "Your uncle knows he isn't going to get his way. He'll leave us alone now."

Before that night was over, Josie chose to reveal a family secret that had been kept from all the Miggliores in my generation. "It was the only thing that Rose and Anthony and I could ever agree on, and Paul, too, when he was still around—not to tell you all the truth about your grandfather."

"Papa Miggliore?" I said. "You mean how he died?"

I had a feeling it would either be that or something about his mistress, but I didn't want to be the one to bring that up. Was I about to hear that my grandfather had put this woman up in a fancy Vieux Carré apartment or even set up house with her like an Italian Wilkie Collins? Did he have a separate family in Carrollton or on Saint Charles Avenue or somewhere my poor grandmother would have never thought to venture? Did I have a slew of half aunts and uncles out there I didn't even know about?

We were still in the kitchen with the last food from Mama Miggliore's icebox spread on the table before us. I had gotten up to get myself something to drink.

"Get your tea and come into the living room," my mother told me. When I joined her, she patted the place next to her on the sofa. "Come sit by me," she said.

I did, and what she told me shocked me more than anything my prurient adolescent imagination could have concocted: Papa Miggliore was still alive!

Those stories she had told me about the cosche—how it was through his association with that shadowy group in the Old Country that her father had managed to get ahead—were just the tip of the scandalous iceberg.

"I told you I suspected things weren't quite right when I was a girl," my mother said. "But when I said I didn't know nothing for sure, that wasn't true—at least not after all that commotion when I was twenty."

That would have been 1937, the year the Miggliores' world turned upside down; for in that year, she went on, Papa Miggliore met his fate—not death but a litany of local and federal charges including bootlegging, racketeering, and conspiring to assassinate the mayor of New Orleans.

"Everything we had," Josie continued, "the whole A.M. Enterprises we were so proud of, it was just a front for them terrible people and all they did."

"But what about Mama's visione?" I protested. If she knew Papa was still alive, why would she see him in her vision?

That vision—or, more accurately, my reaction to it—was the very reason my mother had chosen this precise time to tell me the truth.

I was but fifteen and still believed in miracles the day my grandmother died. The impact of her deathbed vision on my developing psyche would have been tremendous, and my mother knew this. It was all I could talk about in the Plymouth the entire way home that evening: Little Joe and Papa Miggliore and the Holy Family all in the same room with us. And then the part about Mama Miggliore wanting someone in the family to become a priest and her looking right at me. How could it not mean something for her to do that, inspired as she was by all those worthies hovering around her like images on a Correggio fresco?

"She didn't know," my mother said.

Didn't know? Didn't know what? Didn't know what she was saying? Didn't know about the cosche? I was confused, so Josie enlightened me.

"She didn't know he was still alive," she said.

"She didn't know?" I said. It didn't make sense to me. How could she not have known that her own husband was still alive?

"We didn't want her to know," my mother said. "We thought she'd be better off thinking he was dead than knowing about the disgrace. That's why we never told any of you all neither." She meant me and my cousins. "We knew you'd all have a hard time understanding how things were back then. And then we were afraid one of you might slip and say something in front of her, and we thought she might pick up on the English in time and maybe understand, but she never did."

"So how did you keep it all from her?"

"It wasn't so hard," Josie said. "Not back in those days."

My mother went on to explain that they managed to keep everything from Mama Miggliore by shipping her off to Italy in the midst of the arrest and trial and then informing her of her dear Angelo's sudden "death" upon her return.

"Thank God the war wasn't started yet," Josie said. "I don't know what we would have done with her then. Probably what Anthony said.

He wanted to buy some property he heard about in Houston and set Mama up there. He heard Houston was going to be bigger than New Orleans soon. 'It would be an investment,' he said. 'At least when this is all over with, we'd have something to show for our money, not like throwing it away on some trip to Europe.' You don't know how many times he threw it up in our faces all the money we would have made when Houston was getting bigger and bigger and New Orleans just kept getting rattier and rattier.

"But Paul was still around then and wouldn't hear nothing about making his mother leave her home for good. He was the oldest, you know, the only one who was really a grown man at the time."

Ironically, if Mama Miggliore had moved to Texas, she would have been closer to her husband, who eventually ended up in a federal penitentiary just south of Dallas. When she returned from Italy, the trial was over and she was never the wiser. My mother was right: by 1940, with none of the city's newspapers or radio broadcasts in Italian, keeping the secret from my grandmother was easy.

"The poor thing never had any friends," my mother said. "We were everything to her. She never talked to nobody else, just the family."

"But what about the monument?" I asked. My mother knew I was talking about the monument to her father that Mama Miggliore often mentioned. I remembered seeing it myself years before. It was somewhere in the country.

Josie just clicked her tongue and gave me a dismissive wave of her hand. "There isn't no monument," she said. "That was just a gazebo in City Park they built where some pirates met with Andrew Johnson before the Battle of New Orleans."

"Andrew *Jackson*?" I said. But to Josie that didn't matter.

"Anthony had a plaque made with Papa's picture on it, and he'd just stick it on top of the one that told about the pirates whenever we'd bring Mama out there."

"But I saw it too," I protested.

"You were young," she said. "You didn't know where you were any more than she did. Why do you think we never bring you out there no more?"

It was the old Italian way: the children protecting the mother. And Josie had more to tell.

"This is the part I'm so ashamed of—what we did when we knew they were going to put Papa in jail."

I feared what was coming. Was I about to hear a tale of bribed officials, threatened witnesses, or worse? Did my mother and the family wind up selling their souls to the dreaded cosche?

"They were going to take everything away from Papa and fine him so much we would have had to live in the shanties with the niggers," my mother said. "The lawyers said the only way out was to say they weren't married."

"You mean they were divorced?" I asked, struggling to comprehend what my mother was telling me.

"No," she said. "Worse. We had to say they were never married in the first place."

She went on to explain the incredible and convoluted plan that de Salvo and Papa Miggliore had cooked up to save his estate from being devoured by punitive government officials. My grandfather, with the foresight that would have been unbelievable in anyone but a Sicilian with a crooked lawyer, had for years been putting everything in Mama Miggliore's maiden name, Ellen Fortunato.

"That's why he never let anybody see the books," my mother said. "Because then we would have known that it was all hers—all the money, the businesses, the property, everything. If she knew that, she could have kicked him out on the street like a dog instead of having to beg for a washing machine."

With the businesses and property all in my grandmother's name and no clear link between them and Papa Miggliore's illicit activities, the only way the government could touch anything was by fining my grandfather and taking advantage of Louisiana's community property laws to collect—which of course would be impossible if the couple wasn't married. Josie explained more of the details:

"He told them all he only *worked* for Mama. He just managed all the businesses for her, he said. Can you believe it? Proud and bossy as he was, to have everybody think he was nothing more than a hired hand working for a woman! There just wasn't nothing Papa wouldn't do for money, even to lower himself like that."

My mother paused and asked me to get her a glass of tea. That was very unusual for her. The only times she had ever asked me to get her anything were when she was flat on her back sick in bed. It was as if in her mind things had changed that day. Her mother was gone and I was fifteen—old enough to start taking care of her. I didn't even know how much sugar to put in her tea, so I brought the bowl back with me.

"They didn't believe a word of his lies, of course," she continued after taking a sip as if there had been no interruption. "But what could they do? There was no proof. Mama married him in San Guiseppe before she came over. They'd never find that little church, even if it wasn't blown up in the war. And even if they did, Papa could have easily used his connections to bribe a poor parish priest. I wouldn't put it past him to have planned all that out from the beginning, just to cover himself."

I asked why "they" never asked Mama Miggliore if Papa was telling the truth. I wasn't sure if "they" meant the police, the FBI, or some other group.

"That's another reason we had to send her to Italy," she said. "For fear they might do that. But they never got a chance. By the time she came back, the lawyers had worked everything out."

What Josie meant was that the government was caught in a kind of double bind, a Catch-22 of sorts: If Mama and Papa weren't really married, Mama Miggliore's testimony was useless to them; and if they were, she couldn't be forced to bear witness against her own husband, even so much as to say, "Yes, he is my husband." It was the most absurd and beautiful of legal technicalities, and de Salvo only had to pay off one or two crooked judges to get the scheme to work. So with Louisiana not recognizing common law marriages, there was absolutely nothing they could do but let Mama and the children keep all the money.

"We've got them by the balls!" Anthony is said to have blurted out when de Salvo explained it all to them (only Josie didn't quote him exactly; she said the "you-know-whats").

"God forgive us," my mother sobbed. "We called ourselves a pack of bastards and accused our mother of a sin we knew she'd pour a pot of boiling red gravy over herself before committing—and all for money."

Mama Miggliore stayed in Italy for quite a while. Every time she was ready to come home, my grandfather had Paul or Anthony cable Sicily with another stalling tactic. The excuses they used were so ridiculous it's amazing anyone would believe them; for example, one said that New Orleans was in the grip of a peculiar strain of influenza that was known to become particularly virulent when mixed with the breath of someone who had recently inhaled the air of southern Italy.

"Poor Mama," my mother said. "She was just an ignorant thing, no schooling. She would have believed anything they said. And they knew that would get to her. You know how she lost my sister Grace in that big epidemic. That was twenty years before, but a mother never forgets. She would have stayed away for the rest of her life if it meant keeping harm from her children."

My mother told me that finally, after nearly two years, my grandmother came home. "They were starting to talk about war again over there. I told them I wanted her home or I was going to go get her myself and tell her the truth. Paul met her ship in New York. He told her on the train back to New Orleans that Papa was dead. He said she cried all the way home. She wouldn't even come out of the compartment to eat."

I thought about what Mama Miggliore must have felt at the moment of her death when she was expecting to be reunited with Papa only to find out that he wasn't there but instead was in jail in Texas. And I wondered if it's possible to be humiliated and disappointed in Paradise. Incidentally, my grandmother didn't have to wait long to be reunited with her husband, that is assuming the Lord counted the twenty-five years he spent in prison as his Purgatory. He died in 1962. I never met him.

My mother didn't seem to want to talk about those things anymore. She took both of our glasses of tea back into the kitchen and rinsed them clean. I remember the ice cubes dropping into the sink like stones. On her way to bed she spoke her last words of the night. "We made a fool of our mother," she said. "Pray to God she forgives us."

CHAPTER FOUR

BEHIND THE LEVEE

So the reactions of my mother and godparents to Mama Miggliore's *visione*—those awkward looks of shame and discomfiture—were explained. There had been no miraculous visitation by the Holy Family, no reunion between my grandmother and my otherworldly Uncle Joe, no transcendental colloquy between wife and long-departed husband. What we had all witnessed in that room were simply the hallucinations of a dying old woman.

Between that realization and the more mundane shock that my grandfather was still alive, I barely slept that night. As I thought back over the way my mother and her generation had always spoken of Papa Migglio-re, I realized that I should have known that something wasn't right. They never actually referred to him as being dead or alive; it was always something like "before Papa left us" or "when Papa was still around." My grandmother herself was the only one who actually spoke of him as being dead.

It may seem incongruous that despite the exposure of my grandmother's deathbed visions as delusional wish fulfillments and the consequent erosive effect that had on my own faith, I still became a priest. Perhaps I felt more compelled by the circumstances to fulfill one of her wishes myself and, in so doing, restore a bit of the dignity that my mother and godparents had robbed her of. What difference did it make if her wish were sanctioned by the Holy Family or not? My grandmother wanted me to take Holy Orders; that much was certain. And so I did.

It is only in recent years—the eighties, I believe, though it may have begun in the seventies—that religious, especially male religious, have had to defend their choice of a vocation. That was certainly not the case during my seminary days in the sixties, when there was still a plenitude of vocations, or even when I was ordained. But then came the seventies and the precipitous drop-off in seminarians, not to mention the exodus of full-fledged priests from the Church. In 1959, the year before I entered Saint Jerome's, there were 381 such institutions in the United States, each the size of a midsized high school, cranking out eager young priests like dashboard statues of Saint Christopher. Twenty years later, a scant one-third of them were still open. The rest were either sold, let out as nondenominational retreat houses, or reserved as retirement homes for aging religious—an option that will probably not be necessary much longer as for every two old priests who die today, only one is ordained. There were sixty thousand priests in this country when I was in training; today I am one of but twenty-five thousand.

So who can blame people for looking askant at those of us who remain, as if only a peculiar aberration of human nature could explain a man's choosing such a life in the post-Reagan era. I've become quite adept at handling those "Why did you want to be a priest?" questions. I know they don't mean the same today as they did twenty-five years ago.

I'm versatile enough in my creativity to tailor my responses to suit the questioner, who seldom fails to betray his own preconceptions in the tone or wording of his query. The demographics of the whole issue are really very interesting. For example, consider the shallow, self-centered Baby Boomers. They don't for a minute fool me with their cynical, disingenuous little "So, Father, why did you choose the priesthood?" when what they really want to know is why I didn't go to law school or get married.

I've found that the best way to put these people in their place is to discreetly let them know that I came from money. In New Orleans it was usually enough to drop the Miggliore name. Even if they knew the truth about my grandfather, they would usually be nonetheless impressed; for these people, having a relative in federal prison is practically a badge of honor, the price of success. Mentioning that I adopted my uncle's name when I took Holy Orders was another useful strategy: What better way to gauge someone's character than by what "good friends" he claimed to be with Anthony?

I've had such grand fun with women who ask. Sometimes they're attracted to me, especially the divorced ones, single mothers in their forties. I know it's not a physical allure, not for a fleshy thing like me. It's more what they see in their college professors when they go back to finish that degree they gave up on to have children or the authors they stand in line for at book signings: simply the company, however fleeting, of an intelligent man they have nothing to fear from because they know on some instinctive female level that they have nothing to offer him.

It was these single ones—the widows and divorcées—that tended to call me Tony and ask me why I had chosen the priesthood rather than educational administration or a life in academia. Knowing their proclivity for romanticism, I concocted a story of myself and a lovely young girl I had met in college. I even gave her the name Ellen, after Mama Miggliore, so that I wouldn't forget it. We had been graduate students together; I was working on Henry James; she was studying the Brontes. One autumn she traveled to the north of England to research her dissertation. I begged her to wait until the spring, when I was planning to go to Italy for my own research. We could have rendezvoused in Paris, perhaps seen Belgium, where Charlotte Bronte had once succumbed to a tragic and unrequited love.

"But Ellen was willful," I'd say, wistfully smiling. "She went to England that autumn. And she caught a chill on the moors." The Lord saw fit to take the only girl I had ever loved, and knowing that I would never love so fervently again, I chose service to all His children. "I never finished my PhD," I'd add mournfully. "I never made that trip to Italy."

Older women were a different story—especially the very old ones, of my grandmother's era, the Italians and Hispanics in particular, who still burned votive candles and said novenas to Saint Jude. For them, as a young man my soul had been a wayward barge drifting ungoverned down the river (I found that the river motif worked better in New Orleans than the standard desert theme). Then one night Saint Peter or the Virgin Mary or what have you came to me in a dream and gave me direction.

I even made up one such dream: I am behind the levee trying to build a castle of mud on the bank of the Mississippi. But one ship after another (some bearing the names of famous companies, symbols of ambition or worldly pursuits, others seemingly filled with idle pleasure seekers frolicking on the decks) keeps passing too close to the shore, the rippling surges of the great river lapping at my feet in their wake, rolling over my work and reducing my castle-in-progress to an amorphous bump like an ant pile in the grass. With these people nothing could be too obvious, nor need I have worried about mixing metaphors. Saint Peter then appears in a pirogue and tells me that there are trout and redfish the size of men to be caught just around the next bend in the river but that he needs a helper to get them into his boat. He couldn't find anyone to aid him in the great city, where the fish were needed the most. I resist just a bit, but in the end go with him.

The old women love it. There is a special quality to the lifelong New Orleanian, a unique, almost charming, ignorance that makes possible a wide-eyed fascination with, and even an endearing faith in, the most hackneyed and preposterous of stories.

I know that some would criticize me for telling such tales—bald-faced lies they might call them. Who can we have faith in if not our priests? But what should I say—that I became a priest not because of a vision or an epiphany, but because a birthmark on top of my head—a random configuration of broken blood vessels beneath the surface of an infant's scalp—convinced a superstitious old woman of my destiny? Or perhaps they might be more inspired if I said that as a fat and friendless fifteen-year-old, I selected the relative sanctity of the seminary over the cruel and judgmental world of high school.

Much of this came out in the therapy I was forced into years later, but as childhood waned into adolescence, it became obvious that the traditional male life choices were simply not suited to me.

As I've said, I didn't have friends as a child; I had cousins. And with sixteen of them, what more did I need? If I've given the impression thus far that I wasn't fond of them, that's true. There was, of course, one exception: one cousin that I loved and admired enough to make up for my contempt for all the others—Anthony's oldest, Tony Junior. Two years older than I, he was always going through the stages, passing youthful milestones that the rest of us could look forward to. I recall his First Communion. I was four and totally in awe of my cousin in his navy blue slacks and white sport coat. I thought about nothing but him for days thereafter, begging my mother for a coat like Tony's. I was there at his Confirmation three years later as well. He was one of the tallest boys in the group, already evincing that strong, lean athlete's body.

My cousin's entering high school led to a new pastime for the Miggliore grandsons: our excursions behind the levee. Although Mama Miggliore's house was just blocks from the river, I had only been to the levee a handful of times. Uncle Paul, probably to get away from Aunt Nita and the rest of the adults, sometimes took a few of the children there to fly kites. But we never actually saw the river; the trees grew so thick and tall that the only sign of it was the masts of the biggest ships that floated past.

Tony excelled in every sport that rewarded quickness and height: he stood out at basketball and track (a sprinter with those muscular thighs, not one of those consumptive-looking distance runners). But his favorite was swimming. I was thirteen when Tony first led us to what became our own private spot on the river. He'd change into his trunks at Mama Miggliore's after the dinner or birthday cake or whatever it was that had marked the occasion for the family gathering and then lead us through the neighborhood and to the river. He was always barefoot and shirtless. A group of young girls who lived along the route used to stare at him, whispering and giggling whenever they saw him. Unable as I was to so much as remove my shoes in front of others and expose my pink, hammy feet, I could never emulate his gloriously unabashed public na-kedness, but I idolized him all the more for it.

Our destination was an old rusted barge that we had made our meeting place. Like the river itself, it was invisible from the levee, ob-scured by the thick growth of trees and weeds that in the summertime was almost impenetrable. Nonetheless, Tony had somehow found it, and in time he and the rest of us, his doting disciples, had worn our own path to it through the brush.

The barge was two-tiered; metal stairs without a rail—a perilous climb—led to the upper level, essentially the roof, but serving as sundeck and diving platform for anyone brave enough to risk the deeper water. At first that was only Tony; the rest of us could only watch from the deck or the muddy shore as he took his plunges. It was probably only fifteen feet or so, but he might as well have been leaping from the crest of the Huey Long Bridge for the impression he made on us.

Looking back on it all today, with my experience working with young men his age, it was in his boyish eagerness to show us what he could do that I find such a delight. He had an exhibitionist's pride in his own developing physique, typical of adolescent boys. I'll never forget the first time he took his trunks off in front of us: He had just made one of his magnificent dives and stayed under the cloudy water longer than usual. Just as we were wondering if his head had become lodged in the mud and we had lost him forever, the suit floated to the surface, Tony himself a second or two behind. I was mortified for him, not realizing that he had been under the water removing it on purpose, and I turned my back to spare him at least that much humiliation. When I heard him sloshing back to the shore and remarking on how good the water felt, I turned around again and saw him standing there before us, wiping his brow with the trunks as if that were the only use he had for them. That vision of him standing there, naked and glistening bronze, is the picture I will always have in my mind of Tony Junior.

A thin line of brown hair led from his navel to the bushy growth between his legs. He called it his "happy trail" and asked us all what we thought of it. Ronnie and one or two of the others ventured to approach him and tug on the hairs. Tony didn't stop Ronnie when his hand went a bit lower; he just looked down at him, and then at me, as if wondering why I stayed back. Then he put his suit back on.

In time the younger ones were following Tony off the top of the barge. Tony always went first so that he would be waiting for them in the water. Sometimes they were naked, following his lead, but by comparison to him they looked ridiculous, gangly and awkward, all bony arms and legs, hairless and unworldly as newborn marsupials. Ronnie took special delight in running around exposed. His nudity, unlike Tony's, always seemed unnatural and gratuitous to me. Whereas Tony only swam or sunbathed nude, Ronnie would strip as soon as we were safely behind the trees and remain so until it was time to return to our grandmother's, even when we'd venture away from the barge and hike through the woods, exploring new territory. It was as if he wanted anyone and everyone—even strangers we might happen upon in the woods—to see him.

I never disrobed in front of my cousins, nor would I jump off the top of the barge, at least not of my own power. My inability to swim confined me to the shore and my self-consciousness precluded my removing any of my clothes in front of the others, even so much as to take my shoes and socks off and let my toes wallow in the soft mud beneath the shallowest water.

In truth it wasn't just a Biblical modesty that kept my clothes on. I was ashamed of my body—and not only because I was fat, although that was enough to keep me covered until I saw my cousins and realized I had another reason to hide myself. It seemed a curse at the time, as if God had slighted me for no reason; but later I understood that it was His gift to keep me pure.

Tony never teased me like the others for not being able to swim or for being embarrassed to take off my clothes. But one day after all the others had jumped and safely found their way to the shallow water, he came for me. I was in my usual place—out of the sun, perhaps fifty yards from the water's edge, sitting on the trunk of a fallen cypress that must have been overwhelmed by the force of a great storm. Unlike the flamboyant Ronnie, Tony seldom strayed far from the water without putting on his trunks, so it caught my attention that he let them dangle from his hand like an old rag as he came out of the water and walked toward me. When he got close, he tossed them on the tree next to me. I thought he was going to use them as a seat, but instead he held out his hand.

"Come on, it's your turn," he said to me. I took his hand without a word and let him pull me to my feet. My heart beat almost painfully, and I feared he could see my fleshy chest jiggling through my shirt, drenched as it was with my own nervous sweat. Tony led me to the barge, never letting go of my hand. Or was it I who wouldn't let go? When we walked past the others, I saw Ronnie's eyes fixed on the point of our clutched hands like a cat teased by a dangling trinket.

I kept my eyes on Tony's body as we climbed those redoubtable stairs to the higher tier. On the first steps I watched his feet. Even they were tanned. He seemed to climb on his toes, his heels never touching the stairs. I had never noticed the tufts of golden hairs that sprouted from his big toes. His calf muscles pulsed like my heart with every step. There was hair on his lower legs, but his thighs were still smooth. Halfway up, I closed my eyes. Blood seemed to be rushing to my head, and the fear of falling nearly overtook me for a moment. A few more steps and I opened my eyes again to follow the cleft of Tony's broad back up to his shoulders, the nape of his neck where his tan was its deepest and a light fuzz stood out in contrast.

We had made it to the top. Tony stepped onto the platform and led me to the edge. I was afraid he was going to abandon me when he released my hand. What would I have done if he had jumped alone and left me standing there to follow him like the others? I knew I wouldn't be able to do it, but descending those steps on my own was just as unthinkable.

Tony had no intention of abandoning me, though. He had only let go of my hand so that he could turn and face me.

"It's okay," he said. "The current's not until you get out in the middle of the river. It's like a lake here." He took a step toward me. "Come here," he said.

Then he put his arms around me and lifted me up. He actually picked me up like he would a girl or one of those skinny little ones. Fat, blubbery me! I locked my arms around his shoulders and went completely numb. Then he let out a rebel yell in his deep, confident voice and we were in the air. The collage of emotions swirling in my addled brain—fear, euphoria, love, complete surrender, and trust in another—found their way like a circulating fluid from my head to my loins.

It happened as we struck the water. Something was coming out. I could feel the spurts but didn't know what it was. Blood? Would the wa-

ter be red from me? Poor Josie, she had never told me about these things.
It was the first and only time.

The river surprised me with its warmth. I had expected it to chill
me like the stream from a garden hose or the first jets of a shower on dry
skin, but instead it seemed to welcome me like a warm bed in winter.
We couldn't have been under for more than a few seconds, but I've spent
hours, probably days, reliving them in my mind over the nearly two score
years that have passed. My body was coming back to life. Free from sight,
sound, and gravity in that underwater world of touch, my hands felt
Tony's hair, his shoulders and back, the smooth, tight cheeks of his buttocks. My mouth managed to find his chest and bonded airtight around
a nipple; it was hard and concentrated like a snap on my winter coat.

"You did it," I heard Tony say. I hadn't even realized that we
had bobbed to the surface. I was still holding on like a baby monkey to
its mother, tasting Tony's skin, but I let go when I knew the sun was on
us again and the others could see. Tony didn't seem to mind; I think he
would have let me nestle there forever.

I know Ronnie was jealous by the way he looked at us as Tony
was taking me by the hand toward the barge and later as he led me out
of the river and back to the shore. It shouldn't have surprised me that
Ronnie would try to get even. He had always been jealous of me: for my
excellent grades in school and for my special place in Mama Miggliore's
esteem—which place, by the way, I believe led to his ambivalent attitude
toward my birthmark.

In our childhood, he was forever making fun of it or feigning
revulsion to it in front of others. But when we were alone, as we often
were in those early days—Italian cousins of an age might just well be
siblings—and there was no reason for pretense, his fascination for it was
obvious. He always wanted to know what it felt like. Did it hurt when I
got a haircut? Could he touch it? Once when he was at my house and we
were doing homework together (i.e., he was copying mine), he grabbed

a piece of onionskin paper out of his book bag, pressed it down hard against my buzz cut, and traced my "holy mark." Then he took to his crayons and colored it Indian Red. I firmly believe that he only took up dancing because he wanted to do something that my pudgy, uncoordinated self would never be able to match. Years later, when he was doing hair after the dancing didn't go anywhere, he found it his place to recommend ways to make my birthmark less noticeable, especially after my hair had begun to thin: skin creams, hair coloring, even hats and hairpieces.

Ronnie must have begun planning the incident he orchestrated behind the levee almost immediately after Tony and I took our plunge. The gathering at Mama Miggliore's that day was in honor of one of Anthony's younger children's birthday. Since we were too old for the children's games that had been planned for the party, Ronnie summoned me and Tony to the porch and suggested that the three of us break away for some fun at our secret place. I couldn't wait to go. This was just a matter of weeks since the plunge, and I had been praying ever since that it would happen again. Mama Miggliore lacked the strength by then to spend much time with even her favorite grandchild, so I didn't feel any guilt about neglecting her. But I was disappointed when Tony didn't seem to want to go. He said it wouldn't be right for him to miss his little brother's party. Then he turned his back on us and rejoined the family.

Ronnie seemed unaffected by Tony's dismissive attitude. He went to his mother's Cadillac and grabbed something from the back seat. On his way back to the house, he waved it in my face. It was a pair of Tony's swimming trunks. What was Ronnie doing with them?

"I'll get him," Ronnie said, and he followed Tony into the house. It wasn't long before he came out again, smugly letting the screen door spring shut with a loud clap to announce his triumphant return.

"He's putting on his suit, so get ready," Ronnie said to me.

"I thought he didn't want to go," I said.

Ronnie walked down the porch steps and to his mother's car

again. "He needs a favor and I told him I wouldn't help him if he didn't," he said. He had gone to the car to get the sheet that Rose always kept on the back seat to keep it from cracking in the sun. "Here, hold this," he said, and he tossed it to me. It was bright yellow like the car.

"What kind of favor are you supposed to do for him?" I wanted to know.

"He met some bitch he's trying to impress, and he always needs money for gas and the drive-in. Things like that," Ronnie said. "He showed me a picture once. I wasn't impressed. She has this crooked nose like somebody smacked it with a tap shoe, and her eyebrows are too thick. I didn't say anything, though. I didn't want to hurt his feelings. But he could do so much better. He met her at a CYO dance, so I guess it figures she'd be a dog."

Although it hurt that Tony would go to Ronnie instead of me when he needed something, I understood. Before Mama Miggliore died and the estate was parceled out, the grandchildren's standard of living was for the most part a matter of their parents' resources. Everyone—Paul, Anthony, Rose, and Josie—had a comfortable house, and their children's educations were taken care of, but beyond that, you would hardly know we came from money. For entertainment and luxuries, we were left on our own. By the way, it wasn't considered a luxury that Anthony's and the Fishwife's houses were three times larger than Josie and mine; they used the old excuse of their bigger families to arrange that.

I know Tony would have come to me for help before going to Ronnie if he hadn't known that of all the grandchildren, I was surely in the weakest position to do anything for him. Time or attention I would have given him without limit, but money was another story. My mother's only income came from the paltry salary Anthony paid her for working a few hours a week in the music store. The little pension she got from my father's job with the bread company isn't even worth mentioning. Anthony, forever rubbing it in that she had married a poor Cajun, liked to tell my mother it wasn't enough to buy the sandwiches for a decent wedding.

In contrast was Rose, who could blow her big nose with ten dollar bills once she married into the Cuchinottos and all their fish money. And Tony had to know, as we all did, that she gave her precious Ronnie anything he asked for.

"This time he wants more," Ronnie said.

"More money?" I asked. "For what?"

"He wants Uncle Anthony to lend him the money for a car so he can take Miss Crookednose out whenever he wants, but he said he won't help him unless Tony comes up with half the money himself. You know what a cheap old fuck Uncle Anthony is."

I did indeed, but I didn't know how Ronnie had planned to use our uncle's parsimony to his own advantage.

"How much does he need?" I asked.

"Two hundred dollars. The car's only four hundred. It's a used MG. Just two seats—one for Crookednose and one for Loverboy."

I thought of my little ceramic elephant bank at home, where I'd squirrel away the dollar bills Mama Miggliore gave me and the quarters from Josie for cleaning my room and dusting the house. I doubted there was a fifth of what Tony needed in it.

Ronnie went on to tell me that although he had the full two hundred dollars, he wasn't going to let Tony have it all at once.

"I'm going to milk this for all I can get," he said.

He had already given Tony fifty dollars the week before, telling him it was all he had at the time but that he'd be able to get him the rest—fifty every month or so—as long as Tony agreed to a few conditions, like sleeping over at Ronnie's house. "He's already come over twice," Ronnie gloated.

I couldn't believe it. Tony hadn't spent the night at my house since we were children and his parents went on a second honeymoon in Biloxi. "What do you all do?" I asked, too naïve to imagine what a little sissy like Ronnie could possible do all night to keep a dynamic young athlete like Tony from being bored to tears.

"You'll see," said Ronnie. "That's what this is for." And with that, he grabbed the yellow sheet from me and told me that at some point after we had gotten behind the levee, he was going to lead Tony into the woods to a little clearing we had once found on one of our little forays.

"I'm going to tell you to stay where you are so you can let us know if anybody's coming," he instructed me. "Tony might not go along if he knows you're going to be watching. But you can sneak up on us and see. I'll make sure his back is to you."

I still didn't know what Ronnie had in mind for me to see, and I was afraid to ask—afraid that whatever it was should have been so obvious that I'd look ignorant and obtuse. The only thing I knew for certain was that Ronnie had used money to coerce Tony into spending time with him. Pathetically, I began to survey my own resources. I couldn't think of any way to multiply what I had in my elephant bank except by selling my records, which nobody would want now that Rock and Roll had made Johnny Ray a has-been.

Once we had made our way to the barge, Ronnie wasted no time stripping and trying to get Tony to climb the steps and jump off with him. Tony wasn't interested, though. He kept his trunks on and used the excuse that he had just eaten and didn't want to dive, so he'd wait in the water for Ronnie to jump, in case Ronnie needed any help. I could tell our big cousin wasn't in the mood to play with Ronnie; he must have had enough of him during the week. I stayed in my usual place, on the defeated cypress, hoping Tony would come for me again.

After his jump, Ronnie swam over to Tony and said something to him. They were too far away for me to hear, but I saw Tony look over toward me before replying. Then Ronnie led him out of the water and toward the trees. Just as he had planned, Ronnie told me to stay where I was and be a lookout. I was to call them if anyone unexpectedly came near. Ronnie took Tony's hand and led him into the woods.

I debated whether or not to follow. Would I be betraying Tony if I did? Certainly Ronnie wanted him to believe that they would be alone. But I wanted to know what they were doing, and so I got up. It was perhaps a hundred yards from my seat on the cypress tree to the clearing. I had never negotiated the trek on my own; Ronnie or Tony had always blazed the trail. Along the way I was nearly driven back by the thickness of the weeds, the brambles that pricked at my arms and legs, unseen rocks that impeded my progress and nearly caused me to sprain my ankles, swarms of wasps and mosquito hawks. I was Phoenix Jackson, the old woman in the Welty story, making her way through that Delta thicket, past a roll call of hobgoblins. Once Tony had spied a snake along this trail and pointed it out to the rest of us. Ronnie had shrieked like a melting witch, and Tony kicked at the creature with a brave bare foot until it slithered its sinister self out of our way.

I forged on, but not, I am ashamed to say, to do some good for an ailing child like old Phoenix. Rather it was the selfish conviction that I, like a wayward character out of Hawthorne, would see something forbidden in those woods that urged me on. I regret that I didn't read the signs in nature and turn back.

A subtle change in the density of the brush some paces ahead indicated that the clearing was at hand. A few more steps and the dominant greens and browns of the brake began to take on a preternaturally yellow hue. It was the Fishwife's cover sheet. There was only one unobstructed path into the clearing, a natural alcove between two willows where the vines and brambles and other parasitic growths had somehow not intruded.

As it turned out, Tony wouldn't have seen me even if Ronnie hadn't arranged for his back to be to the entrance of the clearing because his eyes were closed in what I at first mistakenly took to be an attitude of indifference. He was on his back, his knees bent and pointing straight to the sky, his feet planted firmly on the sheet like a sunbather on a beach. His arms were at his sides. His trunks were bundled into what served as a pillow for his head. Ronnie was on his knees, caressing one of his big cousin's calves and picking at the hairs on Tony's shins until he saw me and put a finger to his lips as if I were not too breathless to make a sound. Then he put his belly to the sheet like that slithering snake and began to play his fingers along our cousin's thighs. Tony answered the touch by opening his legs just enough for Ronnie's head to fit between his knees. As Ronnie's kisses moved farther and farther up those smooth, muscled thighs, Tony's legs spread even wider until they seemed to go limp in a welcoming surrender.

I began to feel dizzy, as I had that day atop the barge with Tony. Blood was rushing to my head, but instead of proceeding in its circuit to my loins, it stayed there and began a throbbing in my brain as if desperately looking for a way out. Tony's only reaction when Ronnie took him in his hand was to slowly raise an arm from his side. I thought he was going to swat Ronnie away like one of those annoying mosquitoes that seemed to come out of the river itself in hungry hordes at dusk. But all Tony did was ball his hand into a fist and use it to prop up his head above his makeshift pillow. Perhaps he was looking at Ronnie, but with his head now raised as it was, I could no longer see if his eyes were open.

Tony was in Ronnie's grip now. I could see it arching back on his belly like a supple gymnast from its furry base to rosy tip reaching nearly to his navel, a tiny pool of sweat. A little drop glistened at its tip; that, too, I took in my innocence to be sweat. I had seen it many times behind the levee; it had always seemed thick and full and healthy, swinging freely between those thighs—never a tiny fingerling like the younger boys' or a shrunken and puny ugly thing. So until Ronnie pried it from Tony's belly, I couldn't tell that anything was different.

I had never seen one like that, nor would I have dreamed of touching it. But Ronnie did something more than that—something I had never imagined one human being might do to another. I got even more light-headed watching, so much so that I had to brace myself against one of the willows for support. Whether what I was witnessing was in essence good or evil, I knew it was not meant to be done before an audience, but Ronnie obviously enjoyed that part, affectedly sighing and cooing like an infant with a pacifier. I hardly knew what to make of the sight. I wasn't repulsed by it; indeed it struck me that Ronnie, in his attitude of worshipful, almost prayerful submission, had only found a new way to show Tony the respect and deference that he deserved. It was when Ronnie started to touch himself and I knew he was just as intent on gratifying his own selfish drives as honoring Tony that my emotions turned to anger and disgust. After indulging himself for several minutes, Ronnie saw fit to announce my presence.

"He wants his turn," he said, and Tony looked over his shoulder and right at me. I expected some kind of adverse reaction from him, like scrambling to his feet with embarrassment and trying to force himself, wet and swollen, back into his trunks; or perhaps he would go berserk and physically punish Ronnie and me. Instead he seemed to sense my apprehension, as he had that day by the water.

"It's okay," he said, reaching out to me with the hand that wasn't propping up his head. With his upside-down smile that was both inviting and frightening to me, Tony was actually beckoning me to join them.

But I couldn't. Not because there wasn't anything in the world I wouldn't do if Tony asked me, but because of Ronnie. In my mind Ronnie had made it all dirty—corrupt and impure. I wanted to take Tony's hand again as I had dreamed so many times, but not with Ronnie there stroking himself like a grinning satyr. So I turned on my heels and left them without a word, my head pounding as I walked back to Mama Miggliore's house alone.

My grandmother's death occurred only a few weeks after the incident with Tony Junior and Ronnie behind the levee. There were no birthdays or family functions in those intervening weeks, so I had no occasion to see Tony again as I so badly wanted to. And of course he wasn't there at the deathwatch, which made that horrific day all the more traumatic for me. Not until Mama Miggliore's funeral did I get my next chance to see him, but he spent all of his time with his father; he must have known I wouldn't dare approach him as long as he stayed close to Anthony.

I believe he was ashamed that I knew all about him and Ronnie. He must have taken my reaction behind the levee—my failure to take his hand, the tortured look I must have had on my face from my aching head, my silent flight back to the house—as a moral repudiation. Perhaps he might have even thought I told my mother what I had seen, and he feared being shamed before the family. Although we never discussed it, he must have known that the bad blood between his father and my mother had gotten worse with Mama Miggliore's passing. If I were the vindictive type, I might have thought to use him to hurt my vengeful uncle.

People come to us priests with their baggage as if we're all psychotherapists. One thing I've noticed as I help them through their issues is that there is always an incident, often occurring in late childhood or adolescence, which determines the direction of the rest of their lives. In my case it was Tony's break from me, occurring virtually concurrently with the death of my grandmother. There is no telling how my life would have been different if I had had Tony with me through my developmental years instead of being pulled into Ronnie's orbit. I might have gone to high school instead of Saint Jerome's seminary, maybe even followed Tony to LSU and even roomed with him there.

Many of these insights regarding Tony Junior came from a therapist I was seeing a few years ago, after an unfortunate series of events that unfolded after I led a group of boys on a three-day retreat near the Tchefuncte River in 1988. By then Ratchett had managed to make enough political and financial connections to succeed to the archbishopric of the city. Rev. Manresa, a lazy-eyed Jesuit from Boston, and a *psychiatrist* no less, had his office on the thirty-third floor of a high rise on Poydras. He was probably taping our sessions in addition to the reams of notes he took every time we got together.

Manresa was always black-suited and seated behind a prodigious mahogany desk that must have been ten feet wide. He never rose to greet me or walk me to the door after a session, prompting me to wonder if there might be something wrong with his lower body. He had an oddly pronounced brow, almost Neanderthal in its protrusion, which could have been an indication of at least partial dwarfism. Then there was that lazy left eye, which as you looked at him at his desk always drifted over to a wall with a large aquarium and a window facing the river, so that he never seemed to be giving his patient more than half his attention. My chair—it was a recliner, but I seldom used that feature—faced the window and the fish. Sometime in the middle of each session, Manresa would ask me to feed them. The food was in a tin in a cabinet beside the aquarium. I wasn't sure if the feeding was part of my therapy or more evidence that my doctor was hiding something behind that desk.

I was always wary in my conversations with him; I wasn't about to trust a Jesuit. Manresa took an almost voyeuristic interest in my child-hood, so naturally many of our sessions focused on family issues, particu-larly my relationship with Mama Miggliore and my cousins. Perhaps it was purposeful on my part, but I believe I let my guard down whenever the subject of Tony Junior came up. Manresa must have found me the ideal subject on those occasions, as I rattled on an on about his beauty and strength of character and what a despicable little deviant my late cousin Ronnie was (yes, Ronnie had died two years earlier). I must have described Tony to Manresa a dozen times, his strong legs and beautiful chest, how he looked climbing barefoot up the steps of the old barge. But he never stopped me; he never said, "Yes, we've been over that already. Let's go on to something else." Was he conjuring images of Tonys he had known himself, the salient evidence of his interest safely hidden behind the desk?

So, why was I seeing this Manresa in the first place? As I mentioned earlier, the sessions came about as a result of the Tchefuncte retreat ordeal. My direct superior at the time told me that he wanted me to "talk to someone," but I suspected that Ratchett was behind it; and given all the recent events that have led me here to Kattannachee, I'm convinced I was right. Forcing me into therapy was just an early strong-arm tactic to humiliate me after Tchefuncte. Manresa was no doubt handpicked by the archbishop himself: otherwise why a psychiatrist? I wouldn't doubt if the archdiocese was shelling out two hundred dollars an hour into the Jesuit's coffers. Wouldn't a psychologist with a PhD have served the purpose for perhaps half the price? Or, for that matter, even a fifty-dollar-an-hour counselor? Going right to the top seemed more than a bit extreme.

And it made me more than a bit suspicious. It all makes sense now, though, given what I know about their plotting. Circumstances that I will explain in time made it impossible for them to act against me after Tchefuncte, but wouldn't it make a useful bargaining chip for them later to force me to comply with their demands if they could show that I had been under psychiatric care? (And don't think me paranoid, because that is *exactly* what they did!) Further, by sending me to a high-priced shrink, they could maintain that they spared no expense in getting me "help" should I say or do anything in the future to compromise the Church's reputation.

At least I was somewhat on my guard, not foolhardy enough to completely tell all to one of Ratchett's handpicked lackeys.

"And do you remember what you were doing when you learned of your cousin Tony's death?" Manresa subtly asked me during a session. We had been talking about the years after Mama Miggliore's passing, when Vietnam was raging and Tony enlisted in the army.

"No, I couldn't even tell you exactly what year it was," I said. "Sometime in the late sixties, I think." Of course I was lying. I could have told him the exact day if I had wanted to—April 16, 1970, outside a village called Cam Hoa, a hundred or so miles south of Saigon. You won't find it on any map today; the place was leveled during the battle and never rebuilt. I still have an old map with the village on it. I used to track Tony's whereabouts during the war. Whenever I managed to hear through the family where he was, I stuck a pin with a white head on it over the spot. There's a black pin over Cam Hoa.

Manresa would never know any of that. He was setting me up with that question about what I was doing the day I found out. He already knew about Tony's death. We had talked about his and Ronnie's respective fates early in our sessions. He was just trying to find out how much Tony had meant to me. Cleverly, he had me feed the fish just before asking the question so that he'd have more than just my tone of voice to gauge my reaction. Would there be a break in my feeding routine? Would I tremble and spill too much food into the water? Would I walk any faster or slower, trip and lose my balance on my way back to my chair?

Except for a little difficulty getting the tin open, causing me to spill a few flakes of fish food onto the carpet, I believe I showed no reaction. I wasn't going to let that conniving Jesuit know how much Tony had meant to me.

"We wrote to each other for a few years," I told Manresa. "First while Tony was at LSU and then when he went overseas the first couple of times. After a while, we just stopped. By the time he died, I hardly thought of him at all anymore."

"And did you keep his letters?" asked the wily Jesuit.

I had to be careful here. If I said yes, he was likely to ask to see one or two, and of course they never existed.

"No," I said. "I threw them away along with a lot of old papers in the seminary"

As far as my taking the name Anthony Miggliore upon ordination, I told Manresa that it was in honor of my godfather. Whether he believed that or not was his problem. He couldn't challenge me without tacitly admitting at least an indirect connection to my uncle through Ratchett. I had him there.

Whatever that prying little manipulator thought he knew about me, he would never know how Tony's death had really affected me. How could either he or that heartless archbishop whom he was reporting to possibly have understood the truth—that when I heard Tony was dead I felt what I can only imagine one feels at the loss of a lover. I couldn't go anywhere or see anyone; even the company of my own mother was intolerable to me. For weeks I made excuses to avoid our Sunday dinners that had become customary in the later years of my studies. I told her I had to go to some church or another as an "observer" or that I was needed on a weekend retreat or that I had to write a paper on some abstruse topic like the Schism of Aquilea.

Eating was my response to the depression, a natural one in a black hole of obesity like New Orleans. I started to gorge myself on the most unredeemable foods: doughnuts, cheeseburgers, tamales, foot-long hot dogs peddled by unkempt street vendors and frustrated poets. Later, once my depression had subsided and the overeating had simply become a habit, anything Italian would do. By the time I was ordained a few months later, I thanked God I could wear the surplice: It was about the only thing short of a pup tent that would cover the seventy pounds I had gained.

CHAPTER FIVE

ORDINATION

It was during those months between Tony's death and my ordination that I really learned New Orleans, its streets and neighborhoods, its restaurants, the language of its people, the places where it never sleeps. Mine had been a life of Catholic insulation until then. The most volatile decade of the century had just ended, and I had spent it reading Tertullian and Aquinas and learning to give absolution for sins I'd never had the chance to commit. My wanderings took me from Mid-City to the Quarter, searching not only for food, as I was eating more and more after Tony died, but for the company of people whose experience had been nothing like mine. I'd walk for miles, and when I was too tired or bloated from a meal, I'd hail a cab. Money wasn't a problem since my mother had gotten her full share of Mama Miggliore's estate and didn't know what else to do with it except make sure I had everything I needed, which at that time was primarily food and conversation.

The latter was as easy to find as the former. New Orleans is a city teeming with people waiting for someone to talk to, and a surprising number of them are young. Every generation of our youth seems to have something they're running away from. At that time it was Vietnam. There were so many young men—boys really, barely out of high school. I must have met a different one every night: boys from all over the South. Canada was too far away, so they came here. "You can disappear here," they'd say. "It's better than leaving the country." Then they'd tell me their fathers had disowned them, called them cowards when they said they wouldn't fight. I told them I had just lost someone close to me over there, and a few said their fathers would have preferred that. I often gave them money because I thought it was the only thing I had to offer them.

They'd call me Mr. Broussard. Though I was only a few years older than most of them, I wasn't aging well. Not only was I heavier than ever, but my hair was starting to thin. Ronnie was cutting it at the time. He had taken up cosmetology after his pathetic little New York dancing career fizzled out after a couple of years. All the while he was up there, the Fishwife made sure everybody heard about her son who was "in the theater in New York," even though we all knew he was only there because of her money. By then Ronnie's father, Uncle Eugenio, was dead of prostate cancer, so Rose was rolling not only in Miggliore money, but in a tidy share of the Cuchinotto fish fortune as well. She often disappeared herself for weeks at a time, using Ronnie as an excuse when she was really in seclusion after another nose job. By 1970 she had finally traded Mama Miggliore's nose for Sophia Loren's and had resumed the face-lifts. The cancer that would ravage her surgeons' handiwork and leave her sculpted features in ruins was still a few years in the future.

"They're nominated for a Tony!" she crowed to my mother on the phone when one of Ronnie's shows managed not to close inside of a week. It turned out that the award, which they didn't win in the end, was in lighting or makeup or some other silly category that the cast has nothing to do with and nobody cares about anyway.

"Oh my God I can see it!" Ronnie shrieked one day in 1970 after I had climbed into the styling chair at the salon and removed my hat. He had been cutting my hair since he moved back from New York and his mother put him through cosmetology school. Once he got his license, Rose financed the opening of "Mr. Ronnie's," his uptown shop. He billed himself as a "hair aesthetician" and claimed to have worked with dozens of celebrities. On the shop's walls were autographed glossies of stars like Carol Channing, Mitzi Gaynor, and Juliet Prowse. Of course Ronnie had never been within hacking distance of these people's hair, much less ever appeared in any of their shows. He told me he had managed to get the pictures signed at various social functions—fundraisers for the arts and even a few private parties if he could manage to tag along with someone on the guest list.

I had taken to wearing hats in response to my incipient hair loss, which I attribute to anxiety over Tony's passing. Instead of sleeping at night, I'd lie awake with an icepack at my bedside, ready to apply it to my head when the tension felt like someone was aiming a heat lamp at my scalp. Those often became the nights when I'd get out and walk the streets until I found some relief in talking to a young stranger.

The recession of my hairline had proceeded apace in those months after Tony's death. I tried to control the situation with hairspray, but that only worked indoors; it was useless on the windy streets of New Orleans, where hats were the only solution.

"What?" I asked, looking at Ronnie's gape-mouthed expression behind me in the mirror. Naturally my damage control had been con-centrated on my hairline since that's what I saw in the mirror. Not until that day in the shop did I realize what was going on in the back. Ronnie was staring at the top of my head with such alarm and revulsion that I thought I had lice.

"That thing on your head," he said. "I can see it right through your hair!"

It was still a few moments before I realized that he was talking about the nevus, my port-wine stain, the "holy mark" that had distinguished me as a child in the eyes of our grandmother. Once Mama Miggliore was no longer around to call attention to it, and the longer hairstyles of the sixties had served to cover it up, it had ceased to exist as a practical thing in my life. Now with my hair falling out in clumps, it was back. And who of all people would be the first to notice it but Ronnie!

"Look!" he said, grabbing another mirror and holding it up so I could see.

Through the illusory distance brought about by the two mirrors, it wasn't very clear to me. What I saw seemed to be a discoloration in my hair, as if someone had stuck a wad of bubble gum in it.

"It doesn't look all that bad," I said. "Do you think if we let my hair grow a little longer it might cover it up?"

"No," Ronnie said. He started poking at my head with a comb and making faces like he was picking ticks off a dog. "There's not enough hair to grow it long. You'd look like Bozo the Clown."

We discussed various treatment methods over the ensuing weeks. "I heard peanut butter's good," Ronnie said. "It's all protein, and so is hair."

So I started eating peanut butter like a toothless elephant. Not even bothering to spread it on bread, I'd just take it by the spoonful, as much as two jars a day. I'd follow each serving with a handful of chocolate mints to get the smell off my breath. After two months, I had gained twenty pounds and had less hair than ever.

Next Ronnie tried "electrical massage": From a cabinet next to the sink in the private stall he always saw me in, he pulled out a long, wand-like corded instrument with a cushioned, bulbous tip that vibrated when he switched it on. I noticed it was already plugged in when he took it out; there must have been an outlet inside the cabinet. It was as if he wanted the thing always at the ready, for what purpose I didn't dare imagine. With me, though, the vibrating tip was applied to the thinning areas of my scalp with the intent, Ronnie stated, to "stimulate the dormant follicles." Of course the idea was absurd and fruitless as far as waking up any sleeping hair roots, but the massage felt good nonetheless, especially when Ronnie rubbed the gizmo directly on my birthmark, which seemed to have become more sensitive over the years that it had been covered with my hair and now reacted more gratifyingly than the rest of my scalp to the stimulation.

"Did you know it changes color when I rub on it?" Ronnie asked. He had the wand right over the nevus, so between the sound of the motor reverberating between my ears and the relaxing pleasure of the vibrations, I barely heard him.

"What?" I asked.

"Your purple spot," he said. "It changes when I rub it."

"It probably just blanches from the pressure."

"No," Ronnie said, "it's doing just the opposite. It's going from a pale mauve to something darker, almost crimson." He switched off the wand and started rubbing his finger over it. "It even *feels* different," he said. "Like it's swelling up and standing out from your head."

I remembered Mama Miggliore's long-ago prediction that over time my "segno sacro" would gradually morph into something undeniably significant, an unambiguous emblem of my distinction. I thought my hair loss might be a part of that process, like the shedding or molting process that some creatures go through, ushering in a new stage of life or the advent of their true essence. The idea that my "holy mark" might become my most prominent physical feature, changing colors and swelling to obscene proportions like a crimson tumor, made me more determined than ever to cover it up.

We discussed dyes, but Ronnie concluded that changing from my natural medium brown to anything darker would just make me look balder than ever. Going lighter would make the thinning less obvious, but it would only cause the birthmark to stand out more conspicuously, like a landmark in a lifting fog.

"Aren't there any colors that would blend?" I asked desperately.

"Blend with that thing?" Ronnie sniffed back. "Nothing that would look the slightest bit natural. You'd look like something out of *Batman*!"

Finally we decided that the only tenable option was a piece. I abhorred the idea of wearing a toupee while still in my twenties, but it would serve to improve my looks and cover what I had begun to think of as my disfigurement. And besides, in my line of work, people weren't often likely to be running their fingers through my hair. Fortunately, I had the money to afford the best, a nine hundred dollar "unit" (Ronnie said it was his price, but I had my doubts) handmade in Italy from human hair with an incredibly light, nearly transparent cap. Following Ronnie's advice, I ordered two: one to wear and one to keep at the shop for him to style and prep for my next visit. He measured me for my first ones that summer; the pair came in just in time for my ordination on September 27, 1970.

For the next several years, no one but Ronnie saw my holy mark, hidden as it was beneath my piece. Despite seeing the nevus on a regular basis, though, my cousin couldn't resist making a comment every chance he got: how big it was, what color it appeared to be this time, how much more it seemed to stand out as my hair got more and more sparse. Eventually he started to wax mystical about it, positing notions nearly as absurd as our long-dead grandmother's regarding its significance, only couched in the quasi-intellectual psychobabble of the seventies.

"You know, if something inside of us needs to come out, it's going to come out," he said to me out of the blue during a regular visit to the shop in 1974. I remember the year because I had just begun my tenure at "the Den," a house for homeless high school boys, a position I happily remained in until the early eighties. Although Ronnie hadn't prefaced his remark with any specific reference to my birthmark, he had just taken off my hair and I knew what he was talking about. He had lately begun to see it as something that I should be proud to show the world. Like Rudolph's red nose, it was a singularity, not a thing to be ashamed of. He started trying to talk me out of wearing hair.

"It's who you are," he said. "Not this." And he tossed my hair irreverently into the sink for its washing. It landed upside down and was slowly swallowed beneath the suds like a bedraggled corsage.

Ronnie must have read every psychological self-help book that came out in those feel-good-about-yourself days and spent hours theorizing about how it all applied to me.

"If you could only see how red it's gotten," he said at one visit. He held up his little mirror for me, but I wouldn't look. "It's your passion," he insisted. "You've kept it hidden so long—first under your fat."

I must have started at that because he retreated just a bit.

"Oh I know it sounds cruel, but it's true. That's what we do. First you covered yourself up by gaining weight, then hiding away in that school [St. Jerome's, the seminary] all those years, and now under this black suit and that hair. But we can't keep our true selves bottled up forever. They've got to come out."

I almost stopped him and demanded to know what he knew about my true self. And as for emotions, I had hardly felt any since Tony died, but I wasn't going to bring that up. It would only get Ronnie started on the old days, maybe even take him back to the levee again. So I let him babble.

"I know we all thought Mama Miggliore had some crazy ideas about you and this thing, but in our Western culture, we don't pay enough attention to the old ones and their wisdom. She just saw everything in religious terms, but she was on to something."

Another time he tried to get me to believe that the "something" that Mama Miggliore was on to might be explained through phrenology. He claimed to have just read a book about it.

"Phrenology?" I said, as if my cousin truly might be insane.

"Yes," he said. "It's the study of the shape of the head. Phrenologists believe that the personality can be mapped out by studying and measuring the shape and contour of our skulls."

"I know what it is," I said. "It was a nineteenth century fad, like séances. Nobody believes in it anymore." I didn't want to encourage my cousin by mentioning all of the intelligent figures of that century who had put their faith in that quackery. Walt Whitman, for one, absolutely swore by it. One of his biographers said he even donated his brain to be studied by phrenologists after his death. As the story goes, a careless technician dropped the organ and splattered the Good Gray Poet's gray matter all over the laboratory floor.

"When was that book written," I asked sarcastically, "1860?"

"Excuse me, Father Smarty Pants," Ronnie countered, hands on his bony hips, "but try 1974! I saw the author on Mike Douglas just a few weeks ago." With his finger he traced the outline of the mark's hourglass figure on my head. His nails were long like his mother's. "I bet we could find somebody in the Quarter doing phrenology readings."

"I don't doubt that," I said. "Aren't they still practicing voodoo down there?"

Ronnie gave me a dainty slap on the shoulder. "Stop that! I'm serious. I just know the doctor who wrote the book would have something to say about this thing. I'm going to write him a letter."

Whether he wrote that letter or not, I don't know, but the subject of phrenology wasn't brought up again at my next visit. This time Ronnie's opinion was that the truth lay deeper, below the surface.

"This thing is a sign of something," he said. "Something inside of you. You can keep trying to cover it up, but eventually you're going to have to face it. It's going to come out." Then he added with a histrionic flourish, "And you're going to be miserable until it does."

I wasn't miserable, I could have told him. Granted, it might have been for the first time in my life, but I wasn't. I had just started a master's program in American literature at Tulane, and I was optimistic about my new position at the Den; there were some sad and wonderful boys there and so much good work to be done.

It was all so absurd. I thought I had heard every cockeyed birthmark theory when I was a child, but now Ronnie was making it out to be some kind of portentous symbol out of Hawthorne and I a Catholic Arthur Dimmesdale. The analogy of the sinful, disgraced priest plagued my sleep that night, precipitating a terrifying dream.

It was Easter in New Orleans and, for reasons unclear, I had become the most exalted priest in the city (a rival to the archbishop?), chosen to carry the Cross in a televised re-enactment of the Stations that began with a public sentencing by Pilate (the mayor of the city) and a mock scourging before a crowd in the French Market. After being draped in a magnificent violet cloak and capped with a papier-mâché "crown of thorns" by two beefy Saints players dressed as Roman legionnaires, I began my circuitous trek through the Quarter that was supposed to culminate in a glorious Crucifixion at noon in Jackson Square, after which I would celebrate Mass in the Cathedral before television cameras and the largest Easter crowd ever assembled in the city.

Wielding the vertical portion of a fiberglass cross and followed by a crowd of worshippers, I made my way down Esplanade and into the Quarter at Decatur, where a contingent of the "women of the city" offered me their tears and a drink. After I admonished the women to weep not for me but for themselves and their children, the crowd applauded and began to strew petals of spring flowers in my path as I turned down Ursuline to the sounds of the cheering multitude, solemn strains of Easter hymns from speakers lining the streets, and the clicking of a thousand camera shutters like locusts in the oaks at dusk.

Somewhere along the way, though, after I had "fallen" for the second time in front of an oyster bar on Royal, the tenor of the dream took a nightmarish turn. It started when I began to sense a discomfort on my scalp, which I at first attributed to my makeshift headdress. But that wouldn't explain the change in the demeanor of the crowd, which was beginning to appear amused and distracted as my discomfort became a searing heat as if someone were focusing the sun's rays onto the back of my head with a magnifying glass.

By Saint Philip the crowd, which had so lately been admiring witnesses to the solemn Passion Play, was completely transformed into a jeering, foul-mouthed mob, laughing, cursing, and pointing at me as if I were the village hunchback or some defiler of virgin innocence. It was no longer Holy Week, I came to realize, but Mardi Gras, its irreverent and antithetical precursor; and I was soon covered not in azalea and magnolia petals but horse droppings, offered not sips of cool mint tea but doused with cheap beer and spoiled seafood. My violet robe was now a garish purple and gold calico costume of the cheapest polyester, my crown a foolscap with bells atop. The "holy women of the city," who had been following my steps since Decatur, singing hymns of the Resurrection and offering to dab my brow with cool, disposable cloths, were gone. In their stead appeared a wicked chorus of Bourbon Street hookers—cruel and dissipated expressions painted on their heathen faces, taunting my obesity, holding up their little fingers to mock my manhood, and dancing an obscene jig with corrupted, half-naked men to a hideous hybrid disco mix of Professor Longhair.

At the Square, instead of the rest of my cross and the television cameras that were supposed to record my speech at the end of the symbolic journey, a nightmarish tableau awaited me. Stocks out of Puritan New England had replaced the equestrian statue of Andrew Jackson. Ratchett and my Uncle Anthony were among the hateful crowd surrounding what was looking to become the scene of my humiliation.

Once I was secured helpless in the stocks, a shirtless, black-hooded and muscle-bound Negro grabbed my foolscap to strip it from my head. One of the bells had become entangled in my hair, which the Negro brute yanked off with the cap in one fell and humiliating swoop. As the brute stood by, brandishing his trophy like the scalp of a vanquished foe, I could see what had turned the crowd so viciously against me: My birthmark had become a red-hot brand, searing a hole in its own image completely through my hairpiece. Noticing that the hourglass shape of the hole had turned the wig into a hideous and hirsute visor, the Negro fitted the ersatz carnival mask to my face, turning me into a mortified werewolf before the cruelly cheering crowd. I awoke just as the throng had set upon me, yanking me from the stocks and stripping me of my garments. They drove me to the river, where they forced me onto an anchored barge—the very one my cousins had played on as children—and sent me drifting naked down the river.

As chilling as that dream was, I couldn't let it upset me. It was just Ronnie's stupid little allusion to the birthmark as symbol coupled with my rereading of *The Scarlet Letter* for one of my classes at Tulane that brought it on. I had a great deal to console myself by: I had just recently begun to do some very good work among the boys at the Den with the promise of much more to come. And one undeniable fact proved that I was no Dimmesdale and Ronnie's theory was a pail of hogwash that showed my cousin to be no more an intellectual than he was a dancer: Unlike Hawthorne's weak and hypocritical cleric, I had been true to all of my vows for over four years. I had committed no sin.

My ordination was auspicious enough; seven of us began our religious lives in Saint Louis Cathedral that warm Sunday morning in September 1970. Ratchett had only recently become archbishop of New Orleans. After using every connection he had managed to make in twenty years, he became right-hand man to his predecessor, an Irishman named Fallon who had won the city's affection and admiration by ministering to Allied soldiers on the battlefields of Europe during the war. Perhaps it was a way of giving final absolution to the Germans that the aging Archbishop Fallon picked Ratchett as his successor, sending him to Rome as his proxy toward the end to ensure that he'd make the proper connections over there as well.

He was quite young to lead the Catholics of New Orleans, probably still in his forties by my reckoning. He spoke no more to me that day than he did to my six colleagues. No one would have known by his aloofness toward me that he was so well acquainted with my family. Of course none of the Miggliores were there except my mother. Like a cancer in remission, Anthony would maintain his distance from me for many more years, waiting for just the right time to strike again. Rose had conveniently chosen that week to visit Ronnie in New York, where he was rehearsing for another embarrassing production that closed almost before it opened.

After taking Holy Orders, the seven new priests assisted Ratchett in celebrating our first Mass, which was televised locally. We each gave a reading from scripture. I had my mother in mind when I chose mine, thinking how she'd be alone in the pews reserved for family of the newly ordained, watching her only child begin a path that could only take him further from her side. I wanted to look in her eyes when I read the passage, but when the moment came, I couldn't. Instead I just passed my eyes over the throng of strangers and settled them finally on the television cameras. "Did you not know that I need to be at my father's work?" I read from Luke. Minutes later, she was the first to receive Communion from my hands. I wondered as I placed the Host on her tongue if she might be thinking of Danny, her husband, my father the bread man. We didn't discuss that afterwards when we walked through the Quarter to lunch on the patio of the Court of Two Sisters. From there, I was off to Holy Gates.

CHAPTER SIX

HOLY GATES

My first assignment was in the suburbs, a dozen or so miles outside the city limits in Jefferson Parish. Holy Gates was a new parish when I arrived, having sprung up in answer to two demographic phenomena of the sixties: the Baby Boom and white flight from New Orleans. The forced integration to which the city capitulated early in the decade was a great boon to the Church, which responded by building dozens of churches and schools in the surrounding Parishes, ensuring whites a safe, legal, and at first inexpensive alternative to the inner city.

At Holy Gates I was assistant pastor, chaplain of the convent, and principal of the school. I'll never forget the first time I saw Holy Gates Elementary. I thought it was a carpet warehouse or some sort of military storage facility. Only later did I realize that all of the schools built by the Church during that era looked like this: twin, two-story, flat-roofed rectangles with ceramic facades and adjustable windows running the length of the classrooms. Structurally I would compare them to a marine barracks with all the architectural panache of a terrarium. The suburban ethos of the population the parish served was as conservative as the buildings indicated, and I doubt I would have ever gotten over my disdain for it had I remained there for twenty years, as the pastor of the place, whom I was appointed to assist, was destined to do.

Father John Foley was a hunter, a football fanatic, and, in general, a poorly educated middle-aged Irish inebriate when I arrived at Holy Gates; and he stayed there until his liver finally gave out in the mid-eighties. He hailed from Bunkie, a wretched little hole in the middle of the state that I experienced first-hand on my ignominious road to Kat-tannachee. It was just a brief stop for lunch at what must have been the oldest Dairy Queen in the South, but those thirty or so minutes were enough for me to understand why someone from that place would try so hard to drink himself to death. Central Louisiana has never been known for its outstanding literacy rates, and Father Foley, not unlike many religious of his generation, had no academic degree. The man could hardly speak a grammatical sentence if he were inspired by the Holy Spirit Himself; his malapropisms ("*Hollow* be Thy name") were legendary. Once, in a sermon based on the Prodigal Son theme, he tried to draw an analogy to the "salmon swimming back to Capistrano."

Yet the people loved him, holding him in the highest esteem for no apparent reason that I could discern except for an inexpressible regard for the amount of liquor the man could consume. He would drink absolutely anything (at Christmas, the bottles—gifts from wily parishioners—piled up on every table and countertop in the rectory like votive candles in a cathedral), but his favorite potable was beer. About the only time he didn't have a can in hand was on the altar, and even there I had some suspicions. I even found a bottle cap on the floor of the confessional once.

"I had suffered a stroke a couple of years ago," he told me one day, the nuances of the past perfect obviously and hopelessly beyond him. "So you might notice me walk unsteady or slurring my sentences a little sometimes." Resisting the temptation to comment that with sentences like that, slurring would be a blessing, I let him go on to tell me that his symptoms were supposed to be controlled by the medication he took for his "condition," but he sometimes had to stay off the medicine because it caused him severe headaches.

The parishioners, of course, knew nothing of this, and I was forbidden to breathe a word to anyone. After one particularly suspect performance at nine o'clock Mass, during which he delivered a thirty-minute homily, ranting almost incoherently about the impending Saints/Rams game, and calling for the intercession of Saint Jude to ensure that the "hornied enemies" would be put in their place and the game decided in favor of New Orleans, I offered to clean up for him so he could go back to the rectory and "rest" a few hours before the televised game. What I really wanted to do was sniff the chalice, which I did. And if what I got a whiff of wasn't Jack Daniels, may my nose rot from the sinuses out like my aunt's and fall off like a clump of Play-Doh. Incidentally, the Saints lost that game in a typically humiliating shutout; perhaps Saint Jude was as unimpressed with the pastor of Holy Gates as I was.

"These people don't want any part of that Vatican II bullshit," Father John told me one afternoon not long after I had started. "They want their priests to be priests and their nuns to be nuns." He was having a beer, of course, and had given me one too. I despise beer and only pretended to drink with him, excusing myself every few minutes for the bathroom, where I'd make a point of pouring the stuff into the toilet loudly enough so he'd think it was running right through me.

He was talking about a controversy that had recently erupted regarding the length and color of the habits worn by the nuns who served the parish. The Theresitans are a Spanish order founded between the World Wars by Theresita Albara, a young Spanish woman and ardent anti-Communist. By 1970, the order was no longer active in Spain, but it had missions in Mexico and Central America, as well as staffing the school at Holy Gates, their sole outpost in the United States.

The Theresitans had always worn black wool from head to foot. The only visible body parts of a good sister in full livery were her hands and the oval of her face. The movement to change began with the mission in Central America and spread to Mexico without igniting the slightest protest so that by 1970, the Theresitans of Latin America were sporting light gray cotton habits with hems rising about one-quarter the distance from ankle to knee. The new veils, which were available in either gray or white, were distinct from the rest of the habit so that they could be detached whenever temperatures or other matters of reason dictated. The populations served by the sisters south of our borders were so grateful for the Theresitans' efforts toward their medical, educational, and spiritual needs that they could not have cared less about what the sisters were wearing.

Such was not the case at Holy Gates. When one of the sisters returned from a visit to the Yucatán mission clad in the new outfit, the uproar from the parishioners was such that she might as well have shown up in a see-through negligee.

"It might be okay in Nicaragua where they're out in the sun all day," said one man, "but what do they need to dress like that around here for?"

"All they do is teach all day and then pray and watch TV in the convent at night," said another. "And what did we bother raising all that money to air condition the classrooms for?"

"If they raise their skirts, aren't they going to have to shave their legs?" one woman noted. "I don't think nuns should shave their legs."

"What about the veils? If they take them off, we won't even be able to tell they're nuns!"

"What's next? Miniskirts?"

I suggested a compromise of wearing the light habits in the summer—perhaps only when school was not in session—and sticking with

black for the rest of the year. Granted, southeastern Louisiana isn't exactly Nicaragua, but our summers can be quite sweltering when you're
bundled up like the Grim Reaper.

The parishioners showed little interest in my opinion and for the
most part took their gripes to the pastor. Foley tried to reason with them,
but his powers of diplomacy were as ineffective as his rhetorical skills on
the pulpit. When some members of the congregation began threatening
to pull their children out of the school and tear up their personalized
Sunday donation envelopes, he put in a call to the archdiocese.

Ratchett, of course, was wise enough not to get involved in such
a petty squabble, but he sent an arbitrator, a visiting monsignor from the
archdiocese of Houston who was teaching economics that semester at
Loyola. The monsignor, Ratchett wrote in a letter to the parish, would
not be speaking for the archdiocese, but the archbishop knew him well
and trusted that he would be able to find a solution to the problem. It
was vintage Ratchett, keeping his own hand and a half clean in case the
negotiations failed, but maintaining just enough of a role to take credit
for any success.

The monsignor was obviously well briefed on the political situation at Holy Gates because he didn't waste any time meeting with the
parishioners, who sent a delegation to the rectory the evening he arrived,
greeting him and proposing a general "town-hall" type assembly later in
the week to discuss the problem. The cleric was a skillful Church bureaucrat, yet he was transparent enough to a knowing eye like mine. He
graciously thanked the delegation for the suggestion, duly praised them
for their sincere concern for their parish, assured them that he believed
he could settle the matter by talking to the good sisters, and petitioned
their prayers for his success.

Father Foley and I soon learned wherein lay the reason for the
monsignor's smug confidence in his negotiating powers over the Theresitans. The ever-politically astute Ratchett had apprised him of the useful

fact that there was something far more important to these nuns than having the most stylish habits.

"I've come to understand that there is a nascent movement among the Theresitans to have their foundress included in the canon of the saints," the monsignor said to us almost incidentally after the lay delegation had left and I was serving coffee from the Gorham service, spiking Foley's cup with a shot of rum, a consideration for which I was acknowledged with a furtive wink as soon as the first sip had passed his lips.

"I believe that the sisters' commitment to that cause could be a very useful bargaining chip for us," added the visiting priest.

Foley questioned that. "You mean that if they go back to their old habits, we can promise them that Theresita Albara will be a saint?" Even to him it seemed too far-fetched a pledge.

The monsignor smiled. "No, of course not," he said. "I'm sure they know that such a promise can come only from the Holy See. The process of canonization is long, complicated, and unpredictable at best. And between us, expensive and political as well." He took a calculated sip of his coffee at that, as if those last two adjectives were the thrust of his point. "That's where the archdiocese can help them."

The deal that Ratchett and his power brokers had authorized was that if the Theresitans would help restore tranquility to the parish by pledging to return to their black habits and veils for five years, the archdiocese would use its considerable resources to promote the cause of Theresita Albara. After five years, the issue of the habits would be up for renegotiation. By then, the politic monsignor assured the sisters, one of two eventualities would surely have come to pass: Either the people of Holy Gates would have come to accept the changing ways of the Church since Vatican II, or the Order of the Theresitans would have gained enough attention and popularity ("clout" was the persuasive word he used) throughout the region, and perhaps the nation, via the successful furthering of the cause of their foundress to get their way with the stubborn parishioners anyway. The sisters were convinced and dropped their protest, as well as their hems, immediately.

Even someone like me, who had never witnessed a canonization movement firsthand and knew only the basics of the process through the requisite Church history courses I had taken in seminary, knew that the odds were stacked against them. Since the thirteenth century—when Gregory IX decreed that the recognition of sainthood would thereafter be strictly a papal prerogative—through 1970, only about three hundred canonizations had taken place, roughly one every other year. The reason that there are literally thousands of saints in the official canon is that before Gregory put the reins on the process, any deceased persons who were considered "holy" by their community and around whom a cult of worship or idolatry arose could be a saint. Since the pope had usurped the power of canonization, many locals were upset that their parochial heroes and heroines couldn't so easily be added to the canon, so the Church concocted a new distinction, preliminary to official sainthood, to mollify them: a candidate could be "beatified" (declared "blessed") before the ultimate honor, sanctification.

"Fortunately for us, Theresita Albara's cause is a relatively new one," the monsignor said to Father Foley and me at an early strategy session, once the deal with the nuns had been signed (yes, he got it all in writing). "At this stage, even the possibility of beatification is extremely remote."

He went on to explain that the reason he considered the long odds fortunate was that the further along in the canonization process, the more expensive and politically sensitive the whole ordeal becomes.

"At first it's all pretty cheap and innocuous," he said as we sat in the parlor of the rectory enjoying a plate of peanut butter cookies Sister Amelia had baked for us. Amelia wasn't bright enough to teach—not even elementary Spanish to the lower grades—so she did the cooking and housekeeping for the convent. Part of the arrangement that the archdiocese had made with the order was that in addition to their teaching duties, the Theresitans would see to their own domestic needs, including providing meals for the pastor and assistant pastor. Foley explained to me that it was really a good deal for the parish. Sad as it is to admit, parochial teaching salaries in those days were so pathetic that it would have been more expensive to hire someone to cook and clean than to pay another full-time educator. We both agreed, though, that we would have tried our best to keep Amelia even if it meant dipping deeper into the collection basket or teaching a class or two ourselves. Her cookies were absolutely to die for!

The monsignor continued lecturing us on the economics of sainthood. "When a cause is just getting off the ground, the main focus is PR, getting the word out to the public, letting them know about the Servant of God."

"The Servant of God?" asked a confused Father Foley.

The monsignor obviously took pleasure in the pretense of authority, using jargon to elicit questions he knew he could answer. I had lately done some reading on the subject of saint making and knew that everything he told us that night was information readily available to anyone with a library card. And there he was, another of the Church's frustrated little men who would spend his life toiling and spinning for the glory of those far more artful and ruthless than he, holding court like the postulator general of the Jesuits.

"Yes, the Servant of God is the one whose cause is being forwarded. In this case, Theresita Albara herself." He took his first bite of Amelia's cookie. "These are excellent," he said. "You know you could probably sell these."

"We already do," agreed Father Foley. "Twice a year at the school bake sales—spring and fall. They're our top seller. She always has me bless the dough before she starts baking."

"That's an interesting angle," commented the monsignor.

"You told the sisters the archdiocese is going to help them," I said. "What exactly are you planning to do for them?"

"Yes," he said, "that's what I was getting to. At the beginning of a cause, it's like anything else—the Nobel Prize, the Heisman Trophy, or what have you—your candidate can't win if nobody knows about him. So it's all about PR and publicity. Only at the local level. That's where it has to start."

Father John pointed out that the sisters had been doing little things along those lines since they arrived at the parish. "Every year for Theresita's birthday they have the children write poems and draw pictures of her to take home to their parents. They start with that famous photograph of her. You know the one where she's sitting at her desk next to a radio and there's a picture of Christ on the wall?"

"Yes, I've seen it," said the monsignor.

"Well, they have a contest to see who can draw that picture the best," Foley added. "I'm always the judge."

The monsignor looked at his watch, but Father Foley didn't take the hint.

"Last year one little girl drew Theresita to a tee," he said. "I mean everything right down to the chewed up fingernails and that little spot on her lip. But she had Christ looking like one of the Beatles. What's the one who married that Jap woman who looks like the missing link?"

"John," I said.

"Right, John. With that stringy hair and beard and those granny glasses. Only she didn't put the granny glasses on him, but it looked just like him all the same. She would have won, only everybody kept saying, 'What's that Beatle doing on the wall?' so I just couldn't give it to her. Besides, a couple of the sisters didn't think she should have drawn the spot on her lip. They said it was probably just an imperfection on the film because it's not in any of her other photographs. But it still could have been a cold sore."

"Indeed," snorted the monsignor, bug-eyed for a split second. It would prove to be the first of a handful of subtle glimpses into his true opinion of Theresita. He recovered his façade of equanimity, though, before I was able to read any significance into his telling little ejaculation.

"It's no wonder they haven't made much progress toward their cause," said the monsignor. Then he got the conversation back on track by telling us that the archdiocese was going to let the sisters design a holy card and pay to have a few thousand copies made. "His Excellency has been so kind as to allow the sisters unrestricted use of the printing facilities at Loyola. That should do nicely for the holy cards and maybe even some little brochures of Theresita's life and career."

"What would we do with those?" asked Father Foley.

"Various things," said the monsignor. "We can have them added to the reading materials in the various parish churches around the area. I'm sure the archbishop would even agree to feature them in the cathedral for a week or two. And the sisters could always just walk around and give them out to people. Do you have any malls around here?"

"Yes, a couple within a few miles," I said. This was around the time Canal Street started going to the dogs and I began searching for other shopping venues for my mother.

"Those will probably do nicely. And Catholic bookstores usually don't mind placing a stack of things like that on display. The trick is to get them near the cash register, next to the impulse items like Godiva rosary beads at Easter."

"I've never had those," said Father John.

"Oh, they're fabulous," said the monsignor. "And they've made a fortune." He reached for another cookie. "These could be right up there with them too."

We discussed the Theresitans' case at more length. One point they had in their favor was that in the past century and a half or so, a high percentage of successful causes represented the founders of religious orders. That would stand to reason since those candidates had in the membership of the order the advantage of one of the basic, though unofficial, prerequisites of sainthood: a group of followers absolutely devoted to the cause, a ready-made "cult of worship," as it were. There was another side of that coin, though. Since such a cult could hardly be considered a disinterested group, the Church, especially in recent decades, had begun to place more emphasis on the candidate's amassing a following *outside* of the order—in other words, among laymen. As the monsignor came to spend more time at the rectory over the next few months (his temporary tenure at Loyola was for a year), he became more and more prone, especially over drinks with Father Foley, to breach his confidence with the archbishop.

There is a certain species of small-time bureaucrat within the Church that I've come to recognize, the ecclesiastical answer to the company man. The monsignor was a typical example—absolute in his loyalty to his masters, but so pathetically desperate for attention and esteem from others that his discretion is at best questionable. He loved to mention his dinners and social functions with Ratchett, his power lunches with the Loyola brass. Through his indiscretions, I gradually became aware of Ratchett's true agenda with regard to the Theresitans' cause.

At first there seemed to be nothing suspect about the archdiocese wanting to confine the sisters' crusade to a strictly local level; it made good strategic sense, both logically and economically.

"Every movement needs a logistical focal point," said the monsignor to us one night early on, in one of his pontifical moods. It was around the end of the year, and we were enjoying a plate of beignets that Amelia had prepared especially for the holidays. "Like a test market for a new fast food burger—if it can't get off the ground there, no need to waste more time and money on it."

He went on to deliver a monologue on the fiscal side of sainthood, noting the outrageous expense of the process once it moves past the parochial level: researching, writing, publishing, and distributing the official *vita* of the candidate; launching a national and worldwide publicity campaign; hiring a legion of lawyers to argue the case in the Vatican.

"And I thought all they had to do was work a couple of miracles," Father Foley managed to say with a mouth full of beignets. He could consume one in two great chomps, like a Great Dane attacking a ham sandwich, and with about as much delicacy.

"It's actually *four* miracles," corrected the monsignor. "Two for beatification and two for canonization." He could have stopped there, but instead he made an observation that seemed totally irrelevant and academic at the time. In retrospect, though, I can see that it was quite discreetly calculated. "Unless the candidate was martyred," he said. "Then the Church waives the two for beatification."

"Theresita wasn't martyred, was she?" inquired Foley. It was precisely the question the monsignor wanted to hear.

"Hardly," he sniffed. Father Foley had given him the opening he wanted. It was another of those cryptic indications of his true underlying attitude toward "the candidate," an attitude that certainly must have reflected that of his bosses. But what could the Church have against Theresita Albara, a woman well known to have nursed soldiers during the Spanish Civil War and who died of leprosy contracted ministering to the peasants of southern Mexico?

The monsignor was not yet ready to explain himself, nor did I feel that the time was opportune to press him for information. His type tends to talk when they're ready. In any event, he immediately changed the subject back to financial matters.

"Anyway, the real miracle is raising the money," he said. "Moving a cause all the way through to canonization nowadays can easily cost a million dollars."

"Jesus, Mary, and Joseph!" said Father John, a puff of powdered sugar bursting from his mouth like a little steam engine.

"Too bad she wasn't a Jesuit," I said.

It wasn't long before the monsignor was ready to start spilling the beans about the Church's real position on the Theresitans' cause. He joined the pastor and me for dinner on New Year's Day 1971, and I was able to use the holiday as an excuse to exploit his weakness for tequila just enough to discover why the Theresitans had come to Louisiana in the first place.

"Doesn't it seem strange that an order whose niche has for decades been aiding the dirt poor of Latin America would suddenly stake out a claim in the United States?" he asked us. "Let's face it, New Orleans may have a shitty standard of living by American standards, but it isn't exactly a hotbed of malaria and dysentery."

"Maybe if they wanted to work with whores and drug addicts," said Father Foley.

"Right," agreed the monsignor. "But even then, why the suburbs? Why not the inner city—the projects or the French Quarter, where all the pimps and junkies are? It's like a doctor who studies for years to treat the lame and diseased and spends his whole career doling out Pepto-Bismol on a cruise ship."

He had a point. I had wondered about that myself and had always concluded that the order's true motivations must have had something to do with money. Was the archdiocese kicking something back to the Theresitans' treasury—perhaps a percentage of each Sunday's collection plate or a cut of the students' tuition—in exchange for their services? What I learned from the monsignor was that it all had to do with the cause.

"Frank made a deal with them," he said, toadyishly referring to Ratchett in the familiar to impress us with his place in the "in crowd." I wondered why he wasn't joining the archbishop for New Year's dinner. "Frank" was no doubt breaking bread with some stinking-rich denizens of the Gardan District, and "Frank" wouldn't want to be bothered with the company of an insignificant bootblack like this little monsignor. In fact, "Frank" might have been sharing New Year's fare at that very moment with my own uncle, for all I knew.

The deal that Ratchett made with the Theresitans dated back to the mid-sixties, before he had been elevated to his lofty seat. Back then, when the parish of Holy Gates was first organized and the archdiocese was shopping around for an order of nuns to staff the new school, Ratchett traveled to Mexico and met with the mother general of the Theresitans.

"She was most interested in securing an outpost in the States," the monsignor said. "Especially in a mainstream, middle-class place like this."

"Why?" I asked.

"For the cause, of course," he said.

His next point made so much sense I felt silly for not having deduced it on my own: In the modern world, especially since the great wars, moving a cause through the canonization process is greatly facilitated if the candidate can amass a following among intelligent, educated people.

"When it gets past the local stage, some of the worldliest minds the Church can enlist—lawyers, doctors, and scholars of every imaginable discipline—have to be convinced," the monsignor explained. "Theresita Albara wouldn't stand a chance if the only people favoring her cause outside of her own order were a bunch of tapewormed illiterates."

So the two religious made a neat little symbiotic pact: The archdiocese was able to staff its new school without having to pay a dime to the order, and the Theresitans got the foothold above the Rio Grande they so badly wanted. The deal was good for ten years. (I realized it would expire in 1975, the same year that the archdiocese said it would allow the nuns to renegotiate their agreement regarding the new habits.) Ratchett also promised that in the event he became archbishop, he would use his influence to further the cause. It is unlikely that he would have bothered to make good on that part of the arrangement had it not been for the crisis of the white mini-habits.

Just how far Archbishop Franklin Ratchett was willing to stick his neck out for the honor and glory of a dead Spanish nun I found out as 1971 continued. His office kept the limited promises it had made: Holy cards were printed, encouraging the faithful to pray for grace and favors through the intercession of the candidate, and pamphlets eulogizing Theresita's life were distributed to churches throughout the River Parishes.

I became a kind of part-time student of that life myself. One of the more capable nuns in the convent, Sister Ysabel, who had done the research for the little biographical pamphlet, heard that an official vita of the candidate would eventually be necessary, so she took it upon herself to produce one. She had immersed herself in the lives of several other prominent saints to prepare for the task. Since I had done the proofreading and helped her with the English for the pamphlet, she asked me to do the same for the larger project. I accepted, happy to be involved in any kind of learned exercise once again. Since coming to Holy Gates after ordination, I had spent most of my time on pedestrian tasks like overseeing the custodial staff, evaluating teachers, and meeting with disgruntled parents. Conversational topics with Father Foley rarely departed from football or fly-fishing. For intellectual stimulation, I had taken to reading a chapter or two of Henry James before bed each night. That habit would eventually lead to the masters program at Tulane, but that was still a few years away.

Through Ysabel's research, I learned that Theresita Albara had been born in the rural south of Spain, somewhere between Granada and Cordoba. The year of her birth was 1890, a time when the landscape of the central and southern regions of Spain was dotted with the great latifundia, the magnificent estates of the nation's wealthiest landowners, of which Theresita's father—Don Alonzo Sanchez de Albara—was one. Sister Ysabel's vision of nineteenth-century Spain seemed to me to be analogous to a romanticized portrait of the Antebellum South: an idyllically pastoral land of contented workers (*braceros*) serving under the most kindly and paternalistic of masters. All would remain well so long as all concerned recognized and remained in their place. Doing its best to ensure that that would continue to be the case as far into the new century as possible was, of course, the Catholic Church.

Theresita Albara was, by Sister Ysabel's account, a most devout Catholic, convincing her wealthy father to build a chapel on the grounds of the latifundium, where she could worship daily even though a priest visited the estate only on Sundays. She was an only child, so Don Alonzo made sure she was well educated, hiring the best tutors from schools in the region, and later even from the universities, so that she would be able to assume the duties of the master of the estate when his time was up.

"Theresita was devoted to her father, but more so to God," Ysabel wrote, in order to explain the candidate's stubborn refusal to take a husband. The story cited by Sister Ysabel was that her mother, who died of unknown causes when Theresita was only eight, admonished the girl on her deathbed to abjure the ways of the world and give her life to Christ. "So Little Theresita," wrote Ysabel, "who could have had her pick of the finest young gentlemen in the south of Spain, entered a Carmelite convent outside of Granada on her twenty-first birthday, June 8, 1911."

The next twenty-five years, during which Theresita did little more than pray, fast, and, because of her unusually liberal education, assist with the schooling of the younger nuns, makes for rather dull reading. I recommended that Ysabel spice up this section of the life, perhaps with one or two stories of sassy, recalcitrant novices that Theresita was able to inspire with a fervent search for inner light. She could probably procure a few accounts with not too much digging or maybe by publishing a call for letters or relevant accounts in a few Catholic periodicals in Spain. Some of these women with stories to tell might easily have still been alive in the early seventies.

After 1936, though, no embellishment of the life of Theresita Albara is necessary. The outbreak of civil war in Spain ensured that the life of no wealthy Catholic would be dull, even one whiling away her days within the sheltered confines of a convent. The war between the Republicans and the Nationalists (or, as the rest of the world came to see them, the Communists and the Fascists) aroused three passions fomenting within Theresita's soul: her craving for intellectual stimulation, her love of her father, and, most importantly (at least for the purpose of the vita), her devotion to the Church.

"Little Theresita refused to believe that through the mundane duties of a simple nun she was serving God to her fullest when the world outside the convent walls was turned upside down and the very future of His Church in Spain threatened by the godless minions of Stalin," wrote Sister Ysabel with just a bit of stylistic assistance from me.

With that transitional paragraph, Ysabel was ready to begin work on the most important phase of Theresita's life, her service to the Nationalists' cause during the Spanish Civil War. The biographer's work, for reasons that I will clarify shortly, was never completed. But she did manage to put together an outline, the high points of which are as follows:

A. 1935: The great latifundium of Theresita's father is taken over by mobs of braceros. Her father disappears.
    1.   The private chapel is desecrated and then burned.
    2.   Human bones, perhaps belonging to Don Alonzo, are found among the ashes.
B. 1936: Theresita's Carmelite convent, her home of twenty-five years, is ransacked by Communist-controlled agents of the Second Republic.
    1.   Theresita escapes Granada as bloodthirsty mobs of Communists burn churches, murder priests, and ravage scores of innocent nuns.
C. 1937: Theresita organizes a heterogeneous mix of refugee nuns into service in support of the defenders of religion [the Francoists].
    1.   The nuns fan out between Granada and Malaga on the southern coast to aid Franco's African Army's march through Spain.
    2.   Hundreds, and perhaps thousands, of Franco's wounded soldiers are saved through the care of the selfless nuns.

D. 1938: Little Theresita gains fame throughout southern Spain as the satanic leftists are forced out of power a city at a time.

    1.   She meets with Franco and Cardinal Isidoro Goma, the "Primate of all Spain," who personally blesses her in the name of the Holy Father.

E. 1940: With the devotees of God and nation restored to power in Spain, Theresita petitions Cardinal Goma to allow her to found a mission in the New World.

    1.   Over their foundress's modest protests, the nuns insist on the appellation "Order of the Theresitans."

    2.   The Theresitans establish their first American teaching mission in Nicaragua, enlightening the blighted natives in the areas of diet and hygiene, as well as spiritual matters.

F. 1942: The Theresitans expand into southern Mexico.

    1.   Theresita herself founds a small clinic in Las Madres, south of Villahermosa, to give comfort to destitute lepers and consumptives.

    2.   Within two years she contracts both diseases.

G. 1946: Little Theresita succumbs to disease.

    1.   The grateful natives of Las Madres carve her a casket of beech wood.

    2.   Her body is placed beneath the altar in the small chapel adjacent to the clinic.

"What a pile of horse shit!" screeched the monsignor, dropping the papers on the coffee table with a disdainful flourish. I had just showed him the outline and completed chapters of Ysabel's manuscript. It was the summer of 1972. By then his temporary appointment at Loyola was over and he was back in Houston full-time, except for intermittent visits to New Orleans to monitor the progress of the cause and report to Ratchett.

Predictably, there was little to report; if the sisters were making any headway at all, they were doing so at a glacial pace. One area that the monsignor insisted on checking out personally during his visits was the contents of the "Miracle Box." This was a modified suggestion box carved out of oak by a parishioner who did cabinetry work. On the front of the box was a painting of the candidate done by the winner of the 1971 Theresita drawing contest. The box was padlocked, and only the monsignor had the key.

We kept the Miracle Box in an alcove of the church adjacent to the baptismal font. Parishioners who had prayed successfully through the intercession of Theresita were encouraged to deposit documentary evidence of their results in the box. To expedite this, the sisters kept pads of preprinted forms next to the box. I designed the form myself, including space for the petitioner's name, the special request, the date that Theresita's aid was first invoked, a list of any other heavenly personages the petitioner had called upon for the same favor, and dates and evidence of any miraculous interventions, including witnesses. I had the winner of the drawing contest add a little art to the printed forms: a tasteful little tableau depicting a small family kneeling in prayer around the bed of a sick child. Hovering solicitously above their heads was the haloed visage of Theresita. A single tear on her cheek bespoke her humanity and empathy for the prayerful, while a subtle yet telling smile on her lips indicated hope for a happy resolution to the family's crisis. Although the printing of the forms was done gratis by the archdiocese, the monsignor recommended we fix a collection box to the wall of the alcove near enough for people to make a connection. It was a splendid idea: At its peak, that box was taking in an average of nearly fifty dollars a day, far more than any other in the church, even the ones by the votive candles.

The responses we got in the Miracle Box typically ranged from the unimpressive to the absurd to the pathetic. The batch we went through during the monsignor's summer '72 visit was not in the least unusual. The documented "miracles" included housewives winning at one of the local bingo nights after a "lifetime of trying"; students passing tests without opening a book; a man finding his social security card in perfect condition in his cat's hairball; and a young man whose pregnant girlfriend had a miscarriage after he prayed to Theresita every night for two weeks for either Louisiana or Mississippi to legalize abortion.

"That one sounds more like the work of Theresita," sniffed the monsignor after reading the account of the timely miscarriage to Father Foley and me. We were in the living room of the rectory, munching on tortilla chips and bean dip that Amelia had made from scratch. I had brought the Miracle Box in from the church and, after the monsignor had opened the padlock, dumped the papers onto the coffee table. John had the Summer Olympics on the television. They were featuring swimming and gymnastics. It was the night Mark Spitz caught the nation's eye.

I had let the "horse shit" remark pass without comment, a bit abashed that it might have been a reflection on the quality of the writing of the vita, of which I bore considerable responsibility. But now it seemed that it was something else entirely, something about Theresita herself that he had been keeping as tight-lipped about as a frustrated, self-absorbed little bureaucrat was capable of but might finally be ready to reveal. That night I found out what it was, and I realized that financial concerns were the least of the archdiocese's reasons for wanting to keep Theresita's cause confined to the local level.

I knew that Father Foley became even more garrulous than usual after a few drinks, and I recalled that the monsignor's little "slips" had always come when he had had a few himself, like on that New Year's afternoon. They were having beers with their chips and dip, but it was obvious that a few cans of Dixie weren't going to be enough to loosen the monsignor's tongue. So I offered to mix up a batch of margaritas; it seemed the perfect complement to our little repast and a neat transitional prop in case I needed one to steer the conversation around to a certain deceased Mexican nun.

By chance it was Father John and his mania for sports that played a part in getting the monsignor to talk. The Summer Games were in Munich that year, and that got us on the subject of Hitler's infamous snubbing of Jesse Owens in 1936. A discussion of world politics in the thirties naturally followed, from which point it was but a minor leap to the real reason Theresita Albara would never be numbered among the canon of the saints.

"To put it bluntly," the monsignor stated baldly, "she was a heel-clicking Nazi!"

He then picked up Ysabel's manuscript from beside the couch where he had contemptuously tossed it earlier that evening and began to refute one by one the hagiographic myths that the scrivener nun had penned about her idol.

"First of all, what's this 'Little Theresita' business?" he said. "You've seen her pictures. She was as big as Mama Cass. She could have fasted for a month and nobody would have known the difference."

Of course even the Catholics wouldn't consider obesity a strike against an otherwise reputable candidate for sainthood. There had to be much more serious objections.

"Let me go mix up another pitcher," I said, gathering up the margarita glasses. John had just excused himself to relieve his overactive bladder once again, so I knew I wouldn't miss anything while I was in the kitchen chopping ice.

When I returned, the monsignor grabbed Ysabel's manuscript and began frenetically flipping through its pages. "Listen to this: 'Her followers came from everywhere, not only sisters from her own ravaged convent, some of whom had suffered the most unspeakable indignities at the hands of their rapacious tormenters, but laywomen as well, from the fairest milk-skinned maidens to the coarsest furrow-browed matrons, all determined to aid Theresita in her mission to deliver Spain once again into the hands of the army of the Lord.'"

On the television a Russian boy with magnificent arms was doing a ring exercise in a form-fitting jumpsuit. His body seemed to make
a perfect cross—his sturdy arms extended a full 180 degrees and his
feet pointed to the ground. When the camera moved in for a close-up,
though, his bulging eyes and quivering lips revealed the pent-up tension
that was only barely below the surface.

Father Foley took a sip from his replenished glass. "How are we
doing on the Cuervo Gold?" he asked me.

"We're down to the last two bottles," I said.

"Remind Amelia to put it on her list," he said. Besides cooking,
Sister Amelia did the grocery shopping for the rectory and convent.

The monsignor continued with the story of Theresita and her
early followers.

"'They all had lost something dear to them at the hands of the
Republicans,'" he read, "'homes or loved ones, for the most part. But a
core contingent—a group who became known as *Las Innocentas Dolores*,
had been robbed of something which, especially in a country like Spain,
is far more precious to a woman.'"

The Russian boy was twirling around on the rings now. It seemed
his arms should have been twisted like a wrung-out dishtowel.

"Ysabel doesn't mention this," the monsignor went on, "but
Theresita herself was one of these Sorrowful Innocents."

"You mean she was raped?" said Father Foley.

A satisfied smirk spread across the monsignor's face, and I was
naïve enough to assume that Theresita's uninvited deflowering was all he
had on her. In my opinion, it shouldn't have mattered anymore.

"Perhaps that was something shameful in those days," I said,
"but nobody is going to hold that against her in 1972." I might have said
"almost nobody" had I remembered that we were in a parish that was
about to kick its nuns out of the country for exposing their stockinged

ankles.

"That's right," agreed Father Foley. "They're making TV movies about things like that now."

"There's more," the monsignor said. "Some of the Sorrowful Innocents had something more to be sorrowful about."

The television cameras had cut to a scene of a barefoot Romanian boy who was doing backflips and rolling around on a massive padded mat like an ecstatic at a Protestant revival. When he finally came to rest, a few toes were off the mat. The commentators said he'd forfeit some points for that "loss of control."

"Do you want to know what Little Theresita and her gang of the disgraced were really doing during that war?" asked the monsignor. He put his margarita back on the coffee table. He was one of those infuriating people who refuse to use coasters. You could put a dozen of them on a table and he'd avoid them like land mines. "They were running around the south of Spain spreading the clap to as many Republican troops as they could lure into a sleeping bag!"

At first neither I nor Father John comprehended what the visiting cleric was telling us, but as we listened with speechless mouths agape, the hideous reality gradually settled upon us: Theresita had rounded up all of the Sorrowful Innocents she could find who had contracted a venereal disease from their attackers and organized them into a pox-infesting vengeance squad.

"And the Church knew about it?" asked an incredulous Father Foley.

"Apparently all was fair in love and war," said the monsignor. Never had the cliché been more apropos.

"I can't believe Rome would have sanctioned such a thing," I protested.

"Probably not Rome itself," answered the monsignor, "but we believe that in all probability Goma did."

I noted his use of the word "we," including himself among the Church's movers and shakers. He probably meant Ratchett and a few of the crowned heads even higher up the ecclesiastical ladder.

"Goma? The Primate of Spain?" I said. "What makes you think he knew about it?"

"The cardinal was a rabid Fascist," answered the monsignor. "Not to mention a vicious anti-Semite. His rhetoric was legend. He once called the Jews the 'bastard souls of the sons of Moscow.' And his complicity in the Sorrowful Innocents' campaign would explain why he was so anxious to get Theresita and her followers out of the country after the war. Better for him politically, once the conflict was over and it was time to begin re-establishing the Church's pre-eminence in Spain, to have all of those fallen women five thousand miles away. Sister Ysabel's contention that Theresita petitioned the cardinal to allow them to go to America is a sugarcoating of the truth at best. Goma forced them out to cover his own ass."

We talked awhile about the political climate of Spain in the late thirties, concentrating on the unholy union between the Church and the Fascists. It turned out that Franco was not the only political leader whose attention Theresita and the Sorrowful Innocents had caught. Letters were purported to exist between the renegade Spanish nun and Mussolini himself.

"And they want to make her a saint?" said Father Foley. "Those nuns down there in Mexico must have had too many of these." He held up his glass as if in a toast and gave a little laugh.

The monsignor didn't laugh, though. And from the way he leaned forward on the couch and made eye contact with first me and then the pastor, I could tell he relished this moment, about to reveal the Church's real position on Theresita Albara.

"Trust me that what I am about to tell you comes from the highest authority," he said. Then, picking up on Father John's facetious observation, he continued, "They'll be sipping margaritas in Hell before the Church makes that little Fascist whoremonger a saint!"

At that he stood up for no apparent reason, unless he realized that he had said too much and hoped that by his movement he might signal a change in the conversation. He turned his attention to the Olympics. The evening's gymnastics coverage was completed, and the television cameras had turned their attention to a large indoor pool, at the head of which seven or eight young men were stretching in preparation for a race, contorting their bodies into sundry positions.

"Ah, swimming!" said the monsignor. "That's more like it. I've never believed gymnastics belonged in the Olympics."

"I like to watch it now and then," said Father Foley. "Not like football, but once every four years is okay."

"Oh, it's entertaining," admitted the monsignor. "And the gymnasts are no doubt very talented. I just think if you need a judge to tell you who won, you don't have a real sport."

"That would include figure skating," I observed.

"Right," said the monsignor. "They may as well make ballet an Olympic event too."

"I like that women's event where they prance around on that little two-by-four," said Father Foley.

"The balancing beam," I said.

"You see," said the monsignor. "How can something be a sport if only women can do it?"

The network announcer was introducing the young male swimmers. As the camera focused on them one at a time, I marveled at their perfectly smooth bodies—not a hair anywhere on them, not even when they rotated their immense shoulders around 360 degrees like windmills and you could see their underarms. I didn't realize that swimmers shaved their bodies until a few years later when I got to know some boys who swam for the high school I'd eventually work at. Before then I thought that only incarnated Ken dolls could be swimmers.

Another thing about these boys struck me: They could stand there almost nude in front of all those people and the television cameras with absolutely no abashment. They were my first reminder that night of my cousin Tony—not only the swimming, but the ease and fluency about their nakedness. I didn't want to think about my poor cousin then or to let the conversation degenerate into mindless sports talk, so I turned away from the television and tried to resume the discussion of the Theresita issue.

"Why hasn't any of this come out?" I asked.

"Because there hasn't been any reason for it to," explained the monsignor. "In the worldwide scheme of Church politics, Theresita Albara is a nobody. Cardinal Goma ensured her anonymity decades ago by getting her out of Spain, the only country in the world where there might be people who gave a damn about what she had done during the war."

"But if it looked like the Church was seriously considering her candidacy for sainthood . . ." I said, picking up on his reasoning.

Father Foley finished my thought in his own quaint little homespun way: "The shit would hit the fan."

"Exactly," said the monsignor. "If Goma could have envisioned in his wildest imagination that anyone would try to beatify this bitch, he would have exposed her as a war criminal in 1939 and cut his losses. That would have been far less embarrassing."

Prompted by a naïve comment by Father Foley regarding why something that had been kept quiet for over thirty years could not continue to be hushed up, he expanded upon the process of canonization, specifically the scrutiny under which all serious candidates are placed.

"They actually pay lawyers to play the Devil's Advocate," he said. "They pore over the record of anything the candidate said or did, especially anything she wrote, that might be antithetical to Catholic dogma. They'll dig up any dirt they can to block the *nihil obstat*."

"What's that?" asked Father Foley.

I wondered if he didn't know the Latin or was simply ignorant of its meaning in this context.

"The official Church declaration that there is nothing objectionable to the candidacy," said the monsignor. They'd have an absolute field day if Theresita's cause ever got that far. Believe me, they wouldn't miss a trick. Everything from being Mussolini's pen pal to her fatal illness would come out."

"Her fatal illness?" I asked. "You mean the leprosy and TB? I realize those things don't make her a martyr, but couldn't it be argued that they make her somewhat of an ascetic?"

I was playing the monsignor's game, impressing him with my knowledge of a rather esoteric subject. I knew from my own research with Ysabel that true martyrdom is quite rare in the modern world, but that there are a couple of other categories of potential saints based on their suffering for the faith: confessors and ascetics. Confessors had actually been imprisoned but survived, while ascetics were those who had willingly subjected themselves to extreme hardship and privation. I was going to argue that Theresita's volunteering to leave Spain to work among the poor and diseased of Central America and Mexico would at least qualify her as an ascetic, but the monsignor cut me off with an impatient wave of his hand.

"Please," he said, "Theresita didn't have leprosy. She died of the syphilis she brought with her from Spain. Maybe they should make her the patron saint of that!"

As my mind tried to assimilate yet another shocking truth, an outrageous image occurred to me: Theresita as the patron saint of VD, her image on an assortment of salves and ointments being dispensed to prostitutes lining up at her shrine in Mexico, successors to the Sorrowful Innocents selling the same to hookers and their Johns on Bourbon Street, competing for turf with those shaven-headed Hare Krishnas.

"They already have one for that," said John.

"A patron saint for syphilis?" I asked.

"Saint Fiacre," said John, slurping a mouthful of bean dip off a tortilla chip. "Syphilis and other kinds of VD."

He had a nasty habit of redipping something that had already touched his mouth. I try not to be overly persnickety, but whenever I'd see him do this, I simply couldn't eat another bite.

"They use him for barrenness and sterility too," he said. Then with a mouthful of cheesy bean mush: "Oh, and hemorrhoids."

That John would have known something like that might have surprised me in my early days at Holy Gates, but I had long since gotten used to it. I can recall an incident in the fall of 1970, my first year there: The Saints were at home in Tulane Stadium and John didn't have tickets to the game, so he asked me to join him in prayer to Saint Clare of Assisi that it would be a sell-out.

"Why Saint Clare?" I asked him.

"She's the patron saint of television," he said. "If the game sells out, it'll be on."

What connection the Church had found between television and the twelfth-century nun who founded the Poor Clares I couldn't imagine, but John probably could have explained it if I had asked. I eventually came to see that his fluency with the roll call of the saints was no more a sign of prodigious erudition than was his ability to name any professional athlete by the number on his uniform. His talent made him less a learned historian of the Church and more an idiot savant.

"Why did she have to die of that?" John asked. "Couldn't she have gotten treatment?"

"A nun with syphilis?" answered the monsignor. "Think about it."

As I couldn't think of anything to say and my two fellow priests had turned their attention again to the Olympics, I had a few moments to turn everything—the whole affair with the Theresitans and their tainted foundress—over in my mind. It was clear to me that Ratchett had taken advantage of the nuns by dangling before them the unattainable carrot of canonization for their heroine in return for what amounted to a ten-year indenture. I could imagine him huddling with their mother general down in Mexico, convincing her that there was no more fertile ground in all the United States to plant the seeds of a sanctification movement than New Orleans. He might have even shared with her a few statistics that I recall learning in seminary: Did you know that in 1965, New Orleans bought, used, or consumed more dashboard statues, rosaries, holy water, and Eucharists per capita than any other major city in the United States or Canada? Amidst such pious dedication to faith, how could Theresita lose?

I don't know how much Ratchett knew about Theresita Albara's story when, as a priest, he first made overtures to the order, but I gathered from the monsignor that by 1970, when the controversy of the white habits surfaced and by which time he had become archbishop, he was privy to the whole shameless tale. When at that point he promised them five years of his full support, he knew, of course, that the expiration of that term would come in 1975, the same year that he could send them all packing their habits, white or black, for Mexico with no questions asked.

Five years is a millisecond relative to the canonization process. According to the monsignor, there were nearly one thousand backlogged causes waiting to be heard in Rome in 1970. Ratchett knew that even with the most auspicious response from the locals, Theresita's cause would never progress beyond the parochial level in that amount of time. And imagine if it had and the Devil's Advocates in Rome had been unleashed to expose everything: What would they have found but the cause of a Nazi sympathizer who had engaged in the most unspeakable crimes against decency being supported by the archbishop of a major American city who himself had German roots. It would have been an unthinkable nightmare, even if no one had thought to raise the issue of the hapless Catholics who had been gulled by this cynical plotter into praying for miracles to a wretched woman who in all probability was paying for her unatonable sins in the flaming pits of Hell!

That enlightening evening with the monsignor came to an end, at least on my part, shortly after the truth came out. There might have been more discussion of the Theresita issue had I not been forced to retire for the evening—not due to the horror of the whole twisted and sordid business, but from a headache, the first of its kind in many months, brought on by something on the television. Rev. Manresa, my Jesuit therapist, would call such episodes panic attacks when I described them to him years later. I experienced them periodically in the early seventies whenever something triggered a memory of my cousin Tony Junior, though I never admitted that part to Manresa. As far as that prying busybody was concerned, they resulted from the stress of a childhood flashback precipitated by something I was doing in my unaccustomed capacity as a parish priest. I told him I had one, for example, the first few times I administered the last rites to an old woman with any kind of thick foreign accent and when I heard the confession of a boy who had committed sins of the flesh with his friends in their garage.

That night with Father Foley and the monsignor, the trigger was the Olympic swimming coverage. I was able to remain focused at first; thoughts of the sport itself and even the sleek forms of the swimmers, though they reminded me of my cousin, weren't enough to cause an episode. Tony had been dead for two years by then, so I wasn't a complete basket case. But before the second or third race of the evening, the announcers introduced the new American star.

"There's Spitz," said Father John. "They say he could win five medals."

"Maybe more," said the monsignor, and the camera focused its attention on the muscular athlete with the beautiful Mediterranean features. The resemblance to Tony nearly rendered me breathless: the same thick, wavy brown hair, slim yet muscular build, even the little mustache that I knew from photographs Tony had grown after he went overseas.

I wasn't the only one to notice the resemblance. Ronnie talked about it every time I visited the shop and even kept that famous poster—the one of Spitz in his swimsuit with all those medals resting on his sculpted chest. The way he had his hands so confidently on his hips gave me chills whenever I looked at the poster. It was so nearly the same attitude Tony had presented that day behind the levee when he beckoned me atop the old barge with him. Of course Ronnie would have to vulgarize the image with two moist and full lips scratched in scarlet lipstick over the bulge in Spitz's bikini.

My anxiety over seeing the image of my cousin alive on the screen, leaping into the pool and making his way through the water like the son of Poseidon, took its usual form: Blood rushed to my head until my scalp felt ablaze with feverish tension. It was as if some sadistic acupuncturist were pricking my head with a thousand red-hot needles. A similar reaction followed every time I saw the poster in Ronnie's shop, prompting more comments from my little harpy cousin on the redness of my birthmark. It became less pronounced over the months as I got used to seeing the picture until he finally replaced it with one of Robert Redford.

I had to get away from the television. Without another word to my two colleagues, I slipped into my bathroom, took off my clothes and hair, and got into the shower, letting the cool water douse the fire that seemed to be emanating from my brain out through the pores of my head. I went to bed while John and the monsignor continued watching the swimming coverage. To drown out the sounds of the television, I played a Johnnie Ray cassette I had made from some of my old records. I fell asleep to "Here Am I, Broken Hearted."

As Archbishop Ratchett must have known it would, the drive for the canonization of Theresita Albara died out before it had a chance to become an international *cause celebre*. The issue that sounded its death knell, however, I doubt even he could have predicted. Sometime in 1973, a few of the sisters in the convent, led by Ysabel, decided that Theresita's cause might be spurred by a relocation of her remains to New Orleans. Such an act, officially termed a "translation" in Church parlance, could be done with the consent of the custodians of the remains (in this case the Theresitans in Mexico) and the local bishop of the diocese.

Ratchett gave his consent, but with the characteristically politic condition that no undue publicity be drummed up that could turn the issue into a media "event." When the remains arrived, late in 1973, Ysabel wanted them placed under the altar of the Holy Gates church, making it, as she insisted, a true "altar" in the literal sense of the word as defined by the Church in the eighth century. Father Foley, after consulting with the monsignor by phone, told them the casket would have to be kept in the foyer of the convent, which is where it remained for some weeks, attracting little or no attention until Ysabel decided that it should be opened and the remains inspected for any signs of divine favor.

The biographer nun was still at work on her soon-to-be-aborted vita. In her research into the lives of other saints, she had learned that quite a few of them had been discovered to be "incorrupt"; that is, their bodies, in whole or part, had not suffered decomposition after death. Such a discovery can be quite a boon to a cause of canonization, and there was no doubting the sisters' determination to see that coffin opened.

The best the archdiocese could do was ensure that the discovery be done under controlled conditions, closed to the public and witnessed by a carefully chosen few so that if the expected results came to pass, the Church would be spared any embarrassing publicity and damage control efforts could be kept to a minimum. On the other hand, if what was found in that coffin could in any conceivable way be construed as miraculous, and a crowd and horde of cameras were on hand to witness and record it, word would spread like wildfire, possibly igniting the fuse that could lead to an intolerable explosion of publicity. With just a few nuns and priests on hand, Ratchett just might be able to hush things up.

In the interests of both the living and the dead, and in order to
get on with parts of my story more pertinent to my purpose (i.e., how I
landed here in the wasteland of Kattannachee), I will be mercifully brief
in rendering the conclusion to my stay at Holy Gates. The coffin was
opened early in 1974. Five witnesses were present: the monsignor, Father
Foley, and I, along with Ysabel and one other sister. John said a private
Mass before we processed over to the convent and gathered in the foyer.
The school's Negro maintenance man was on hand to remove the bolts,
but John dismissed him once his work was done. The monsignor opened
the lid himself.

The simplest and kindest way to describe what we saw inside
that coffin is that Theresita Albara was no more incorrupt after death
than she had been in life. I will not waste words on a morbid descrip-
tion of the corpse, but the scene was positively Poe-esque: the monsignor nearly losing his grip on the lid upon first beholding the horrific
sight, John coming to his aid with an old, yet sturdy, pair of sportsman's
arms, Ysabel kissing the crucifix of her rosary and crossing herself with
it, and the other nun screaming something in Spanish and dropping to
her knees, presumably in prayer until she collapsed farther onto all fours
and commenced heaving all over the parquet tiles of the foyer bits of the
Eucharist Father Foley had placed on her tongue just minutes before.

I took it upon myself to see to the prostrate nun, helping her
into the living quarters, where we were met by a few of her colleagues
who led her, still doubled over and speechless, deeper into the private regions of the convent. I recognized a few "*Que pasos?*" among their frantic
chirpings. Returning to the foyer, I saw to the cleaning up of the mess
without further defiling the Eucharist.

The seminary can only prepare a young priest for so many exi-
gencies, and I confess that I improvised for this one. Calling for a pan
of water and some paper towels, I blessed the water, wetted the towels,
and wiped the floor clean. I then asked the sisters for a plastic baggie into

which I put the used towels. They seemed satisfied that the situation had been handled with proper reverence. Afterwards, I shoved the baggie into my coat pocket. I didn't want the nuns to see me toss it into the trash; they probably thought we had some kind of sanctified receptacle for just this kind of emergency.

While I was busy with the cleanup, Ysabel was engaging the monsignor in a debate over the disposition of her foundress's remains and exactly what their revolting condition meant. The monsignor had closed the lid of the coffin once again and called for the Negro workman to seal it once and for all; yet Ysabel pleaded with him to allow the body to be further examined, in effect to have it dissected, as evidence of divinity might yet be found. The nun insisted that it was sometimes only certain organs of the body, and not the entire corpse, that were incorrupt; and she cited several examples from her research: Saint Catherine's head, Saint Anthony of Padua's tongue, Saint Clare of Montefalco's heart and kidney stones, and so forth.

The monsignor wasn't about to countenance a makeshift autopsy performed by a desperate nun on a putrefied corpse, neither at that moment nor anytime in the future. He told Ysabel that any invasion of the body would have to be sanctioned by Rome; even the archbishop himself couldn't order it. Whether that was true or not, I don't know, but in any event, Ratchett did order the speedy return of Theresita Albara to Mexico. A broken Sister Ysabel couldn't bring herself to return to the writing of the vita, and the cause was allowed to die a natural death. By Christmas of that year—several months before the expiration of their contract with the archdiocese—the Theresitans had returned to Mexico. Before the resumption of the school year in January, Ratchett had replaced them with a few lay teachers and a handful of Carmelites on loan from a high school in Baton Rouge.

By then, of course, I had left the suburbs once and for all and returned to New Orleans, where I had just begun the next phase of my career. Eight of the happiest years of my life lay just ahead.

CHAPTER SEVEN

THE DEN

I left Holy Gates at the conclusion of the '73–'74 school year. Many a young priest just starting out would have been eternally grateful to start his career in a place like that—a spanking new facility with air-conditioning and every modern amenity, nuns to prepare meals, a maintenance staff to perform menial tasks, such as cleaning and keeping up the grounds or fixing anything that broke. I laugh when I consider how Ratchett must have thought the contrast would be unbearable to me, that after four years of ease and comfort at Holy Gates, I wouldn't be able to suffer a move to a drafty old house in a run-down inner-city neighborhood of mixed ethnicities. But I had a feeling, an intuition of faith perhaps, that with this place and the work I'd be doing there I might finally be realizing the true potential of my vocation.

I was further strengthened by a book I had read while Ysabel and I were researching the careers of modern saints: *The Life and Dreams of John Bosco*. The famous Italian saint, known also as the "Apostle of Youth," would become one of the great inspirations of my life as a priest. Born in rural Piedmont in 1815, Bosco was ordained, as was I, at age twenty-six. He had no clear mission until one day Our Lady appeared to him after he had witnessed two young boys fighting. She instructed him to "Go among them and work." At his peak, he had over six hundred boys in his "oratory." He was given no church by the politically minded local diocese, so at first they met in a meadow.

Bosco is perhaps most famous for his "forty dreams," symbolic yet prophetic intuitions which he shared with his boys in an attempt to steer them away from sin. Many are quite horrific scenes of bodily carnage, representing the death of a soul; for example, a monster slobbering over two boys who had left the oratory for a "dissolute life"; stampeding elephants trampling sinful boys; a flock of crows mauling boys who had exchanged impure stories and pictures, plucking their eyes and ripping out their tongues. I would have many occasions to return to Bosco's life and to implore his guidance while at the Den.

I actually thought a Boscovian meadow would have been an improvement when I first beheld the dilapidated building that would become the Den and my home for the next eight years. The house was located on Ganymede Street, between Magazine and Annunciation—the heart of the old Irish Channel—half a dozen blocks from the river and a dozen or so from the southwestern fringes of the CBD. Most of the houses in the area dated from the early years of the century, but you wouldn't find them on any guided tours of the city's scenic residences. The Den had most recently been the cash cow of a slum lord who had used a government grant to acquire it during the Crescent City's perversion of urban renewal in the sixties, then allowed it to slip further and further into disrepair until it finally crossed the threshold of condemnation in 1969. From that point, it lay abandoned and boarded up like a pest house, home only to vagrants and the cats they kept to chase away the plague of rats that teemed from the nearby wharves of the river.

The Channel before the war had been somewhat of New Orleans's answer to Harlem but on a smaller scale—proud, working class, and ethnic. The name "Irish Channel" is somewhat of a misnomer: Even in its heyday of the twenties and thirties, there were as many poor Italians who called it home as there were Irish. In fact, according to my mother, Uncle Eugenio's family, the Cuchinottos, came from there.

"Of course they moved out and bought a house in Lakeview as soon as the fish business took off," Josie said. "Otherwise Rose would have never married Eugenio. Could you see her living in a house with one bathroom and no tub!?"

No, the Channel had never been upscale enough for my Aunt Rose, but it had at least been a decent place to live and bring up children. In later years, though, the Channel went downhill, until it finally began to resemble Harlem in more than just spirit: The Italians and Irish sold or rented their grandparents' houses to blacks and Hispanics; businesses closed down; a wretched housing project swallowed up a whole block.

When I first saw the Den, its windows were still boarded shut as if a major hurricane were bearing down on the city. But it was May, so of course that was impossible. I was accompanied by a thin young man with glasses and fashionably long hair, who I eventually learned from our conversation was a year from ordination. I met him at Notre Dame uptown, and together we drove (in a sleek new Lincoln, part of the fleet at the archbishop's disposal) to the site of my new home: down Carrollton to Saint Charles, then Magazine east toward the Channel and the city.

Despite its outward appearance—the shut-up windows, graffiti-laced façade, weeds growing rampant, an iron fence and gate in need of a coat of black paint—the house on Ganymede was in decent condition on the inside. My young driver had the key and let us in. The slum lord had turned the building, which had originally been two large apartments, one atop the other, into a fourplex; so there were four full baths, two upstairs and two down—perfect for what the archdiocese intended the structure to be used for: a boardinghouse for homeless high school boys.

The final interior renovations were nearly complete: The wall separating the former blighted apartments A and B had been removed, leaving a large living and dining area in the front, two bedrooms (one of which would be mine), and two baths. My quarter of the house was already complete and ready for me to move in, which I did within a few days. The two downstairs kitchens had been merged into one, reminiscent of what Papa Miggliore had done to appease my grandmother when he started making money. Upstairs, where the kitchens were no longer necessary, there would be one great room along with the two bedrooms and baths. That upstairs great room would be ideal for games and relaxation. Apparently someone had already planned that because in one of its corners, I spied a folded-up ping-pong table, apparently new. The only piece of furniture yet to be moved into the house, it stood there alone, in quiet anticipation of the joyous times to come in that place. I would make a point of spending as much time in there as I could. Saint Bosco had always said that priests must engage in recreation with boys. "There can be no love without familiarity," he wrote. "If a boy knows he is loved, he will love in return. And if the Superior is loved, he can get everything—*especially from boys.*" (Italics are mine.)

I found out from my driver/guide how the Church came into possession of the house. The city, in an attempt to clean up some of its most neglected neighborhoods and reverse the dangerous trend that saw its slums gradually encroaching on affluent and historic areas, began in the early seventies to offer seized and abandoned properties inexpensively to individuals or organizations that would agree to refurbish and maintain them. The deal included tax concessions and (if the buyer paid cash) even a schedule of reduced utility rates.

Let it never be said that I fail to give the Devil his due: Franklin Ratchett, if nothing else, has always been an excellent man of business.

Who could ever say that the Germans aren't among the best in the world when it comes to fiscal sense, organization, and, yes, even sheer leadership ability? Under his hand, the archdiocese snatched up several of those old Channel properties, converting the largest into an apartment building and leasing several others to a variety of small businesses. Shrewdly tempering his savvy sense of economics with a concern for public relations, Ratchett must have realized that he'd better appear to be doing more with the Church's resources than making money hand over deformed fist; hence Boys' Chance, the original name for the Den.

Boys' Chance, when filled to capacity, would be home to twelve boys, four to each bedroom. So as not to overwhelm me that first year, there would be only six boys for the '74–'75 school year, all freshmen. Two more would be added every year thereafter until the house was filled. And of course there would always be the possibility of an unscheduled addition at any time if a qualified boy in need of help came to the attention of the school.

The school, by the way, was Pope Paul VI, an all-boys high school on Magazine, but outside the Channel, in a more respectable locale between Napoleon and Louisiana Avenues. In 1974 its faculty were predominantly laymen and women, although a Redemptorist priest still held the position of principal, and there were a couple of Christian brothers on staff, as well as a few aged Missionary Sisters of the Sacred Heart, the order founded by Francis Xavier Cabrini, who also staffed an elementary school and a girls' high school named for their canonized foundress. One of these nuns, a Sister Angelina, took a liking to me as soon as I told her I was a Miggliore and invited me one evening to the Cabrini Mother House, near the Fair Grounds and across from Saint Louis Cemetery, where I enjoyed a splendid dinner and toured the facility where Mother Cabrini herself had once lived and run a home for Italian orphans.

My dinner with the Missionary Sisters was one of the few home-cooked meals I would have between the time I left Holy Gates and when

Boys' Chance officially opened and we had a full-time cook; the others came thanks to my mother, whom I visited once or twice a week that summer. The sisters didn't seem to be bothered by my taking second and third helpings of their pork roast and fresh corn on the cob. Over dinner and coffee, we enjoyed a pleasant conversation and shared all the latest archdiocesan gossip. Rumors regarding the fate of the Theresitans had spread through the local religious grapevine, and naturally the sisters were eager to hear my side of that story. I managed to sidestep the issue by blaming the failure of the Spanish order to take root here on a "clash of cultures."

"You know they wouldn't even eat corn," I said, holding up a half-eaten cob as a convenient prop. "They said in Spain they feed corn to their animals."

"Oh, goodness!" said the sisters.

Naturally they had heard rumblings of an aborted cause as well.

"Well, much of what I know about that is confidential," I told them. "But I can say this: The Theresitans are going to have to face the fact that Sister Albara, her plenitude of virtues notwithstanding, was no Francis Xavier Cabrini."

The Missionary Sisters smiled and nodded their gray-veiled heads at that.

Afterwards, I returned to my room at Boys' Chance and planned my academic comeback. It may have been the names of the streets I strolled through in the waning weeks of that spring as I was acclimating myself to my new surroundings in the Channel that inspired me to further my education in the liberal arts: Calliope, Melpomene, Euterpe, Terpsichore. Surrounded by the muses and not having seen the inside of a classroom in years, except to observe the teachers I supervised at Holy Gates, I hungered for a return to academia. I didn't want to return to Loyola, where I had taken courses while in seminary; I had had enough of those pompous Jesuits even before they made one of them my shrink.

Fortunately, Tulane was equally convenient—just a brief walk to Saint Charles and a delightful five-minute streetcar ride beneath the splendid oaks. Tuition was half-price for ordained priests, but I would have enrolled anyway. My mother had been living frugally in a small house in Carrollton since Mama Miggliore's death. It was a comfortable little house, but certainly beneath her means considering what her share of the estate had amounted to. So I'm sure she would have paid the tuition if I had needed to ask.

I decided to focus my studies on the nineteenth-century novel. My first course that summer was a seminar on Dickens, an appropriate beginning since the writer had such an affection for destitute children and I myself would soon be dealing with a house full of homeless boys. The course proved not to be as satisfying as I had hoped, as it was taught by a dumpy looking, menopausal lesbian who was writing a book about Dickens (a "feminist re-evaluation") and who was convinced that the defining event of the great novelist's life was his taking up in midlife with an eighteen-year-old actress and leaving the wife who had borne him ten children, all because the wife had gotten fat. The man-hating professor—nicknamed Frankenstein's Mother by the graduate students due to an earlier book she had written on Mary Shelley—would perch her ponderous self atop the table in front of the class, chain-smoking Virginia Slims in open defiance of the university's prohibition that was stenciled in red letters and two languages on the wall behind her.

I made the mistake of wearing my collar to the first meeting of the seminar, unaware of this woman's animus toward the Church. Although she was never openly hostile toward me, and indeed came to admire the excellent work I produced that summer, my presence seemed to be a constant reminder to her of the Church's unforgivable exploitation of women and minorities. Did the class know, for example, that the Catholic Church once taught that sex with women could stifle a man's intellectual development or that priests in the nineteenth century helped propagate the viciously sexist belief that female orgasm unleashed vene-real toxins?

It was a busy summer, my time divided between reading for "mi-sogynist subtexts" in Dickens to appease Frankenstein's Mother—lest she settle her feminist vendetta against Holy Mother Church with me—and getting the Ganymede house ready for the boys, who would be arriv-ing sometime in August, once the school had screened the applications of dozens of hopefuls, reviewed their elementary school transcripts, and considered testimonials from teachers and parish priests.

Late in July, Martha, our cook and housekeeper, arrived. It was a most welcome day. She had been the baker on the cafeteria staff at the high school for years. The schedule she kept over the next eight years would have taxed the energies of most women her age (she turned fifty that fall). God only knows how early she had to rise to take care of her own household of seven children and catch the three buses it took to get from her shotgun on Piety Street—near the Industrial Canal—to the Channel, but she was always at the door of the house by six in the morning. She had her own key, and the sound of her clattering pans and silverware in the kitchen, plus the heady smell of her chicory coffee (the best I had had since Wanda's day) were my alarm clock. After preparing breakfast and doing the dishes while the boys got into their uniforms, she'd ride with them in the van the school sent to pick them up every morning at seven thirty and put in a full shift at the cafeteria. Once her duties there were done, usually around two in the afternoon, she'd return to the house by the Magazine bus, tend to some housework, and finally prepare the evening's meal before getting back on that first bus for the long ride back to Piety Street.

Martha had two breakfast menus, which she alternated through the week: scrambled eggs, bacon, or sausage, and the most scrumptious honey dipped biscuits I have ever tasted in my life on Tuesdays and Thursdays; pancakes on Mondays, Wednesdays, and Fridays.

I can even remember her dinner menus. Traditional New Orleans red beans and rice with hickory sausage and homemade corn bread on Mondays. Fried chicken and mashed potatoes served with what I'd call a velouté sauce, but what Martha ingenuously referred to as "flour and drippings," on Tuesdays. Spaghetti and meat sauce with a cauliflower or broccoli casserole and garlic French loaves on Wednesdays. Inch-thick pork loin chops bursting with sage- and thyme-spiced corn bread stuffing, served with glazed carrots and fried potatoes sprinkled with basil on Thursdays. And, of course, on meatless Fridays, catfish fillets dipped in cornmeal and parmesan cheese, fresh red potatoes cooked in crab boil and smothered in butter and basil, sweet ears of corn, and a basket of golden-brown hush puppies bursting with green onion.

There was certainly no guilt over hearty appetites in that house, no fasting to atone for sins—not with Martha and a slew of teenaged boys around. She had those massive hips that they tend to get at that age, so even though I gained weight myself, I was never made to feel self-conscious about it. Not like back in minor seminary, where my weight became an issue the very first day in the refectory. As we waited silently in line for our first meal, Father Pedeaux, a niggardly, cadaverous little priest, stood watch over the serving lines, making sure none of those growing boys took in more nourishment than Pedeaux himself would have needed to sustain his scrawny, pinched little body: a sliver of fish or meat, one spoon of rice or potatoes, a slice of unbuttered bread. If Pedeaux had his way, we would have been starved those four years of minor seminary, sustained on the Eucharist alone, like those neurotic ascetics the Church so loved to elevate to sainthood.

"Your lives of sacrifice have begun, boys," he told us with his bony, lantern-jawed grin. And to me and the other more corpulent boys: "You're going to need an alb the size of a bedsheet and a cincture that could lasso an elephant if we don't get you down to size."

"*Deo gratias,*" was the only response we were allowed to make.

In contrast, the boys of the Den seemed to love me more with each extra inch Martha's wonderful cooking added to my waistline; some even came to use my belly as a pillow at TV time. The seventies really were the last decade of innocence before the witch-hunts began, you know. Back then a man could still get close to boys without fearing that his reputation might be sullied by some puritanical hypocrite more envious than outraged, or that the objects of his selfless attentions—the boys themselves—might react to his paternal affections with hysteria and paranoia, brainwashed all their young lives by idiotic counselors and TV movies harping on all that good touch/bad touch drivel.

What happened? I've asked myself that countless times. Significant social changes used to take decades, even centuries, to effect. Yet it seemed the whole world had degenerated from trusting and ingenuous into something cynical and suspicious in just a few trips around the sun. What caused it all? Why did everyone stop trusting men? Was it Watergate? Vietnam? The feminists? Some perverse ripple effect from Vatican II? Why all the suspicion? Do you realize that in the state of Louisiana if a man my age so much as mentions his penis to a boy under seventeen, even in the most innocent of contexts, he can be arrested, handcuffed, and led to jail without a question asked? Just imagine it!

And imagine this: What do you think someone would have to go through in the eighties and nineties to secure a position in a place like Boys' Chance? When I started there in 1974, I was praised by everyone— the sisters, the lay teachers, the other priests on staff at the school (none of whom knew that Ratchett and the archdiocese had more or less forced my hand). My "volunteering" was seen as the noblest of sacrifices. How wonderful that someone like me really wanted to be there for those poor wayward boys, they all said. Today, merely applying for such a position would precipitate an endless process of background checks, psychological profiles, finger printings, computerized dirt digging. Insanity!

A case in point to illustrate how far down the road of institutionalized paranoia we have led our youth in the last couple of decades: During my years at the house, I often had to go to the school on some kind of business regarding one of the boys—relaying a message or delivering a forgotten book or what have you. In order not to disrupt the boy's day, instead of interrupting one of his classes or cutting into his lunchtime, I made a point of timing my visits to coincide with the end of his physical education period, once whatever instruction or activity for the day was complete and the boys had returned to the field house to dress and shower. The field house was a small building adjacent to the gym, serving as an equipment storage facility for the school's athletic teams, as well as dressing room, first aid center, and shower facility for P.E. classes. Its door was always open; I could enter whenever I chose, mingle with the boys innocently cavorting in their various stages of undress, seek out the boy I needed, and conduct my business at a pleasant, leisurely pace. The attendant at the field house in those days was a scruffy old former football coach, an Ernest Borgnine type with a ridiculous Brylcreemed comb-over and a thicket of hair sprouting from his ears and nose and 360 degrees around the collar of the only shirt he ever wore—a school-issued T, bearing the image of a snarling grizzly bear, the iconic mascot of all the school's teams.

"Well, hello there, Father!" he'd always greet me with a smile in that booming voice that coach types always seem to have. "Boys, say hello to Father Tony, and watch your language while he's here. And what can we do for you today, Father?"

We had a good relationship, the old coach and I. He was of that old school that never forgot a favor—one kind turn would ensure his loyalty forever. He enjoyed my visits because I was always willing to relieve him for an hour or so while he "ran an errand." I knew he was going to a bar around the corner on Camp Street, but I never let on. I enjoyed the interaction with the boys: passing out towels and jockstraps, making sure there weren't too many shenanigans in the showers, seeing that the seniors weren't too frisky in their "initiation rites" over the hapless freshmen.

Contrast that free and open policy with what I encountered a few years later, in the mid-eighties. By then the archdiocese had me teaching English, taking advantage of the advanced degree I had earned at my own expense. The first time I had call to look for a student outside of class—a baseball player who had missed a Walt Whitman quiz—I once again chose the locker room as the most unobtrusive place; but this time I was given an entirely different reception: First of all, the door to the P.E. room was locked from the inside, so I had to knock. And when it was finally answered, an arrogant young baseball coach refused to let me past him, demanded my business, said he'd send the boy to my classroom as soon as he dressed, and shut the door in my face. I could have been a Camp Street wino looking for a handout for all the respect that hooligan showed me. Only a teasing reminder of the thick, humid ambience of a locker room, only a whiff of the heady generic soap they stock the showers with, escaped that officious sentry. Times had indeed changed.

In early August they finally arrived, those first six residents of the house. I can still recall their names: Kenneth, Steve, David, Jeffrey, Michael, and Jason. They were all children of broken homes—at a time when divorce still carried with it a stigma of humiliation. Alcoholism was a common bond: Four had alcoholic fathers, all of whom were estranged from the family; two of those had mothers who also drank to excess; Michael had been living with a drunken foster father until his parish priest, suspicious when the boy missed several days of school, went to the house and discovered the family living in filth and the boy malnourished from eating nothing but potato chips for a week.

Jason was the most streetwise of the six. Almost a year older than the rest, he would be sixteen before the end of 1974. He had been living with an elderly great aunt, the only living relative he knew. When she became too enfeebled to hold her cashier's job at Woolworth's and her government checks proved insufficient to support herself and the boy, Jason took matters into his own hands, spending his after-school hours and Saturdays shoplifting from every department store on Canal Street. He once told me that this was easy, being young and white: "The floor walkers were so busy watching all the niggers that nobody paid any attention to me." When his take from the stores wasn't enough, he'd trade himself for money in the Quarter. He had missed a whole year of school on the street after eighth grade, hence the age discrepancy. His dark hair was stylishly long, not cropped above the collar per Catholic school regulations.

Jason was in many ways one of the most special boys in my life, the first to really open up and establish a deep and intimate bond with me. Through Jason, I believe I finally realized, at the age of thirty, that I had genuinely important work to do, that I could be an important part of another human being's life. Even today, from a perspective twenty years removed, it still pains me to recall the ultimate tragedy of that boy's life.

It was delightful to observe the six of them those first few days in the house, quietly observing me and each other, testing for strengths and weaknesses, eventually choosing roommates, deciding who'd get which bunk, establishing their positions in the TV room. Like young gladiators, they knew no other way to measure themselves against each other than through physical tests of strength: arm wrestling or weight lifting contests. It was a shame I wasn't taking an adolescent psychology class that summer because I could have written a fascinating little study of role-establishment rituals among adolescent males.

I was too busy anyway coming up with a feminist theme for my major paper for the Dickens class. I had chosen to work on *Great Expectations*, my thesis being that Pip's sister had been having an affair with Orlick, the journeyman blacksmith, into whose abusive arms she had fled in a misguided effort to find the emotional and physical fulfillment that was impossible with her impotent husband, Joe Gargery. She was essentially a sympathetic figure, I argued, victimized by two diametrically opposed, but equally culpable, men: Joe, whose failure as a husband and lover turned her into a frustrated harridan, and Orlick, who with his phallic hammer finally smote her into submission, silencing her shrewish bitching, which was in reality a sad cry for help from a desperately unhappy and trapped woman. Frankenstein's Mother was delighted with my paper, remarking that with a little work it might even be publishable. My return to academia was (if you'll pardon the Orlick-inspired pun) a smashing success.

Perhaps it was an omen of the historic significance of the day that on the very first afternoon that the boys and I were gathered in the great room upstairs, rather awkwardly watching an *I Love Lucy* rerun since not even Jason was ready to assert himself and take control of the channel selection, the network broke in to announce the president's resignation. At least that event, as catastrophic as it may have been for the nation, spurred a more significant conversation among the boys than had Lucy's prancing around in a vat of grapes.

"Why is he quitting?" asked one of the boys.

"Because of Watergate," said Jason. He alone of the six was dressed for a New Orleans August: barefoot and clad only in shorts and a T-shirt emblazoned with a hideous image of Alice Cooper with a snake around his neck. The others could have been dressed for church, obviously trying to make a good impression despite the season.

"Do you all know what that means?" I asked.

A couple of them nodded. One said, "The break-in."

Michael admitted that he wasn't sure. "I know it's on the news all the time," he said, "but I'm not sure what it is."

"So, who's going to be president now?" someone asked.

"The vice president," said Jeffrey, who would prove to be the most talented academically of that first group.

"Agnew?"

"No," said Jason. "They got rid of him a long time ago."

"Ford," said Jeffrey.

It was obvious that a few of my new charges could benefit from a briefing on current events, so I provided a short one. It must have sounded more like a sermon from the pulpit, though, the priest in me reaching for a moral lesson and didactically culminating the little lecture with a general admonishment to all of the necessity of having leaders we can trust.

"So how did he get elected in the first place?" Michael asked.

"Because he said he'd end the war," Jeffrey said.

"Did he?"

"Practically," said Jason.

The dynamic that had already begun to develop between Michael and Jason was obvious: Michael would ask a question and look instinctively to Jason for the answer. Even if Jeffrey answered first, Michael would still look to Jason for confirmation. His propensity to see in the older boy an idol was clear.

"At least he ended the draft," Jeffrey added.

"So what?" said Jason. "Anybody that's afraid of the draft is a pussy."

A couple of them looked at me when he used that word. Was such language permissible in the presence of a priest? I decided that given the multiplicity of roles I would be playing in these boys' lives, I'd be ill-advised to stifle their free expression. This was to be their home, and they needed to feel comfortable here. I chose to lead by example rather than by dictate.

"I'm enlisting as soon as I graduate," Jason continued. "What's the worst that can happen anyway? You go off and never come back."

"You'll have to get a haircut," Jeffrey noted.

"I don't care. It'll grow back," Jason said. "I gotta cut it for school anyway."

Michael watched Jason run oversized hands through his hair. I couldn't help noticing that if Michael had had Jason's hair, he could have passed for a girl—a slight, fragile build, no trace of facial hair, long lashes whose fanlike movement betrayed his eyes as they took in the totality of the older boy's body, not missing even the most discreet gestures as Jason asserted himself as dominant member of the group: the rubbing of the soles of his bare feet (they were big like his hands, sturdy and wide at the toes but well padded like a baby's), the gratuitous lifting of the T-shirt to reveal the line of dark hair below the navel. Did Jason notice Michael's attentions as well as I, and was that the reason he chose Michael as his roommate?

"You wanna bunk together?" was the way he put it.

Michael didn't answer, but turned his submissive eyes to me, as if silently pleading for my assent.

"Is that okay, Father?" Jason asked. I said it would be fine and told them to take the downstairs bedroom next to mine. I thought that, given Jason's history, it might be best if I kept a closer eye on him.

The opening of the school year was still a few weeks away. The boys and I spent the time getting the house in order; there were still a few finishing touches to be done to the outside, such as a new coat of paint for the iron fence and getting the yard in presentable condition. There must have been a ton of debris accumulated around the grounds from the years of neglect and abuse: broken shards of Fats Domino singles, Mardi Gras beads, a brassiere, condoms, baby bottles, countless syringes, a book about Louis Armstrong—New Orleans Public Library stamped on its sides.

It was during those early days that the subject of the house's name came up. The place had been christened Boys' Chance by the archdiocese, but that appellation was universally rejected by the original six, who declared it to be entirely too pathetic and sentimental for a home for boys their age. Jeffrey suggested the Grizzly House, in honor of the school's football team.

"Grizzlies don't live in a house," Jason objected, "except in fairy

THE HOLY MARK *151*

tales."

"What do they live in then?" challenged Jeffrey.

I answered that one. "A den," I said. Perhaps *Oliver Twist* was still on my mind from the Dickens seminar, but in any event, Boys' Chance became the Grizzly Den, or simply "the Den." A large piece of plywood, formerly used to batten down one of the downstairs windows against the intrusion of vandals or hurricane-driven projectiles, was salvaged from the cleanup and used to make a sign, which the boys fastened above the main entrance to the house. Michael, who predictably turned out to be the artist in the group, painted the name in giant calligraphic lettering and reproduced with stunning detail the snarling image of a grizzly's head I located after poring through the school library's *National Geographic* collection.

My eight years of blissful contentment had begun. Besides the joy of working with a succession of lovely boys during my tenure at the Den, I was able to devote my days while the boys were in school to the pursuit of my own education. Buoyed by my success with Frankenstein's Mother, I became determined to earn my advanced degree, eventually focusing my studies on Henry James after considering and then ruling out Hawthorne (too judgmental), Whitman (too indiscreet), and Crane (too fatalistic).

I preferred the earlier, more youthful James, the James of *Daisy Miller*, *The American*, and of course, *Roderick Hudson*, the work I chose for my thesis. I knew those weren't his masterpieces, but I was drawn to them nonetheless for their paradoxical contradictions in worldviews, their fascinating blend of optimism and tragedy. The tired old James of the bloated syntax and interminable sentences never appealed to me; to be honest, he bored me. I saw in those later books the fruits of a bitter and frustrated life, a life of blind, almost ascetic devotion to the mind.

At Tulane I took an average of three classes per semester, completing the course work toward my master's in 1977. I was then free to work on my thesis throughout 1978.

My days immersed in the intellectually stimulating ambience of Tulane, my nights with my boys. Is there any wonder that as I reflect upon my half century in this life, I find so little to compare with those years at the Den? How precious indeed to find that rare intersection of professional responsibility and personal, spiritual accomplishment—and to be graced with more than a fleeting, tantalizing glimpse of it! That realization has brought me strength, even here in Kattannachee, when I become embittered with those who sent me here, for I doubt in all their miserable lives put together they had eight years as happy as mine in that house.

I am reminded of the parable in Luke 8 of the farmer going out to sow his seed. Much of the seed fell upon rocks and thorns or was carried off by birds and came to nothing; but some fell upon fruitful soil and yielded a hundredfold. Such have been my twenty-five years as a priest: a few fruitless years in the barren suburbs of Holy Gates, then gratification at the Den. There would be still more fruitless years to come before I would find fertile ground again in the nineties, once I learned to thumb my nose at the Pharisees and their hypocritical proscriptions and more or less take my ministry into my own hands. I need remember that lesson and the parable of the farmer, too, especially here and now, in this remote outpost they've consigned me to. Luke also wrote that no prophet is accepted in his own country, so perchance there might yet be fruitful seed to be sown even here in Kattannachee Parish.

My favorite time with the boys was the evening hours between eight and ten. Homework and chores having been done before and after dinner, this time was set aside for baths and recreation. We would all gather in the great room for ping-pong and television, and the boys would take their turns in the bathrooms. A local furniture store had donated a comfortable L-shaped sofa unit, and from my reserved place in its corner, I oversaw the activities of the room.

Cleanliness was an absolute imperative: I insisted that each of the boys submit to an inspection after his shower. Never would I intrude upon their privacy for this. I always waited until I saw a tousled head protrude from a steamy doorway and heard the familiar refrain of "Ready, Father Tony." Then I'd smell their hair, check their nails, and see that they put on fresh underwear before allowing them to dress and rejoin the group.

In no time at all they had dispensed with their pajamas and were comfortable spending these hours before bed in their underwear. They had become brothers. And what a lovely sight they were, barefoot and shirtless—perfect in their innocence. The idea that I'd be there to watch them grow—to turn fifteen, sixteen, then seventeen, to first touch steel to their virgin cheeks—filled me with a sense of purpose. They would never be more beautiful. And like all beautiful things in creation, they would never be more deserving of attention. I had never had a pet in my life, but now I had a houseful: a kitten curled up on the sofa to my right, one to my left, two puppies at my feet.

In time I began to notice a competition for my attention: The boys learned that the first to shower could be the first to claim the spots next to me on the sofa, to have their bare chests and shoulders rubbed by my hands, their thick, full heads of hair mussed by my fingers. There was always a foot or two sticking up from the rug, eager to have its toes plucked and tickled. To keep their contests for the showers from degenerating into boyish shows of brute strength—wrestling matches, battles royal, and the like—I had them draw straws every night. How often in life do we get to feel like a prize?

Still they couldn't seem to get enough of me, inventing any excuse for me to touch them: challenging me to wrestle, getting me to inspect a pimple on a back, pull a splinter from a foot, massage a cramping calf or thigh, measure a bicep after a workout. They devised a new game, a twist to blind man's bluff: blindfolding me to test my sense of touch. Could I identify them by distinguishing the feel of a single body part—a head, a hand, a foot, a chest? It was all clean fun, always instigated by the boys, who chose the featured body part. The nipples and buttocks were as intimate as the game ever devolved. In fact, when one boy made a crude suggestion ("Let's see how good Father's hands really are!"), the others immediately issued him a sound and harsh rebuke. I felt as if a brigade of young hearty knights had risen up in defense of my honor.

My sheep hear my voice. I know them and they follow me.
                                                    —*John 10*

A priest must minister to his flock. He does not choose them; they are chosen for him. His duty is to know them so that he can serve their needs. The needs of teenaged boys can hardly be compared to those of the sick or the aged or to those who have chosen lives of prayer and ascetic deprivation. They are special. Yet they must be tended to.

I believe that was my problem at Holy Gates, the reason I felt so unfulfilled: I didn't have a flock there. It was more of a herd—families going to church as if it were a movie theater or the Piccadilly, habitually frequenting the same Masses every Sunday, the parking lot filled with their station wagons and VW buses; competing to see who could get me or Father Foley to more dinner parties, as if that would be their ticket out of Purgatory; lining up at Saturday afternoon confession like middle-class refugees from a bombed mall.

Listening to those ridiculous confessions was such an odious task. Pathetic when not merely trivial—nothing but cheating schoolchildren and lying old women, deceiving themselves about the successes of their children—they bored me to the point that I took to bringing a novel or crossword puzzle into the box with me. I'd strain my eyes by the light of the tiny bulb while they'd recite their litany of insignificant transgressions. It was such an empty, useless charade. My prescribed penances were usually a few Hail Marys and Our Fathers. Occasionally, a long-winded old harridan would provoke me to demand an entire rosary or even a novena. I can remember one particularly absurd woman droning on and on, some nonsense about lying to her out-of-town sister that she didn't have room in her house for a holiday visit because somebody—perhaps the sister's husband—was a bed-wetter. I lashed her with a double rosary.

Was that the role of the priest—to wait passively within the shelter of a rectory for his flock to sin, to mumble some tired old shibboleth, and then send them out to do it again and again? At the Den I realized that I could do the real work of a shepherd: I could *prevent* the straying of my flock!

I shouldn't have been surprised that Jason would be the first; so many factors made that likely: his age, his dominant personality, his recent life on the streets, the disciplinary problems he had presented me with almost from the start. Yet I was nearly breathless with surprise when late one night after the rest of the house was asleep and I had punished him for a serious infraction against one of the other boys, Jason came to my room.

I had been keeping a special eye on him since that first day in the great room when we witnessed Nixon's disgrace together, not only because of what I knew about his history but because of the obvious propensity I saw in him to lead. I knew he could be an influence on the others—for good or bad. It was his relationship with Michael that I found especially unsettling, indeed dangerous. The bond that had begun that first day when Jason took Michael as his roommate only strengthened with time. The two were always together: Michael helping Jason with his homework, watching Jason lift weights, fetching errant ping-pong balls when Jason played a match. The pair were always the first to retire to their room for the night, often long before the official lights out of ten thirty on school nights and one a.m. on weekends. It wasn't unusual for

Jason, in the middle of Monday Night Football or a movie of the week, to rise from his seat, slap Michael on the back of the head, and say, "Let's go." He'd then lead the way downstairs. Michael couldn't have been more compliant if he had allowed Jason to take him by the hand. I could only imagine how little resistance he'd be able to offer the older boy once they were alone.

My decision to put the two of them in the downstairs bedroom next to mine was a fortuitous one. I had disallowed televisions and radios in the boys' rooms to encourage study and society; therefore, little of their activity was able to escape my ears. Also, by my order, there were no locks on any of the bedroom doors (except my own, of course), so if by the sound of heaving pillows or squeaking bed springs I knew they were getting particularly rambunctious, I could quickly intervene. What I invariably saw was Jason getting the better of the weaker boy, straddling Michael's prostrate form and tickling his bony ribs or buffeting his cheeks with playful slaps until they glowed red like a Reubens child's.

"Look, Father, Michael's wearing rouge," Jason might say when I'd walk in, bringing the blush to his captive's cheeks all the more. Or "Listen to him scream like a little girl, Father."

The contrast between those two, especially when they were re-moved from the rest of the group, was always striking. Michael's frail, bony form straining futilely against Jason's muscles; Michael's fair skin made even paler by his black hair and Jason's golden tan; Michael's un-derdeveloped body hiding inside his pajamas while Jason cavorted bare-chested in his jockey shorts.

In seminary we had been warned of the dangers of these "par-ticular friendships," and the priests did everything they could to discour-age them, especially once a young man had begun his novitiate. The final lines to the Act of Contrition come to mind: "I firmly resolve with the help of Thy grace to sin no more *and to avoid the near occasion of sin.*" It was that "occasion of sin" that the master of the novices was determined to circumvent during that most Spartan of seminary years. A young man is generally nineteen or twenty when he begins his novitiate. Several years of minor seminary (not much more than glorified Catholic high school, except for more theology and Latin) are behind him, and he is in theory ready to part ways with his frolicking boyhood and address himself to the contemplation of a life of prayer, discipline, and chastity.

Father Pedeaux, the little anorectic skinflint who lorded it over us in the refectory, had by the end of my minor seminary been elevated to master of the novices. Apparently he had starved the boys enough to accumulate a tidy surplus for the Church and therefore merited the promotion. With the same zeal that he had tried to discourage the feeding of the stomach, he then sought to stamp out the stimulation of the flesh. Novices were to sleep four to a room instead of two, there were no doors on the dormitory rooms in the novitiate wing, and never were a pair to be left alone—not in the bathrooms, not in the library, not even in the chapel. Contact sports of any kind were forbidden.

I don't fault Pedeaux for his efforts; it seemed to me even back then that his energies that had been so unfortunately misdirected when he had charge of the refectory had at last found an appropriate channel. If anything, I'm convinced the priests had erred in allowing the younger boys the freedom that they did. The outrageous antics that went on among the minor seminarians were nothing short of scandalous: wrestling in the showers, naked pillow fights in the dorm, group masturbation, even ejaculation contests (the fastest, the farthest, the most in an hour).

None of this was unknown to the priests. Many of the boys told it all in confession and were absolved with a benign penance of a Lord's Prayer or two and a mild lecture that soon they would be leaving behind their boyish ways to follow in the path of Christ. The dorms and showers were patrolled, of course, but the cleric/sentry (this was Father Couvillon in my day) always rang a bell when he made his rounds. The major malefactors in my dorm room always kept a dummy game of Scrabble set up on a table near the door and took their places around the board at the first sounding of Father's alarming bell. Not once did Father Couvillon question why two or three of the "players" were nude or what was so physically demanding about a game of Scrabble that would leave them red-faced and panting like young stallions.

I always excepted myself from their play, just as I had with my cousins behind the levee—and not merely out of fear of exposing my body. By my early seminary years, it was becoming obvious how little I shared with the other boys my age. Unlike them, I never felt the merest stirrings of temptation, even when my hearty peers were channeling their lusty energies right under my nose. The sights and sounds of it all just gave me a headache, or more often a nervous itching on my scalp—the uncontrollable urge to wash my head.

Nor did the good fathers ever laud me for my restraint. If anything, I was made to feel all the more an outcast. When in confession I had only sins of omission to divulge, those priests would grill me for my perceived smugness and interrogate me for what I must have been hiding. "We can sin in thought as well as deed," one of the priests might say to me, as if like Padre Pio he knew our sins even before we confessed them; or "Remember the Seven Deadly Sins, my son, and one of them is pride." Many times during those years I considered confessing what had happened to me when I took the plunge off the barge in my cousin's arms that day, but I never did. I wasn't even sure it was a sin, as no willful act had precipitated it. I will never confess it now—better to have some part of Tony with me still, even if just a little black spot on my soul.

I became determined at the Den not to see repeated the errors of the minor seminary. In short time I became not just a passive force for good—reacting to transgressions and impotently issuing unheeded admonitions—but a proactive one, anticipating and eliminating the wrongdoings.

Again, Jason was my first challenge, the progress I made with him among my greatest joys. Early on he presented problems on a number of fronts. The prospect of the inappropriate relationship that was forming between him and Michael was only one side of the double-edged sword that was Jason. The other side was his growing antagonism with the rest of the group, especially Jeffrey. It was almost as if he felt the need to balance the amity that flowed from his disciple Michael with enmity from everyone else. The boy was definitely self-destructing.

I admit I was slow to act and might not ever have done so had it not been for an incident that developed between Jason and Jeffrey. Jeffrey was the ambitious one in the group. The parish priest who had recommended him to the house had mentioned his many virtues, but made special note of his honesty and industry. Jeffrey's history in brief was that his father had been an offshore oil worker until he died of bone cancer when Jeffrey was eleven. The mother, who had never worked and had little to no marketable skills, was forced to do shift work as a waitress at a twenty-four-hour Pitt Grill. Despite pulling double shifts regularly, the money wasn't enough to meet the house note, so she and Jeffrey ended up in a single-bedroom apartment across the river in Gretna.

Jeffrey's dream was to help his mother buy another house. He tried to realize his goal by working after school and on weekends at any job a boy his age could handle: grass cutting, car washing, bottle collecting. I never met the priest who became the family's patron and can't recall his name, but he was no doubt touched by Jeffrey's dedication to righting a wrong that he perceived to have been unfairly visited upon his family. The concerned cleric nominated Jeffrey to Boys' Chance in an effort to take the burden of housing and educating him off of the mother's shoulders.

Jeffrey's industry could hardly have escaped my notice even if the priest hadn't noted it in his recommendation. The boy had an almost Puritanical work ethic. If every waking hour wasn't spent productively, something had to be amiss. Rather than see his acceptance into the house as enough of a help to his mother, he seemed to be infused with even more of a compulsion to earn money so as to get her out of that apartment even faster. When he asked my permission to help the school janitors on Saturdays for a dollar and a half an hour, I gave it. His grades were above average, and I saw no reason why he had to begin his weekend by sleeping until noon like the others if he didn't want to.

In retrospect I can see that between Jeffrey and Jason a classic good angel/bad angel scenario was developing. The two boys' predicaments had been markedly similar: both innocent victims of improvident families. But their chosen solutions led them down divergent paths: one working his young body to exhaustion, cleaning and running errands for any merchants who would hire him, the other stealing from those very merchants and hiring out his own body on the most depraved streets of the city.

Every moral lesson inculcated by our faith—from the fall from grace to Cain and Abel and on down to the life of Christ—teaches that the wicked will always be envious of the good. Persecution only masks a deep-seated jealousy within the hearts of the abusers. Of course that realization has helped me deal with my own plight. And it also explains why Jason would sin against Jeffrey.

When Jeffrey came to me one Monday morning with the disconcerting news that his pay from three Saturdays' work at the school had been pilfered from his wallet, I imagined I felt much as our Lord must have when He discovered that a first sin had dashed His hopes for an eternal Eden. I called the group together to let them all know what had happened and to clarify the gravity of the situation.

"A sin against one is a sin against all," I said. "Never again can there be complete trust in this house."

Further, I said I expected a complete accounting from the culprit after school that day—only upon that condition could severe disciplinary action be avoided. They had the rest of the day to think about that. Meanwhile, between my own two classes at Tulane, instead of remaining at the library to do research or study in one of the courtyards, I returned to the Den and searched the boys' rooms. An hour of rooting through chests of drawers and probing under mattresses yielded several forbidden magazines but no money.

The break in the case came that evening after supper when Michael came to me and admitted that he knew who had taken Jeffrey's money but begged me not to force him to tell. Since Jason was in the shower at the time, it seemed clear whom Michael was referring to. It was even more obvious when I noticed that Jason had brought a pair of pants with him into the bathroom; he had never been one of the more modest in the group. In short, I discovered the money within one of the pockets of those pants.

When threatened with expulsion from the Den, Jason shed his tough façade and regressed to a frightened little boy, fearful of abandonment, before my eyes. He dropped to his knees in tears, grabbed me around one of my thighs, and like a young Romeo at the feet of Friar Lawrence, begged for a punishment short of banishment. The money, he pledged, would be paid back tenfold. So moved was I by the tearful pathos of the scene that I nearly forgot whom I was dealing with. Surely this boy, considering his spotted history, was eminently capable of manipulating adults.

Who sheep resembled, but they dissembled (their hearts were not sincere)
Who once did throng Christ's lambs among but now must not come near

How could I know if Jason was sincere in his remorse? I placed my hand upon his head as he remained crumpled and sobbing at my feet, his blond locks still soft like a child's, belying the maturity of his tanned and muscled shoulders. Surely we all deserve the benefit of any doubts, and this boy's crime was hardly too heinous to be forgiven. Yet it had to be answered. As I considered the proper discipline to mete out, my mind came to settle on the pants Jason had brought with him into the bathroom (they were still in a little pile atop the toilet seat where I had found and searched them) and the pockets within which he had concealed his ill-gotten gains.

I pondered the proper action to take, telling the boy I would render my decision when the group returned from school the next day. Hawthorne's work came to mind: particularly the public acknowledgment of sin to effect absolution. The proper punishment would have to reinforce the themes of deceit, covetousness, and concealment while focusing attention on a tangible object that could be taken as emblematic of the whole affair. The pants would be ideal: symbols of the transition into manhood, which Jason, by his irresponsible act, had so patently failed at, and at the same time the means by which he concealed his crime. By depriving him of the pants, I could at once teach a lesson in honesty as well as maturity.

I can't take full credit for the solution I decided upon. The idea was based on a memory from my minor seminary days. Once again it involved the little skinflint Father Pedeaux, during his days as overseer of the refectory. One of the boys in my class—an athletic one, tall and well-muscled—was in the habit of buying extra rolls from other boys, shoving them down his pants or into his shirt, and secreting them back to his room for a forbidden bedtime snack.

Pedeaux learned of the boy's scheme quite by accident. Once we were all served and seated, he'd position himself at the refectory exit, making sure that silence was maintained in the courtyard on our way to our next class and seeing that nothing went into the giant trash receptacles except an empty milk carton. Not a morsel of food was to leave the refectory. When a wayward roll tumbled from the boy's pants leg right under Pedeaux's pointy little nose, the priest—as if he had been waiting for such a transgression and knew exactly what he would do—took immediate action. After chastising the poor boy in a tone of voice certain to draw everyone's attention (not difficult since we were all perforce silent)—calling him a selfish glutton and insisting that only through a single-minded self-indulgence could he have acquired such a strapping and virile body, Pedeaux called for a potato sack from the kitchen, cut three holes in it with a knife he fished from a bin of soiled silverware, and had the boy strip naked before the entire room.

"Did Christ have a body like this?" Pedeaux asked, pointing to the boy's strapping physique. He then had him don the sack.

"Now try and sneak food away under that!" said the priest.

The boy had to wear the sack for the rest of the day and in the refectory for forty days. And for each of those forty days in the food line, Pedeaux had him raise the sack to his chest to ensure he was wearing nothing underneath before he would allow him anything to eat.

I had no access to potato sacks, but an oyster sack should do just as well, so I paid a visit to my cousin Ronnie at his shop the next morning. It wasn't time for my hair to be serviced; I just knew Ronnie would be able to get me a sack from his father's seafood business, which was by then being run by one of his brothers, Uncle Eugenio being long dead from his cancer.

"Whatever do you want one of those for?" he asked. "Are y'all getting into burlap again?" Ronnie had begun, sometime in the seventies, to affect an exaggerated Southern drawl, the phony kind one might hear in a Hollywood movie but absolutely nowhere else on earth, least of all in New Orleans. A few of his former dancing cronies from New York had come down for a visit, which I suspect precipitated his linguistic mutation. No doubt he had played the part of the rural and naïve expatriate all the while he was up there and couldn't be caught out of character back home. I'm sure the "little Southern boy" routine got him plenty of mile-age with visiting businessmen in those seedy French Quarter pick-up bars he frequented.

As for his burlap remark, I made up some ridiculous excuse about needing the sack for a Nativity scene the house was painting (it wasn't even Advent!). Fortunately, Ronnie didn't press for more details. He was too excited about going to a disco in the Quarter that night where some big star was appearing. I believe it was Gloria Gaynor or another one of those Negro sex singers who were getting popular with that crowd at the time. He told me to pass by again after lunch and he'd have the sack.

Back at the Den, I cut holes in it for Jason's arms and head and waited for the boys to return from school. They were unusually quiet that afternoon, even Jeffrey and those who were not connected to the incident at all. Perhaps they feared provoking me before I passed sentence on the malefactor, as if like Titus Andronicus my wrath might generalize to the innocent. Jason himself went to his room and remained secluded until dinner. Even Michael kept his distance. Did he fear Jason knew we had talked? Dinner passed as silently as a meal in the seminary refectory ex-cept for my announcement that I was calling a mandatory house meeting in the great room at eight o'clock. I excused myself from the table, saying I would be in my room praying until the meeting and that I was not to be disturbed.

I made a point of being a few minutes late, knowing this would make an impression, as I have always been known for my unwavering punctuality. As predicted, they were all waiting for me in silence; the tele-vision set was not on, nor could so much as clanging barbells or a bounc-ing ping-pong ball be heard. I entered the room without a word, carrying a small traveling case, which I set at my feet as I took my customary seat in the corner of the couch.

I only wish I had thought to record the exact words of my ad-dress that night, for they were quite effective. I noted that in all the time we had spent together in that house, I had never become angry until the incident at hand and alluded to the story of the moneychangers in the temple. I knew they were wondering if I was going to expel Jason from the Den. (Is that what the traveling case was for?) Gradually I worked my way from the theme of trust to that of forgiveness. But I noted, of course, that forgiveness could only come with repentance.

"Can we hate the sin and yet love the sinner?" I asked the boys. They nodded their assent. Jason, who sat on the rug cross-legged, looked down at his bare feet and grasped his own toes. I repeated the question, this time singling out Jeffrey. "If you can forgive, then certainly we all can." He nodded once again.

The boys were riveted in place, their eyes never wavering from me except for an occasional glance at the case, which I had brought in mainly as a prop to guarantee everyone's attention and which I reached for with great and obvious significance at the word "repentance." Of course the oyster sack lay within.

For the first time that evening, I directly addressed the fallen boy. "Jason, you have not lost our love, but you must again earn our trust," I said, unfolding the sack. I then pronounced sentence, taking as my precedent Pedeaux's judgment upon the young athlete of years gone by. For forty days he would wear nothing but the sack from the minute he returned from school until he dressed for classes the following morning. I directed that he begin serving his sentence immediately.

And virtually immediate was the transformation in Jason: His character and demeanor—I should say even his very personality—underwent a marked change from the moment he donned the sack. Gone was the supercilious façade, the false bravado he had wrapped himself in like a chrysalis. It had been his custom before the incident to claim his space before the television in the great room by sprawling out on his back on the rug clad only in his gym shorts, raising his knees to view the screen through the V of his firm thighs and cupping his hands behind his head to show the tufts of hair beneath his arms.

Ironically, the sack covered more of his body than the shorts he had been used to cavorting in. Yet the result was a newfound modesty of posture. Before the television, he now knelt with his feet carefully folded beneath his haunches so that only his toes were visible behind him. He was almost prim in the way he carefully tucked the burlap between his knees— like a blushing maid at a picnic. My spirits were buoyed by the sense that I had effected a change for the better. Yet there was much more to be done, which I discovered after only a handful of the forty days had passed.

It was Sunday night, the end of the first weekend of his sentence, that Jason first came to my room. How could he have entered without my hearing him I will never know. I'm usually the lightest of sleepers; since minor seminary and the shenanigans of my roommates assaulting my slumber on a nightly basis, the slightest noise has ordinarily awakened me. On an average night in the Den, my sleep might be interrupted half a dozen times by the sounds of restless boys: a healthy stream of urine, even in an upstairs commode; the ringing of water through old pipes as a nocturnal thirst was quenched; the gasp of the refrigerator door during a midnight kitchen raid.

Jason must have virtually floated into my room. Not until I heard him whisper "Father" did I open my eyes and see him standing between me and the closed door, clad only in the oyster sack, which, amidst the dark shadows of my chamber and in my half slumberous state, I mistook for a tunic or an alb and the apparition before me a herald angel or some celestial specter or other. Was I having an "experience," like one of those apocryphal episodes I so often cited when busybodies enquired into the source of my vocation? Or was I hallucinating like my poor old grandmother on her deathbed? Had my heart stopped in my sleep and was this apparition my escort to the other side? My right hand clutched my chest at the thought.

As my eyes came into focus in the dark and I was able to make

out the stenciled words "Cuchinotto Seafood" and the image of a smiling, bewhiskered catfish on the front of the specter's "tunic," I began to
get my bearings. Before I could so much as ask the reason Jason had come
into my room, he had pulled the sack over his head. "I can't sleep in it,
Father," he said as it dropped to the floorboards beside my bed. True to
the letter of my fiat, he wore nothing beneath it.

A sudden sharp itching on my scalp sent the hand that had been
braced against my breast reflexively to my head. My heart nearly did stop
when I realized that I was exposed in front of this boy. Of course I was
in my pajamas, but I wasn't wearing my piece. Not in years had anyone
except Ronnie seen me without it. I looked instinctively over my shoulder to my dresser where I kept it pinned atop a Styrofoam head, on the
face of which I imagined for a moment the grinning visage of my harpy
cousin, relishing the sight of this lovely boy and my humiliation.

I turned back to Jason. He was coming closer. My hand was
still forming a makeshift cap on top of my head. He reached for it as he
climbed into my bed. Then he lay on his back beside me and placed my
hand on his upper leg, where the thigh merged with the groin so warmly.

"It's okay," he said.

Did he mean for my hand to be where it was or for him to see
me like that? I didn't know, but my mortification soon disappeared. I
took another look at the dresser. The Styrofoam head wore no mocking
expression; it was faceless now, peaceful again.

Jason kept my hand immobile on his thigh and started telling
me of his days and nights on the streets, of the scores of men he had
been with and how empty it had all made him feel because he knew that,
despite what they all said, none of them really loved him. We had never
discussed any of that, even in confession. He told me the things he would
let them do to him. Sometimes he would steal their money or jewelry, he
said, because they had stolen something even more valuable from him.

"I want to be with somebody who loves me, Father," he said as he squeezed my limp hand and moved it just enough.

I closed my eyes so that I couldn't see it. How many years had it been—fifteen, sixteen—since I had seen Tony like this with Ronnie lying there defiling him? I had turned and run that day. Ronnie with his little mind games had told me time and again that I had been running from that time and place ever since, that I had run into the seminary and had never stopped. I thought of running again that night, as I suppose many of us do when we stand at the threshold of something momentous.

My enemies will never believe this, but until that night I had never been in bed with another human being save one of my own cousins—and I was thirty years old. Some dangerous deviant! They never knew about any of the boys at the Den, though they tried their best to dig up all the settled dirt they could after Tchefuncte. I know the wicked spin they would have put on it, too: that I had lured them all to my lair like a cunning wolf. In truth I was completely aghast when I realized what Jason wanted and had no idea how to respond. Should I follow the letter of Church teachings and admonish the boy for the grievous sin he was flirting with? Should I tell him that what he wanted was impossible and that he should trust in God and seek solace in prayer? Should I shame and reject him as an unregenerate sinner?

My prayers for guidance were answered when Jason released my hand and it remained fixed to his thigh as he placed his own hand on my head. The prickly tingling was stronger now as Jason forced my head down to join my hand. It was then that I finally realized what that feeling meant, that it was really a message emanating from my birthmark. Mama Miggliore, even in her ignorant, superstitious way, had been right: I had indeed been marked for a special kind of life. My unsightly nevus was a holy mark after all, my own special gift from the Holy Spirit—a unique charisma all my own. Ronnie, too, had been right in a perverse sort of way: He had called it the mark of my "passion" and that it would have to be released if I were ever to find happiness.

The word "passion" has many meanings apart from the vulgar, carnal connotation that my depraved cousin attached to it: the passion we feel for our work and for our ideals, the suffering and Passion of Christ before His death on the cross—neither of these meanings would occur to those who would condemn me, and I can hear them snickering at the absurdity or bristling at the blasphemy if I alluded to them myself. Yet I know they both apply. Jason was a sinner, and I knew the hold he had over Michael. From the seminary I also knew what that kind of hold could lead to. It had undoubtedly already come to that, most probably every night in their room. I could have turned a blind eye to it all like those foolish, bell-ringing sentries and let it go on again and again, confession or no confession. Or I could have issued a stern rebuke and dismissed him from my presence, even expelled him from the group. But either of those choices would have yielded the same result: He would have returned to seeking other outlets, further damning himself and corrupting others.

When one is starving, he will steal; when desperate, he will kill. We must eliminate the need or the sinning will never end. But how can a need such as this one be eliminated without compounding the wrong? That was the focal dilemma I prayed to resolve.

And my answer came in what I dare to describe as a glorious epiphany. As a good Catholic, I had always believed that Christ had died to take the sins of the world upon Himself. But believing is one thing; understanding is quite another. There are many mysteries that we must believe—the trinity, transubstantiation, the creation itself. We earn salvation through believing them, but only when we truly *understand* them will we enjoy that salvation.

That night I finally understood as well as believed. After over thirty years on this earth, my duty as a priest ministering to a straying flock was at last clear. In however limited a way, I had been given the opportunity to walk in Christ's footsteps. By offering up myself, I could take the sins of this boy and those like him upon myself.

I continued my work with Jason throughout his remaining years at the Den. The results were astounding: noticeably less hostility toward his housemates, far less time spent alone with Michael, practically no disciplinary incidents, even an improved academic performance. In short, he became by far a happier boy.

And he was just the first of many. By the time the Den was fully occupied with its capacity of twelve boys, there would be at any given time two or three coming to me for special attentions. Of course I couldn't wait for them to take it upon themselves to initiate the contact; that would have been egregiously derelict of me. In time I became quite adept at spotting the ones who, like Jason, were most in need. If in doubt, I could always search their rooms for pictures or magazines or other signs while they were at school. Generally it was the ones at the end of their second or beginning of their third year that I focused on. They would then be about sixteen, the age when Saint Bosco had warned they are most susceptible to the allure of "attachments" and "bad books" and at the greatest risk of falling into the pit. I instituted a new policy of mandatory counseling sessions with them at that age. We'd meet in my room on specified nights—always at bed time so as not to interfere with their social or academic concerns—and talk about dangerous issues that I knew were or would soon be paramount in their lives, issues which if not addressed could lead to very serious problems. These meetings became confessionals of a sort, with my absolution conditioned upon their pledge never to act upon any impure thoughts or feelings except in the privacy of our sessions.

"If there is a sin," I told them, "then let it be mine."

I knew there was none, though. A sin is not real unless it exists in our minds; we must *believe* we are sinning. My boys would remain innocent as long as I relieved their minds. As for myself—I will defend my own actions to my death, though I answer to no one, save my ultimate

Judge. Let the others say what they will. Like Pharisees with their choplogic and trick questions, they would accuse me of acting in my own
self-interests, of being driven by my own self-gratification. If I cared a
pennyworth about what they believed, I could shut them up with a word
or single glimpse. To think I was so ashamed of my body as a child, and
now I know it was all part of His plan: to make it impossible for me to
be guilty of what they say. So I know there is no sin in what I did with
my boys, unlike what Ronnie did to Tony in that dreadful scene behind
the levee—lusting and rubbing himself against Tony like a drooling satyr,
Tony reaching out to me.

Yes, I had a passion for my boys, but it was a passion of sacrifice,
not of salaciousness. Like a true gift, it was selfless; it asked for nothing
in return. Never did I use any of my boys for my own pleasure, though
many wanted to repay me. "Let me do you," they'd say, so innocently
ignorant of the absurdity of the very thought. Jason was the first, though
he took longer than most—five or six visits—before making the offer.

"No," I'd always say, and gently remove a strong and eager young
hand or restrain an anxious head. I will die pure. I know this and I rejoice
in it. Mine would forever be an ecstasy of the soul. Those who doubt me
will answer to a higher Judge.

Blessed is the man who finds no cause for offense in me
—Matthew 11

CHAPTER EIGHT

ROUSSELL HOUSE

The archdiocese closed the Den in 1982 for financial reasons. The city's economy—like the rest of the state's, at the mercy of the price of a barrel of oil—was suffering pitiably. Blue- and white-collar families alike were moving en masse to greener Southern pastures like Atlanta or Houston, whose leaders had the foresight not to rest their economic hopes on tourist dollars and a single industry. The exodus was reflected in declining school enrollments in every Parish in southern Louisiana. The end of the Baby Boomers' educations only made things worse: schools closed like public pools at the advent of integration. Pope Paul VI High itself was threatened. Drastic cuts were made; good teachers found themselves selling shoes or perfume at Maison Blanche, tending bar, or delivering the *Times Picayune* to anyone who hadn't canceled his subscription to try to save his house.

The archbishop was subject to much well-deserved criticism for fiscal policies that fell abysmally short of being charitable.

"The Church is the largest private landowner in New Orleans," the critics cried. "Why doesn't he sell some property or a few solid gold chalices instead of closing good schools?"

"They own that whole block behind Jesuit," others said. "They're just hanging on to it to make a killing when property values go up again. It's a sin!"

"He thinks all he has to do is wave that deformed hand and everybody's going to feel sorry for him," yet others chimed in. "Well not me. I'd cut off my own hand to save my child's school."

Amidst all the brouhaha, continued outlay on projects like the Den, judged by many to be too liberal and unnecessary, was out of the question.

They were sad days, that early summer of '82, when we were packing up everything for the ultimate farewell—a final folding of the ping-pong table, dismantling of the bunk beds and weight machine, carrying off of the giant sofa unit. Most of what was still useful went to a retreat house for nuns in Covington. The rest—a bin of kitchen utensils, trash bags filled with linens, a few unsteady lamps, a couple of boy-stained mattresses that would be difficult to explain to the nuns—was simply left on the curb for anyone to take.

I should have seen the handwriting on the wall in 1980, when they told me the Den wouldn't be taking in any more boys until the economic picture brightened. They were probably planning to let the numbers dwindle by attrition so that in four years the place would simply close with a whimper. The worsening recession must have made them pull the plug in the midst of their four-year plan. There were only six boys still living at the Den when it closed. A couple were able to find a home with relatives; the rest were parceled out to foster homes or a Catholic social agency.

We had to be out before the Fourth of July. When I returned on the holiday for the last of my own things, the Den was once again just another boarded up building on Ganymede Street. It was as if a beautiful dream realized had been run through a VCR in reverse to a hapless and futile conclusion. My sense of honor to the past led me to keep up with the status of the building within which I had experienced so much joy for eight years. Thank God it never degenerated into the miserable rat hole it was before my arrival. But that was only because Ratchett saw its potential as rental property, leasing it first to Tulane as an off-campus frat house, then to a CPA firm. Today it is occupied by one of those national coffee shop chains. They host poetry readings there on Thursday nights.

Sometimes I attended, listening to the young, unkempt, and self-centered poets hold court on the tragedy of life while I dipped a chocolate-coated biscotti into my frothy cappuccino and remembered all the boys I had known in that place. Dozens of them over those eight years. And in all that time, not one unpleasant incident or ugly rumor. For years they returned to visit me, seeking me out to surprise me in the classroom or at my office at the school, even years later at the old nuns' home. I've even met some of their families, grateful to me for helping their loved one through some difficult years. Not once were my motives suspected or my dedication questioned. Perhaps one of them might find out where I am today and while on business in Shreveport or Monroe, or perhaps even Dallas or Little Rock, make a detour to Kattannachee to give me a hug and tell me how much I meant to him, and when he sees what the Church has repaid me with, return to New Orleans and speak out for his old mentor.

Besides the whittling down of the numbers at the Den, an early clue that the eighties would be a decade of trials was the fate of Jason. He was, in a way, like my firstborn. We had even celebrated our graduations together in 1978. I took him to Galatoire's on Bourbon, where we shared a bottle of champagne. He was of age, of course. The dinner was compliments of a gift certificate my mother gave me in celebration of my master's degree. Yes, dear Josie was still around and in good health throughout the seventies, though between my responsibilities to the boys and my classes at Tulane we communicated mostly by phone and saw each other only sporadically. She was still seeing her sister and even having her hair done by Ronnie, so I knew she wasn't starved for family attention. Nevertheless, it was somewhat inconsiderate of me to see so little of my mother during those years. And I would live to regret it.

Tragically, Jason and I lost touch soon after he left the Den. My error was in believing my work with him was done. Our private counseling sessions had become fewer in his senior year, but that, I came to find, was normal; most of my boys needed fewer visits as they got older and left their wild boyhoods behind. Since there were always new younger ones craving my attention, I tended to let the older, more settled ones go their own way. In Jason's case, though, I should have been more solicitous.

I knew that after graduation he was waiting tables in a little Italian place in Lakeview that sold pizza by the slice, and I even saw him there one night during the Christmas holidays in 1978 when I stopped by after an outdoor Advent service in City Park. He told me he was sharing half of a double off Robert E. Lee with a friend and planned to enter UNO in the fall, once he had saved a little more money. I gave him a hug and a five-dollar tip (I only had one slice of pizza—it was a bit doughy—and a root beer). He seemed rather thin to me, but I didn't give it much thought; it seemed only natural that the boys would lose a little weight once they left Martha's cooking behind. Two years later I saw his picture in the paper. I don't regularly peruse the news, but it was December 9, 1980, the day after that pathetic lunatic shot John Lennon in New York, and I made a point of picking up a *Times Picayune* to read about it. The Lennon story continued onto a page opposite the local police reports, and there, sandwiched between a photo of an Amazonian black woman claiming to be a voodoo priestess, who was running an illicit massage parlor across the river in Algiers, and an account of another tourist stabbing in the French Market, was Jason's face—hollow-cheeked and unshaven, but still recognizable.

It was just another drug-related shooting, according to the paper. Jason was found in the passenger seat of a Datsun in a high-crime area of Gretna between the river and the Westbank Expressway with gunshot wounds to his cheek and neck. He bled to death before they could get him to the hospital. The driver of the Datsun escaped; the car had been stolen, so it was impossible to trace him. The police never found Jason's killer. I called a few times, identifying myself as a priest who had once known him, but the detective on the case told me they had precious few resources to expend on "this type of crime."

I went to the coroner's office and secured permission to view the boy's body before the state interred him. I couldn't bring myself to touch his ravaged face, but I held his feet and kissed them through the sheet as I prayed for his soul.

That night, when one of the boys came to my room, I made him promise to stay close forever.

"I will, Father," he said.

"Even after you're gone from here, away at college, or even working," I said, "you'll always be important to me."

"I know, Father," he said.

I hope I will be forgiven for exacting from a boy whose name I can't even remember today a promise that was so unlikely to be kept, and for seeing, moments later when I closed my eyes over him, the face of Jason in my mind.

As I alluded to earlier, Jason's fate was a mere precursor to the disaster the eighties would be. After the Den closed, I began to have more contact with my mother. It seemed that during those years of my preoccupation with the boys and my studies, Josie had become an old woman. She turned sixty-five in 1982, so I took her to Venezia's, her favorite Italian eatery in Carrollton, to celebrate her birthday and to try to put a happy face on my odious new teaching position. While we were there, she presented me with some very distressing financial news.

Perhaps it was because I was remiss in my filial duties that my mother, as she got older, began more and more to seek out the company of her sister. Italian women will always go back to family. In my mother's case, her brother Anthony was, of course, out of the picture; he hadn't spoken to her in over twenty years, and even if he had broken with his own hateful character and made overtures toward his younger sister, his snubbing of my ordination was in 1982 still fresh in her mind. It had only been twelve years. Besides hearing her rehash that incident for the umpteenth time over spinach bread and veal parmesan, I learned what many of my cousins were up to, including Paul's children, whom I hadn't seen in years. But our meandering conversation came to settle upon Rose and what happened to the money.

I can't help but believe that there was a bit of spiteful nose-cutting involved in Josie's striking up a series of pathetically ill-advised financial arrangements with a sister who never knew anything about money except how to spend it on herself and her own spoiled children. My mother didn't even know where the money was going; she just kept writing checks to Rose and trusting her judgment. Rose had pat little explanations for what became of all the money. Starting in the mid-seventies, they first invested in rental property in New Orleans East, which was supposed to boom with economic expansion in the coming decades, sporting the third-largest shopping mall in the country, but turned into a sprawling slum when whites took flight in droves after 1980.

"It's just horrible," my mother sobbed over her artichoke salad. She was wearing a sleeveless dress, something that she just shouldn't have been doing anymore; the flesh of her upper arms was sagging like a jellyfish by then. "We took a ride out there last week, over the Industrial Canal. Nothing but blacks. You'd think it was Canal Street!"

Rose also claimed that a great deal of money was lost in the silver market when they didn't get everything out before it crashed. Then they bought stocks on margin and lost another fortune.

I didn't believe the Fishwife's story. I was convinced then, as I am to this day, that the whole thing was a setup masterminded by Anthony to get his hands on more Miggliore money and gain a modicum of revenge on me and Josie in the bargain. He knew my mother would never trust him, so he used Rose as his proxy. She could claim to have taken just as heavy losses as my mother but with no apparent effect on her lavish lifestyle, thanks to all the fish money.

"So, what's left?" I asked her.

"The house," she said, "and some money I had in bonds that haven't matured yet. Enough so I won't have to sell the house and so you'll have a little something when I'm gone."

If I had known what was going on, I would have stopped her. She could have put the money into CDs in those days and made twelve percent!

"Oh, I know, Joe," she said to me. My mother never took to calling me Tony. I imagine it would have been too much to expect her to refer to her only son by a name she associated with an estranged brother and a dead nephew. "I should have told you what I was doing, but you were so busy with those boys."

And there was the rub: I had slighted her, so she was forced to turn to her sister, a patently self-destructive act characteristic of Italian women, intended to punish and elicit pity at the same time. My mother was getting even with me for neglecting her, but the most difficult part for me to accept was that in her attempt to make me suffer, she had, whether wittingly or not, helped my execrable godparents do the same.

They would do it to her too—at least Anthony would, hounding her with his insatiable sense of vengeance until she would languish penniless in that hole of a nursing home in Chalmette like a toothless charwoman in a Dickens novel. His confederate, however, would not live so long. Sometime in 1982 or '83 Rose was diagnosed with a rare type of nasal cavity cancer. It was just a barely noticeable lump under her jawbone then, but it would eventually spread to the cheek, the nasal vestibule, and even the eye socket. It became quite hideous in the end. I can't be sure of the year it started, but I know I had begun my hapless teaching job when I got the woeful news.

That job was only the first of three slaps in the face—each more stinging than the one before—that I would suffer at the ungrateful hands of Ratchett and the archdiocese once the Den closed. As if the working conditions I would be subjected to weren't bad enough, they couldn't even vouchsafe me a decent place to live. You would think the largest private property owner in New Orleans could manage to find for one of its most learned and respected priests a more befitting dwelling place than a roach-infested dormitory for disabled wards of the state.

Ratchett must have been beside himself with glee: aiding my uncle's bloodlust (for I know now that every turn of the screw was powered by Anthony's wicked hand) and saving precious dollars for the archdiocese in the bargain. The old apartment house they put me up in is on a corner of Tulane and Carrollton Avenues, one of the busiest, not to mention seediest, intersections in the city. A virtual hub for public transit riders, since converging at the site are lines from the four corners of the metropolitan area—Gentilly and the Lakefront to the north, Saint Charles Avenue and uptown to the south, downtown and the Quarter to the east, Airline Highway and the suburbs to the west. The stench of bus fumes wafting their way to my third-floor window with its scenic view of a bowling alley and thrift store became as common to me as the sounds of street people shouting at each other in their incomprehensible dialect—some sort of Spanish/urban hybrid.

The Church seems to have owned the property since the beginning of time. At one time, in fact, the entire block was in the archdiocese's possession. Its history is quite storied: A tent city was erected there after the Battle of New Orleans. Priests and nuns worked in shifts around the clock for weeks caring for both British and American wounded. Later, however, the property was not put to such commendable use. During the Antebellum period, a Monsignor de la Roussell oversaw its lease to a consortium of cotton factors who supplemented their already prodigious incomes with slave auctions within earshot of the monsignor's Carrollton office. Pressured by Rome to avoid a scandal since the Vatican, under Gregory XVI, had officially reaffirmed its condemnation of slavery in 1839, the wily de la Roussell sold off most of the land to the factors and a company that built a whiskey factory just before the Civil War. The Church made an unholy killing practically on the eve of the hostilities that would ravage real estate values throughout the South for decades.

The present building, named Roussell House in honor of the good monsignor, who would have been pleased by the progress of the property in the twentieth century, was originally a convalescent home erected between the World Wars and staffed by Poor Clares. In the sixties, the federal government requested that it be allowed to use the facility as a permanent home for disabled veterans. I've heard that the lucrative lease runs into the second decade of the twenty-first century. So why bother paying for an apartment or upsetting the status quo at some rectory when I could be tucked away free of charge among a score of paraplegics and amputees and the Church could make itself look as if it gave a damn about those poor people by staffing the place with a priest?

An exhaustive chronicle of my life at Roussell House would fill its own volume, but that would take me rather far afield of my present purpose, which is to summarize my six years of teaching and how they led to the unfortunate Tchefuncte incident. I will digress only long enough to tell the story of Old Sydney, a poor old Negro and one of

Roussell House's least fortunate. Let that be emblematic of my six years in the place.

Old Sydney was a quadruple amputee. I met him at the end of that summer of 1982. His room was on the first floor of Roussell House. Usually he kept his door open so that he could call out to passersby for help whenever he needed anything. In my case that day it was a cigarette.

"Hey, Joe!" he called. "Can you help me with a smoke?"

I wondered how he knew my given name, but more compelling than my curiosity about that was my irritation at being addressed so disrespectfully by a complete stranger.

"I have never smoked," I said. I was expected at the school that morning to meet with a few members of the English Department to discuss reading lists. It was my intent to pause in his doorway only long enough to issue that mild rebuff. I wasn't even planning to make eye contact, as I had learned during those years of roaming the city's streets after Tony Junior's death that looking at these beggars only serves to encourage them. But before I could move on, he spoke again.

"Good for you, Joe," he said. "But I have my own."

So why bother me, I was about to say, until my eyes moved instinctively to the bed where the voice had come from and where I beheld for the first time the decimated body of Old Sydney.

"I just need a little help lighting up," he said, flapping his discolored stumps three or four times like an agitated penguin. I was momentarily reminded of Red Skelton's sea gull routine and almost broke into a nervous laugh at the awful sight of this poor man. The stumps were an ashy white, perhaps from psoriasis or something else peculiar to amputees, quite in contrast to the rest of Old Sydney, whose skin was otherwise as black as the tar that must have caked his lungs from decades of smoking three packs of Lucky Strikes a day.

The open pack was on a little metal nightstand beside Old Sydney's bed. Also on the stand was an ashtray, a plastic bottle of K & B hand lotion, and a box of straws, which he used as a makeshift cigarette holder. He needed me to shove one of the Luckys into a straw and light it for him. He could take it from there. With the extra length the straw provided, Old Sydney could clasp the thing between his stumps and reach it to his lips. A faint odor of some sort lingered in his room. It wasn't quite strong enough for me to recognize, and I dismissed it for the time being as perhaps coming from the cheap lotion on the nightstand or some sort of prescription ointment for whatever was wrong with the skin around his stumps. God forbid he might ask me to rub something on them.

What I eventually learned about Old Sydney was that he had been born, one of eleven children, not far from Ville Platte, in the central part of the state, in 1917. He was a sailor during World War II and lost his arms when a big gun he was tending to exploded near some Pacific island in 1944. His legs were spared in that catastrophe but couldn't survive the combination of his genetic predisposition to diabetes and his coming to live with a sister in New Orleans, the most diabetes-friendly city in North America. By 1970, he had lost both legs to the disease.

I asked him who had told him to call me Joe since I didn't go by that name anymore. He only laughed and said he called everybody Joe until he knew better. I often didn't wear my collar on summer days when I had no duties to perform, but through our discussion of my names, he learned I was a priest.

"Tell me somethin', Father," he said to me. "You think I oughtta be a Catholic?"

"That's really a matter of conscience," I said. "What faith were you raised in?"

"Oh I don't know," he said. "Baptist, I guess. Like my parents. Ain't most people what they parents was?"

"Usually," I said.

"Tell me, you a priest—you think them Catholics could do something for me?"

"I'm not sure I know what you mean," I said.

"I mean what do Catholics do for people like me?" he said. It was amazing how dexterous he was with that straw and cigarette, even leaning over the nightstand and flicking the contraption with his yellowed teeth so that a red hot ash dropped squarely into the ash tray.

"They own this building," I said, unable on the spot to think of anything else.

"Well, I guess that's something," Old Sydney admitted. He went on to ask me about a form the residents were required to fill out every year. One of the series of questions on the form was the religion of the resident. "You think if I put down Catholic they might do a little more for me?"

"It's probably just for statistical purposes," I said. "I doubt it would make any difference."

"Then I guess I'll just keep putting Baptist," Old Sydney said.

Just before I left, he asked me if I would "give the room a spray for bugs" and directed my attention to a decrepit little dresser, the only other piece of furniture in the room besides the bed and the metal nightstand. On top of it were several cans of aerosol insecticide and a black and white Phillips television set that, judging from its antenna and separate UHF control knob, must have been fifteen years old. In close proximity to the dresser were two other objects which I found odd considering Old Sydney's limitations: a broom and a purple tennis shoe.

"Did you see a roach?" I asked him.

"Not today," he said, but he insisted that I spray anyway. I did so, and what filled the air was the same odor I had detected upon first entering the room, only more intense than before. Old Sydney, it turned out, harbored a keen loathing for cockroaches, exacerbated, I'm sure, by his utter helplessness against them.

He did what he could to protect himself from the roaches. His room, never completely free of the patina of roach spray, was awash from

dusk till dawn in fluorescent light in an effort to trick the nocturnal creatures. The shoe and broom were always there for whoever answered his
cries, like a mallet and stake, ready to slay the monsters.

By day, other obsessions gripped old Sydney. He was a lusty old
soul with pathetically no outlet for his passions. He never wore clothing
and was prodigiously proud of his huge purple-black member, which
often popped into view like a balloon from beneath his sheets when he'd
ask me to reposition him in the bed. During one of our conversations,
I happened to mention that he and my mother were the same age. For
weeks he harped at me to introduce them.

"Tell her I'm the perfect man for her," he said to me as I was
shoving another Lucky into a straw for him. "It still works fine, and I can't
never run around on her!" He laughed until he choked on his own smoke.

A few of the more ambulatory residents of Roussell House who
killed the roaches for him also took turns in what was euphemistically
referred to as "relieving Old Sydney." That was what the hand lotion was
for. One of the men told me he knew that it was technically a sin but that
God was sure to understand. "He can do it himself if he flips over in the
bed and rubs himself long enough, but he ends up making a mess on the
sheets," he said to me. I more or less gave him my dispensation, but with a
strong admonition that no gratuitous pleasure should accompany the act.

Old Sydney died while I was still at Roussell House. The cause
of death was respiratory failure, no doubt a combination of smoke and
the insecticide that forever permeated his room. They called me in to
anoint the body, which for some reason was fully exposed, the cover
sheets turned down to the foot of his bed as if in readiness for an autopsy
and not the last rites of the Catholic Church. I had never seen all of Old
Sydney at once, but there he was, his ebon body and all four stumps
against the bedsheet, like a great beached starfish, blackened by the sun.

My nights at that depressing hole might have been more toler-
able if my days had been spent in pursuits more beneficial to the mind

or body, or at least amidst more salubrious working conditions. As soon as it was clear that my beloved Den would close, I applied to the archdiocese for permission to pursue a PhD in American literature with a concentration on the early Henry James. My master's thesis on *Roderick Hudson* had been well received and even garnered a polite letter of refusal from an assistant editor of the *Henry James Quarterly* when I submitted it for publication. He took issue with my attributing much of Rowland Mallet's fascination with Roderick to Rowland's childhood obesity. I have no doubt that I could have expanded my thesis into a book-length dissertation without much problem if I had just been given the opportunity.

By 1982, after four years away from a classroom, I was quite thirsty to return to an academic watering hole. I am reminded here of Roderick's statue *Thirst*, his miniature study in bronze of the beautiful naked boy drinking from a gourd, which captured Rowland's fascination early in the novel. To Roderick, the bronze symbolized youth and all its trappings: health, strength, innocence, curiosity—all that we sense slipping away as we approach middle age. I was thirty-eight in 1982. I had no more boys to watch over, and when I asked them to allow me at least to quench my intellectual curiosity once again, they denied me. It seems they had other plans for my return to the classroom.

Essentially their intent was to consign me to the ranks of the petty high school pedagogues for the rest of my career. I should have been a Jesuit. Then I wouldn't have to go begging like a mendicant friar to those penny-pinching archdiocesan bureaucrats for every little thing. One letter to the Provincial and they'd send me halfway around the world to study Tibetan philology if I told them I'd add another degree behind my name. And all I wanted was to go to Tulane, a mere bus and streetcar away from that miserable pest house they had me living in.

"You don't need a PhD to teach high school," they said, dismissing my request.

And indeed I didn't! In fact I was absurdly overqualified with my master's for the classes they gave me: three freshman sections and two slow-track American literatures. I begged for an honors section so that I could assign an early James novel—perhaps *Daisy Miller*—and maybe read *Leaves of Grass* in its entirety. But I was told those sections were assigned by seniority. I'd be archbishop before I'd lead an intelligent discussion of Whitman at that place.

As I mentioned earlier, the recession of the eighties hit the education community like the smiting hand of God. Not only were schools that had been around for a century forced to close, but those that survived resorted to desperate measures to remain open. Admission standards were lowered if not dropped completely. No high school entrance exams screened the scanty applicants of the eighties. No letters of recommendation from parish priests or elementary school administrators were expected any longer. No transcripts were perused by directors of admissions. The ticket to getting into a Catholic high school in New Orleans by 1982 was simply an eighth grade diploma from anyplace that could legally issue one and at least one parent or guardian with a decent credit rating.

To say that Pope Paul VI was scraping the bottom of the local gene pool to fill its classrooms is no exaggeration. The school was taking in everyone from the borderline retarded to the certifiably sociopathic, and naturally the worst of the worst ended up in the "slow track." Perhaps that was why they wanted a priest in that classroom: to administer the last rites over the brain-dead.

I would be ashamed to reveal the reading list for my so-called American literature course. I had met that summer with the chair of the school's English Department—a fortyish, anorectic-looking woman who never used makeup and wore her hair in that hideous frizzed style that was so popular at the time (recall Streisand circa 1980)—and mentioned that I planned a historical survey beginning with some Puritan poetry and a few readings from Cotton Mather's diary. We'd continue with a couple of Enlightenment texts (I had always wanted to take a group through *Common*

Sense in its entirety). This would lead naturally into the Romantic period, when I would assign a Cooper novel and then tackle the Transcendentalists. Finally, after Hawthorne, I would conclude the year with the realism of Crane and perhaps even James and one or two of the moderns.

The woman laughed.

"Things have changed since our day, Tony," she said. "You're not leading a graduate seminar. These are kids."

I will not dwell on the woman's presumptuousness in addressing me so familiarly at our first substantive meeting, nor on what it said about the changing times that a priest at a Catholic school should have to answer to the likes of her. The list of "suggested texts," which she then handed me, I will comment on, though. It was laughable. Had the educational establishment in the eighties lost faith in its students to the point that it considered them utterly devoid of higher cognitive processes, intellectually incapable of reading a book that didn't deal with sports, dating, or eating disorders?

I had absolutely no autonomy as an educator; all decisions were made by Ms. Frizz or some higher administrator. I couldn't even design my own quizzes. All testing materials were standardized, as were the so-called "review sheets" that were to be distributed to the students before every test, essentially reproducing the questions that would be asked and providing the answers. I made the mistake that first year of ambitiously trying to introduce my American lit students to *Walden* and even photocopied a portion of "Economy" for a class reading. But the boys just saw Thoreau as some sort of feral wild man running around naked in the woods.

"How can you live in a cardboard box?" they asked. "Wouldn't it get wet?"

Finally I gave up and assigned the book that was on their original reading list, a novel about a Vietnamese pot-bellied pig that could solve algebra problems.

Again, my purpose here is not to belabor the frustrations of those unproductive years. I could easily fill pages with a tedious litany of episodes from my hapless places of residence and work: e.g., the drunken serenades from the tenant adjacent to my quarters in Roussell House, a navy veteran of the second war who drank himself into inebriation on Taaka vodka every night, singing along with his scratchy collection of Rosemary Clooney records. To this day, when I'm trying to read or meditate quietly, I can hardly keep the phony Italian cadences of "Come on-a My House" from swirling through my head.

The event that led to the dropping of the curtain on my years at Roussell House and my career as a high school instructor was the Tchefuncte incident in 1988. Saint Theresa of Jesus once wrote that more tears are shed over answered prayers than unanswered ones. I prayed nightly for those six unhappy years that I would once again be given the chance to work among needy boys and influence their lives as Saint John Bosco had a century before me and as I had so assiduously attempted at the Den. Certainly the Lord could not have intended for one of His servants of my abilities to languish away as a nondescript drone in the hive of educational bureaucracy.

My faith in His wisdom persisted. He was merely testing my fortitude. I had only to persevere through these trials and my prayers would be answered. That answer did indeed seem to come with Tchefuncte, but in its aftermath, I was left not with a newfound sense of purpose and rebirth, but with an all-too-personal sense of the wisdom of Saint Theresa.

CHAPTER NINE

TCHEFUNCTE

The Tchefuncte (pronounced Chi FUNK tuh) is a tiny river in south-eastern Louisiana running north to south along the border of Tangipa-hoa and Saint Tammany, two of the so-called Florida Parishes just below where the chin of Mississippi rests like an adoring spaniel upon the toe of Louisiana. The river, sometimes called the "Little Tchefuncte," is seldom more than ten or fifteen yards wide and extends a scant forty or so miles through this predominantly rural part of the state before emptying itself into the great Lake Pontchartrain, upon whose southern shore the city of New Orleans lies.

The river's environs feature one of the last unadulterated pine sa-vannahs in the Gulf South. Its cypress-lined banks, especially at its more secluded northern end, make it an ideal getaway for hikers and a mecca for ornithologists and naturalists. Fishing and boating predominate at the Tchefuncte's wider mouth, near Madisonville, one of the larger towns on Pontchartrain's north shore. During my purgatory at Holy Gates, I often had to assume the double duties of pastor and assistant on Saturdays while Father Foley and a few parishioners with boats whiled away the day on the little river, fishing for largemouth bass and imbibing beer by the case. John always joked that he was going along to "bless the fleet."

Just a few miles south of the source of the little river, in the remote northeastern corner of Tangipahoa Parish, the Benedictines built a retreat house before the war for members in their last year of major seminary. When their own numbers began to drop off and age, they converted the facility to a retirement home. By the seventies, necessity had again forced the Benedictines' hands, and they began to rent the property for retreat purposes to other orders of priests and nuns, as well as to lay groups of various denominations. Its location, a mere hour's drive from New Orleans, yet a world away from the urban chaos, made it an ideal getaway for groups of jaded students from the city's schools. Like many local high schools, Pope Paul VI was using Tchefuncte as the site for its three-day senior retreats. Approximately eight to ten students were scheduled per retreat. A priest (usually the campus minister) accompanied each group.

By 1988 I was one of only three priests on the faculty, so you might think that I would have been called upon to share in the retreat duties regularly. I had discreetly volunteered my services several times over the years, only to be told they didn't like to take anyone out of the classroom for the retreats. It was a flimsy excuse—as if they couldn't find some moron who could count twenty-five heads and press the play button on a VCR!—but the campus minister, Father La Grange, had no teaching duties, so I couldn't really argue with it. Apparently my exemplary record of eight years with the boys at the Den counted for nothing, yet another example of the Church's blindness to the talents of its personnel.

Father Etienne La Grange had personally led nearly every retreat since the school began holding them at Tchefuncte in the seventies. The handful he had missed since I joined the faculty were handled by Father Michael Labruzzo, who also coached the wrestling team. Father La Grange was spending more and more time with his elderly mother down in Thibodaux that year. He was actually nearing retirement age himself and would soon return permanently to his roots in that French-speaking area to the south. Father Labruzzo had managed to step in every time, but one Wednesday, Etienne's old mother took a nasty fall when she let go of her walker to stir a gumbo pot, and Mike was committed to lead his squad of wrestlers to an important regional meet in Lake Charles. So, for the first time, I was asked to go to Tchefuncte.

My preparations for the retreat included a visit to the school's senior guidance counselor for a briefing on the particular situations of the eight boys who would be attending. I had taught a few of them: two fat boys, their last names Finn and Finney, had been in my class their first year. As chubby freshmen, the luck of the alphabet ensured that they would be seated together, and as the years went by, their friendship grew in proportion to their bellies. By their senior year, they were enormously obese but as jolly as a pair of smooth-faced Santa Clauses.

For the most part, the ersatz psychological profiles of my eight temporary charges were rather unremarkable. Several had seen their parents through separations or divorces and were being shuttled from one household to the other on alternating weeks like work crews on an offshore rig, but such arrangements had become so common by 1988 that the children were more or less expected to cope without professional help. Divorce by the eighties was practically a rite of passage for their developmentally growth-stunted parents.

There was one boy, however, whose case the counselor made sure I was intimately familiar with. We had set up an emergency meeting that Thursday morning in his office in the middle of my one and only free period, during which I usually ate because I spent the noon break on my "lunch duty": patrolling the stairwells for fights and vandalism.

"We're a little worried about this one," he said to me before apprising me of the student's situation. The boy's name was Sean. He was, I learned from the counselor, the type that the culture of high school was perfectly suited to serve: handsome, a dark-haired six-footer; athletic, a swimmer no less; intelligent, boasting a GPA in the top decile of the class of 1989; and talented, having appeared on stage in several student productions over the years. Of course I hadn't taught him—since only the most hopeless dullards and underachievers were placed in my basic sections.

"Sean's younger sister recently attempted suicide," said the counselor. "I think she's sixteen, a junior at Cathedral Academy, and he's taking it pretty hard."

"Was the girl depressed?" I asked.

"I can't tell you everything I know," he said, "but it's a very unhealthy home situation. The girl swallowed half the medicine cabinet while the mother was passed out. Sean found her and brought her to the hospital, just in time from what I've heard. The mother was useless. She's at least admitting to her own problem now. The father is an attorney. Apparently he wasn't home."

The way he arched his brows at the word "apparently" and then averted his eyes to a nearby shelf of books on adolescent anxiety disorders made me suspect that the part of the story he wasn't at liberty to discuss involved the father. Did he believe the man was only pretending to have been away during the crisis? Or perhaps he knew the man was gone but conducting some illicit business, perhaps rendezvousing with a mistress. That would explain the mother's drinking. In any event, he refocused our discussion on Sean and explained the decline in the boy's attitude and performance since his sister took the pills. He had begun to miss swim practice, and several of his teachers had reported a drop in his academic performance as well.

"And he turned down the lead in *Bye Bye Birdie*," the counselor added. He had grabbed a yearbook from one of his shelves. "Here, look at this," he said, and he showed me a picture of the boy. "Look at that hair. Can you see it slicked back in that fifties style? He would've been perfect as Conrad."

I had never met the boy, but I did recognize him from the picture. It was of the entire swim team, posed with their coach in warm-up suits beside the pool where they must have just won a competition. Sean was on one knee in the foreground with another boy I didn't recognize, one hand on the trophy. His bare feet were beautifully shaped, large but not oversized like a clumsy, gangly boy's. The team jacket he wore was unzipped to his waist and opened just enough to reveal one nipple on a firm, smooth chest. His hair was indeed striking, even in the black and white image: so dark it wouldn't even have to be dyed for the play. The boy appeared to have all the looks, the confidence, the poise to make a perfect Conrad Birdie.

"I'm not saying you have to do anything special with him over the weekend, Father," said the counselor. "But this is a very unhappy kid right now, and you should be aware of what's going on just in case he decides to open up over there. Sometimes these kids do that. They end up coming out with stuff we had no idea was going on."

The only other advice he gave me was to take special note of Sean's reaction when he opened the "surprise" letter from his parents. As a traditional feature of the senior retreat, Father La Grange always had the parents write letters to their sons, usually focusing on the predictable themes of pride or confidence or what have you. The letters remain in the custody of the retreat leader, at whose discretion they are distributed to the boys. I took the counselor's caveat to be an advisory that I should deliver Sean's letter under private circumstances.

I brought a yearbook back to my room at Roussell House that night and looked at other pictures of Sean. My favorite was a shot of him in the pool. He appeared to be swimming right into the camera, the caption indicating that he was doing the breaststroke. Only his head and the rounded muscles of his shoulders were visible above the water. Wet, his thick black hair seemed even darker and more impenetrable. It masked his scalp like a shower cap. Countless drops of water teemed off his body. Frozen crystal by the camera, they seemed to hover around him like preternatural points of light or the aura of a saint.

For the first time in years, the itching on my scalp returned that night. It had been so long since I felt it that I doubted its message at first and tried to wash it away with shampoo and muffle it under baby powder. Like Padre Pio with the stigmata, I greeted the return of my own peculiar sign with a certain degree of anxiety and trepidation. In fact, I'm sure that was the reason I dreamed that night of my dead cousin. No, not Tony Junior, as might be expected considering the pictures of those handsome young swimmers I had fallen to sleep looking at and the impending prospect of spending time in an isolated spot near a river with a group of boys about the same age as my older cousin in those bygone days behind the levee. In retrospect, I should have seen it as an omen of foreboding that Ronnie would appear to me on the eve of the Tchefuncte disaster.

He was a scant two years in his grave at the time. The godlessness and dissolution that had ruled him for decades finally cost him his life in 1986. I don't know when he discovered he was HIV positive—probably around the time the Den closed because I recall detecting a subtle change in his demeanor around that time; he stopped apprising me of his escapades in the French Quarter discos and tea dances and of the nameless multitudes that sojourned in his bedroom. No more pictures of him and his drag friends at the gay carnival balls. He tried as long as he could to hide the truth about his health, claiming to be on a cruise or visiting friends in New York when he was really just too sick to work or see anyone.

"Are you losing weight?" I'd ask him now and then in the shop when I had become suspicious.

"Oh yes," he'd say, attributing it to a new diet he had picked up from the talk shows or an exercise regimen he claimed had him running around Audubon Park like a hyperactive shih tzu.

By 1985 there was simply no denying the reality of his condition. Chalking it up to the latest health fad would have at that point been absurd; only the most deluded soul in the throes of anorexia could have chosen to look the way he did. He finally started to confide in me, even calling me at Roussell House to talk or entreat me to have coffee or dinner with him. Was he coming to me because I was a priest, or was he seeking a connection to an earlier time of life, before the irremediable third act of his tragedy?

I doubt that I was much comfort to him. Oh, I listened to him—I've always been good at that. Usually he just talked about the others he knew who were dead or dying: hairdressers, bartenders, dancers he had known either locally or in New York. I had never met any of these people, but some of the names were familiar to me from other stories he had told through the years, juicy snippets of their all-night debaucheries during the seventies, calculated to ensure that I knew what I was missing.

Naturally I muttered the usual sentiments and platitudes we conjure when someone is facing a great trial or grief, things like the insignificance of this ephemeral life compared with the next, the impossibility of fathoming the motives of God, the apparent absence of justice in this world. Hopefully Ronnie was so racked by guilt and absorbed by his own misery that he couldn't tell I didn't believe a word I was saying. Divine justice here was abundantly clear and eminently deserved. Could anyone possibly believe it a coincidence that my cousin and his mother would be stricken at nearly the exact same time by two horrific diseases that had nothing in common except for being perfectly complementary to the sins of their victims? Was this not obviously the smiting hand of God in action?

Here was my cousin—that worshipper of youth and beauty who once frolicked with those sleek bodies on the stages of New York, that profaner of all things obese who used to ask me for my old T-shirts so he could use them as drop cloths when he remodeled his apartment—looking at forty-one, with his wasted body and sunken cheeks, like a Dachau survivor. Meanwhile, his mother, who used to ridicule me for my unsightly birthmark and spent untold thousands of her husband's money and her own Miggliore inheritance to make sure she didn't end up with the same face and nose as her mother, was living out her life in seclusion. The cancer had left her by the mid-eighties with not much of a face and no nose at all. The whole cruel turn of events was absolutely Biblical in its magnificence.

The sketchy reports I received of my aunt's condition came through my mother, who curiously was the only person Rose would allow to see her. Josie visited her sister three times a week for the last two years of her life but always waved me away when I pressed her for details. It was just too horrible, she said.

Rose lived long enough to bury her youngest child. His funeral was the last time I saw her, though she kept her ravaged face hidden beneath a huge black hat and veil. She spoke to no one, not even her own children. I had wondered if I might see Anthony there, but he claimed to be out of town on business. Rose died within a year of Ronnie. She had directed her surviving children that she was to be cremated and that only they were to attend the service. Not even my mother, who had nursed her during those awful last years, was allowed to attend.

Although Ronnie and I were both grown men in my dream that night before Tchefuncte, its setting was a surreal hodgepodge of scenes and places from our common past. I was sitting in the chair in his shop at the beginning, wearing a yellow hair-cutting cape over my clothes and looking into the mirror at Ronnie, who was standing behind me, working on my exposed scalp with his comb and scissors.

"I want you to hear my confession," he said to me.

And then I was walking with him through the woods behind the levee. The yellow cape he had snapped around my neck was still in place, but to my immense distress, I realized I was wearing nothing beneath it. We made it to the swimming place, but the old barge was no longer there; in its place along the bank of the river was a church. Ronnie and I entered it together, and, absurdly, it became the cathedral where I was ordained. Its immense space was empty except for the two of us. We walked a ways toward the altar, past various statues, holy images, and Stations of the Cross. Finally, beneath the depiction of the seventh Station, where Christ falls for the second time, my cousin dropped to his knees and wrapped himself around my legs.

"Tony always loved you and not me," he wailed. "But I bribed him and blackmailed him to keep him away from you."

I stood in judgment over him as no doubt it had always been intended I should. I was no longer naked; the yellow cape was now a full suit of holy vestments, complete with chasuble, as if I were about to celebrate Mass.

"I deserve to die," Ronnie cried, and at that moment there was a change of scene. I suddenly found myself in Mama Miggliore's bedroom, still dressed for Mass, only something had been added to my regalia: the miter of a bishop. I have no idea what part of my psyche that came from; I have certainly never entertained the slightest ambitions to ascend the Church hierarchy. The politics would be far too offensive to my conscience. Perhaps the hat was a symbol of my inherent superiority to the basest of my relations. In any event, though, I must admit I wore it in the dream with impressive aplomb.

Ronnie was prostrate in my grandmother's massive old bed, imploring my forgiveness and absolution. We both knew that the only penance that could save his tortured soul was death, so I splashed him with holy water, like a triumphant Dorothy vanquishing the Wicked Witch, and he was gone.

I awoke to the predawn darkness of my little room in Roussell House. It was four thirty in the morning, but I was much too anxious about my dream to get back to sleep. What had it all meant? Surely my symbolic dispatching of the memory of my cousin could only augur good things for me. In my heart I had forgiven my cousin for trying to make me believe, as he did, that mine was a false life, for all that nonsense about my pent-up passion and how I was doomed to misery unless I faced up to it. I had finally faced up to him, and I was ready to assume my responsibilities at Tchefuncte.

The theme of the retreat, "Our Inner Voice," had been chosen by Father La Grange weeks before. The boys were asked in their theology classes to consider what it meant to them personally and to discuss it in group sessions over the weekend. As retreat leader, I was given free latitude to dwell on the theme to whatever extent my discretion dictated. The only requirement was that I bring it up in at least one general meeting.

I liked the theme. Besides the obvious attribute that it would encourage the boys to think and talk about what was going on inside of them, it suited me personally. I saw in it the opportunity to expose the boys to some philosophy and writings that I was never able to touch in my shallow, watered-down literature classes, like Emerson's infallible conscience and the Romantics' rejection of extrinsic authority. It had taken me so long to understand and heed my own inner voice; so much time had I wasted listening to false prophets and interpreters.

I drove the school van to the retreat site myself. Pathetic as it sounds, it was the first time in my life that I had been to the north shore of the lake, although it lies a mere twenty-five miles from New Orleans. I mention that only to stress how poorly traveled I am, thanks to the niggardliness of the archdiocese. In all my years in the priesthood, the only place they ever sent me was to Atlanta for the Southern Convention of Catholic School Administrators while I was at Holy Gates; and I only got to do that in place of Father Foley because deer-hunting season was opening in Alabama and John wouldn't have missed that to see Christ come down off the cross. If I had sold my soul to the Jesuits, I'd probably be in England right now working on my second PhD or researching a book on Henry James.

The drive across the lake with the boys was a pleasant one. It was a beautiful September morning, so bright and clear that the shore of Saint Tammany was visible scarcely halfway across the bridge. The van could seat eleven comfortably: the driver and front row passenger, plus three rows of three passengers, unless any were exceptionally obese like Finn and Finney, who took up the rear seat themselves, where they munched blissfully across the lake on immense bags of caramel popcorn that Finn's father had provided as a bon voyage gift. Sean had the window seat directly behind me, so that if I trained my mirror just so, I could unobtrusively observe him at will. He wore a baseball cap and blue-tinted sunglasses that complemented his perfect complexion but made it difficult for me to see into his eyes. One of the boys brought a cassette tape and insisted I play it all the way across the lake (a frighteningly hideous musical group called Twisted Sister); but Sean listened to his own music through headphones. Sometimes I could see his lips moving to his own private lyrics. Seldom was his attention drawn from the placid waters of the lake to anything going on inside the van. The school counselor was right: Here was a boy with much weighing on his mind.

We arrived at Tchefuncte at just after nine thirty that morning. The Benedictines must have been divinely inspired when they picked this place for their seminarians' final getaway. It was pure bucolic splendor, several miles removed from the main highway beyond Covington. Locals peddled Creole tomatoes, watermelons, and jumbo shrimp from the beds of trucks parked along the rural roads that took us west toward the little river.

A magnificent vista of orchids greeted us as we drove through the open gates of the grounds, past the image of a haloed Saint Benedict himself in his customary cowl and tunic, smiling down from a great billboard, his arms outstretched and the backs of his hands raised to the approaching motorists, as if bidding a fatherly welcome to all. Alas, even this sylvan paradise was not beyond the reach of the malign hand of infamy. Some cowardly vandals had despoiled Benedict's image by painting over three fingers and the thumbs of both hands so as to make them indistinguishable from the background of the picture, effectually erasing all but both middle fingers so that the saint appeared to be greeting the approaching motorists with a double-barreled obscene gesture. The overall sacrilegious effect had obviously been calculated to outrage the two groups of visitors most likely to see it—Catholics on retreat and ornithologists on expedition—for beneath the offensive image the scoundrels had scrawled with the same paint they had disfigured Benedict's hands the following caption: "I'm going to shoot two birds today!"

The boys could hardly fail to take notice.

"Look, he's flicking us off!" one of them exclaimed.

Everyone lunged to the right for a gander out the windows. Even Sean took notice, removing his headphones and, at least for the moment, joining the group.

"Who is that?" one boy asked. "Is he a priest?"

"It's supposed to be Saint Benedict," I said. "But that is obviously not the message that he intended to send us."

"Ha, ha!" laughed all the boys. All except Sean, that is, who commented, all too prophetically as it would turn out, "Maybe it was."

We drove up to the main building of the retreat complex and were met at its door by our host, a tiny, oily-haired Benedictine by the name of Millburg, the only permanent staff member of the facility. He had a cowlick that resisted control even by its own grease. I later learned that his real name was Guidry and that, as an avid ornithologist, he had taken the name Millburg upon ordination to honor Saint Milburga, an eighth-century abbess and patron saint of birds.

The retreat complex consisted of a chapel, two cabins that could sleep a total of sixteen visitors, and the main house with several private bedroom/bathroom suites, one of which was Millburg's permanent residence; another would be at my disposal for the weekend. The main house also included a spacious cafeteria and dining room and a small but comfortable library with some exquisite Natuzzi chairs, a sofa in deep maroon leather, and a respectable collection of books, especially in the areas of history, theology, and philosophy. Additionally, several coffee table books on ornithology adorned the sitting area.

Millburg led the way to the boys' quarters to get my charges settled in. I was already looking out for an appropriate place to be alone with Sean so as to properly gauge his reaction to his parents' letter, as the counselor had bid me. It was obvious, though, that the boys' cabin would not answer the purpose. There was but one great bedroom with four bunk beds in the building. If I wanted a private moment with any of these boys outside of a shower or a confessional, I would have to make other arrangements. There was the second cabin, but I couldn't count on that; since our group only needed one, I assumed (correctly, I later discovered) that the other would remain locked and inaccessible for the weekend.

The boys were allowed a few hours of free time before lunch. They had been prepared in their theology classes for the great deal of "down time" that they would have over the weekend and were coached as to how to spend it. They were encouraged to explore the grounds and more or less stake out their own private space for prayer and meditation. After seeing that they were settled in their cabin, I told them to split up and get to know their surroundings. We would all meet for lunch in the main house at one.

Meanwhile, Father Millburg gave me a guided tour of the complex. Besides the principal buildings I've already mentioned, there were several other tiny, yet beautiful, gazebo-like structures dotting the many acres of the grounds. Millburg referred to these as "stations." I managed to take a peek into several of them. They were all nearly identical hexagonal structures with a window on every other side. I would estimate each to be not much more than one hundred fifty square feet in area. A porch with a single rocking chair, encouraging solitude, encircled each station. At the center was a tiny room accessible through but one doorless aperture. Inside could be found a solitary prie-dieu with a missal on top. A framed portrait of an event in the life of Saint Benedict hung on one of the walls. The stations, like all the buildings at Tchefuncte, were immaculately whitewashed. I'm sure this was meant to symbolize peace or the cleansing of the soul or some such thing, but I felt all that whiteness gave the place the appearance of a state-run sanatorium.

I later learned that the Benedictines kept a full-time staff of maintenance people—gardeners, maids, cooks—to keep up the place from Monday through Thursday, but for the weekend retreats, Father Millburg alone would see to the guests' comfort. The cooks had prepared our meals in advance so that all Millburg had to do Friday night was heat the oil and dip the already filleted and breaded catfish into it. I wished I could have met the women responsible for Saturday's spaghetti and meat sauce so that I could have told them that by my taste their recipe was rivaled only by my dear mother's.

"Rarely have I sampled such a perfect sense of oregano and basil," I remarked that night to Father Millburg.

"Oh, it's all fresh, you know," the little priest said. "They grow all that stuff out behind the grotto."

The grotto was a little fabricated cave of red brick that Millburg showed me as part of my Friday orientation. It was built to memorialize the cave outside of Rome where Saint Benedict was said to have lived as a hermit out of disgust with the undisciplined world, but I'm sure it resembled Benedict's original in only the most stylized way. Actually it looked more like a brick igloo to me, but at least the landscaping was nice. The Benedictines had made commendable use of a few ferns and hawthorn bushes.

Once inside the little igloo, I found it to be one of the most private and isolated spots on the grounds. The structure had only one entrance and a single window of stained glass. On the window was depicted the rather odd scene of a man and a bird. The man I gathered to be Saint Benedict from the images I had seen in all the little stations and on the desecrated billboard. The bird might have been the Holy Spirit, except that the third member of the Trinity is usually represented by a dove and this bird was as black as a lump of coal. It looked more like a crow. Perhaps the artist was making a point about the stereotyping of goodness, like the creators of those Negro Barbie dolls. In any event, Benedict seemed immensely pleased to see the little creature, which appeared to have just alighted upon the branch of a nearby tree and had a small apple wedged between the pincers of its beak. There were two pews in the tiny room, facing a tidy little altar on which sat a copy of the life of Benedict and a marble bust of the saint.

The odd picture on the window was just one indication of the special regard in which birds seemed to be held at this place. Throughout the grounds, I couldn't help noticing the abundance of accommodations for the creatures: There were birdhouses and birdbaths at practically every turn. Wooden signs hammered into trees here and there provided visitors warnings against feeding the feathered denizens of the grounds and gave instructions as to what to do if one was found in distress. Harming a bird was absolutely forbidden and punishable by immediate expulsion and lifelong banishment from the grounds.

During my ensuing conversation with Millburg, I learned of the priest's interest in the creatures and that it was, of course, he who had put up all the bird signs and facilities. He began talking to me about his avian avocation after I remarked that the middle of a grotto honoring Saint Benedict seemed an odd place for a birdhouse.

"Oh, to the contrary," insisted Millburg. "Birds were very important to Benedict. Don't you know the story of the raven?"

I had to admit that I didn't, so Millburg edified me with an explanation of the story behind the strange picture on the stained glass window.

"While Benedict was living the life of a hermit in the cave outside of Subiaco, he was fed every day for three years by a raven. Without the intercession of that dear winged creature, the saint would have surely starved to death."

He pronounced the word "winged" with two syllables, a telling indicator of the type of romantic mind that could believe such an absurd and obviously fabulous story, typical of the rot I had read in all those lives of saints I suffered through with Sister Ysabel.

"How interesting," I said. "Is that what made you choose the Benedictine order?"

"That and Saint Milburga's being a Benedictine abbess," he said. "Are you familiar with her story?"

Again I had to admit my ignorance.

"She had wondrous powers over birds. They would refrain from damaging the local crops at her command."

"That must have made her very popular with the peasants," I noted.

"Oh yes," Millburg agreed. "She was very popular and beloved by all. Much like an early version of Saint Francis, only with an exclusive concentration on birds."

The poor man must have been as hungry as Benedict himself for someone to listen to all of this. His greasy cowlick seemed to stand up even more than usual, like the plumage of an anxious woodpecker.

"And I know I may be stretching it a bit with this," he said, "but the other patron saint of birds is Saint Gall, and Saint Benedict is the patron of gall stones."

He looked at me for a reaction. I just said "hmmm" and arched my eyebrows, which was all the encouragement the little zealot needed to continue.

"Saint Gall once performed an exorcism," he said. "And a flock of demons fled the possessed woman's body in the form of blackbirds."

"You should write about all of this," I said. "I wonder if anyone has ever done a book on birds and the saints."

"I don't know," he said. "I should do some research into that."

"Oh yes, you really should," I said, wondering how much longer until one o'clock.

Millburg continued to regale me with bird stories from the Bible and lives of the saints, some of which were marginally interesting, such as the tale of Saint Cloten, the seventeenth-century Jesuit missionary who was rescued from his torturers, a tribe of savages in western Africa, and carried to safety on the back of an ostrich. Millburg eventually segued into his beloved hobby of bird watching. In particular, his expeditions of late had been focusing on a rare species of woodpecker—the ivory-billed variety. No sightings in the United States had been confirmed since the seventies, and the bird was generally believed to be extinct until a few were observed in Cuba in 1986, an event that Millburg described as a "spectacular discovery that shook the bird world."

"If they're in Cuba, they could be here too," he said. "They love the swamp forests."

Later that night, over coffee in the library, my host showed me sketches of the ivory-billed.

"Audubon said they reminded him of a Van Dyke in flight. Notice the signature markings—the yellow irises, blue feet, the deep carmine at the back of the male's head."

I looked at the picture. The bird appeared quite unimpressive to me: It was basically black and white, so that it probably looked like a flying penguin at a distance. The signature markings Millburg had noted looked discrete and incongruous, as if they had been painted by numbers. In profile, the bird looked puzzled and stupid. Was the entire "bird world" in a tizzy over this thing?

Well, no matter. At least Millburg would be kept busy chasing the feathered will-o'-the-wisp all over eastern Tangipahoa for the better part of the weekend. He had an expedition planned for Saturday and Sunday.

Little of consequence took place that first day at Tchefuncte. After lunch—a bountiful fare of cold dishes: meats and cheeses plus egg, shrimp, and potato salads—we processed in silence to the chapel, where Father Millburg and I said Mass together, followed by the retreat's first official group meeting. The boys weren't yet ready to open up, but they listened attentively as first Father Millburg and then I spoke about heeding the inner voice.

Millburg retold the story of Benedict and the cave, only in this version the raven not only brought the hermit food but spoke to him as well, foretelling that Benedict would go on to found twelve monasteries and influence the entire Christian world. I pictured the scene—a filthy and emaciated recluse in a dank and dingy cave living on regurgitated worms or larvae or God only knows what and listening to a cawing bird reciting a grandiose vision of his future—and nearly vomited my pastrami from the combination of revulsion and hysteria. The boys, though, seemed riveted with interest. The two fat ones, Finn and Finney, even ceased for the moment munching on the breadsticks they had squirreled away in their pockets after lunch.

At the risk of losing my audience by not delivering a story as fantastic as Millburg's, I chose to illustrate the inner voice with an example more rooted in our own time and place—my dear deceased Mama Miggliore's vision for her grandson.

"My grandmother knew of my calling before I did, even from the moment of my birth," I said. I discreetly left out the part about the birthmark. The boys would naturally want to see it, and in those days I would have sooner exposed myself on the altar at High Mass than take off my hair in public. Instead I said I was born with a caul—those things are always an omen of something or other—which my grandmother insisted was a religious *cowl* placed over my head by an angel as an unequivocal sign of my calling.

Surprisingly yet significantly, Sean was the only boy to raise a question about my story.

"But Father Tony," he said, "your grandmother wasn't God. How can what she said be your inner voice?"

At first I was a bit piqued by the comment. They had all just swallowed that babbling bird story without a peep, and the first thing they question is the wisdom of Mama Miggliore! Did he think Millburg's stupid bird was God? Maybe I should have said my grandmother lived on a dairy farm in Tickfaw and a talking cow had foretold my ordination!

I bit my tongue, though. This was the first time Sean had spoken to me directly and I thought it best, for the sake of the relationship I was hoping to foster with him, to be patient and strive to understand what had prompted the question. Why would these young people listen en-raptured to the most far-fetched fable and then doubt the words of their own elders? I concluded that the issue was a matter of trust, in Sean's case most probably rooted in whatever was going on with his father, and I ap-proached the question accordingly.

"You're right, Sean," I said. "My grandmother's voice was not the voice of God, just as the voices of your parents are not the voice of God. My grandmother's was just one of the many voices I heard in my youth, some of them quite contradictory." Here I thought of those other voices of my childhood, my covetous godparents and the young Father Frank, and I knew the message I had for this boy.

"The key is knowing where the source of truth lies," I said. "In essence, our inner voice tells us whom to trust. For me, there was never a doubt that my grandmother was right and those other voices were leading me away from the truth."

"What did those other voices, those bad ones, tell you?" asked one of the boys.

"Oh, various things," I said. "That I was nothing special, that I should work in the family business like my cousins, many such things. We hear those voices all our lives."

I was still hearing them then, a different chorus but with a message just as false and hurtful: that I was suited for no work more important than that of a classroom drudge. Indeed I'm hearing them to this day, condemning me to this life of exile, doomed to say Mass in a trailer before a congregation of narcoleptics for the rest of my life.

"You too must sort through the voices that you hear and follow the right one," I said, again directing my attention to Sean. "It may be a voice that you haven't heard yet. Or perhaps you are just beginning to hear it now. I don't know. But when you hear it, it will touch you in a special way. It will communicate to you in more than just words. You will feel things you have never felt before. And you will know without a doubt."

The boys were free to recreate for most of the latter part of the afternoon. Eventually they all gathered along the bank of the Tchefuncte, where the little river passed through the Benedictines' property, a few hundred yards from the main house and near one of the little "stations," which a few of the boys, including Sean, used as a makeshift cabana to change into swimwear.

I joined them there as the late afternoon sun was just dipping below the cypress trees on the western side of the river and seated myself on the porch of the little station before gathering the boys for dinner. From my place in the solitary rocking chair, sipping a tall glass of Father Millburg's mint tea, I had a keen insight into what the sainted John Bosco must have felt as he gazed upon his oratory of little Italian boys over a century ago. Not since my nights overseeing the great room at the Den had I had a taste of Saint Bosco's ecstasy.

Now here within my sight were eight boys, free of the trammels of school and work for perhaps the last time before surrendering their innocence to the world. All were shirtless except Finn and Finney, who had plopped themselves on a fallen cypress trunk like two giant manatees and dangled their meaty feet in the water. Four played a barefoot game of volleyball around a frayed net that appeared to have been picked at by a few too many of Millburg's winged wards. In the little river, Sean and one other boy splashed and chased each other like children. The other boy, though muscular and athletic himself, tried time and again to swim away but was no match for Sean's strength and speed in his watery element. Sean was dressed for the contest: He wore nothing but one of those tiny swimmer's bikinis. He caught his prey by the legs and tickled his bare feet until the boy screamed with glee and begged for my intervention.

"You need to know your own limitations, Sammy," I called to him. "You wanted to swim with the sharks. Don't complain when you get eaten by one." The other boys hooted their approval, and I held up my glass of tea as if to salute them while Sean gave Sammy's foot a playful bite and dragged him helpless through the water by his ankles.

Saturday morning I prepared a hearty breakfast of bacon, eggs, and fresh cantaloupe for the boys from Father Millburg's bounteous kitchen. Our host himself had risen before dawn and embarked on his wild woodpecker chase long before the rest of us began our day. The better part of the morning and early afternoon was devoted to prescheduled activities: Mass, a group meeting, a thirty-minute recess, private meditation, lunch. I made a point during breaks in the program to take a moment with each of the boys to give them their "surprise" letters from home. They all seemed pleased and sometimes moved by what their parents had written. A couple insisted on sharing theirs aloud with me; most walked off reading and rereading theirs. The most emotional response came from an unlikely source; Finn, one of the jolly fat boys, dropped his jovial façade and cried on my shoulder after reading what his father, another large man, had written.

"I know these years haven't been easy for you, son, as they weren't for me," Finn the Elder wrote, adding a list of cruelties he had suffered during his own school years, all of which were apparently completely unknown to the boy. I remembered the man from a parent conference three years earlier. Too big for the student desks, he had stood in the back of the room, smiling and nodding as I gave the standard PR speech, putting on a happy face about the wonderful opportunity the young men of Pope Paul VI were offered and how much I looked forward to working with their sons. Afterwards, he came up to me. "Guess who I am," he said, and we both laughed at the resemblance, not just the size but the round red face, the enervated gray eyes and curly orange hair. Seldom do I feel thin next to another human being, but this man was absolutely immense. Though no older than the rest of the parents, he leaned dependently on a cane as he walked, whether due to an orthopedic condition or simply to support his weight, I don't know.

I won't quote what I remember from the letter; though touching, it was a bit rife with platitudes and clichés. The father praised his son's strength in facing his lot without complaint and making the most of his life. I was able to relate to some of that. Never had I burdened my mother with the verbal pinpricks I had suffered from Rose or Ronnie or my classmates in grade school, even though they had continued well into the seminary—until Pedeaux, that sadistic lord of the refectory, temporarily starved me down to 180 pounds.

By mid-afternoon, I had distributed the letters to all the boys except Sean. I wanted to wait until the perfect time for our conference. It came during the long recreation, when all the boys were gathered once again near the river and Sean was swimming laps between its banks. The scene from my spot in the nearby station was virtually the same as Friday's: a veritable Twainian tableau, with a volleyball game on the grass and boys frolicking in and around the water. Sammy was back in the water but had apparently learned his lesson and forgone getting into another hopeless aquatic contest with Sean in favor of splashing the sated and inert Finn and Finney with water.

Sean was swimming alone, as seemed only appropriate since anyone else in the water would appear in comparison to his graceful elegance as absurd as a desperate flailing fish in a boat. I had his letter in my lap as I rocked myself almost into a monomaniacal trance watching him from the porch of the little station. I lost track of the number of times he traversed the width of the little river, but he appeared focused and disciplined like a sleek amphibious soldier on a mission, probably counting inwardly toward a predetermined goal he had set for his body. What was so striking was the sheer physicality of him, like pure skin and muscle, his body a fourth classical element along with the air it breathed, the water it propelled itself through, and the fire heating it from within. The idea of a soul and a mind accompanying that form was almost an adulteration. He wore only that tiny strip of cloth again, but even that seemed to be too much. If he had been nude, even the most prudish of schoolmarms would have marveled at the pure natural beauty of the scene.

I couldn't bring myself to summon him out of the water; even the business of the letter seemed too mundane to disturb him with—like beckoning the model for Michelangelo's *David* off his pedestal to fill out a tax form. So I waited for him to emerge on his own.

When at last he did, he reached for a yellow towel he had placed by the water's edge and patted himself dry, first his chest and shoulders, then one leg and finally the other. His thick black locks he shook dry with a powerful shudder that left him with his head thrown back in an attitude of seeming ecstasy, his eyes closed and face to the sun, whose attentions he seemed to have all to himself.

My own eyes remained fixed on him, despite my fear that he would open his and see me. Of course I could always say I was just trying to get his attention to talk about the letter, which incidentally I had opened and read there on the porch, careful to hide it behind a book of the Rule of Saint Benedict that I had procured from Millburg's library after lunch.

The letter was from his father, most unusual in a two-parent family. Normally the mothers pen the missives in the plural and both sign them. But for this seemingly seminal occasion, a three-day event that would take her son away from home and at least symbolically mark the juncture between the subordination of adolescence and the independence of manhood, Sean's mother was altogether silent. Oh, I suppose one could blame the woman's drug problem or say she was distraught over the daughter's attempted suicide, but surely the father could have found her in a lucid moment and gotten his wife's signature on the paper; and besides, it was *his* daughter too. At the very least the man could have mentioned the mother, if only to say she shared the sentiments he was expressing. Two of the boys in the group were from broken homes, but their parents had sent separate letters. Another oddity was that this letter was typed—even the signature, "Dad," without complimentary close. I found that grossly insensitive, especially considering the family's circumstances. It was becoming apparent that Sean's family was indeed broken, but in a different, more insidious way.

As for the letter's content, that too seemed egregiously inappropriate. It focused almost entirely on the writer, as if the rest of the family were mere supporting players in a production that was all about him. The mother was a cold, selfish woman whose substance abuse and frigid nature had driven him to seek affection in "perhaps inappropriate places." The sister's desperate act was a tragedy that no one felt more sharply than he. They needed to stay together as a family now more than ever if they were going to help the girl recover and try to heal "her and all of our wounds." He devoted a lengthy paragraph to an exposition of all he had done for the family, how tirelessly he had worked to build a successful practice so that they could live in a beautiful home (he even gave the number of bedrooms and square footage as if he were placing a classified ad) and Sean and the sister could go to the best schools, learn to ski in Aspen, and have their pick of colleges. The only personal note about his son was a reminder that he could have any new car he wanted upon graduation.

The whole letter seemed to be part excuse, part bribe or threat, as if the power to destroy the perfect picture of prosperity that he had taken great pains to paint in the letter lay with the boy. I recalled the sense I had that the school counselor didn't trust this man. He was a lawyer and so knew exactly what to say and what not to (recall the absence of a signature). There was obviously a great deal for an insider to read between the lines. All clues pointed to a mistress: the frigid wife, the blameless husband seeking illicit love, the devastated daughter. Would to God that the truth had not turned out to be so much worse.

Sean spread his towel on the grass between the volleyball players and the river and lay down in the sun. He faced the water, though, not the rest of the group, as if he had no more interest in their play than the most perfect and accomplished athlete would have in the clumsy struggles of street urchins. At first he sat up with his ankles crossed; it was the first time I noticed he wore a bracelet on one of them. His sinewy arms braced him, elbows locked and palms flat against the towel, the muscles of his back and triceps in exaggerated stress. What thoughts were going through his mind as he gazed across the Tchefuncte? Was he thinking of his despondent sister? His desperate, pathetic mother? Was he perhaps listening for the inner voice I had told him might sound at any time?

A minute or so and he lay back on the yellow towel, his arms at his side and knees drawn up and perpendicular to the ground. Then he relaxed his legs, opening them as if to invite the sun to kiss his inner thighs. At that point I rose from the rocker. With the letter in my hand, I silently approached him; I didn't want him to move until I was closer. Not until I was standing almost directly above him, blocking the sun and casting his supine form into shadow, did he become aware of me. Reflexively, he closed his legs and propped himself up on one elbow. One knee he bent to rest the sole of one foot—the one with the bracelet—on the ankle of the other. I could see how perfectly smooth and bronze his skin was. The bracelet dipped to the middle of his heel. Even his feet weren't untouched by the sun; if any different from the rest of his body, perhaps they were just a shade more lightly golden. Was he smiling at me or merely squinting from the brightness of the light around my head? That image of Tony Junior lying on the sheet in that clearing behind the levee came back to me, only it was different this time: Ronnie wasn't there to debase the scene. I had buried him and his stultifying influence. It was Tony alone that I saw, reaching out to me and smiling.

Sean lifted a hand to block the glare. He was smiling; I could see it clearly then. "Hey, Father," he said, and I asked him if he had had a good swim.

"Great," he said. "The water's so cool and I don't smell like chlorine!

He asked me if I liked to swim. In response I told a little white lie—that I hadn't swum in years, but as a boy I had enjoyed diving into the river near my grandmother's house. I have noticed that even the most taciturn boys can become perky and garrulous if I can somehow manage to steer the conversation to a sport or hobby they have an interest in, especially if I can demonstrate even a rudimentary interest in it myself. Sean wanted to know how deep the water was, the height of the "platform," what kind of dives I did, how far the swim to shore was, how long it took, etc. I told him we could talk more about that later, but for now I needed to show him his parents' letter. I didn't let on that I knew it was from his father alone. When I suggested we go for a walk, he rose and I led him to one of the covered paths along the river. Before we disappeared into the trees, I glanced back to make sure the other boys were accounted for.

When Millburg showed me the artificial grotto of Saint Benedict, I silently noted that it might be the most ideal place on the grounds
for a tête-à-tête with one of the boys. Accessible from only one direction
as the walking path dead-ended at the little shrine, the site was perfectly
secluded. The river itself abutted the grotto on one side, and the surrounding woods were quite dense; it would be impossible for anyone
to approach through the trees without being heard. Finally, the "igloo"
offered one last defense against intrusion. Unlike the little stations, with
their 360-degree porches and windows all around, the igloo was totally
sealed in brick, save for the single excrescence of a doorway, which incidentally rendered its interior, when viewed from the sunlit outside, absolutely pitch black. It was to the grotto that I, therefore, led Sean.

Out of either modesty or respect for me, Sean had wrapped the
yellow towel around his waist before we made our exit. Its bright banana
color in contrast with his golden skin and dark wet hair brought to mind
a virile Polynesian dancer. I imagined him bending backwards beneath a
limbo stick or moving his body in perfect synch to a chorus of rhythmic
drums, his muscles pronounced by the lurid glow of a score of tiki torches.

He walked along the path on my right, and the towel was tied
in a knot over his left hip, where the bikini was at its narrowest, so that
the tie completely obscured the little suit, and as he walked, the slit in
the towel revealed nothing but a side of naked skin from his ribs to his
braceleted ankle.

We made small talk on our way to the grotto, mainly about
Sean's swimming. He told me about a few upcoming meets and his hopes
to make the team at LSU. I snatched the opportunity to mention that I
knew he had missed a few practices lately.

"There's been some stuff going on," he said. His head drooped a
bit, and I could clearly see the vertebrae protruding from his upper spine.
There was a down of fine white hairs where they met the back of his neck.

"You mean with your sister?" I asked.

"That's part of it," he said.

"Is that why you didn't want to be in the play?"

"I didn't think I'd be into it right now," he said.

"You'd make a wonderful Conrad," I told him, and I touched him for the first time—just a light, three-fingered touch on that downy part of his neck. As I had hoped, it provoked a smile, which encouraged me to give him a supportive little squeeze.

We had just made it to the clearing of the grotto when I brought the letter out of my pocket. "Why don't you read this and then we can talk some more," I said.

Sean took the paper and paced the clearing of the grotto as he read it. At one point he leaned his back against the little birdhouse and put his free hand on top of his head. He started rubbing his right shin with the sole of his left foot as if he were scratching himself, but the way his toes were curled told me that the gesture was emotional, perhaps rooted in anger or frustration. The letter was two pages, single spaced, and Sean kept darting back and forth between them as if he were doing a handwriting comparison or checking for inconsistencies, always putting his hand back on his head as he read the same passages over and over.

There was a wrought iron bench beside the birdhouse. No doubt Millburg had spent hours perched upon it, reading the life and works of his beloved Benedict and feeding his little feathered friends who had stopped for a rest at the sanctuary. Sean sat himself on the bench and cursed his father under his breath—but in a kind of affected stage whisper (I recalled he had done some acting), obviously intended for me to hear. I took my cue and joined him on the bench.

"Do you want to talk?" I asked. A touch of some sort was appropriate here, but it was important that I be careful. The boy was angry and upset, and those emotions would be seeking an outlet. I needed to proceed with caution and help him find a harmless release, lest they be directed at me, a psychologically apt substitute for the villain father.

Remembering the precedent I had established just minutes before, I thought it would be safe to place my hand again on the downy nape of his neck. When that gesture was met with no resistance, I repeated the little squeeze. It worked, for he immediately began to open up.

"That son of a bitch. He thinks I give a shit about a car. That son of a bitch."

As much as I deplore profanity and have tried to keep my story gratuitously free of it, I quote Sean here only to give a sense of the boy's state of mind. Although his language became quite vulgar and abusive toward his father, so that I will have to paraphrase much of our exchange, I was encouraged by Sean's honesty with me, recalling from my days at the Den how the use of gutter language among boys in the presence of an authority figure can be a sign of the elder's acceptance by the group. It's all very tribal.

And in keeping with that observation, perhaps it was appropriate that we retired to the "cave." Sean was getting more and more upset as he railed vitriolically against his father, and I feared that despite our distance from the rest of the group, he might attract some attention. I led him into the little igloo, and we sat together in the second pew, between the door and the only other light source in the tiny room: the stained glass image of Benedict and his patron raven.

Sean was vague enough about his father's transgressions—accusing him of betraying the mother, ripping the family apart, causing the sister's suicide attempt—that I continued to hold to my rather obtuse theory that the man kept a mistress and had somehow been exposed. My counseling of the boy therefore proceeded upon that assumption: I began with an exegesis of the Garden of Eden story and the resultant fallibility of all men since that primordial fall and segued into Christ's forgiving Mary Magdalene. Just as I was warming to my subject with an inspired didactic speech on the weakness of many men for the charms of tempting Jezebels, Sean stopped me and delivered a stunning coup de theatre.

"He doesn't have a girlfriend," he said. "He was f------ my sister!"

Here Sean stood up and in his frustration grabbed a prayer book from the back of the pew before us and threw it—whether purposely or not I don't know—directly at the bust of Benedict. The statue turned out to be made of cheap plastic and not marble as it appeared, and it toppled over and fell off the little altar. Sean stood there above me, flexing his fists and panting as if he had just set a state record in the hundred-meter breaststroke.

Having no Bible stories at the ready that would quite fit this development, I silently touched Sean by one of his hands, which was still pumping like a beating heart. He tightened his grip around one of my fingers, as if I were his only link to salvation, and I pulled him back onto the pew beside me. Through his plaintive sobbing for his sister and defiant cursing of his father, the whole ugly story came out.

The base man had been molesting the girl right under the noses of his wife and son since the child began high school. The abuse roughly coincided with the wife's problem with pills and liquor; however, which of those issues was the chicken and which the egg would not be easy to determine—if indeed it even mattered anymore. On the night of the sister's suicide attempt, it was actually the father who discovered the girl's near-lifeless body, no doubt on a visit to her room to conduct more of his unspeakable business. He left the house without alerting anyone, though, hoping for the girl to die and the blame to fall upon the substance-dependent mother, a significant proportion of whose pharmacopoeia was later pumped out of the girl's stomach.

"The m----- f----- kept my mother doped up all the time," Sean said. "He kept her going to this f------ psychiatrist so she'd never know what was going on."

But Sean knew. He was aware of every one of his father's awful visits to his sister's room. It was the brevity of this one particular visit that made him go there himself that night.

I could feel the boy's anguished guilt. Placing my arm around his bare shoulders, I let him vent until he had told me the whole story. When no words were left, save for more damning execrations against the father, I coaxed his head onto my lap and massaged his scalp, sifting his thick, raven locks through my fingers. My other hand rested upon his chest. He was still breathing heavily, and his strong, vibrant lungs, swollen in their capacity from years of competitive swimming, made the effect even more dramatic. My hand rose and fell with his heaving chest like a raft on an unquiet sea. I rubbed the smooth muscle around the tiny buttons of his nipples, attempting to quiet the storm. He was immaculately groomed. His face was boyishly smooth, the shadow of a beard at his sideburns and under his chin betraying an incipient manhood to the sight but not to the touch. As my hand strayed from the firm, rubbery mound of his chest to beneath his arms, I could feel that he shaved there too; barely a hint of stubble was detectable.

My touch must have been a comfort to him because his breathing began to quiet. His eyes were red and moist, and when I asked him to close them, he obeyed. I loosened the knot in the towel that was still tied around his waist and lightly tapped his thigh. "Lift up," I said, and again he complied, not a hint of resistance, not even the opening of his eyes. I used the towel to pat them dry. Then I lifted his head from my lap and knelt by his side.

"Lie on this," I said. He opened his eyes and let me slide the yellow wrap under his back and shoulders. For his head I folded the top of the towel into a makeshift pillow. I sat at his feet and lifted one of his legs onto my lap. His foot was large and shapely. I rubbed the concave of his arch with the palm of my hand. The sole was soft, like the cushion of a kneeler. The nails of his long toes were pink and perfectly uniform. There were a few hairs around his ankle that had been missed by his razor. I tugged on them playfully, drawing a much-needed smile, though his eyes remained closed in an irrefutable sign of trust.

As I stroked the long, tight muscles of his calf, I asked him if indeed he didn't feel better having opened himself up a bit to another. He nodded his assent and I assured him that whatever we shared that day would be held as sacred as the bonds of a sacrament.

"If we are to hear an inner voice, it must speak to us alone," I said, perhaps a bit overzealous to work the theme of the retreat into our counsel.

There was some silence while I petted his knee, hoping he'd remember my words from group—that the inner voice does not always come to us in the form of words. I won't be so vulgar as to describe the signs of his need coming from his young body; they were unmistakable as he lay there in his swimsuit. It had been so many years since I had been called to minister to a boy like that that I became afraid. My head started to ache, and I began to shake and perspire. My breathing became heavy and belabored as Sean's got more relaxed, as if I was taking his anxieties upon myself. A tickling sensation on my scalp alerted me that the unthinkable was about to happen: My piece was coming loose from the anxiety and perspiration. Panic nearly took me over, the fear that it might fall off and land on Sean. I pictured it coming to rest on his stomach, like a hairy bird's nest fallen from the rafters; and I shivered at the humiliating prospect.

Whether it was because he felt my trembling, smelled my fear, or simply wanted to know why I had stopped rubbing his leg, Sean opened his eyes and saw me frantically trying to get my hair to stick to my head, pressing desperately with both hands like an anguished migraine sufferer. Instead of gawking at the ridiculous sight, though, he reacted with a sweetness that I had as yet not known he possessed.

"It's all right," he said, reaching up with one hand so that it joined my two, which were still shaking atop my terrified head. "It doesn't mater." And he helped me remove my piece, not even looking at the shameful thing but keeping his eyes locked on mine, an almost beatific smile on his lips, even as we let my hair drop to the floor behind our pew like a dead and harmless thing not even worthy of our notice.

For the next half hour, I was back at the Den, fulfilling my life's calling—giving, comforting, satisfying. Why must our glimpses of heaven on this earth be so fleeting? Despite what anyone would later say to the contrary, there was no doubt of Sean's wholehearted acceptance of my ministrations. He embraced me with all his being—his body and soul. The sad events to follow would not be "consequences" of what happened in the grotto that day, as my enemies would so hypocritically maintain, but the result of a malign meddling and perversion of the truth. Alas, though, I have but God and Saint Benedict as my witnesses. Let me be judged by them alone.

Approximately twenty-four hours remained of the retreat after my session with Sean. They passed rather uneventfully: dinner and another group Saturday night, breakfast followed by quiet contemplation and a final Mass Sunday before returning to New Orleans. Father Millburg monopolized most of my time Saturday night after the boys had retired to their quarters, regaling me ad nauseam about the various sparrows and finches he had seen on his little avian safari. Alas, there had been no sightings of that precious woodpecker of his. I dearly wished there had been; perhaps it would have kept him out for the night. Instead, as I sat there in the library trying to reflect on the progress I had made with Sean and contemplate the future of our relationship, he kept shoving Polaroids of tree holes and birds' nests in my face like he had just returned from a pilgrimage to Medjugorje and saying things like "Can you believe what perfect little engineers they are?"

My hope that Sean would seek me out in my classroom or perhaps look for me after school to talk were not fulfilled. Although we did pass in the halls Monday, and I made a point of being visible in the cafeteria when I knew he'd be having lunch, we did not speak. I did not see him at school Tuesday, so I checked the absentee list in the discipline office and found his name on it. When he was again absent Wednesday, I sought out the counselor to see if he had any information. Perhaps the family situation was deteriorating even further, depressing the boy to the point where he couldn't even come to school.

"I'm not at liberty to talk about that situation," the man said to me, his dismissive demeanor my first hint of the horrific events that were to follow. He hadn't even offered me a seat. I tried to tell him that Sean and I had gotten close during the retreat and that I believed that if I spent more time with him, we could have a real breakthrough; but he cut me off and told me I would have to talk to the president of the school about "that issue." When I mentioned that I had some incriminating information about the father, he rose from his chair, took me by the elbow, and practically shoved me out the door like a Fuller Brush man.

Why the president of the school? The principal, not the president, oversaw all curricular and disciplinary matters. It was to him that the faculty and students reported. The president occupied a fiscal position; he stayed in his office in the upper floor of the administrative wing, counting money and making business deals, seldom gracing the halls of the school except to glad-hand the wealthy parents on PTA nights. What interest could that chinless money changer possibly have in this affair? He was a priest, though, and by 1988 a mere layman held the post of principal. I should have sensed the political implications of that fact from the start. As it turned out, I didn't have to seek out the resident High Pharisee or even call his secretary to request that he vouchsafe me a few precious minutes of his time, for I was summoned to his lofty counting house the very next morning.

I arrived punctually for the nine o'clock meeting but was kept waiting in the lobby of his office suite for nearly an hour. When I told the secretary, who had that dour, ex-nun look about her, that I had a class at ten, I was informed that it had been "taken care of" and that Reverend Father President would be with me shortly. So I took my seat again and continued to peruse a few issues of the *Clarion Herald* and *U.S. News*, which were scattered on the visitors' waiting table. At nearly ten o'clock, the door to the president's office opened, and from it emerged a young priest whom I knew only vaguely by reputation but would soon come to have every reason to despise as a mortal enemy.

Walking past me without the slightest acknowledgement and slithering out the door was Theodore Weed, about to take his place as the third member of what I have pronounced the "Anti-Trinity." In the fall of 1988, I knew only vaguely of him, as I was, of course, living at Roussell House and not staying at the residence with the other priests who staffed the school. He was considerably younger than I. As matters began to unfold, and I could see that he was going to be not just a peripheral character in my life but indeed a redoubtable nemesis, I made it my business to learn that he was fifteen years my junior, born in 1959, the year of my grandmother's death.

He was the youngest of several sons, all scions of a powerful New Orleans judge. His brothers all went on to distinguished careers in law and politics, two later winning seats on the councils of Jefferson and Plaquemines Parishes. They were all tall and prepossessing figures, debonair and mustachioed like Clark Gable or Omar Sharif. All except Theodore, that is—the runt of the litter. Skinny and hairy like a monkey, he was prematurely bald, but not neatly and uniformly, more like a mangy dog or the butt of practical jokers who had mixed a depilatory with his shampoo. Not that the greasy little man ever washed his light bulb of a head, with that huge cranium tapering to a tiny pinched mouth and imploded chin. His tiny feet and hands could have been a child's except for the black hair, thick as a werewolf's, on his knuckles. He was far too unimaginative to be a lawyer and ugly to be a politician, with his rickety joints and pointy yellow teeth like a Graham Greene villain.

Why a duplicitous little misfit like Weed would become a priest in the first place wasn't as unfathomable a mystery as it might have first appeared, at least not by the eighties. Unable to compete with his successful brothers, but jealous by nature and craving their distinction and prestige, where else was he going to turn but to the Church? Its hierarchical structure would have attracted his type. With something akin to a corporate ladder to climb, there might be a future for a brown-nosing little yes-man like him. Perhaps he might even work his way up a few rungs and tread upon a few lowly subordinates.

He was already doing something like that in 1988. Along with his seminary work, he had taken accounting courses at Loyola and eventually earned a degree with which he was able to secure a position in the school's finance office and spare himself the ignominy of teaching. Now, with an office on the top floor, not far from the president's, he could consider himself part of administration and turn up his nose—hairy tufted nostrils and all—at the rest of the staff.

Of course I didn't know all of this yet as our paths crossed for the first time that morning in the administrative waiting room. As for the president himself, I had had precious little to do with him in my six years teaching after the Den closed, making me all the more anxious to know why he, and not the principal, had wanted to see me. It soon became obvious that the Church wanted to keep the ugly little issue that was unfolding under wraps and "in the family."

I will probably never know the complete truth of the matter, but the president's version of it was that Sean had revealed through confession what had happened between the two of us in the Grotto of Saint Benedict.

"The archbishop has been monitoring the situation," said the president, "and I can tell you that His Excellency is very disappointed, as am I, that someone whom the school placed in a position of trust would exploit a vulnerable child for his own advantage."

So Ratchett was in on it too! I might have known. I was suspicious of the confession story from the beginning, and once I knew that the grand master of the cover-up was involved, I was convinced it was a lie.

And what a masterful one at that! Their plan was becoming clear to me. The seal of confession protected the boy's identity, but not that of—as the president put it—"a culpable adult who cognizantly led him to sin." One word from the grand inquisitor and I would be strapped to the stake, faggots flaming at my feet. Clearly they wanted me to believe that Sean had made his confession to Weed, a totally preposterous idea. As if a dynamic young athlete, one of the most popular boys in the school, would confide in an anal little bean counter like him. I surmised that Sean must have gone to the counselor to talk. To *talk*, I say, not to "confess"; he was probably ready to tell the man the truth about the father, thanks to the headway I had made with him at Tchefuncte. No doubt the counselor, piqued and jealous at the progress I had made with the boy in spite of his own failure, grew suspicious and prodded the poor boy for irrelevant details of our session together: "So, what made you decide to talk to Father Tony about this? . . . Did it come out in group? . . . Oh really, you had just come from a swim? . . . And tell me about this secluded little grotto?"

They're all master interrogators. Sean probably thought he was talking to someone he could trust, as he had with me. He was ready to share with this man the truth about his father and finally put a stop to his family's torment. Instead, the focus was shifted onto what the boy had done with me. Never mind that it was through my methods, my intercession, that the boy had finally opened up and felt that inner voice that he had failed to sense for so long. He must have left that office feeling guiltier than he had over allowing the father's abuse to go on for so long. It was all so pathetic.

And so typical of the Church. The counselor must have taken his information straight to the president, who told him to keep quiet and not speak a word about the matter—especially to me. That would explain my rude dismissal from his office that morning, his practically shoving me out the door like a harping solicitor. The introduction of Weed into the picture smacked of Ratchett's handiwork: using a dispensable toady like that to ensure his own and the president's deniability. There was surely a connection between Old Judge Weed and Sean's father, who of course was a lawyer, although I never got around to investigating that angle. But in few cities do birds of a feather flock so exclusively together as in New Orleans; the two men probably shared drinks at NOBA socials on a regular basis.

Weed's brushing past me without notice as he left the president's office suddenly made sense—not that I would expect much in the way of social graces from the little worm, but his obvious avoidance of even momentary eye contact was telling. Clearly he already knew who would be waiting outside that door. They had been talking about me—probably getting their instructions via telephone directly from Ratchett.

Although I'm sure that my doom had already been decided, the president would only tell me in his office that morning that I had been relieved of my teaching duties effective immediately and that I was going to be reassigned with due speed. I would be given the remainder of that day and the next to prepare to move my effects out of Roussell House.

But where to, I wondered. The rectory there at John Paul came to mind. There Ratchett could easily have the president and his network of informers like Weed keep an eye on me, but keeping me around the school would have been awkward since they had in effect just fired me from the faculty. And what work would they have me do—fill the concession machines and empty the dollar changers? They had an old half-wit Christian Brother doing that at the time, but he must have been eighty. I wouldn't have put it past them to have me take his place; it would have been the perfect insult for someone of my stellar academic credentials. And I'd be reporting to Weed in the finance office. How appropriate!

They made me wait through the weekend before discovering my

real fate, and I must admit that considering what they suspected me of, it was every bit the coup de grace I should have expected from them. They were making me the live-in chaplain at a home for retired nuns in Gentilly. What better way to punish one suspected of delighting in dalliances with young boys than to maroon him among a bunch of drooling, incontinent old scolds! And on top of that, they set me up with that lazy-eyed psychiatrist, too—the Jesuit dwarf Manresa with his fish-feeding therapy.

The real truth, though, is that I could have weathered it all—Ratchett and his spies, the gropings of that simian psychiatrist, those senile old nuns, and even more—if Sean and I had only been able to build on what we had begun at Tchefuncte, but my work there had all been for nothing, even less than nothing when all was said and done. I tried to phone Sean's house several times that week, but all I got were recordings, even from the children's number. Before I had moved my things out of Roussell House, I learned that the family had gone into seclusion because Sean had shot himself in the bathroom with the father's gun.

I don't know how I managed to bear another loss. As we do in moments of desperation, I let my mind carry me back helplessly to other forlorn moments of devastation. Poe called this "perverse," that uncontrollable urge of ours to batter our anguished souls with exactly what they need the least: more pain. I thought first of Tony Junior, then the sad fate of Jason, the first boy I had really reached all those years before at the Den. Now this third blow.

I kept calling the children's number, even after they had moved me into the old nun house, just to hear Sean's voice on the recording. Eventually it was replaced by the sister's, the weak, mousy sound of a victim. I heard through teacher connections that she was cutting herself. Ironically she had survived, though, as had the father. I'm sure the school knew about him from that unprincipled counselor's reaction when I broached the subject, but with Sean no longer around, the rascal's guilt was a matter of my word against his; and they knew I couldn't come forward without risking that everything that transpired between me and Sean would be dragged through a public slime pit. There had probably been a meeting between the school and the father—or more likely between all of their lawyers—wherein the whole ugly matter was declared a standoff.

How the Church always loves such an outcome: allowing it to protect its own interests and those of the wealthy and influential, however putrid the reek of guilt surrounding them, at the expense of the innocent and powerless—like an expendable faculty member and a beautiful boy's memory. The father had effectually killed his entire family—his son was dead, his wife an addict, and his daughter no longer able even to feel pain. Yet he was able to continue his successful law practice while I was upended, forced against my will to see that stoolpigeon shrink and wait on a bunch of old women like an overqualified attendant in a senior citizens center. That sorry place would prove to be my last official Church appointment before Kattannachee. The horrendous decade of the eighties couldn't possibly be over too soon.

CHAPTER TEN

CONSOLATION

Originally, Gentilly was a plantation owned by two French brothers Dreux in the early nineteenth century. Today it is a large chunk of the greater New Orleans area lying just north and east of the city. Its name is virtually ubiquitous along the northern fringes of the city between Bayou Saint John to the west and the Industrial Canal to the east. Everything from flea markets to auto body shops to washaterias bears the name Gentilly.

The neighborhood of Gentilly Terrace was developed in the early twentieth century on beautiful terraced lots along Gentilly Boulevard. To passing motorists, the houses of Gentilly Terrace present a strikingly regal view, resting several feet above street level, a most unusual phenomenon in a city so otherwise topographically monotonous as New Orleans.

Our Lady of Consolation was founded in 1978, when a childless widow of a well-known surgeon willed the house her parents had built when she was a child to the archdiocese with the stipulation that the property be used as a rest home for aged female religious. The usual lawsuits ensued, jilted heirs claiming anyone who would give everything to the Church must by necessity be a doddering incompetent, but the archdiocese almost always wins those things, especially with a cagey manipulator like Franklin Ratchett at the helm, forever cultivating close ties with wealthy old women like this and being able to produce the letters and photographs to prove it. The place had been open for ten years when I moved in.

I knew little of that eastern area of New Orleans, but I learned that I was near one of the city's many cultural/demographic crossroads. My awakening came on my first Sunday afternoon at Our Lady of Consolation. It had been a tradition before my arrival for the more ambulatory sisters in the home to be taken for a "ride" after Mass and Sunday dinner. The sisters cackled their admiration for the lovely lawns and gardens as we drove east on Gentilly Boulevard a little ways. A couple commented that the neighborhood had always reminded them of their early "communities" (nunspeak for convents). Most of these old nuns had begun their religious lives as mere girls when the southern part of the state was dotted with rural convents. The sisters spoke fondly of places like Saint Martinville, Grand Coteau, Eunice, and Ville Platte. Most of these women didn't come to New Orleans until the sixties or seventies, when the Church closed their dwindling little "communities" and shipped them here to try to stanch the flow of young nuns out of the convents and maintain some semblance of a religious presence in the city's elementary schools. It seemed that we had only driven a few blocks when the oaken canopy over Gentilly Boulevard gave way to barren utility poles and crass billboards advertising cheap vodka and Negro cosmetic products.

"Lock your doors," admonished one of the sisters, for I had unwittingly crossed over the unmarked but altogether psychologically real boundary between Gentilly and what had become known in recent decades as "New Orleans East." The sisters were unanimously adamant that we take advantage of the first available U-turn and fly back to the protective arms of Our Lady of Consolation.

"We'd better go back," said one.

"Father Fitzgerald never took us this far," added another.

It was as if they had become once again the belles of their Southern girlhoods, as loath to venture across the tracks into the Negro section of their little towns as to tell their fathers they were running away to join the gypsies or elope with a Jew.

The street signs I noted, as I was looking for a place to turn around before one of the sisters had a stroke, indicated that Gentilly Boulevard had become Chef Menteur Highway, the appellation by which the street would be known for several more miles through the black areas of New Orleans East and beyond the Vietnamese settlements even farther east before it became the two-lane Highway 90 to the Mississippi Gulf Coast.

The sisters were obviously relieved when I managed to turn around before crossing the Industrial Canal, the Rubicon of New Orleans East. Once we were safely headed west, beneath the protection of the Gentilly oaks, they began to lament the change in the area's demographics since the seventies.

"My nephew used to live in a nice apartment on Lake Forest," one of them said. "And not too long ago either, when I was teaching at Saint Michael the Martyr. Now they've turned it into Section 8 housing. He had to move to Metairie. It's just a sin."

"I used to have my hair done out by Michoud when they first opened the house," said another. "Now it's a Vietnamese pool hall."

"Oh no!" said a third.

"Yes, and I heard there's a massage parlor upstairs where they used to keep all the beauty supplies."

"Oh, Blessed Mary!"

I don't want to give the impression that the sisters harbored any un-Christian racial prejudices. Several of them had taught black children, volunteered at Charity Hospital, even brought Thanksgiving baskets into

the projects. Ministering to other races in their underprivileged environ-
ments or being served by them in one's own is a far cry from ethnic as-
similation, and truly it's about as much as we should expect from these
old women, considering the worlds they came from.

I know it's getting ahead of my story, but while I'm on this subject, I can't help but think of what they did to my poor mother, abandoning her in that racially mixed nursing home in Chalmette, across that
hideous green bridge from New Orleans East. You can't even tell the help
from the visitors in that place. You can see what malign plotters they
were, arranging for me to live in a house full of elderly women so that I
would intimately learn their psychologies, then condemning my poor old
mother, who wouldn't know New Orleans East from Nairobi, to those
women's most dreaded fear while ensuring that I would remain hundreds
of miles away, powerless to help her.

But again, I stray ahead of my narrative. I would remain at Our
Lady of Consolation for seven years. To a casual observer, it might appear
to have been a genial assignment, benign at the worst. The accommodations were spacious, a decided step up from the rat hole they had me in
at Roussell House. I had my own bedroom and private bath. There was
a cozy little patio and garden behind the house, where the sisters grew
fresh mint and basil—plenty of sun for two hibiscus trees and some magnificent pink and white camellia bushes. In the evenings, when it was not
too muggy or cold and I could steal a few minutes away from the women,
I liked to read Faulkner on the patio's chaise lounge and allow myself to
be whisked back by his verdant prose and the soft, mesmerizing scent of
night jasmine. Every three years the Church supplied the house with a
new Lincoln, which I had little official use for besides bringing the house-
keepers to the grocery and the sisters to their doctors and, of course,
out for their little Sunday afternoon rides. I certainly wasn't overworked.
Theoretically, I was supposed to say Mass every morning at seven, but
there were seldom more than three or four women at the place in any

condition to attend; so after a few weeks, I began asking those few to sign up for the mornings they'd like to participate, and if no one asked for a particular morning, I'd sleep in with the rest of them.

Though my stay at Our Lady of Consolation was a year shorter than my tenure at the Den, it would seem ages longer. Despite the apparently pleasant living conditions, I soon felt surrounded by death and decay, trapped in that house like a desperate character in a Southern Gothic world of dentures and Depends. Unlike the Den, where the years passed in a blink, like a burst of youthful vigor, Gentilly was a timeless eternity, the weeks and months distended like the bellies of those torpid old nuns.

My first three years there, before I began the street mission that saved my sanity, were especially otiose. Perhaps it was because the sisters reminded me of my own mother; Josie was over seventy by then and would inevitably need care herself before long. Who was there to provide it for her besides me, and where would the funds come from now that she had poured nearly all of her Miggliore money down her scheming sister's drain? Would we have to sell the house? It was the only property we had left.

It hadn't really occurred to me before, but I had passed midlife myself, in my mid-forties when I moved into Our Lady of Consolation. I was overweight, as usual, and would be even more so in time from the inertia of the old nun house, beginning to sag at the jowls and chin, and bald, of course, though I was covering it up in a more permanent way since the embarrassing slippage at Tchefuncte.

I needed to find a new stylist since Ronnie died. For two years I had been chopping at the fringe myself and gluing my piece down with a foul-smelling do-it-yourself concoction I'd pick up at Sally's. After my encounter with Sean in the grotto, though, I began visiting one of those hair replacement salons for a weave. My piece was then more or less permanently attached to my real hair, and I'd only have to look at my bald head when I'd go in for a tightening every six weeks or so. No more groping for my hair in the middle of the night for fear someone might see me exposed if I paid a little visit to the kitchen for a midnight snack, not that those myopic old crones would have even noticed. Nor would I have to worry about Sister Rita snatching it in one of her arm-flailing seizures or Sister Immaculata, stone deaf and nearly blind, knocking it off as I stooped to offer her Communion, powerless to fend off her curious gropings with a chalice in one hand and wafer in the other.

In any event, whether it was from the oppressive thoughts of my own aging or the more imminent mortality of my mother, those first few years at Consolation were quite a trial for me. I estimate I performed the Anointing of the Sick an average of twice a week. It became a kind of contest to some of the sisters, this keeping score of their sacraments like girl scouts racking up merit badges.

And then there were the doctor visits! If the niggardly archdiocese would have let me spend as much time in classrooms and libraries during those years as I did in waiting rooms—between the proctoscopes and the cystoscopes, the chest pains and the fecal impactions, the loose dentures and the myocardial infarctions—I could have taken my PhD! Couple all that with my own mandatory visits to Manresa, that Jesuit shrink, and it's no small wonder I didn't really lose my mind during those years—or at least become a hopeless hypochondriac. If one of my charges wasn't recovering from a fall that left her with a sprained wrist or ankle or a bruise as grand and dark as an eggplant, another was convalescing from a hip replacement or cataract removal. A musty sweet odor of impending decay, what Faulkner called "the smell of old female flesh," pervaded the house as if the ghost of a senile priest were forever walking its floors, burning incense in an ancient pumpkin and blessing the rooms with the dust of a thousand crushed mothballs.

To make my plight in the old nun house even more oppressive and humiliating, in 1990 the archdiocese appointed that ambitious little baboon Theodore Weed special embassy to the archbishop for the Gentilly and New Orleans East region, no doubt in reward for his complicity in the Tchefuncte conspiracy. A mere two years after passing that test, he had ascended several steps of the Church's stairway to glory, leaving behind forever the workhorses who staff the parochial schools for a cushy position in archdiocesan administration and perhaps earning at long last the right to hold his misshapen head up at table with his overachieving brothers.

He was perfectly suited for the position. The job included acting as "stand-in" for Ratchett at events the archbishop was unable to attend, such as silver and golden jubilees of religious, church fairs, and bingo kickoffs. Weed's function at such affairs would be to greet everyone in the name of the archbishop, expressing His Excellency's most sincere regrets for his being unable to join them for this most important occasion due to some excuse that they always called "other exigent duties in the name of the Holy Father" or some such baloney. He'd then read the "Special Message from the Archbishop," a canned little speech, insubstantial enough to fit any occasion and written by someone on Ratchett's staff, probably a nun with an English degree.

The special embassies also handle investigations into reports of Church improprieties and complaints from parishioners about the management of parish schools and properties, conveniently allowing Ratchett to give a politic response like "I'm not aware of the specifics of that issue, but one of my staff is looking into it" when probed by reporters. Then, of course, there are all those perks that come with being even a minor player in the arena: lunches with monsignors, teas with mothers superior, a driver at his whimsical disposal, a staff of young seminarians eager to please, trips to places like Acapulco, San Francisco, and Vancouver as part of Ratchett's entourage at the annual Conference of North American Bishops. I could go on, but as special embassy, Weed's predominant responsibility would be to "visit" the various Church properties and institutions in his assigned region and report his findings directly to the archbishop. For his inspections of Consolation, he would arrive at midmorning. He never drove himself—that would have been beneath his dignity—and he always sat in the back seat, reducing his driver (always a handsome young seminarian) to the level of a chauffeur.

He always stayed for lunch, and it sickened me to see everyone fawning over him like Padre Pio incarnate. Now and then one of the dizzier nuns would address him as Your Excellency or ask to kiss his ring. I never saw him correct one of them; he'd just smile and proffer his ring (probably that cheap thing they've been giving out at ordinations since the eighties). He'd meet individually with the house staff—the cook and housekeeper and a nurse if one was present that day. The sisters he'd interview privately in their rooms, asking them questions about the conditions of the house: Were they comfortable? How was the quality of the food? Were they receiving sound and adequate "spiritual guidance"?

It may all seem harmless, just part of the job of being the eyes and ears of the archdiocese, except for the more pointed, probing questions I learned he was asking that weren't on his official list. A couple of the sisters who were still sharp enough to see through his unctuous machinations, and who knew where their fealty justifiably lay, told me he had been leveling suspicious interrogatories at them, hardly even bothering to cloak the fact that it was I he wanted information about. One of them, who had a knee fused since childhood and was unable to bend it those sixty-odd years, felt indebted to me for driving her downtown and waiting with her three hours for an orthopedic shoe fitting.

I was out on the patio the first time the two of them came to talk to me about Weed and his snooping. It was sometime in January 1991. I remember because Weed had delivered the archbishop's holiday message to us, basking as always in his own self-importance. Then he blessed the place for the new year, as if I couldn't have done that myself. When he called for his car, I made a point of excusing myself to do some work in the garden. "I'm going to cut a few camellias," I said. "They're absolutely gorgeous right now." I knew he wouldn't follow me after that. The little monster is allergic to flowers! The sisters had made that discovery a few months earlier when they gave him a tour of the house shortly after he ascended to his new position and one of them presented him with a freshly plucked hibiscus. "The way he cringed, you'd think I was waving a toe of garlic in the face of the Devil," she said. They all found it hysterically ironic that someone named Weed would be mortified by the proximity of a flower.

The two nuns joined me in the garden after Weed's car had whisked him away. They must have sensed my discomfiture around him, for as if to soothe my anxiety they brought a pot of coffee and some blueberry king cake. Over the refreshments, they told me what the meddling priest had said to them.

"He wanted to know if you're here when you're supposed to be," said Sister Delia. She liked me because I took her to the beauty parlor every third Saturday morning and didn't tell anyone she had a bald spot the size of a cardinal's biretta; her stylist slipped one day and let me walk into her cubicle before she had put her veil back on. "Do you ever take the car and go off and we don't know where you are?"

"He asked me about phone calls," said Sister Margarita, the one with the fused knee. What she called her "peg leg" stuck straight out like a prong on a forklift when she sat down. Immaculata, the blind one, was forever tripping over it. "Are we ever neglected because you're on the phone, and do we ever get calls from strange people?"

"Strange *men* is what he asked me," corrected Delia. "And he wanted to know about visitors, too, not just phone calls. 'Does Father Tony allow strangers to come into the house?' was how he put it."

"Yes, he asked me that too," said Margarita. "It was like he wanted to know if you ever bring friends here to visit. I wanted to say 'So what if he does?' What business is it of his?"

What business indeed, I thought. But even though I was pleased to see that they were coming to share my antipathy for that bête noir Weed, I felt it prudent on my part to appear temperate, lest they become suspicious as to the root of our enmity.

"I've known Theodore for years," I said. "We worked together at the school." I rose to pour us each another cup of coffee. "If I don't seem myself around him, please don't blame him. You see, we lost one of our students to suicide—a boy Theodore and I both knew."

"Oh, dear," said Delia. Margarita crossed herself.

"Perhaps we remind each other of that sadness," I said.

"We're so sorry, Father," said Margarita.

"I know," I said. "Theodore is very young, you know, despite his looks, and I know he wants very much to meet with His Excellency's approval in his new position. Between us, he was a great disappointment to his father."

"Oh, yes, the judge," said Delia. She hadn't had a chance to swallow her last bite of king cake when I mentioned the man, and some purple sugar seeped out of her mouth. "He almost became mayor back in the sixties, remember?"

"Yes, I remember," said Margarita. "He was so handsome. Why didn't he ever run again?"

"He knew better," said Delia. "New Orleans will never have another white mayor."

"You can say that again," agreed Margarita. "Christ will come down off the cross before that happens!"

"Exactly," resumed Delia. "Why do you think all his sons moved out to Jefferson and Plaquemines?"

Margarita shook her head and patted down the napkin she had draped over her peg leg.

"My nephew, the lawyer, knows him," continued Delia. "Don't tell anybody, but he told me he's crooked."

She finally wiped the purple sugar from her mouth with a finger, and for a moment she was Oberon's grandmother, an aging fairy with her fingers dipped in magic dust for a spell she was too superannuated to effect.

"I heard one of his brothers might run for Parish president," said Margarita.

"Which one?" asked Delia. "The one on the council or the one who used to be mayor of Kenner?"

"I'm not sure," said Margarita. "I get all those Jefferson politicians confused. It seems like they're all related to each other."

"At least they're all white," said Delia. "I'll ask my nephew."

"Anyway," I said, "as if it wasn't difficult enough for Theodore, knowing that he couldn't live up to Judge Weed's expectations, the loss of that boy was quite a blow. Theodore was his spiritual advisor, you know—so that was like another failure to him. So if he appears overzealous in his new capacity, let us attribute it to the need to please another kind of father."

"We'll pray for him," said Margarita.

"And for the boy too," said Delia.

After that I became ultra-alert to Weed's activities. Delia and Margarita could always be depended on to tell me whatever he said to them, but those two trusty old souls, despite their apparently spry natures, were not going to live forever. Plus Weed was likely to begin tapping some of the others for information if he didn't get anything useful out of them, and a few of those old crones could hold a grudge like Madame Defarge. They were likely to tell stories about me because I didn't show up in their room just once like Johnny-on-the-spot with a bedpan when they screeched out in the middle of the night, or if at confession I gave one of them a stiffer penance than another for an equitable transgression. ("You gave me a dozen Hail Marys just for cursing that *Price Is Right* contestant when she only got a half dozen for passing gas and letting Immaculata take the blame. I don't think that was fair.")

Not that there was much for Weed to dig up—not in those first few years anyway. The only thing he might have discovered was that I wasn't saying morning Mass with the regularity of the sunrise, but it would have been difficult to prove that. I was cognizant of other dangers, though. A few of the sisters might be tempted to talk to Weed simply out of loneliness. Even a repulsive social pariah like Weed could easily endear himself to one or two of those sad old women who might say whatever they thought would please him.

Another possibility that I couldn't turn a blind eye to was that in the absence of incriminating evidence against me, Weed might file false reports with the archdiocese. Just as some of the weaker sisters might condemn me by way of ingratiating themselves with him, so might he seek to advance himself in the eyes of the archbishop at my expense. There was never a doubt in my mind that Ratchett was pulling Weed's strings, nor was it any less obvious that His Excellency had become the substitute father figure in whose eyes the sad little priest so desperately needed to succeed.

1991 would prove to be a watershed in my life's story. I would mark my forty-seventh birthday that year, the twentieth anniversary of my ordination having passed the previous fall. That occasion, though normally a joyous one, seemed at the time only a grim reminder that my better days were behind me and that I had little to look forward to in the coming decades other than presiding over a succession of old women who had outlived God's own purpose for them. I was beginning to doubt the soundness of His judgment. It seemed that for every just and de-served doom—the rotting of my aunt's artificial face, Ronnie's death by the plague of the eighties—there were even more injustices: Uncle An-thony's life of luxury, Ratchett's ascendancy to the pinnacle of power and prestige, Sean's untimely death for which his culpable father would never have to answer, my own mother's penury.

There seemed to be no place for me to turn. My future in the Church was a forlorn specter of futility and disillusionment; I couldn't hope that they would appoint me to even a lowly assistant pastorate at the most blighted parish in Greater New Orleans or vouchsafe me a meaningful ministry. Meanwhile, a cankerous Weed flourished in the de-flowered ground of New Orleans East, and his malevolent patron, Franklin Ratchett, had one more source besides that guileful shrink informing him of my every move.

Yet what future did I have outside the Church for that matter? With little of my mother's share of the Miggliore money left for me to inherit, I couldn't very well doff my collar and thumb my nose at Ratchett and all his sycophants. Yes, I would have a house to live in, but what would I do for an income? Without the PhD that the archdiocese had blocked me from pursuing, my academic options were dismally few. On the college level, I'd be doomed to the dead-end job of instructor, reading wretched essays on the pros and cons of capital punishment by remedial students who should have been driving potato chip trucks. My high school options were hardly rosier: Ratchett was sure to use his influence with every administrator in the city to frustrate my search for employment in the parochial system, condemning me perforce to the Kafka-esque Hell of the New Orleans Public Schools, where "educators" scrub feces off classroom walls and patrol the stairwells for adolescent sodomites. I might as well apply to the Peace Corps and lead hygiene seminars in Somalia.

Adding to my sense of disquietude, my hair was beginning to give me problems. Since I switched to the more or less permanent weave, my piece and I were only separated for an hour or so every six to eight weeks when I visited the salon. Despite the convenience and security the new process offered, I had begun to see its drawbacks. It was very difficult to wash beneath the cap, especially for the first few weeks after a tightening. A month, or even less, after a visit, and the shampoo and conditioner buildup around the perimeter of the cap started producing an odor like rancid oyster grease. The itching could be unbearable. My scalp craved stimulation. There were times when I longed to scour it with a Brillo pad in the confessional box. I came to take such delight at the salon when the girl cut out the weave and shampooed my head that I began to feel guilty of some kind of epicurean indulgence, like a patrician of ancient Rome, pleasured by a hired strumpet. Could I have been any more brainwashed by Catholic preachment?

I was gaining weight again too. Of course I hadn't been what one might call thin since my seminary days, when Father Pedeaux was starving us all into pious submission. But at least the weight gain leveled off in the eighties, after I left the Den and Martha's cooking. There was certainly little opportunity for gluttony while I was taking my meals at Roussell House, where the fare could best be compared to the leftovers at a Dickensian workhouse.

Of course I was busy in those days, too, commuting daily between Roussell and the school and traipsing up and down those halls and stairs for my classes. What did I do at Our Lady of Consolation besides take three full meals a day, watch soap operas with the old nuns, and stuff coconut cake and gingerbread into my mouth all day? With my exercise consisting of helping one of the semi-ambulatories to the car for a drive to the gerontologist, is it any wonder I had blown up like a medieval bishop?

My own physical and emotional health was but one of the multitude of factors that led me to begin my street mission that summer of 1991. Never before in my life, even at the closing of the Den, had I felt as desperately lost and forlorn as in those months immediately preceding my epiphany. Depression stifled my reason like a black hood over the head of the condemned, for condemned I certainly seemed to be, my career in the Church a cruel and pitiful joke. My few brushes with happiness—the Den and then Tchefuncte—would soon be the dim memories of an old man doomed to live out his professional life as a caregiver in a geriatric nunnery.

For months I could only be lifted from the Slough of Despond by the thought of food and the desire to avenge myself on the human harpies who had so plagued me. With naught but sinful conceits to energize me, I wondered if I offered anything pleasing to the sight of God or if I was just a hateful bugbear in His eyes. Though I prayed day and night for deliverance, I must beg forgiveness that there were times when I contemplated joining Sean in the ultimate act of desperation, so little faith did I have that the Holy Spirit would ever come into my life again and shine His light on my poor benighted soul.

But praise be to God! He did come, stealing into my dreams one dark night in June. It had been a particularly trying day. Sister Aquilina, who had taught art at the elementary level since the dawn of Cubism, insisted that everyone rise for morning Mass in honor of her sanctified namesake's feast day. As if rising at the crack of dawn and gathering nine old women and their teeth and various ambulatory aids was not trial enough for one morning, I found Aquilina at the door of the little chapel (a converted sitting room with an attached bath that functioned as a sacristy), barring my entrance.

"I've decorated the chapel for Saint Aquilina's day," she said. "I want us all to go in together."

She insisted that the lights remain off until we had all found seats, which was not difficult since the pews were only three deep in the tiny chapel. In the darkness I could barely discern before the altar three unaccustomed objects on small tables arranged more or less symmetrically, the one in the middle considerably larger than the two flanking it. I assumed the proud old art teacher must have prepared some displays for us, probably visual aids in appreciation of the life of Saint Aquilina.

I was close. It was not the life, but the *death* of the saint on which we were all about to receive a most edifying and unforgettable lesson. Our hostess hit the light switch, and all at once our eyes were accosted by a gruesome triad. On each of the tables to the left and right of the altar was a framed portrait of a male figure who appeared to be trapped in a dark valley and engulfed in flames. Above the flames, a headless girl in blue robes hovered, holding out her head in her hands so that a stream of blood trickled from the severed neck onto the burning man below. The captions read "Diocletian in the Pit of Hell" and "Volusian in the Pit of Hell."

I eventually read the explanations that Aquilina had written on index cards placed in front of the displays and learned the inspiration for the macabre pictures. Saint Aquilina was the young daughter of Christian Phoenicians who was martyred by decapitation at the age of twelve during the emperor Diocletian's Great Persecution in the early fourth century. Her crime was refusal to join the "imperial cult," the joining of which was tantamount to pledging allegiance to the empire and renouncing Christianity. Volusian was apparently a local Roman official—perhaps a governor or magistrate of some sort (the index card merely referred to him as one of Diocletian's local "goons")—responsible for carrying out the emperor's decrees in Phoenicia. The pictures were intended to convey the boundless spirit of forgiveness of the Christian martyr, who would strive to lessen the suffering of her persecutors even by quenching with her own blood the fires that consumed their damned souls.

Our gathering might not have ended in panic and chaos had those two works been the only objects on display. Half of the myopic old nuns couldn't make out the pictures from a distance, and even if they could, they would have hardly found them more terrifying than some of the illustrations from the old catechisms they taught from before Vatican II. (I can recall from the book in use when I was in first grade one particular depiction of a hapless group of men and women surrounded by fire and extending their arms, scorched and welted by the flames, to an angel of deliverance. And this was just Purgatory!) The two pictures, though, being smaller and peripherally located, didn't draw the attention of the larger display in the middle.

It consisted of two basic pieces: a large headless doll—perhaps an old Chatty Cathy, maybe three and a half feet long, counting the head—

and a bare wooden chair modified into a crude model of a guillotine. The doll, obviously meant to represent the martyred girl Aquilina, was lying face up on the seat of the chair, clad in a blood-bedaubed white sheet. Both its legs, as if crippled like Margarita's with the fused knee, extended straight back toward the altar. A piece of cardboard, cut at an angle and spray-painted silver to mimic the blade of the death machine, was glued in place between the posts of the chair. It, too, was stained with blood, which of course ended up being diluted ketchup. The severed head rested on the floor of the chapel like the shrunken victim of a voodoo sacrifice, oddly free of blood, which phenomenon I interpreted as a symbol of the beatific nature of the young girl it represented, but turned out to be a pragmatic concession intended only to keep ketchup stains off of the pine planks.

Neither the crudity of the display (it could have passed for a fourth-grade social studies project on the Terror) nor the absurdity of the anachronism it presented had a pacifying effect on the old nuns. They were rendered either catatonic or hysterical by the sight. All except Delia, that is, who I noticed stood by in stoic silence while the others were either collapsing into their pews or scurrying out of the chapel in an Apocalyptic panic as quickly as their walkers and palsied old limbs would take them.

"I knew she was going to do something like this," Delia said to me later. "I used to teach with her. One year she made her summer school students bring in Barbie dolls and chop off their heads. The parents were furious."

It took hours to restore normalcy to the house. My regular duties were compounded for the rest of the day. Some of the sisters wanted to confess either the profane words they had uttered in their panic or the wicked thoughts they had entertained toward Sister Aquilina for engendering them. Others insisted on receiving the Anointing of the Sick for the strain on their weak hearts. Aquilina holed up in her room all day, probably out of shame, but ostensibly threatening a hunger strike until she got a "formal apology" for what she referred to in the note she taped to the outside of her door as "the disrespectful reception of my tribute to one of the purest saints in the pantheon." It really was, if you'll pardon the rather ironic cliché, the day from Hell.

I didn't expect to sleep a wink that night. Stressful days since Tchefuncte had been staying with me into the wee hours of the morning, scenes of conflict or whatever unpleasantries had taken place replaying over and over in my mind until I was driven from my bed in search of food or a volume of Proust to read myself to sleep. I had even considered asking Manresa, the Jesuit psychiatrist I was still seeing, for a prescription but thought better of that since I didn't want Ratchett, and God knows who else, to know I was on "medication." It should have been even worse than usual since several of the sisters had signed up for Mass again the next morning, and I had the promise of another interminable day looming over me. Would Aquilina really go forward with her hunger strike? Would the others try to get even with her? Would they try to draw me into the conflict? Would Weed somehow find out about the feast day fiasco?

As it turned out, though, when I laid head to pillow that night, I felt a healthy and peaceful kind of exhaustion, such as I hadn't experienced since my nights at the Den. I wondered from whence such a serene feeling, like the aftermath of a day of hard but productive work, had come. I realized later that in those precious few minutes before falling to sleep, I had been in a kind of penumbral region; the quietude I had experienced was something like the aura that comes over a migraine sufferer before an attack, only its antithesis—as if I had been visited by a herald angel, preparing me for the coming of the Light.

The enlightenment that led to my transcending the dismal fate that the Church would have abandoned me to and beginning my own street mission came to me in a dream that seemed to transfix me even before I surrendered to sleep. Even in that penumbral state, I'm certain I can recall imagining myself driving through parts of the city I seldom had call to see. I was leaving Gentilly, the old nuns, and the garish adulteration of New Orleans East behind, embarking down Elysian Fields toward the river I had known as a child with my cousins.

At some point I found myself on foot, and suddenly I was no longer alone; a group of boys had joined my wandering, which still seemed to be pointless and desultory except for a faint, synesthetic promise of imminent purpose. The group of boys grew ever larger in my wake. As I crossed the final blocks before the river—Burgundy, Dauphine, Royal— there must have been a score of them, emerging from the darkness of the Quarter like weary orphans, survivors from a dreadful holocaust, staggering from their caves. The first hope of dawn was signaling downriver, and we followed its rays toward the east, past the Creole cottages and miniature Greek Revivals that line the winding streets of the Faubourg Marigny.

More and more boys joined our odyssey as we continued toward the rising sun. Its rays highlighted the reds and golds in their lovely heads of hair and illumined their smooth, fair cheeks. My dream, born of a restless mind swirling with anxiety and the stress of a dim future clouded with unresolvable conflict, had become a bright Boscovian vision as we crossed the boundary of Press Street and entered Bywater. I might have been the beloved John Bosco himself, leading his adoring flock of boys through a nineteenth century Piedmont village. Some of the stronger ones lifted me off my feet, and my dream nearly became a surreal mélange as I seemed to be weightless and floating between my own time and that of the sainted Apostle of Youth. A donkey was pulling a fruit cart beside train tracks that ran along the river's course, and the boys sat me on its back. I knew not where the beast would take me, but trusted its gentle instincts as it bore me farther toward the east.

The boys followed, a multitude of them now, some of them— the stronger ones who had lifted me onto the animal—walking by my side, clutching me by the wrists and ankles as if simultaneously depending on me for guidance and protecting me from a fall. Others rode in the cart behind us, passing me the most succulent of its wares—peaches and pears that flooded my mouth with an ambrosial taste like nothing since the banishment from Eden. Boys licked my fingers, kissing the juice from my hands.

A bell tolled from somewhere nearby, and we came to a stop. Again the stronger ones lifted me, this time back onto my feet. I had somehow become divested of my dark suit and collar and stood there in street clothes, one with the throng of youth that now surrounded me. They were all reaching out for me, grasping for my hand, hugging me by the waist and legs. When one extended his hand toward my head, I started. Instinctively I shrank back, but in the grip of all those boys, I couldn't move away. The hand was on my head, and I closed my eyes to the humiliation and exposure that I was sure would follow. Then, all at once, a cheer went up, and I knew there was nothing there to shame me. Other hands joined in, all rubbing my bald pate like a magic lantern. They were shouting my name now in a great huzzah, but not "Father Tony." I stood there in the full brightness of morning as I had never stood among my brethren in so many years. And they were calling me "Joe."

I awoke with a racing heartbeat in my room at Consolation, at first flummoxed then dejected by my tedious surroundings. Had my dream been merely a cruel tease, a painful reminder that I was to spend my days among a gaggle of bickering old women, presiding over the dark winter of their superannuated lives and not among the young and vibrant with choices yet to be made, among whom I could make a real contribution?

Before I could sink further into despair, I noticed a glow just perceptible around my window, a few strands of light sneaking through the cracks in my drawn blinds. Was it morning already? Had this dream, which had left me at once forsaken yet oddly energized, held me in its grip all night?

I looked at my clock. Incredibly it was nearly six. Indeed I had slept all night, the first sound night I could recall since before Tchefuncte. It was nearly time to rise and prepare for Mass, a prospect I ordinarily dreaded but faced that morning with an unwonted strength. I had a vague sense that my dream was its source, but there had not yet been time to reflect on its precise meaning. Clearly a change was taking place; as I opened the blinds, my surroundings and my mood were brightened with an untainted light that not even the tedium of a Mass with those old women could dim. For once it didn't bother me that none of these stubborn old nuns would take Communion by hand and that I had been given the gift of consecration only to deposit the precious Host into a toothless mouth that smacked it like a peanut butter cup. No, not even that would spoil my day. Indeed something glorious was happening.

CHAPTER ELEVEN

BOSCO IN NEW ORLEANS

Later that morning, I had a few minutes alone to ponder my vision. Fortunately my literary training helped me interpret its awesome import. My journey toward the river was a movement both backward in time to a more innocent past and forward into a more promising future. The crowd in my wake was a composite of the tattered, hungry boys who flocked around John Bosco over a century ago and the legions of lost, homeless youth who wander the streets of New Orleans today with infinitely more spotted pasts and sophisticated needs.

The street clothes and my being known to the boys as Joe was a clear sign that I would have to disavow myself of the fetters of the Church in order to effect a useful mission. What could the Church do anyway but weigh me down like a millstone with its arbitrary and obsolete regulations, its coercion by fear and guilt? These young lives could not be impressed by a piece of bread and a bedtime story; nor could they be frightened into submission by the threat of damnation, for damned in their own eyes they already were. And why would they turn to a priest anyway? What were we to them by the nineties but agents of a corrupt authority at best, pederasts and sodomites at worst?

Did I want to answer to an ambitious bureaucrat who cared about nothing but his own advancement? Did I want the continuance of my work to depend on the archdiocesan bottom line? Hadn't they closed the Den as soon as it was no longer, as they put it, "fiscally prudent" to keep it open, despite the good that was being done there, and weren't they doing the same to schools and churches across the city that were beloved to thousands? Even Bosco himself had no church when he began his work. His oratories were held in a meadow with no walls to limit or confine; the Italian sky was his Sistine ceiling. No, the Church was clearly the problem.

My dilemma was clear: I had been blessed with a God-given talent for working with youth. To waste such a talent would be tantamount to a sin of omission. At the same time, I knew that the Church would never again let Father Anthony Miggliore exercise that talent. At long last, I had the solution. I wouldn't even have to resign from the priesthood; I'm sure the Church would understand that such a move would not have been "fiscally prudent" anyway, now that my Miggliore money was all but gone. I would keep my day job, so to speak. Even one as antipathetic to my real ambition as was my position at the old nun house could hardly keep me down if by night I was able to soar to new heights of self-actualization. By the end of that watershed day in June, the details and logistics of my plan were still to be worked out, but the basic framework of my future was clear: For the first time in over twenty years, I was about to become once again Mr. Broussard!

In order to effect my transformation, I had to assume a nocturnal identity free of the trappings of the priesthood and the baggage of Father Tony Miggliore. Step one would be to do something about my miserable hair. I must have gone through a dozen pieces and enough money to refurbish the cathedral since my ordination, when I first started covering up. The euphoria I felt in my dream when the boys touched my head—the lightheaded exhilaration of having nothing to hide—would never be mine as long as I continued to wear that shameful and duplicitous mask.

At my next tightening, I inquired about my options and chose to switch to a "clip-on," allowing me once again to remove my piece at night, as I used to do before Tchefuncte. The horrid itching would be solved as well; I'd finally be able to scrub my scalp in the shower again. I didn't even care if one of the old sisters yanked it off in the throes of an apoplectic dementia, so giddy was I over my happy prospects for the future. By day I could be the devout Father Miggliore, selflessly tending to my pathetic old charges with the private assurance that by night, as Mr. Broussard, I could spread comfort, hope, and love where it was truly needed: among the homeless youth of the streets.

A base of operations would be in order, a safe haven as it were for the boys I'd rescue. Recalling my dream, I decided to begin looking in the neighborhoods east of the Quarter and quickly found a cozy little Victorian shotgun for lease in Bywater—on Desire near the wharf. The porch was a bit rickety and the screens on most of the windows slit, but it had a refrigerator (though not frost-free), a functioning bathroom, window units for heat and air that actually worked, and the rent was less than I would have paid for a one-bedroom apartment in any other area of the city that was safe to walk at night.

I wanted nothing of opulence. Recalling Thoreau's admonition to "simplify, simplify, simplify," I limited my furnishings to a couch, a recliner, a Formica dinette set, one double bed, and a tiny chest of drawers, all of which I picked up at a flea market on Saint Claude Avenue. Sadly, the population of boys I would be serving might never have learned to love or trust, and I couldn't be there at all times to guard against the inevitability that one of them might take advantage of the one person who had befriended him; so there would be nothing there to tempt them into crime, nothing that anyone would bother to break in for. Secondhand T-shirts and shorts stocked the chest of drawers; towels and a robe would always be on hand in the bathroom in case anyone needed a shower. Other than that, the place would be as barren as the cell of a Trappist monk.

As if taking her place in the Lord's plan for me, my mother suffered a minor stroke that summer—nothing terribly serious, but enough to keep her bedridden for a few weeks and give me an excuse to take some time away from Consolation. During her convalescence, she decided that now that she was in her seventy-fifth year, it would be a good time to let me take over the management of her affairs, not that there was much left to manage besides the house and a tiny income from what was left of her share of the Miggliore estate. In any event, she had the lawyer bring the papers to the house, relinquishing power of attorney to me. In a fatal faux pas that I should have had the foresight to avoid, she stuck with the same family firm—de Salvo and Sons—that had handled the Miggliore business since my grandfather was around. Mike de Salvo, of the third generation of these dago shysters, charged her $250 an hour when any hungry kid fresh out of Loyola Law School could have done the job for a fraction of that and kept his mouth shut.

Besides tending to Josie and the legal matters, I spent those couple of weeks away from Consolation getting to know my new surroundings down by the river. Bywater is not unlike many of New Orleans' neighborhoods that adjoin the river in that it was originally settled when the Spanish and French plantations that had occupied the land broke up in the nineteenth century. What makes the area so special is that it has changed so little over more than a century and a half. Of course other parts of the city try to boast of such timelessness—the Quarter, for example, and the Irish Channel—but their historical quaintness is all for show, an artificial creation of preservation groups and council resolutions to propagate an illusion for tourists, while behind the flimsy façade lies the ugly specter of commercialization and civil rights acts gone hay-wire—Pakistani carriage drivers in antebellum livery rolling past a Greek Revival McDonalds. Bywater is still untouched by all that nonsense, one of the few lower middle class neighborhoods in the city that has managed to retain its racial purity to this day. I truly could have been a nineteenth century Bosco in this little pocket where time had stood still. The descendants of the original immigrants to settle the little tract of land along the Mississippi (literally "by water")—mostly Irish and German artisans—are still there, their sons among the fair-skinned boys of my dream.

Patrick was the first of them that I got to know. The dark-haired son of a jolly but drunken longshoreman, he lived in another shotgun on Independence Street, a few blocks from the Desire house. His mother was a graveyard shift clerk at a 7-Eleven on Franklin Avenue. I met him the day I took the house. I was carrying a few boxes of miscellany I had picked up at the flea market—clothes, kitchen utensils, some cheap Pyrex plates—when he came up to me with a cigarette in his hand, shirtless and in jeans that were too short for him despite being pulled down several inches below the elastic of his boxers. Tiny gold rings pierced both of his ears. A lower tooth was missing, but otherwise he was a beautiful boy, those raven curls so unexpected yet not uncommon among the Irish.

He helped me with the boxes and asked if I had anything else for him to do, that he'd work for "smokes." A Negro with a pickup truck had approached me at the Saint Claude flea market and offered to deliver the furniture for thirty dollars, and I was expecting him any minute; so I told Patrick he could help carry everything into the house. Afterwards, I gave him one of the T-shirts so that we could have sandwiches at a little place on Chartres near the railroad tracks.

Over lunch I learned his story. He was seventeen, the younger of two children; his married sister lived across the Industrial Canal where she and her husband sold used tires. His father, the longshoreman, did shift work at the Poland Avenue Wharf and was usually intoxicated when

he was off, so between that and the mother's working all night and sleeping by day, the boy was unsupervised more often than not.

At first I was surprised that a young man from a two-parent
household could be so idle and directionless, but I came to realize that
his story was typical of the culture of that area and the working class
neighborhoods even farther to the east in Saint Bernard Parish. He had
dropped out of high school in his junior year. As far as future educational
plans, he could only say that he might try to get a GED "someday." His
only occupation was occasional work with his father when they needed
an extra hand on the wharf to unload cargo from some foreign port. Last
week it had been bananas from Costa Rica.

"That's how I got this," he said, pointing with a french fry to his
missing tooth. "Got hit by a flying winch."

He told me more about that incident: that he had been knocked
unconscious and that his father had gotten "a few bucks" from the dock
people in compensation, with which he bought his son the pair of athletic shoes he was wearing and used the rest on back rent and Wild Turkey.

"It's okay, though," he said. "It didn't hurt that much, and I
think it looks pretty cool."

That much was true; it certainly didn't spoil his looks. To the
contrary, the little tittle of imperfection, like a mole on a Hollywood
siren, was just what he needed—a tiny speck of vulnerability. The first
time I held his hand, I noticed how small it was, yet soft and full like
a child's. His lovely dark hair put me in mind of poor Sean, and that
night I dreamed again. I was with Patrick on the wharf, watching him
at work, heaving cargo from the deck of a ship across a walkway plank
to the dock when suddenly the ship seemed to shift; boxes were falling
into the river, and the water became a yellow logjam of bananas. Patrick
dove in to retrieve as many as he could, but it was Sean who emerged,
laden with bunches of the fruit like a Polynesian god of plenty, depositing
them at my feet. We were no longer on the dock, nor were we beside the

little river at Tchefuncte; my wild associations had carried us back to the
levee behind Mama Miggliore's house. Another shift and there was my
grandmother with her new husband the day she landed in this country,
unable to speak a word of its language but still comprehensible if anyone
could hear the word she kept repeating at this wonderful and mesmerizing sight: "Bananas, bananas!"

I spent as much time as I could at the new house that first week.
Of course I had to check in with Josie at least once a day to monitor her
progress and see that she had something to eat. Usually while I visited,
I'd fix a pot of red beans and pickled pork or a shrimp jambalaya—something she could spoon out and warm in a microwave for a couple of days.
By late afternoon, I was back at the house with Patrick. How he knew
when I'd be there I have no idea, for my route to Desire didn't take me
past his house and I never saw him on the street. Yet invariably there he
was, knocking on my screen door within fifteen minutes of my arrival,
asking if I had any work for him to do, or if I could give him a ride, usually to a friend's house on the other side of the Industrial Canal in Arabi.
We'd eat at the Burger King or Popeye's on Saint Claude and stop at a
little store run by Vietnamese that sold discounted cigarettes. Soon he
was making himself at home with me: the offers to work ceased, and he
started spending the night when he knew I'd be there, calling me at all
hours to pick him up from somewhere or other.

My original vision of a bipolar existence, changing roles with
night and day, proved untenable in practice, so I settled on a routine of
spending weekends—Friday evening through Sunday morning—in Bywater. I'd return for Sunday afternoon Mass and dinner with the sisters.
Of course I had to get permission from the archdiocese to take this time
away from the nun house, which was essentially a twenty-four-hour post.
For my excuse, I used my mother's continued need for care after her ac-

cident. I told them I had found a sitter for her during the week but no one who would work weekends for any kind of reasonable fee.

I addressed the official request to Weed in the hope that the little man would be flattered and perhaps a bit disarmed by that recognition. I gave Josie the Desire house telephone number with strict instructions not to give it to anyone under any circumstances but to call me herself if someone needed to reach me. As far as she knew, I was doing research for an unauthorized book on the Church's response to urban homelessness and had to tell my superiors that I was caring for her. At least half of that, and who knew—perhaps ultimately all of it—was true.

I suffered from self-doubt. The Den had opened in 1974. I was yet a young man, still in my thirties. Would I search in vain for young men who could still relate to me, still want what I had to offer? Or was I truly past my usefulness and therefore in my proper element at Our Lady of Consolation?

My fears proved to be unfounded. I had merely to establish my presence and the boys, like the throngs in my prophetic dream, came to me. Patrick was an early aid as well. He quickly learned my schedule (I told him I taught at LSU and spent the week in Baton Rouge) and started showing up, especially in that first year, with hungry strays in tow, usually boys he had found in Arabi or Chalmette or who had wandered to the wharf looking for work. I tended to fish upriver: the Quarter, the Warehouse District, the bus and train stations, wherever I might find the most needy and homeless youths—my "Little Olivers" I came to call them, after my favorite Dickens novel. I'd buy them some food, bring them to the Desire house, and listen to their tales of abuse and abandonment, foster homes and detention centers. Sometimes I'd give them a little money.

For more than three years, I ministered to those streets, and in all that time there was not a single incident; not one of those boys betrayed me or tried to harm me in any way. They could sense that I loved them; in many cases I was probably the only one. "Mr. Broussard" even earned a degree of fame among them. Many times I went to the house only to find a strange boy waiting on my porch. "Are you Mr. Broussard?" he'd ask, sometimes mentioning the name of another boy I couldn't even place. "I thought maybe I could stay here." And often it was one of my familiar Little Olivers, coming back for "more."

I felt revitalized. The spirit of purposefulness that had animated me at the Den was back at long last—and stronger than ever. The rush of energy that I anticipated all week would reach its apex when I'd drive away from the nun house on Friday afternoon and head toward Bywater, pulling over at some midway point—usually along Elysian Fields—to snap off my hair, shove it into one of Josie's old hat boxes, and close the trunk lid on the wretched thing for the next forty-eight hours. The bliss of sticking my bare head out the car's window and feeling the wind and rain on my scalp would only be surpassed by the crowning touch of one of my young Olivers.

Perhaps the ultimate proof of the righteousness of my street mission was that I was able to draw on the strength it gave me through the week as well, when I was faced with the daily trials of Father Miggliore. In short, I became a better priest. Rising early for Mass was no longer a dreaded ordeal; in fact, I came to look forward to it. No longer did I seek to escape the dreariness of my daily routine through the narcotic of sleep; every day was to be celebrated to its fullest, and I even encouraged the sisters to sign up so as to rejoice with me. What had previously irked me in the poor old women, I now endured with newfound patience and understanding: the slobber on my hands after communion, hearing their sad little sins and shouting penances into deaf ears like an emcee at a bingo parlor, keeping up with their soap operas. I no longer dwelt on my past sufferings, nor did I curse those responsible.

During Mass I managed to get through the Canon, invoking prayers for "John Paul our Pope and Franklin our bishop" without choking on the words. On the contrary, I came to pity the archbishop as we do a former enemy whose malignant reach we believe ourselves to have risen beyond. Weed, too, was beneath my contempt. I had endured the hairy little bootlicker's condescending intrusions into my work at Our Lady of Consolation for months, his stares ranging from villainously condemnatory for what had happened to Sean to smugly satisfied at the price I had to pay. I knew—and even now still believe—that he will be as frustrated in his climb to respect in the archdiocese as he was in his sad efforts to please his father. The Church will spit him out, as it did me, once he proves himself of no further use.

How naïve I was, believing that I could go on like that forever, as if my newfound love of life and spirit of hope were enough to purify every mean and vicious force I had ever faced in my life—and as if there might not yet be some force of evil at work, a counterbalance to undermine my good works. The early Christians had the Romans, Joan of Arc the English, Ignatius the Inquisition. And I had Weed. Of course I realize that my fall could not have been effected without a misstep on my own part, but after three years of my double life of service without a hitch, my guard was down; and Satan and his minions were ready to pounce. I should have never brought those tapes to the nun house.

Why did I make them in the first place? It must seem so senseless, like the perverse act of a psycho in a Clint Eastwood film to ensure his own apprehension. But that wasn't it at all. I did it for the memories. Not that I planned on spending my time looking at the tapes. I didn't even own a VCR. It was just that I knew there could be no permanence in my relationship with those boys. Seldom did I see any of them more than a handful of times, and the overwhelming majority but once. Even Patrick disappeared after the first year or so. He told me one day he was going to work on a tugboat and that he'd be away for a few weeks. I never saw him again.

It was his camera, by the way. He said he had bought it cheap at a pawnshop in Tremé and asked if he could keep it at the Desire house until he sold it. Later he showed up with a stand for it. It was not an uncommon request; he was always bringing things like that to the house, usually electronic gadgets like radios and computer accessories, but now and then a watch or other piece of jewelry. He didn't want to keep anything at home for fear that his father would sell it to buy liquor, and he always promised to give me some money when he sold something. Of course I never expected anything from him and wouldn't have accepted it if he had offered.

For the first year he was the only one on the tapes; he loved being photographed. I must have hours upon hours of him—talking on the phone, striking up playful poses like a bodybuilder, showing off his first tattoo—an incongruous melding of a bleeding thorn bush and the legend "Carpe Diem" between his shoulders. For a month after he got it, he had me rub it with the Vaseline every night I saw him. Sometimes I'd place the camera in its tripod (which he acquired, along with a remote control device, a few weeks after the camera) and train its eye on him for hours while he slept in the bed or relaxed on the old flea market couch with his bare feet in my lap as I shaved his legs (hair seemed to be out of favor with many of them, a happy change from the eighties that made me less self-conscious about my head).

Who can really blame me for wanting some kind of memento of my boys, a little keepsake frozen in time? We would have no correspondence, no ten-year reunions, no yearbooks. The Church had made all that impossible, just as it had made impossible any hope I might have had to be recognized in this life for my selfless efforts. I wanted records of the lives I had impacted. And, yes, I deserved them. Does anyone doubt Mother Theresa kept her *Time* cover?

Nothing could have substituted for the videotaped records of my boys in motion, of the sound of their voices, of their faces and body language as my voice and touch worked a change in their attitudes, transforming the anxious insecurity of the streets into the beatific pleasure of a safe house. No words in a journal—tedious lists of names and dates that would have blended into cacophony over time—would have done justice. It wasn't their names that made them real (They could have been using aliases—few had IDs); it was the *sense* of them. Their bodies told the truth of their stories: their knife-scarred torsos, bodies pierced and decorated like young savages on the crest of manhood, hair shaven or dyed in every color of hope and possibility. All of those images would have been lost without pictures.

Patrick was the only boy who ever knew about the tapes. I didn't actually get the inspiration to use the camera on any of the others until months after he disappeared. When I realized he wasn't coming back, I knew the tapes were all I'd ever have of him, and in time the same would be true of all the others. They would all be gone, and eventually I'd be an old man with nothing but fading memories. That was when I started bringing some of the tapes back to Consolation every week: not to view them (there was no VCR there even if I had wanted to) but just to hold them in my hand at night and savor the memories they held. Sometimes I would fall to sleep clutching one and dream a pleasant dream. Of course I wanted to watch them, but I offered that little frustration up as a sacrifice and promised the Lord that I would deprive myself of that pleasure until I was old and retired like the nuns, with no more work left to do.

Of course I couldn't let the boys know I was taping them without destroying the honesty and spontaneity that I so cherished in them. I had to find a way to conceal the camera. The house was heated by a floor furnace and cooled by window units, so obscuring it behind a wall grill was not an option. There was a convenient hole in the wall between the bed and bathrooms, which I utilized to make sure no one was getting into any mischief while supposedly taking a shower. I made a few enlightening discoveries about some of my guests' substance abuse habits through that little chink (I just had to lift a little flap of loose wallpaper in the bedroom). The possibility of discovery if any of the boys so much as moved the shower curtain, however, precluded the bathroom as a hiding place. The only room in the house that normally had enough clutter to conceal anything was the kitchen, but nothing memorable ever happened in there in the first place, and hardly any of these boys were averse to rooting through the bread box and amidst the bags and boxes on the counter for the "munchies" I always kept on hand for them.

I ruled out the bedroom; perhaps only half of the boys ended up in there, and I wanted to remember them all. That left the living room. I kept the camera hidden under a pile of dirty towels in a plastic clothes basket on the little dinette table across the room from the sofa. The lens was the only part exposed, but still virtually undetectable between two striations of the latticed basket. The only chancy part was checking the little viewfinder to make sure the lens was pointing in precisely the right direction without being noticed. This little sleight of hand I accomplished by pretending to be fiddling with the towels and muttering something like, "When am I going to wash these filthy things?" It never failed me. I liked to use the remote, which I kept in my pocket, to turn the camera on. I'd simply wait until I was in place and tell my young ward to close his eyes before pulling it out.

After Patrick was gone and I started bringing a few of the tapes back to Consolation for the week, I took every precaution to keep anyone else from finding them. I'd keep them under lock and key beneath a few extra surplices in a cherry chiffarobe that I had borrowed from my mother for this express purpose. It had once belonged to Mama Miggliore, and every time I opened it, the scent of mothballs and roach droppings whisked me back forty years to my grandmother's house.

It was incredibly remiss of me to leave the key in the chiffarobe as I did; generally, I kept it locked in the tabernacle of the little quasi-sacristy adjoining the chapel, hidden under the paten. No one said Mass on Saturdays, and I was always back by Sunday, so it could have gone undetected forever. And even if someone had found it, they would have had no way of knowing what it was for. I was only to be gone for a scant hour or two (Immaculata's semiannual cataract measuring). Weed had just paid a visit that weekend, I was told—snooping around "like a little hedgehog," Delia said—and it was only Monday. Surely he wouldn't be back for several days. Sloth was my cardinal sin of the day: I simply couldn't be bothered to bring the key back to the sacristy for that measly trip to the doctor.

Oh, but I would live to rue that negligent oversight, rooted as it was in my own complacency. Weed knew precisely when to strike: after three years of allowing me to go about my business happily unmolested by him or any of my nemeses.

They didn't take long to level their guns. It was only Friday when I was called to the phone, snatched without warning from the sisters in the day room in the middle of *All My Children*. It was Ratchett's office. His Excellency would like to see me at his residence within the hour. It wouldn't be necessary for me to drive myself: A car was already on its way.

I had no idea what was about to happen. The twenty-fifth anniversary of my ordination was approaching. Might this summons have something to do with that? Perhaps a special Jubilee Mass was being planned, or my long-awaited trip to Europe was finally at hand, or the *Clarion Herald* wanted to do a feature on my work at Our Lady of Consolation. Was it even possible that Pharoah Ratchett had decided I had been punished long enough and was going to end my Mosaic enslavement at the old nun house? That would have been a mixed blessing since the job melded so seamlessly with my work in Bywater. Would I be able to get away on weekends if they offered me another assistant pastorate somewhere? Yet another possibility came to mind. The parochial schools had begun to rebound. The local economy had bounced back with the rising price of oil, and the children of the Baby Boomers were now crowding the classrooms. Was the archdiocese planning to open another home for boys? What a glorious way to take the sting out of turning fifty—to return to the Den and save the Desire house rent to boot!

So loath are we to face the horrific that we will continue to deny all signs up to the moment the ghastly truth is staring us in the face. Even when I recognized Weed's driver on the street, I was still in denial, entertaining ludicrous explanations for the special embassy's involvement in the archbishop's business with me. It had been six years since Tchefuncte, and our relationship had become civil—a bit strained perhaps, but cordial. I had even stopped pretending to be working in the garden when he showed up. As they say, the best revenge is living well; and I was happier than I had been in over a decade. All considered, whatever role Weed had played in bringing me down after Sean's tragedy seemed long past and incidental. I knew about his occasional weekend visits to Consolation, but they had never raised my suspicions; it seemed understandable that he would want to see that the house was running smoothly while I was away. He probably wanted to be on hand to attest before the archbishop to my dedicated work with the sisters and to congratulate me on my new assignment. The lending of his car for the occasion seemed an appropriately generous touch. Was it going to be *my* car now—one of the perks of my promotion?

The drive to the archbishop's Carrollton residence took about fifteen minutes. We made it in silence. My driver (yes, I still thought he was going to be "my driver") was listening to a religious talk show on the radio—one of those phone-in programs that have come to dominate the AM airwaves. It was hosted by a priest, Father William Mendaci, a native New Orleanian who loved to boast smugly of how he had worked his way up from his blue-collar Irish Channel roots (his father had driven a milk truck or something) to a chair of ethics at Loyola. As if a Jesuit teaching ethics wasn't ironic enough, the program's topic of discussion was our society's perverse emphasis on appearance over reality, while I happened to know from one of the sisters whose grandniece worked at a tanning salon on Saint Charles Avenue that Father Mendaci was visiting that establishment on a regular basis in preparation for his show's scheduled debut on local television in the fall.

"Why do you think the Catholic schools insist on uniforms all the time?" he lectured a caller in his common Channel accent ("tom" for "time") that made even a PhD sound like a stevedore. "How can we teach kids values ("valyahs") if they think they're losers if their clothes don't come from The Gap or Eddie Bauer ("Bowah")?"

We drove on, Father Mendaci continuing his harangue on the spiritual "valyahs" the good Jesuit fathers had instilled in him as a boy. I met Mendaci once. He spoke a couple of years before at a funeral for one of the sisters whose last appointment had been a clerical position at Loyola. Even there he was a walking advertisement for a Catholic education. Somehow he had managed to dig up one of the old nun's report cards from the little parish school she had attended near Opelousas in the twenties, waving the old piece of cardboard around on the pulpit like a winning bingo card.

As we were pulling into the giant horseshoe drive of the residence, an angry caller was screaming about the double standard at his daughter's high school: "They wouldn't let my child walk across the stage at Mount Olive because she was pregnant, even though everybody knew the salutatorian had an abortion. The Church has a lot of nerve talking about appearances! That butch nun should rot in Hell with her fat girl-friend!"

Mendaci hung up on the man after cautioning him about the laws against "unsubstantiated slandah."

We parked beneath a huge magnolia that shaded the apex of the horseshoe, and when my driver got out, I discreetly checked my snaps in the rearview mirror. I tended to have the sensation of loose hair in moments of nervous stress. Since I had eschewed the accursed tape, the feeling was usually psychosomatic, but when anxious about something, I'd find myself almost compulsively checking my head like a neurotic phrenologist doing his own skull mapping.

Satisfied that my hair at least was secure, I ascended the granite steps to the huge double doors at the entrance to the residence, passing between two Doric columns that guarded the oaken portals. The doors must have measured ten feet from threshold to lintel. There was a brass ring on each and a button on the wall to the side. I pressed the button but heard nothing. Was it out of order or was a buzzer going off somewhere deep within the building? Employing the brass knockers seemed too urgent, like the desperate act of a vassal importuning the protection of his feudal lord. So I waited. Would Ratchett himself greet me at the door? I couldn't remember which hand was crippled and which of mine I should extend. What should I say to him? In my twenty plus years as a priest, I had hardly spoken to him except for brief exchanges of niceties at public functions—confirmations or funerals of well-connected congregants. Naturally, he was at my Aunt Rose's interment, blessing her coffin, which was closed, of course. Even then he barely vouchsafed me the honor of kissing his ring.

His ring! Yes, it was on his left hand. It was the right that was deformed. I can see him now in my mind, his left profile, sitting at the nesting tables in Mama Miggliore's death chamber, sipping Wanda's scalding coffee as if it were a cool beverage, soothing to his demon lips.

I was about to press the button again when I heard something on the other side of the great portal. At last one of the doors opened to the inside, and a gray-haired woman, perhaps in her early sixties, stood before me. She could have been clerical help or some other servant, but most probably a nun. It's difficult to tell anymore—you have to look at the shoes.

She looked at me without expression. In fact, hers was a face that seemed incapable of expression—the product of decades of stifled emotion, of being in the midst of the great and powerful but seeing and hearing nothing. Her little round spectacles and hair cropped like Joan of Arc only added to her nondescript air.

"Father Joseph," she said.

Why did she call me that? I had never been called that. I couldn't tell if it was a greeting or a question, and not so much as an arching of an eyebrow gave me a clue.

"Anthony Miggliore," I said.

She did not correct herself but only lifted her chin the tiniest bit and looked me over through the bottoms of her little spectacles—a "that's what you think" look, as if she knew more about who I was than even I did. It was the most animation I would see from her, even as she led me silently through one hall and then another. We passed the kitchen, and I could see that it was spacious and well appointed—pots and utensils hanging on walls—like an intimate little restaurant in the Quarter. I could smell the fried seafood; a Friday lunch was apparently in preparation. Was I to be dining with His Excellency?

A marble staircase took us to the second-floor hallway, its walls lined with portraits of all the bishops of New Orleans. There was the first—Penalver, the Cuban who was so appalled by the depravity of eighteenth-century Louisiana that he wrote a formal complaint to Pius VI. And then the familiar ones, immortalized in the names of local schools: Chapelle, Blenk, Shaw, Rummel. Finally, there was Franklin Ratchett himself, his image the only photograph; the others were oils on canvas. What a fitting testament to his meretricious administration. If only Luis Penalver could return to whitewash the grime and rot that has come to corrupt the diocese he founded two centuries ago.

Several doors flanked the "Hall of Honors," interspersed asymmetrically among the portraits. All were closed and unmarked. One final door stood at the head of the hall. I knew from the size of the building and the relative shortness of the hall that there had to be a great deal of space behind this door. Perhaps it was the entrance to the archbishop's private suite of rooms. A sensation of anticipation and prideful intimacy washed over me at that thought. I could literally be standing on the threshold of the acceptance and recognition that had so unjustly been denied me these many years. Pretending to be patting down my hair, I stealthily checked my snaps again while the woman knocked on the door.

A muffled voice could be heard from within, unintelligible to me but apparently not to my guide, who tried the brass knob in response. Opening the door just a few inches, she turned back to me and, without making eye contact, gestured with an outstretched arm and open palm, her fingers pointing to my feet and sweeping toward the threshold. Her movements seemed strangely stylized, like a figure from a medieval portrait only partially infused with animation. Apparently I was to proceed. My guide, meanwhile, backed away, then turned and retraced her steps down the hall from which we had come. It was the last I saw of her.

The room I entered was much darker than the hall. Once my eyes adjusted, I could see that I was standing in what was apparently the archbishop's study. It was a magnificent room, not quite square, but perhaps thirty feet wide and nearly as deep. Books lined two of the walls—thousand of volumes, although I never got close enough to inspect their titles. The room had a faint but familiar odor to it that took me back to an indefinite point in my past as only the sense of smell can. Was it a déjà vu—for certainly I had never been in this place before—or was it something about Ratchett that I was recalling from years ago, his clothes or cologne? There were several doors in the study. They might have been closets, but I suspected they were portals to more private chambers.

It was a few moments before I saw Ratchett himself, seated a good twenty feet away from me, his left forearm—the one with the normal hand—resting on the desktop. The other he kept at his side, hidden from my view. The desk was gargantuan and eminently busy, cluttered with stacks of papers, a silver tea service and salver, several glasses and carafes, a slag glass lamp, a computer. An oriel behind the desk must have projected, if my sense of direction was true, onto the back of the residence. The curtains of its three windows were drawn, depriving the room of its only source of natural light. Further, a curious structure directly behind the archbishop drew the eye's attention away from his form. In the darkness it was a monolithic silhouette, about as tall as a man, but as wide as two filing cabinets. It seemed curiously out of place between the desk and the oriel, and I concluded that it had been brought there to answer a particular exigency.

Whatever foolish conceits I still entertained that I had been called to this place on a happy occasion were dispelled when Ratchett spoke his first word to me.

"Joseph," he said. His tone was anything but welcoming, an ominous cross between a summons and a reproach.

And of course that name again. Not since my impertinent cousin Ronnie passed had anyone except my mother used it with me. Hearing it from Ratchett's lips somehow made that elusive scent in the room even more pronounced and distinct. I almost had it as I walked toward the archbishop's desk. It was linked, I was certain now, to something in my grandmother's house; but before I could locate it any more precisely, Ratchett reached with his good hand for the cord of the lamp. The Garden of Gethsemane was the scene now illuminated on its shade. It struck me as disturbingly premonitory at the time, and in retrospect I can think of nothing more appropriate. I couldn't describe anything else about that section of the study now touched by the lamp's light even if I thought it important to do so because I could now see clearly the monolith behind Ratchett's chair; and once I realized what it was—a portable stand for a television and VCR—and what its being in this room at this time meant, I became blinded to everything else around me, only released from my monomaniacal trance by a snap of Ratchett's fingers.

He was signaling Weed to emerge from one of the doors to my right. The door must have been slightly ajar because it made no sound when he opened it. The archbishop said nothing to his special embassy, but only momentarily averted his eyes in Weed's direction and, raising his forearm without lifting his elbow from the desk, gestured with his

index finger, as if beckoning a servant whose attention he took for granted. Weed walked behind the desk and shoved a tape, which must have
been protruding from the mouth of the VCR, into the machine. Then he
snatched the remote from the upper deck of the stand and took his place
to Ratchett's left. Looking to his superior for instructions and receiving
none, he pushed play.

The archbishop did not bother turning to watch the tape. Weed,
however, savored every second that His Excellency suffered it to play,
though he put on an unconvincing display of horror and revulsion at
what he was seeing, holding his hand to his mouth and muttering things
like "Oh my Lord" and "Mother of God." Neither he nor Ratchett addressed me, and at first I thought I might be able to plead ignorance. The
setting was unidentifiable—no one knew about the Desire house, and I
was always careful not to aggrandize myself by facing the camera (here
the little remote had come in handy).

What the viewer saw was a nude young man sitting up on a
couch (I've forgotten this one's name. I found him one night at the bus
station on Loyola, asking people for money for a ticket to some little
town in Mississippi where his grandmother lived. It was an interesting
phenomenon I noticed among his generation—this dependence on the
grandmothers). He had been smoking, but I talked him out of that. I
really was concerned for their welfare. I knelt in front of him, his hands
holding my head down. It was the only way I allowed them to touch me.
One of his legs was draped over my shoulder, perfect toes flexing before
the hidden lens. Wearing street clothes with my back to the camera, I
could have been any portly, middle-aged male.

I felt some hope: I could deny any knowledge of this tape. Re-
gardless of whether they believed me, they couldn't prove anything. Even
if they discovered my fingerprints on the cassette, I could say, "Yes, it was
mine. I had bought it to have some old home movies from my childhood
converted to video as a gift for my mother. Someone must have stolen

and defiled it to frame me." I'd then cast a suspicious glance in Weed's direction. It just might work.

"I'm sure you recognize this scene," Ratchett finally said.

"I can assure you, Your Excellency, I have never seen this before in my life," I answered. And before God it was the truth. I remembered my vow not to look at any of the tapes as long as I continued to work, and I resented these two even more now for forcing me to break it.

But just as my animus was fortifying into defiance, something happened on the screen that dashed my hopes. The boy (I'm thinking his name started with a J—Jason or Joshua?), overcome with the intensity of the moment, all at once threw his head back and cupped it in the palms of his own hands.

"Oh God!" he cried.

They could have been my own words. At the very moment that he removed his hands from my bobbing head, I knew all was lost, for there it was for the world to see: the segno sacro!

I had almost forgotten about my holy mark, especially since Ronnie hadn't been around to harp on it every six weeks at the salon, telling me how red and swollen it had gotten, how someday it was going to be impossible to cover it up, that it would soon be bulging through my piece like a whale under a tarp. But there it was again, the chalice my grandmother had seen at the moment of my birth, only bigger and more protuberant than ever, just as my cousin had predicted. On camera it was more the color of blood than of wine.

"The mark of Cain!" Weed exclaimed.

The archbishop ordered the special embassy to stop the machine. Weed complied, ejecting the tape from the VCR and stuffing it covetously into an inside pocket of his jacket. Ratchett then dismissed him from the room. Both commands were communicated in gestures of his one good hand. He spoke not a single word to his little monkey in my presence.

Once Weed had disappeared behind the same door he had entered through, Ratchett asked me if I would like to remove my piece. I told him that wouldn't be necessary, upon which he rose from his seat. My eyes couldn't help darting straight to his deformity. The nails of his aborted little fingers had been let to grow since I had last seen them, probably in a sad attempt to give the nubby little things the illusion of a normal length; but they made his hand look all the more like the hideous talon of a predatory bird. When I quickly averted my gaze back to his face, his eyes were not meeting mine. Instead he was looking up just a bit, toward my hair, as if to say that we were even—that there was something monstrous about both of us. Silently, he left the room, exiting through the same door as Weed.

Left alone in that immense study, I wondered why the archbishop had not uttered a word of reprimand. Surely he wasn't discussing his plan of action behind that door with Weed. I couldn't believe that he would have arranged this theatrical little exposé without knowing exactly what his next move would be. So, what was he doing? Probably watching me from some surreptitious vantage point at that very moment, enjoying every delicious second that I stood there stewing, biding the minutes until he would return to deliver the preordained coup de grace.

I fully expected to be summarily defrocked; Ratchett would no doubt be returning any moment with papers to sign, or perhaps he'd delegate that juicy little detail to Weed. I'd be disgraced throughout New Orleans. Every priest in the city would know what had happened; Weed would see to that. But they'd never know the whole story, just the Church's perverse side of it. No one would ever know that I had reached those boys the only way I could, that by selflessly giving of my time and attention and expecting nothing in return I had probably touched their lives as no one had before. Now they'd be sending me back to my mother. What would I tell poor Josie—that at the age of fifty I had decided to start a new life? And what would I do without my stipend from the

Church? Was I destined to be an unpaid caregiver for my elderly mother for the rest of her days?

Alas, my future would soon be all too clear, as would the depth of the malignity of those who had orchestrated it. Indeed the greatest tragedians of the Renaissance could not have written a more horrific recognition scene than I was about to take part in.

At first I thought he was a stranger—the elderly man in layman's clothes who emerged from that same door through which the two priests had exited. I surmised he was an archdiocesan official—perhaps in the legal or human resources departments—called in by Ratchett to validate his executive decision. But for his extreme age, I would have feared he was with the police. It wasn't until he looked at me and spoke my name ("Joseph" again), and at the same time I noticed the cigar and was apprehended with full force by its odor, that I realized I was standing before my uncle.

I almost collapsed. The realization that Anthony was taking part in my humiliation was nearly too much for me—not to mention the heady sensations that seeing him again brought on. It was my grandmother's face that I was looking into. Even more so than Josie, he had taken on the physiognomy of his mother in the decades since I had seen him last. There were the huge ears with their pendulum lobes, the bushy brows, the ponderous nose that his sister Rose had tried so hard to avoid herself but in the end would have given everything to have back again. I was too stunned and nonplussed to do the math, but he must have been about the same age now as his mother when she died, which was, of course, the last time I had seen him. He hadn't bothered to attend my ordination, still licking his wounds for failing to break Mama Miggliore's will and stewing over my decision to take his and his late son's name. Now, after thirty-five years, he would have his revenge.

It was becoming apparent why the archbishop had left the room, and it wasn't to ensure a few tender moments of reconciliation between long-estranged family members. The consummate politician, Ratchett was leaving it to my uncle to state the consequences for what was on that tape and to outline whatever choices I had left.

My uncle was remarkably reserved, considering this must have been the climactic moment of the latter half of his mean little life, the culmination of years of scheming and strategizing with trusted old Father Frank. How he must have been dying to tell me what he thought of me: that he had always known I'd come to this, that I had never been worthy to take the name of his son, that I was marked from birth not for auspiciousness but for ignominy, that my becoming a priest was a sacrilege and proof that Mama Miggliore was a senile old crank who was spinning in her restless grave at this very moment.

He held the tape in the hand that wasn't busy feeding that reeking stick into his mouth. Weed must have passed it to him during their little cabal in that room behind the door. He made no mention of it, but just held it there like a prop to remind me of the power he held over me as he laid out the bleak vista of my future.

Obviously there were several parties involved who would prefer that the tape not be made public. The Church didn't need that kind of publicity, and my poor mother might not be able to survive such a jolt on top of her recent stroke, he said. It was hardly necessary to mention what the exposure would do to my career as a priest. (This, at least, sounded hopeful: Was a future in the priesthood still in the cards for me?) Then there were the ramifications to me personally if the District Attorney's office should declare any activity on the tape to be criminal. He admitted that he counted himself among those with an interest in keeping the "scandal" under wraps, calling himself the "patriarch of the Miggliore family" and "safe-keeper" of its reputation.

"But I'll do what I have to do," he added.

His demands were simple. He knew about my power of attorney; he must have paid off the de Salvos to break privilege. I was to immediately sign over half of my mother's estate to him and the other half to the archdiocese. The house and what was left of Josie's share of the family stock would be gone. I would be allowed to remain a priest, but would be "relocated" to an as yet undetermined parish. No mention need be made of my "psychiatric history."

The implied threat in that last little codicil was obvious. If I made any waves, they'd trot out their hired leech, Manresa, who was bound to say whatever they wanted. Who knew, but between him and their threatened criminal investigation, they might be able to fabricate a case to have me institutionalized for the rest of my life.

Anthony promised to see to the needs of my mother for whatever time she had left. What an empty pledge that proved to be. If I refused to cooperate, he would personally see that the tape be made public. Ratchett would deny any knowledge of the incident or the deal. Weed's complicity could easily be guaranteed with the offer of some kind of promotion, perhaps an office in the residence itself; his type always relished the propinquity to power, like house niggers in the Old South. Simply put, I was being blackmailed by my own uncle and the Pope's chosen shepherd to the flock of New Orleans. I signed everything he put in front of me.

My dignity was hardly their concern. They shipped me up here first thing Monday—on a BUS no less! While my uncle and his two co-conspirators were enjoying their seafood repast at the residence, probably toasting their triumph with shrimp cocktails and glasses of Muscadet, I was being hustled off the holy grounds by Weed's driver, who dumped me at my mother's door like an expelled schoolchild. I wasn't even allowed to return to Consolation to say good-bye to the sisters, the excuse being that as it was Friday, my presence would not be expected there anyway.

"They want you to spend the weekend like you normally do," the young seminarian told me. "At your mother's—or wherever."

"Wherever indeed!" They just didn't want me talking to those nuns. I might discover how Weed had managed to get that tape out of there without my knowledge. Could he have possibly sneaked into my quarters without any of the sisters' knowing about it, or had he threatened them to keep their mouths shut? Might one of them have been in league with him?

I could only speculate, for I would never know. They boxed up my belongings and shipped everything up to Kattannachee the next week. Saturday afternoon one of the archdiocese's SUVs showed up at Josie's house with Mama Miggliore's chiffarobe. Mysteriously, all of the tapes it had contained were gone. No one has ever mentioned them to me, but I'm sure Weed has enjoyed countless hours of entertainment from them. A few others were still at the Desire house, so I made one last visit to Bywater to get them Saturday night. As was normally the case, a boy was waiting for me there. I was glad that he was one I knew from previous visits because I wanted to be with someone familiar that night. I held him as long as he would let me. When he left, sometime after midnight, I did as well, taking with me only my little collection of tapes, never to return.

CHAPTER TWELVE

KATTANNACHEE REDUX

The rest of that last weekend in New Orleans I spent with my mother. Josie was understandably distraught at my leaving Consolation. I told her there simply weren't enough retired nuns to justify a full-time priest in the house anymore, and they were sending me someplace where I'd be needed more.

"I want to go too," she said, "I can sell the house."

"Let me get settled in my new parish, Mama," I told her. "Then maybe I can send for you."

She was seventy-seven years old, and I was leaving her to the mercies of a brother she hadn't spoken to in decades. Anthony's promise to see to her needs was as empty as his cold, vacuous heart. Before the ink was dry on the documents giving him control of everything, he had her stuck in that cheap nursing home in Chalmette, a desolate region of junkyards and trailer parks south and east of the industrial canal, which

is absolutely the last place on earth anyone who has attained the slightest social standing in New Orleans would be caught dead. Her bedroom
window overlooks a back street behind a bowling alley. You can hear the
pins falling over the telephone. When I called the manager to complain,
the cheeky woman told me not to worry, that the noise tends to bother
the visitors much more than the residents, who are generally too hard-of-
hearing to notice. At any rate, the room was probably the cheapest my
uncle could find in the entire five-Parish area. Coincidentally, the $1,500
a month Anthony paid for it was, by my reckoning, about as much as the
extra income he would be receiving from the property he had appropri-
ated from his only living sibling.

I arrived here completely exhausted and famished after a nine-
hour bus ride that must have taken me through more wretched little
towns than Huey Long on one of his campaign stumps. Lunch was an absolutely inedible hamburger at a Dairy Queen in Bunkie or Cheyneyville
or some such abominable place. Even if I hadn't been too consumed with
worry and anxiety to sleep a wink, my fellow passengers would not have
allowed it. Why do even total strangers feel compelled to keep priests engaged in conversation every minute of the hour? It's always "Oh, Father,
do you know Sister So and So? I've always wondered what happened to
her" or "You know, Father, I've always wanted to tell somebody that the
best years of my life were when I went to school at Saint Such and Such."
    I had no idea of my destination until I boarded the bus in New
Orleans, and even once I knew its name, I had no idea that I was destined
for the most desolate outpost in all of Louisiana. The bishop of Monroe
arranged for an elderly parishioner to meet me at the bus depot in Ber-
nice, the last stop before Arkansas. The old gentleman drove me to my
new residence in Kattannachee, talking my exhausted ear off the whole
way.

"So you're from New Orleans, Father," he said. "Haven't been down there since right after the war. One of my daughters was married in Memphis, though."

"Really," I said.

"I bet you've got some stories you could tell about your days in the city."

"Indeed," I said. "But I'll take most of them to my grave."

I will not rehash my reaction upon first beholding my execrable living and working conditions in this place except to say again that I found them more ghastly and deplorable than anything I ever expected to see outside of the Third World; nor did I voice my complaints when I met with the bishop two days after my arrival. Over a nice lunch of stuffed eggs and a chicken/spinach salad prepared by Clara, whose honey mustard dressing is to die for, the spiritual leader of the Catholics of Northeast Louisiana discussed with me my duties and welcomed me to the region, adding how pleased he was that Archbishop Ratchett had chosen someone of my experience to take over in the Parish.

He didn't fool me. Not for a minute did I believe that he was clueless of the circumstances that had led me here. He would, of course, want to feign ignorance just in case I brought any opprobrium to his district. The Church had comfortably assimilated the Clinton culture; deniability was the word of the day. The bishop extended his hand through the window of his Cadillac after our lunch. I kissed his ring, and he and his driver were on their way back to Monroe. He has yet to show his face in this part of the diocese again.

My bitterness toward that evil triumvirate back in New Orleans has dissipated considerably in the year that I've been here; I haven't called them the Anti-Trinity in my journal in months. Actually I started to get over it the first morning that I awoke to the smell of Clara cooking breakfast. The sausage I heard and smelled sizzling on the griddle had come from a hog freshly slaughtered by the son of the elderly gentleman who had driven me from the bus depot.

Besides Clara's fabulous cooking, I have other blessings to count. So little is expected of me here that I can almost consider myself in semi-retirement. I only have to say Mass four times a week: twice on Sunday and once on Tuesday and Thursday. More often than not, no one shows up for Friday confession and rosary recitation. Weddings and baptisms are few and far between among my predominately geriatric parishioners. Visiting the sick takes up some time, but not nearly as much as it did with those hypochondriacs and malingerers in the city.

I'm feeling healthier myself. It must be that I'm under so much less stress up here that my scalp hasn't bothered me in months. I'm Father Joseph now, by the way. That was one of Anthony's conditions. And I've left the hairpiece behind. Actually I made that decision before I boarded the bus in New Orleans. I was waiting at the depot, sitting in those pew-like seats before my bus departed, when I suffered an acute attack of diarrhea. So urgent were the cramps that I barely made it to the restroom in time. The anxiety was attacking my head too—the itching again—so I did it. I tore off my piece and flushed it too in one great, purgatorial cleansing.

I've taken to driving around the Parish in my plenitude of spare time. I can take in all of Kattannachee in a leisurely afternoon ride. Sometimes I'll cross into Arkansas, where incidentally I found an interesting spot that I've wanted to return to. Driving down a dirt road off of Highway 82 late one afternoon, I happened upon some kind of construction site. A few abandoned bicycles were scattered among the pieces of heavy equipment that sat resting for the night along the side of the road. Pulling over to investigate, I could hear the sounds of boys at play as soon as I shut off my engine. There were half a dozen of them, frolicking barefoot among the great mounds of earth formed by the backhoes and bulldozers, like urchins out of Stephen Crane—hardly a sylvan paradise, but about as close as one could hope for in southern Arkansas. Some were splashing around in a man-made watering hole, a pool of mud formed from recent rains among the hills of dirt. There was a striking innocence about them that drew me closer until I could see that a couple of them wore nothing but the Arkansas mud that clung to their smooth, lightly muscled limbs. They were most probably Protestants all—no Catholic guilt. The sight brought on a phantom hair sensation, like the pain of an amputee in his missing limb. I still get them from time to time—the illusory feeling that something is loose on top of my head—usually in moments of stress or excitement. I made a mental note to return.

And why not today? It's not as if everyone's falling all over themselves to mark my anniversary. If it weren't for that insulting card from Ratchett's office (probably stamped by Weed), you'd never know anyone even knew about it. Not a peep have I heard from either Monroe or Shreveport; they're making sure to keep their distance. My poor mother probably doesn't remember. She's becoming confused now, asking me things like "Have you heard from Rose lately?" It's actually a blessing, I suppose, that she doesn't really know what's going on and has more or less lost any concept of time. I tell her I'm very busy on special business of the bishop of Monroe or that they're sending me to some important conclave in Dallas or Memphis and that I'll be visiting soon. That seems to make her happy.

Rehashing all these years has certainly stimulated my appetite. It's almost time for lunch. At least I have Clara's lasagna to look forward to. Maybe she'll load it with extra ricotta just for the special occasion. I've put on a few pounds these last few months, thanks to her fine cooking. She's learned all the dishes that I remember from my childhood: grilled scampi, beef marsala, veal scaloppini. Not that I need the extra weight, but at least my appetite shows I'm getting over the depression. Without my piece, I'm beginning to look like Henry James in his later photographs, after he shaved off that hideous Victorian beard. Perhaps

I'll bring *Roderick Hudson* with me on my drive this afternoon, in case there's nothing else to do. I haven't read it since graduate school.

When I join Clara, she wants to see my "holy mark," only she just calls it that "splotch" on my head. She swears it's been changing colors lately, and that has her concerned. She's so short I have to bend over for her to get a good look.

"You have to be careful when those things start changing colors," she says. "It could be cancer."

She wants me to have it burned off with that new laser thing they're using. There's a doctor in Monroe who does it, she says.

I tell her not to worry, that it's been changing like that for years, and that I'd feel almost dismembered without it now. I've told her an abbreviated version of my birthmark and Mama Miggliore's visions, but she wasn't impressed.

"That was just an old woman talking," she said. "You need to let a doctor look at that thing. I have a cousin who had to have something like that burned off his neck when it started turning black."

I insisted that she sit down to dinner with me this time. Bless her heart, the meal she had prepared would have made my grandmother proud: stuffed bracioline, a side of melanzane lasagna, an artichoke salad, even chocolate cannolis and spumone wedges for dessert. As I looked over the wonderful table she had set and smelled the delicious aromas that filled the air, I realized that, although humbled, I might yet be raised again.

He that can make a root flourish below the soil could make fruitful the darkness in which I dwelt.

—Jean-Pierre de Caussade

What did I need with trips to Rome, dinners with the high and mighty, the title monsignor before my name? They had tried before to knock me to the ground—closing the Den, denying me a PhD, shutting me away in the old nun house, and now this. But there is no vindication in vindictiveness, and vengeance must be left to the Lord.

I blessed the table Clara had set, and enjoyed my meal with her. After dinner, besides the blessing after meals, I recited the prayer to Saint Raphael, patron of happy meetings, in hopeful anticipation of a fruitful future:

"O Raphael, lead us towards those we are waiting for, those who are waiting for us. May all our movements be guided by your Light and transfigured by your Joy. Lonely and tired, crushed by the separations and sorrows of earth, we plead for the protection of your wings. Remember the weak, you who are strong, you whose home lies beyond this region of thunder, in a land that is always peaceful, always serene, and bright with the resplendent glory of God. Amen."

I thought of Josie as I kissed Clara and took to the road to Arkansas in my humble station wagon, reflecting on these twenty-five years. They had not defeated me, only made me stronger. My career in service was not nearly over; there could be twenty-five more years to come.

The last might yet be first.